Content Warning

This book contains references to miscarriage.

TREEBLOOD

Andrew Maes

To everyone who showed me support.

Thank you.

PROLOGUE

The sound of the warning bell had been replaced with the screams of terror as the invaders broke into the streets. Men and women screamed as they dragged their children behind them, desperately trying to flee to safety.

Their soldiers fought valiantly to repress the onslaught, but the line would not hold. Most of the creatures had already poured into the city, devouring its inhabitants, clawing at anything that moved.

He could hear it all from inside his room.

And he knew they would not make it.

He hurried to write the last of his notes, scrawling whatever he could that might be of use to any who found them. He had already taken records of his discoveries over the years, carefully documenting them in a secret room, hiding them from his fellow people, knowing they would eradicate them, but hoping future inhabitants would find them. Make use of them. For he and his people were now truly forsaken.

It detailed everything needed to prevent a repeat of their mistakes, to avoid living the horrid life as they did.

And this horrifying ending.

He could barely control the shaking of his hand as the screams continued. Grew. Each shriek striking deep as a blade.

His words were sloppy, but it did not matter. As long as it could be read, it would work.

The Elders had not heeded his warning, and now those of his beloved city would pay the toll. They had been playing a dangerous game from day one but arrogance had ruled their decisions, making them believe they could control the outcome. That they could play God, hold back the enemy with a flick of their hands.

But soon nothing would remain.

The creatures were otherworldly, driven by instinct beyond anything the city had ever witnessed. The monsters lacked common sense, strategy, or any form of thought.

Which meant they also lacked any fear. They would not retreat no matter how their numbers whittled. They were voracious, desperate to reach a goal that none had been able to decipher, to truly know.

He wondered if the creatures themselves knew.

The sound of the door crashing open demanded he abandon his work.

He placed his quill down, rising from his chair on shaky legs.

It was time.

He fled the room, closing the door behind him and satisfied it blended seamlessly enough with the wall so as not be discovered easily, but hopefully the next inhabitants could find it. There was no hope for him, but there might be for those who came next.

He turned to face the woman and her child who had rushed inside, seeking safety where none could be found.

But once these creatures knew where you were, nothing would hold them back.

And they had led one inside.

The tall, gnarly creature squeezed through the doorway, its gruesome features striking fear into any who dared to stare.

He placed himself in front of the cowering woman and her child, knowing it would do nothing to stop the beast.

A second entered his home.

Then a third.

Over his shoulder, he said to the woman, "Tell me, could you hand me that weapon over there?" he gestured to an empty space behind them.

They followed his finger, turning to stare into the void in search of his request.

I pray this will make it easier.

With their backs turned, the creatures descended upon them.

1

East Gate Captain Castor Belden stood ready for the oncoming attack from his position on the bulwark. Across the plains and the few successful farms that surrounded the city of Malvark would soon be trampled by the creatures charging towards their walls. They were mindless beasts, paying no heed to what lay between them and the precious material for which they lusted. The trampling of crops wasn't an act of malice, simply an impediment between them and the city.

Thankfully, their only neighboring city intermittently provided supply packages. Just enough to keep them going.

The warning horn blasted throughout the city at frequent intervals, quickening the pace to indicate how close the creatures were. The bell they had previously used had been consumed by the metal-hungry beasts, and he had watched, transfixed, as the bronze had seemed to melt into their bodies. Castor could not determine how their bodies worked or what was their true goal – if any. For nearly two hundred years his people had fended off the monsters, yet they were no closer to stopping the frequent attacks.

He turned toward the city that he had sworn to protect, scanning what remained. Metal had been banned long before Castor was born, and over the centuries the city had slowly phased out its use from important infrastructure, yet the creatures were able to detect iron and steel no matter how well it was hidden.

Malvark was a city bleak and deflated. A city of dull grey stone and drab wood reflected the depression of the citizens that dwelled within it. They would all be hiding in their homes, wondering if today was the day the creatures swarmed their homes and tore them to pieces.

In a way, that would be a relief.

From his position behind the lines of archers, General Deven's voice boomed. "Bowmen, prepare! The metalurks are nearly within range!"

Castor returned his attention to the incoming threat. A stout breeze pushed up from the plains, a cool kiss against the newly shorn sides of his head. With nimble fingers, he tightened the leather tie in his hair briefly wondering when grey would finally streak his dark brown locks. He ignored the scowl the general threw his way; the animosity between the two cut both ways. Castor may have been the East Gate Captain, but the general took away his command whenever the man was present, and he was *always* present. While the East Gate was a straight run from the forest the creatures called home, and bore the brunt of most attacks, there was no denying the smug pleasure General Deven took in belittling Castor, especially in front of the men.

As the sun slipped behind the horizon, the metalurks' bodies darkened from their usual crimson tone into a dark grey, almost black. From this distance, even the inky dots that stained their skin melded with the shadows. Castor grimaced; their color seemed fitting for the creatures that attacked their city every few days.

"Draw!" the general called.

The bowmen pulled back the string of their livewood bows and took aim, their wooden arrows seeming primitive against the monsters.

Castor wondered what metal-tipped arrows would look like, or how much more effective they would be if the creatures did not feed upon it.

The Voice, the collective that had reigned over Malvark for the last two hundred years, had outlawed the material to prevent giving the creatures more reason to attack. The Voice allowed the use of metal only with express permission from the Gods.

5

Unfortunately, there was no exemption when it came to fighting metalurks.

"Loose!" The general shouted, and Castor watched as the equivalent of pointy branches were released, raining down onto the metalurks. As expected, the attack didn't have much effect. The arrows mostly fell short, and those that hit their marks didn't pierce deep enough to take the creatures down.

Another volley was loosed in the hope of taking down as many of the enemy as possible before they reached the walls.

Few creatures fell before reaching the large livewood gate. They pounded and scratched at its surface, chipping at it bit by bit. Livewood was the city's unique resource, the only place the Gods had blessed with its growth. It was said to be as sturdy as metal and had a unique interaction with its own sap. It was all they had for defense.

The monsters would claw at the door, desperate to get into the city in search of metal. On those occasions when the defenses had been breached, the monsters would normally ignore people unless they got in the creatures' way, which was where Castor came in.

"Cursed atrocities..." General Deven muttered. "Castor! Lead your regiment of Steelwoods and don't allow the beasts to run amok. Keep them contained as best as you can!" The general was clearly displeased with how the defense was playing out.

Castor saluted and ran down the steps to where a band of Steelwoods awaited his orders. Castor hated being called a Steelwood, it was simply a fancy name to give the soldiers who wielded livewood weapons. He suspected it was to give inspiration to the public, to gain their trust, yet the name was misleading— none of them had ever seen steel let alone touched it.

He marched towards his men, livewood spear in hand. Castor gripped the weapon tightly in frustration, feeling like a child playing pretend. The spears were no better than sticks that wouldn't break. Effective for trying to keep as much distance between themselves and the metalurks as possible, but that did not stop him from feeling defenseless.

As Castor led his men towards the front gate, the soldiers atop the wall hefted their wooden spikes, weighted with rocks near the tips, the soldiers would attempt to impale the metalurks that collected at the gate.

Castor inwardly sighed, pushed aside his distaste for the outdated methods, knowing they had to defend Malvark with whatever means available. It was the metalurks fault for Castor and his people being unable to use metal, not the fault of The Voice.

Beyond the gate, ungodly screams and shrieks shattered the night as the metalurks were crushed against the livewood gate and impaled by primitive spears.

Castor's men took their positions in the tunnel that led to the East Gate, livewood spears and clubs held tight as they lined either side. The backup portcullis was dropped; the latticed pattern provided less durability than the outer gate but allowed Castor and his men to attack through the gaps.

It was their last barricade against the belligerent creatures.

When the metalurks broke through the portcullis, he and his men would fight to the death. Behind them stood the few horsemen the city could afford to maintain. Any creature that made it past the Steelwood foot soldiers would be chased down and skewered with longspears. They could not allow a creature to run loose in the city.

Castor shook himself from the distracting thoughts, focusing on the predicament ahead. The air smelled stale as he breathed deep. The scent of the impending fight left a bad taste in his mouth, just as it did with every wave of enemy that attacked his city.

He took the forward position to lead his soldiers in defense of the tunnel. His spear began to feel uncomfortable as he constantly repositioned his grip. The livewood weapon was effective enough to defend against the metalurks, but he still felt suffocated by its use. He longed for the day that his people would rid themselves of the metalurks for good, so that they could once again use metal. As a soldier, he wanted to know the effectiveness of metal, what it felt like to hold in your hand, the possible sense of security one would feel simply by having it at your side.

But there was no end in sight for these. For nearly two hundred years they survived against this menace, and yet they

7

could not gain enough footing to rid them completely. He was proud to be among the soldiers that would carry on Malvark's continuous fight for survival but felt useless as he knew he had no ability to change it.

No one did.

The sound of the lower section of the main gate shattering brought Castor's attention to his enemy. A small hole had formed, revealing the shuffling of feet and the tearing of claws as they broke more pieces off, the hole growing larger by the second. One metalurk was impatient enough to squeeze through the hole on its own, struggling through the small space as the others continued to tear at it. The creature scurried forward on all fours, its smooth head containing no features. It was the embodiment of nightmares as it rushed forwards, its smooth face almost pining as it hurried, its insatiable hunger for metal demanding to be quelled.

But Castor had been living this nightmare since the day he was born into this cursed city.

The creature didn't hesitate as it charged with full speed towards the portcullis. It rose to run on its legs, preparing to impact the gate with all of its might.

Its own momentum only made it easier for Castor's spear to skewer its head.

Castor shook the creature free from his elongated stick. Behind its lifeless corpse, the hole had grown large enough for the rest of the monsters to pour through. Castor once again took in the repugnant air through a deep breath.

Another day, another fight for survival.

* * *

The battle was fortunately short in comparison to their previous fights. It seemed as though the creatures were dwindling in number, and as much as Castor felt guilty for thinking so, he was thankful for the easier days. A few of his Steelwood soldiers had sustained wounds when the creatures made a small break through the portcullis, though fortunately none of the injuries were fatal. They couldn't afford to lose soldiers at every fight.

One of the first laws put in place by The Voice in Malvark was that couples should bear no less than three children. It ensured the city had plenty of soldiers to defend it. Such was the commodity of life in Malvark, there were many laws instituted to protect Malvarkians lives and their way of life, in a time of crisis. Any who dared to murder, steal, or in any way harm another who was also fighting to survive in this accursed city, deserved to be dealt with harshly. This was not the time for petty quarrels or greed.

Castor hated those who put themselves above others. His gaze drifted to the lofty heights of the mansions situated atop a rise on the western side of the city. He knew they weren't hunkered in basements praying for a reprieve, not from where they sat safe behind their gates.

Castor spat on the ground and piled his spear with the other livewood weapons that needed inspection for repairs. Specialized craftsmen would determine which weapon could be repaired, and which would be fashioned into something else. Another key quality to livewood was its ability to repair itself with the very sap of the tree from which it came.

Medics attended the various scratches and shallow wounds of Castor's men, while the remaining soldiers gathered arrows and rocks for reuse in the next confrontation. The large wooden doors that served as the front line of defense had a large chunk missing, but craftsmen were already at work, placing the small chunks of the door together and slathering the livewood tree sap at the cracks – gluing the pieces together.

Treeblood was always peculiar to watch.

It's unique interaction with its own wood set it apart from other trees. Castor watched, transfixed as always, as the sap slowly melded into the livewood, as if blood was coursing back into a body. The mysterious liquid allowed the livewood to be reshaped easily, softening the wood over its slow absorption process. The then softened wood somehow realized its broken pieces were part of something larger, as if it recognized what it was supposed to be and slowly began to reconnect itself.

It was this miracle that allowed Malvark to stand as long as it had against the ever-living threat. Livewood truly was a blessing from the Gods, and a testament to Malvark's imperishable hope for survival.

Castor checked on his men as he waited to provide a report on the day's defense for General Deven. And Castor knew the general would make him wait. By the time the man descended from the wall, the craftsmen had repaired the minor damage to the portcullis in addition to the main gate.

The General had loosened his hair after the fight, and it was now freely flowing past his shoulders. The steel grey held barely a whisper of light brown, and there was a full beard to match. General Deven was a soldier in every sense, his green eyes surveying his surroundings for possible threats; and he walked as if his authority alone would clear buildings from his path. A seething mix of arrogance and confidence that both intimidated and inspired the people of Malvark.

"Castor," the general called as he turned into the tunnel.

"General Deven." Castor saluted.

"Report."

"Minor wounds, no casualties. Metalurks barely broke through the portcullis before we were able to stop them."

"Good. Have the men put on wall duty until they properly recover. Fill in the gaps with whatever reserves we have."

"Yes, sir."

"Is that all?"

Castor ignored the man's sneer. "Yes, sir."

The general nodded and strode away, clearly not wanting to talk to Castor longer than absolutely necessary. Castor should have been annoyed that his superior wanted as little to do with him as possible but was honestly content with their brief yet necessary interactions. General Deven held a special kind of animosity toward Castor, the East Gate captain cared little as to why that was. The General would not do anything to harm Castor's position – there was a grudging, unspoken trust in Castor's ability to perform his duties. As long as the general didn't hinder Castor's effectiveness in leading the Steelwoods, he would shrug aside the man's blatant distaste for him.

"Captain!"

Castor turned to Vance's voice. The man had a minor cut along his forearm from overextending with his spear thrust – an important lesson learned – but was otherwise unharmed. "Vance," he greeted the man, who saluted in return.

"Doc here says I shouldn't participate in the next fight. Possibly two. Scratch went a little deep, so I should rest it for a week."

Castor dropped his gaze to the blood-soaked bandage around Vance's arm. He didn't want to tamper with the wrappings to inspect it for himself, but he trusted his Steelwoods, and he trusted Vance. Besides, what good were soldiers if their superior didn't trust them?

"Any unfit for duty in the tunnel are meant to be placed on the wall," Castor said. "But what good will giving you a bow do if you can't use an arm for a spear? Make yourself scarce from the general's sight for a while, but don't stray too far. We'll need you in case the situation gets out of hand."

"Thanks, Captain. You off to see her now?"

"Just as the sun sets."

"How's she doing?"

"Not too well, I'm afraid."

A frown of genuine concern creased Vance's brow. "I thought she was getting better?"

"I thought so, too. Sadly, she's relapsed a bit."

"Well, let her know we're all supporting her. She can come have a drink with us anytime!"

"Will do. Thanks, Vance." Castor smiled and gave Vance a dismissive nod. He hadn't the heart to tell the man that his sister would never take up another drink, but that didn't hinder Vance's generous intentions.

Castor decided not to delay meeting with his sister; she needed to see him after every fight to ensure that he was still alive. It sometimes grated on him, to fill his sisters' obligation so shortly after every fight, but he knew her anxiety would only grow until she could see him with her own eyes.

* * *

As usual, the library was dark, matching the glumness of the city, but at least the unique scent of old books provided a comforting change.

"You're not hurt, are you?" Maggie asked, worry alight in her eyes as she gripped tightly the books she had yet to shelve in the library where she worked. She visibly relaxed when he shook his head.

Maggie returned to her task, slotting a book into place, satisfied with Castor's response. Her dark brown hair frizzed about her face, complementing the bags under her pale blue eyes from days of sleepless nights. It made his heart ache that she no longer resembled her carefree, joyous former self.

He leaned against the end of the shelves, staring out into the near-empty library. It was calm and quiet, exactly what his sister needed. She had been working here for only a few months, but had quickly settled into her new position, familiar with most of the library's organization.

"You're going to be one day, you know," she continued, slowly putting away another book.

Castor sighed inwardly, knowing how difficult it was for his sister to understand that it was a necessary inevitability. It is true that he felt guilty for making his sister feel so, but he had to set aside her feelings in order to focus on the defense of the city.

"One day, possibly, but you know that I'm aware of that, Maggie. I'm not going to change my mind. Others will suffer if I choose to just leave now."

"I know, I know, it's just... I don't want it to happen." Maggie was now staring blankly at the books, lost in some terrible world of hers. Castor lifted a book from the trolley and gestured for her to take it, wanting to distract her from whatever she was imagining. She hesitantly took the book and made her way over to where it needed to be shelved.

"I know my words sound like a metalurk's claws to your ears at this point, but you need to stop thinking about those things, Maggie. You won't get better if you keep doing it." He hesitated before asking, "Are you still talking to Audrey?"

Maggie pursed her lips, an obvious sign of guilt as she lowered her head and turned slightly away from him.

This time, he released his sigh heavily. "You know you're supposed to keep talking to her."

"But she's not helping me!" Maggie cried.

"Of course she won't if you don't let her." He took a step toward his sister. "Stop convincing yourself that she is always out to get you. She has no reason to, and she really is trying to help. That's what she *does*, so please let her."

Maggie turned away from him again, but he could see that she was not utterly convinced that Audrey was scheming against her this time. He decided not to pursue the topic any further, trusting his sister was berating herself enough.

"The Day of Sacrifice is coming," Maggie finally said, changing the subject.

Castor nodded; he had mixed feelings about the ritual. Sure, it was the only event where the nobles shed blood to keep the city safe, but it was just the same two families who did so while the others continued to live their lives without having to sacrifice a son in order for Malvark to continue its struggle for survival. Castor didn't understand why the Gods would choose such a barbaric method, but who was he to dare question them?

"I know," Castor said. "Which means we'll get a new stock of livewood coming soon. I just wonder what The Voice will decide to do with it."

Maggie shook her head, placing another book on the shelf, her fingers lingering on the spine. "I wonder if the Daolins will continue their streak. It doesn't seem entirely fair that they've won the past three times, yet the Noldins must still fight to decide which son is sacrificed."

Despite Castor's concerns, he spoke the words he always did. "It's the way it is, and the way it must be. The Noldins know this, and I'm sure they're okay with it. After all, it helps the city."

"Even still, they must be worried," Maggie persisted. "Elias is their last son. What will happen if…" Maggie trailed off, and Castor's heart immediately sank.

"Maggie, don't. Come on, you need to keep moving. Keep yourself distracted. Are you reading any new books?"

13

His sister slowly nodded, gaze momentarily lost into empty space before pushing herself to speak. "Yes, though I don't know if you'll like my answer."

"What is it?" Castor readied himself to be upset, then berated himself for doing so. His sister was coping as best she could, and the Day of Sacrifice was always going to be hard for her.

"The history of old Malvarkian laws."

Castor knew he wouldn't like the response; his sister was obsessed with learning about old Malvark, that it was somehow relevant to her and all she'd been through.

Malvark had been an established city before their people had arrived nearly two-hundred years ago. Established, yes, but devoid of a living soul. The previous inhabitants – the old Malvarkian's – had disappeared without a trace. It was a bad omen, but their ancestors had been desperate, needing walls to defend against the growing number of bandits on the land.

So, they had made Malvark their home, and unknowingly traded one threat for another.

Castor's first reaction was to scold her but she was a grown woman, and he knew it wouldn't do any good. Maggie was just as stubborn as he was. So he sighed instead.

"I know you disapprove of it," Maggie said. "But I'm an adult. I'm fully capable of choosing what I want to read."

Castor looked apologetically at his sister. "You are. Sometimes I forget that. I just worry about your obsessions. Sometimes… sometimes they get the better of you."

"I know what I'm doing," Maggie insisted.

"Yes, you do. After all, what good is an older brother if he can't trust his little sister?"

Maggie smiled at him, a brief flash of her old self reappearing before it quickly faded. Castor cleared his throat. "I'd like for you to go see Audrey. Tonight."

Maggie's face sunk. "Really?"

"Yes. I just want to make sure you're doing well. She's a professional, I trust her judgement over mine."

"Alright," his sister answered, disappointment clear in her voice. "But I'm not going to answer all her ridiculous questions."

"That's fine," Castor said. "Thank you. I should let you work in peace. I'll see you again soon." He embraced his sister, squeezing a little tighter than normal.

She spoke in his ear, "Good seeing you."

He knew she was reluctant when it came to Audrey, hoping that she spoke truthfully this time. She had broken several promises before.

In either case, he prayed for his sister.

2

Birdsong woke Elias from his deep slumber. The incessant chirping skewered his ears, the little feathery tyrants wanting to fully embellish the pounding in his head. He should not have drunk so much last night. He stirred in the bed, trying to endure the pain of the birds' morning cheeriness but to no avail. He reluctantly and carefully rose, not wanting to disturb his body further from sudden movements and made his way to the window.

He pulled aside the curtain, and reeled back, wincing against the sunlight that stabbed at his eyes.

Elias dropped the curtain and hobbled over to his bed where he sat, head in his hands. He rubbed his eyes, the irritation telling him they would be reddened. As his sight slowly adjusted to the gloom of his bedroom, the carpet's dark shade of red resolved, the shape and material of his drawers, and the distance of his bed to his desk all became clearer. A chalice sat upon the desk, and Elias knew without looking that it would contain a liquid that held a slight tinge of blue.

Geraldine, you deserve a raise.

Elias shuffled over to the desk and downed the contents of the cup. He lay upon his bed once more as he awaited the liquid to take effect. The throbbing in his head slowly abated until it was no more then he rose, knowing that his father would be upset if he were late to his lessons.

A quick change into his formal attire and Elias made haste towards the kitchens, scooping an apple and a bread roll from the bench and devouring both on his way to his sparring lessons. He had not realized how hungry he was until the first crunch into the apple.

He scratched at his chin; his beard had begun to grow back, but there was no time to fix that now. Elias entered the training room where his father stood with Merek, his teacher. It always amused Elias whenever he saw the two standing side by side. His father was rather short, standing at about five foot four and had thinning, light-grey hair; Merek was towered at six foot three and his thick, black hair was neatly woven. Elias kept his amusement to himself, having been scolded many times for commenting on the disparity.

"Ah, so you have decided to attend today's lesson then." Elias' father did not attempt to conceal his annoyance.

"I'm not that late."

His father shook his head. "The mess of your hair says differently. You have to start taking this seriously now, Elias. No more drinking until the Day of Sacrifice is over," his father ordered, much to Elias' dismay.

"Father, no! You can't do that!" Elias said, dropping his hands from where he was tying his long, light-brown hair. "I am of age and can do as I please now!"

"You must focus entirely on your training," his father snapped. "And clearly abusing alcohol is impeding that. So, you will obey me. You very well know it is for your own good, I shouldn't have to repeat myself."

Elias was tired of arguing with his father; it would not amount to anything. So he would simply have to disobey his father's orders... like he always did.

"Elias?"

"Yes, Father?"

"No more alcohol. Please."

Elias smiled, ignoring his father's hopeful stare. They both knew he would not obey the command, despite how serious the situation. Drinking would cause issues, Elias knew that, but it was his only relief to the pressure that had been steadily building since he was a child.

His father wished Merek good luck and disappeared out the door, neither he nor his son looked at each other. Elias started to strap the pieces of his metal suit of armor on, and Merek walked over to assist, his own armor clinking as he did so.

"Warin is right this time." Merek's voice was a little gravelly from years of shouting during training. Elias did not respond, pretending to focus on ensuring his armor was strapped on properly. He did not wish to engage on the topic. "We are only months away from the Day of Sacrifice. He is right to be worried about you and your habits. If they negatively impact your learning, then you could very well lose."

"Yes, I know that already. Why do you think I drink?" Elias snapped, a little snarkier than he had anticipated.

"The Day of Sacrifice will soon be upon us, Master Noldin," Merek said, ignoring Elias' outburst. "You must take everything with the utmost seriousness from now. You haven't long before your fate is decided."

Elias knew all too well that the Day of Sacrifice was nearing. He had been dreading the day for his entire life.

It was the reason he was born, and it would be the reason he would die.

The Noldins and the Daolins were the two families destined to put forth a sacrifice to the Gods; had been ever since Malvark had become their home. The Gods themselves were presented with a short list of volunteers and had chosen the two families for this highest honor. Every twenty years, a son from each family would duel to the death. The sacrifice that would appease the Gods.

Elias' family had lost the past four consecutive duels.

Needless to say, that record impacted negatively on their family's morale. Elias was the sole male left in his family, other than his father who was excused from the duels due to his age. The future of the Noldin lineage was Elias' burden to carry.

He'd lost his mother when she had given birth to his younger sister, who had sadly passed away only days after. His two elder brothers had also passed away—one to a duel, the other to an illness at an early age, before Elias was born. Now, Elias was expected to either sire a son, or somehow come out victorious in the next duel. Both were great complications for Elias. He had no interest in siring children, and he lacked the confidence in himself to win the upcoming duel.

There were strict rules regarding the families' interaction—the opponents were not allowed to meet until the day of the duel, and the families were to avoid each other unless The Voice called a meeting, and even then, the chosen sons were forbidden to attend.

The chosen sons would simply show up on the Day of Sacrifice, and fight to kill the other.

Elias begrudgingly finished donning his suit of armor, and took up his steel sword, swinging it a few times to loosen his muscles. As much as he despised the training sessions, it usually allowed him to focus his mind on the moment, rather than the future.

He spent some time moving around to adjust to the weight and restrictions of the armor. It had been designed for him on his eighteenth birthday and was a perfect fit. The Voice gifted a set to each duelist as a requirement for the fight. The metal was kept secret from the public, not wanting to cause them further fear than necessary.

It took a while for Elias to be convinced the metalurks could not detect metal through the specially padded training room, but he had to admit that he still had doubts. And if he had doubts, there would be no chance of convincing an entire kingdom.

The training lasted a few hours, longer than usual in preparation for the Day of Sacrifice. Elias' father would be pushing the them to train as much as possible before the day came, wanting his son to break the unlucky streak of the family and lift some of the crushing pressure that came with it.

Merek praised Elias on his efforts and the two removed their armor, which was a process in itself. No assistants were allowed, keeping the secret of the metal to a minimum. The armor was heavy, needing to be durable enough to stop a blade, and Elias found himself once again drenched with sweat. He noticed Merek appeared to be just as exhausted, which was a good sign for Elias.

19

It meant he was at least still on par with his teacher and ready for combat.

They spent some time cleaning their armor, having to maintain it themselves. They kept mostly silent, focusing on their respective equipment.

"You know, if you are nervous about the upcoming event, you should talk to someone," Merek commented as if they had been discussing the topic at length. Elias resisted the urge to retort, taking a moment to convince himself Merek was only trying to help. It was no secret the duel was taking its toll on him, but Elias did not like to say so, let alone hear it voiced.

"Who would I even talk to? No offence, but I can't have you suddenly taking it easy on me because you know about my problems."

"I have already guessed what they are, and I have not taken it easy on you since, but I understand your reluctance. Perhaps your father?"

Elias scoffed at the suggestion. His father was not easy to talk to, having his own worries to deal with. Still, Elias was all his father had left, yet despite it bringing them together, it only drove them further apart. Elias' fate had caused a rift between them that no talking would magically bridge.

"All right, not him either then. Have you any friends you can talk to? I understand you must stay within the household most times, but surely you have gone out and socialized?"

Elias' mood suddenly dropped at the suggestion. He had no real friends outside of the household. Living a sheltered life did little to help. "Afraid not. I have only been to events when we knew the Daolins would not be in attendance, and that was only on rare occasions. Father has not exactly let me out regularly enough to keep in contact with anyone."

"Then perhaps enjoy yourself. Without the drink, I mean. I do not know if your father will heed my advice, but perhaps I can slip him a word that some relaxation might help your fighting form. Go out and enjoy the town, with some escorts of course. Can't have you accidentally running into a Daolin, who knows what they might scheme without your father around."

"Surely, they know that they must leave me alone. No interference or contact before the duel."

"I suppose that depends on whether you believe the rumors or not. About their spy in your father's employ. Nevertheless, you must have an escort when you leave the grounds. Go out tonight and enjoy yourself, Elias. You deserve it."

"Enjoy myself without alcohol? I'm sure you must be joking."

"There is much fun to have without the need of it."

"Oh really? Any suggestions?"

Merek fell silent for a moment, brow furrowed in thought.

Elias chuckled and shook his head. "I knew that there wasn't."

"Well, then you'll have to simply find it for yourself!"

Elias rolled his eyes, though Merek had a valid point. Elias should spend the night enjoying himself.

Stress piled heavier with every passing day. He doubted a night's relaxation would help, but it would at least provide temporary relief, a distraction at least. It had been quite a while since he was allowed outside of the grounds, perhaps he could convince his father to even let him wander town unattended. It was a long shot, but with the upcoming inevitability of the duel, where he may just end up being a sacrifice, his father was sure to be lenient.

Merek bid Elias farewell, and Elias shuffled off to what would fill the second half of his day: lessons on his family's history of duels. He begrudgingly headed towards the room where Madam Martha was inevitably waiting to lecture him on the same lesson for the thousandth time. There was only so much recorded history of their ancestors' duels, and Elias' father was insistent it held the key to learning the technique of the Daolins' champion. It was a tedious lesson, and with his lack of sleep and adrenaline of the sword-training slowly seeping away, he would find it difficult to stay awake during the entirety of the two-hour session.

* * *

As expected, the lesson was long and boring. Elias was scolded multiple times due to his slouching and drifting off, though it did little to prevent him from repeating the offences.

After bidding his teacher farewell and making promises to do better (that he likely wouldn't keep), Elias did his best to shake off the dreariness and decided to find his father to talk about Merek's suggestion.

Warin Noldin was in his usual place in the study, staring into the fireplace, glass of wine in hand, and recently opened bottle on a nearby table. Elias often found his father like this, contemplating whatever was bothering him. As the Day of Sacrifice drew near, his father spent increasingly more time in his chair, wine his only comfort.

Elias gathered a chair near the desk as he made his slow approach and placed it opposite the small table that now bridged the gap between he and his father. The open bottle of wine tempted Elias, its rich scent beckoning him, tingling his tongue.

Elias set aside his lust for the wine and returned his focus to the situation. His father did not acknowledge his presence, just continued to stare into the fire as if it were the only thing left in the world.

"Has Merek spoken to you?" Elias asked, studying the fire that had grabbed his father's attention. The flames flickered brightly, dancing to heat the room adequately enough that Elias began to feel the need to remove his outer tunic.

"He had quick word with me, yes," Warin finally responded, his eyes not moving an inch from the fireplace. His words were soft, his mind clearly not having completely returned from where it had wandered.

Elias waited a moment before continuing. "I wish to explore the town tonight, preferably on my own."

Warin did not respond right away, and Elias could not tell if he was thinking about the request, or if he had already made up his mind when Merek had mentioned the possibility. His father broke his focus on the fire to refill his glass with the wine. Elias did not watch as his father poured, not wanting to give any indication he wanted to go into town to drink.

Which is exactly what he planned on doing.

Warin filled his glass, far past the courteous limit when guests were involved, but Elias was no guest. He sat, awaiting his father's response. Whatever his father's decision, it was obvious Warin was not happy about the situation.

"What will you do in the city?"

"Explore. Walk. Enjoy. Perhaps mingle with people and actually make some friends for once." Elias immediately bit his tongue, not wanting to have sounded as harsh as he did. It was true he blamed his father for his lack of a social life, but he also blamed himself for not being able to make that connection when the proper situations arose. Now was not the time to have an attitude towards his father.

Warin seemed to be contemplating Elias' words, likely debating internally about the consequences. "Drinking?"

"Just for tonight, and then I'll cut back." Elias surprised himself with the answer. More surprised to find himself believing it.

"I suppose that is all that I could ask for." Warin sipped at his wine, either not seeing the irony or simply choosing to ignore it.

"I think it is a fair request," Elias ventured into the silence that followed. "Allow me to enjoy it one more night, and I'll begin working on cutting it out before the duel. Cutting bad habits takes work, but I at least promise to try."

"You wish to go alone?"

"Preferably. I will agree to a small escort if you must."

"Fine. Two guards will walk with you everywhere but keep to themselves. Geraldine, however, will escort you everywhere herself. No arguments," Warin said; it wasn't so much an order but rather a mutual arrangement between two adults. Elias had expected a small regiment of guards and various escorts to ensure his safety, so this was far more than he could have hoped.

"I can agree to that."

"Good. You may leave whenever you choose, but please return before the moon reaches its peak."

"Yes, Father." Elias rose from his chair, pleased with how the conversation had gone and excited to begin preparations to leave.

23

"Elias," Warin called before he could take a step towards the door.

Elias froze at his father's tone, a slight chill cutting through his body. "Yes, Father?"

Warin hesitated, seemingly struggling over his next words. "Please control yourself," Warin pleaded softly, then his gaze returned to the fire.

Elias waited, feeling there was more his father had wanted to say but the room fell to silence bar the crackling of the flames. Elias nodded to his father and made way for the door, his excitement dulled by his father's unspoken words.

* * *

It did not take long for Elias to leave for the city. Excitement propelled his preparations, though they were not many in number. A bath, shave, and change into an appropriate outfit – one befitting a citizen of higher status, but not enough to throw his position in the face of others. Or at least he thought so. By the time he was done, Geraldine had received word from Warin and fetched two guardsmen, who were all standing at the ready at the bottom of the staircase. Elias descended quickly, nearly falling down in his haste, distracted as he was with buttoning his jacket.

"Ready, Geraldine?" he smiled at his maid, though it quickly faded once he realized she was still wearing her work attire. Her usual dark blonde hair was neatly woven into a practical fashion, her face neutral. He had hoped that she would have let loose for a single night.

"Yes, sir," she responded formally, and gestured for the guards to open the door. Elias debated ordering her to change into something more suitable for the night ahead but decided against it; she was likely obeying Father's commands. The two armed guards did not help his case either, drawing attention to him like a metalurk amongst pigs. He took a deep breath in preparation of dealing with the inevitable stares, questions, and conversations of Malvark's people. He always felt uncomfortable speaking with them, with the admiration heaped upon him, like he was some kind of god. He hated it, and it was something he did not need, especially tonight. Tonight, was for enjoying himself, relaxing and drinking.

And definitely not thinking about the Day of Sacrifice.

He strode out the doors with purpose and enthusiasm, already deciding to begin the night by heading to the market square where there would be few stalls giving out meats and vegetables, freshly cooked on the spot. He had heard about it through Geraldine, who frequently visited the markets to restock on food. He wished to experience it himself and praise the folk who ran the markets for the efforts on keeping up the morale in these dire times. He knew his role was important for the people, but he truly respected those who kept up the fighting spirit of the day-to-day struggles.

Despite being born into a noble family, Elias' household was still limited on the amount of supplies they could purchase, and he always imagined others had it far worse.

He made way down through the front gates that marked the end of his property and awaited with anticipation as the guards swung it open for him. He hesitated for a moment, staring downhill at the houses that sat below him, guilt seeping its way in. He hated this view. A reminder of how privileged his birthright was.

Quickly shaking off the feeling, he hastily walked towards the city center, a spring in his step leaving poor Geraldine and the guards to put in the effort of keeping up with his pace.

Geraldine suggested multiple times that he ease himself into it, not only for their benefit, but also on his expectations. True, Elias had not wandered the city for quite a while, so his expectations might have been quite high, but he did not feel the need to dawdle. Even should he be disappointed, there was no point in dragging that out.

As he made his way downhill, people immediately noticed his presence in town, and they began their excited stares and whispers, gossiping about the potential reasons of his visit. He paid them no mind, leaving them to wonder. If he stopped to speak with them now, it would only invite others to gather, and he did not want to be stopped before he even reached his first destination.

Thankfully, the armed guards' appearance was enough to keep people from approaching, their drawn livewood weapons acting as warning enough.

Elias finally made it to the market square, which doubled as the city's center. There he laid eyes on the beauty of the livewood tree the city proudly displayed at its center. Its sight was always a double-edged sword, bringing both joy and sadness to Elias.

It was a beautiful white tree that held a slight pink hue. This particular tree had patches of brown in random places, though Elias had heard previous trees would sometimes bear different colored patches. It was a display of the city's most valued resource and the reason Malvark still stood today.

It was also a reminder of his brother's death.

The tree was replaced every twenty years, the day after the duel. It is brought to the victor, who plants it during a ceremony, in honor of the sacrifice.

He remembered the day it was planted. Even as young as he was, it was not a day anyone would forget, let alone Elias. He smiled at the fond memories of his brother and sent a silent prayer to the Gods that were watching over him.

The tree was littered with different offerings the people gave to the Gods. As the only visible livewood tree the people were allowed to see – the rest, Elias had been told, were grown and harvested in a specific location for efficiency. This tree acted as placeholder for the Gods physical presence, and the people believed the Gods gifted them the livewood tree so they may succeed where the previous tenants of the city had not.

Elias was drawn away from the tree by the sensational smell of freshly cooked beef mixed with various spices, and he approached the elderly man who had been cooking the delectable meat on a campfire. The man's long, thinning grey hair was a mess, but was tied back to avoid it falling into the food. The cook had just finished with the meats, removing them from the pan and piled them onto a clay plate. He stared up at the small gathering of people that had been watching him, each with a plate in their hand.

Elias felt guilty, not realizing the proper etiquette. The elderly man's eyes fell upon Elias, instant recognition reflecting in his face.

"Sir Elias Va Noldin! I am humbled by your appearance at our town center. Come to pray to the tree for good faith in your upcoming duel?" the elderly man spoke with a smile, his voice wheezy from age and likely affected by his profession.

Elias had tried to back away before the man had called attention to him, wincing a little as he heard his own name called out. "Greetings. I am out enjoying myself this night. The attack happened yesterday which means today I can freely explore without having to worry. I was just enticed by your pleasant cooking and was interested. I see you've gathered quite a few admirers." Elias motioned towards the patient crowd, now realizing that many were considerably young. Most wore confused expressions, clearly wondering who he was and why the elderly man had grown excited by Elias' presence.

"Your compliment has surely boosted my spirits, sir. These are just the ordinary spices, a gift I received when I retired. I will tear you a piece to try for yourself."

Elias looked again at the patiently waiting crowd, seeing now how skinny and gaunt some were. His guilt became a lump in his throat. He wanted to decline the courteous offer but seeing the man's face made it clear that tasting his cooking meant a considerable amount to him. Elias reluctantly took the piece that had been prepared, the heat threatening to burn his fingers if he held it for long. As soon as the flavors hit his tongue, he momentarily forgot about the guilt. The meat was tender, and the spices warmed his tongue as he chewed. His stomach warm as he swallowed, yearning for another piece, but he had already taken food from the mouths of others, he would not do so again.

"My good man, it seems the Gods have answered my prayers so soon, this is truly divine. No wonder you have people gathering around like metalurks on metal."

The elderly man gave a wide, joyous smile at Elias' words. "Thank you, sir. I am so pleased you enjoyed it. These are my usual gatherers and I enjoy cooking for them. My meat supply is more than I need now that I am older and have no one else to feed,

27

so I stock up and give it out to whoever needs it. Parents send their children over mostly, but today I am glad that you got to partake. Now I truly know that I am blessed,"

The man's eyes watered slightly from sheer joy, and the lump returned to Elias' throat as the man's words settled in. He should not have taken the food if it was to feed hungry children, but it had meant so much to the man. "Keep up the good work, uh... I'm sorry, what is your name?"

"Jeziah, sir."

"You are doing the Gods work, Jeziah. I compliment you on your efforts and implore others to follow your lead," Elias added, noting that the center was not bustling with people as he had expected. He understood things were becoming more dire with each passing day, but now he could see for himself the impacts it was having as time went on.

He said his goodbyes to the man and apologized to the children who he had cut in front of without realizing, guilt swelling his tongue as he almost stuttered.

Elias continued his wanderings, his attitude soured slightly, but he was determined to continue on and enjoy himself. He had been into town a few times, but never without his father or without an express purpose. It felt freeing to be able to choose his own direction and destinations without the constant voice in the back of his mind telling him he needed to be elsewhere.

Geraldine remained quiet as they walked, clearly here on a professional level. She had occasionally slipped out of her finely polished work personality before, so Elias was hoping she would simply loosen up tonight. He encouraged and teased her, trying to get her to relax just enough so she would smile and begin having fun. He knew his father would have given her strict orders to control him, but he found amusement in trying to break her stoic façade.

By the time they had reached the Everwall Tavern, she was smiling at his antics. Once he had broken through the first time, it became easier to bring down the wall she was insistent on putting up.

"Well, Geraldine, shall we go in for a drink?"

"You know your father wouldn't like you drinking."

"He knows I planned on drinking. I think he accepted knowing that I would do it with or without his permission."

"Then he wouldn't like me drinking."

"Well, I am going in there regardless, and you'll have to come with me. The guards can choose to stay outside or join in as well, but they'll probably dampen the atmosphere in there. So, you come in, sit down, and we'll see what happens."

Geraldine could not argue; she had been ordered to follow him everywhere after all. Her shoulders fell, and she reluctantly followed Elias into the tavern.

Elias had pushed to leave tonight for one particular reason: it was the one night of the month the taverns could sell alcohol freely. Normally, there were limitations dependent on the day, to stretch out the supply as fermentation was a lengthy process.

One night a month, however, the taverns were allowed to sell all their alcohol rather than being restricted to specific types.

The tavern was vibrant with the sound of people chatting and laughing, and in the corner a bard regaling songs. It was precisely the scene Elias was after. Smiling faces, alcohol being shared, laughter, and not a worried face in sight. He led Geraldine through the crowd, people either too drunk or too distracted to recognize him and managed to find a couple of seats at a table. He ordered two ales, knowing that Geraldine would give in at some point if he placed a drink practically in her lap.

Elias could not contain his own smile, a sense of ease falling over him as the alcohol was poured into a couple of mugs. His smile widened as a drunken trio slurred their words as they sung along with the bard, who encouraged their attempts.

He thanked and paid the barkeep and took his seat next to Geraldine, who was obviously uncomfortable. She was used to the cleanliness of a noble's house, not the unkempt mess of a crowded tavern. A man was attempting to speak with her, the alcohol on his breath obvious from the way Geraldine reeled and turned her head.

Elias placed a mug before her, and the man turned his attention towards him.

"Oh, you'ves already got a... a... drink den? I'm sorry, I dids not know you had a... a... a man already." the drunk was tripping over his own words as he exchanged glances between Geraldine and Elias.

"Oh, pay me no mind," Elias said jovially. "We are merely friends. She is all yours, my dear man." Elias smiled, prompting the man to return the gesture and place an arm around Geraldine.

She looked at Elias with annoyance, trying to shrug off the man's arm, but he kept it firmly grasped to her shoulder.

"I think he's lovely, Geraldine. I didn't realize you'd hit it off with someone so soon."

"Sir, please do not encourage him." She then turned to her admirer. "As for you, I'm not interested, so I suggest you leave before I hide metal under your bed tonight." Geraldine plied the man's hand from her shoulder.

"Okay, okay, I get it. I was just… trying to be nice to you." the man stood, grabbing his empty mug and lifting it to his mouth, turning the cup upside down and leaning so far back he ended up staggering into other patrons, who drunkenly helped him stand and laughed at his inability to maintain his own body weight.

Elias smiled as Geraldine pulled the cup closer to her and took a drink. *Well, that didn't take long at all.*

The two continued drinking, talking to random patrons and occasionally joining in song when the entire tavern did. Only one man seemed to recognize Elias and his status but kept it discreet as Elias entertained his questions. He enjoyed the talks until the topic of the duel arose, and the man sensing he had said something impolite, thanked Elias and excused himself.

"I don't think I've had quite enough just yet," Elias said. "Maybe one more cup?"

Geraldine walked off to fetch them both a drink, and Elias looked around at the patrons enjoying themselves before his eyes caught the flicker of movement at the door as it swung open.

A man had entered that demanded his attention.

He was slightly taller than average, his short, dark and curly hair flowed smoothly into a neatly kept beard. It suitably matched his outfit, which mostly consisted of black clothing Elias could tell the regular citizen would not be able to afford. However, the most remarkable aspect was his glistening blue eyes. They contrasted his dark outfit, making them shimmer with color, and the flickering candles only accentuated their brightness.

Elias was immediately smitten.

He had not realized how long he was staring at the man, who had now made eye contact. The man greeted a few others before making his way over to Elias, who decided to stand his ground once he had gotten caught.

"Something troubling you, stranger?" the man's voice was deep and confident, though Elias thought he heard a hint of amusement.

"I apologize for having been caught staring, it was not courteous of me. I was admiring your attire. You dress well, and clearly have a knack for standing out in a crowd, if you don't mind me saying."

The man smiled, which was exactly what Elias had been hoping for. The handsome stranger took a seat next to Elias and looked him up and down. "Not a stranger to fashion yourself. I recognize the intricate pattern in the stitching, a creation of Tarin Albedor, if I'm not mistaken."

"You definitely know your fashion."

"I like to dress sensibly and rely on my clothes to not quickly wear out. He isn't cheap, but he does good work."

Elias nodded in agreement, a little uncertain about where to lead the conversation as it slowly became stagnant.

"You must be of noble blood to afford such attire," the man commented, a little awkward as it appeared he was also struggling about how to carry the conversation forward. Elias thought it was cute that he appeared bashful but felt a thrill inside knowing the man at least wanted to continue talking.

"I apologize," he said. "I did not wish to talk of finances, I made haste with my words before my…"

Elias shook his head and held up a hand. "It is fine, I assure you. I am of noble birth, but not a topic I wish to discuss tonight. Perhaps something else. Are you familiar with your wines?"

The man smiled, straightening his posture. "I think I know my wines quite well. We haven't many distillers who make them, so they are easy to distinguish if you enjoy them well enough."

"Then let us play a game. Wait here a moment." Elias rose from his chair and made his way to the bar where the barkeep had just given Geraldine their drinks.

"Oh, sir, I was just on my way back."

"Take it to the table Geraldine, I have a guest."

Geraldine appeared confused but did as requested. Elias signaled the barkeep and surprised the busy man when he ordered two glasses of each wine he had in stock. The barkeep was skeptical at first before Elias produced the coin, plus a small tip to have it brought to his table.

Elias returned to his seat where Geraldine held back a smile. He knew her well enough, and gave her a quizzical look, but she shook her head slightly to let him know it was nothing of import.

"The barkeep will be along shortly with the game I have prepared for us," Elias stated, the man giving a slight smile at the prospect of what it might be.

The trio spoke as they waited, commenting on the bard's performance, when the barkeep made his way over with another server, producing two trays full of cups with different wines.

"Here you go," the barkeep said. "Two of everything I had in stock. This one here is—"

"I don't mean to be rude," Elias said, cutting the man off before he was able to label the wines. "But I don't wish to know their names or flavors. I have challenged this man to taste them and tell me who and what they are."

The stranger smiled, clearly amused by Elias' little game. The barkeep smiled and wished him luck before returning to the bar.

"I hope you know your wines. If the barkeep did not tell you, then how are you to know if I am wrong?" the man picked up a cup, swirled it before giving it a sniff.

"Are you saying I don't know my wines well enough? Did you hear that, Geraldine? This man has insulted me." Elias feigned hurt, and Geraldine just very stiffly nodded along. Elias thought it odd but could not ask her any questions in front of the gentleman, especially when he was having such a strong connection with this man.

The stranger took a sip of his drink, contemplating for a moment. "Well, drink and prove me wrong then, with your strong expertise. This is from Madam Raelene's distillery. One of her newer concoctions of berries and spices. I believe she kept this one stored inside a livewood barrel. Surprised to see such a high-profile wine in this tavern." He spoke with no hesitation, the confident front producing a cocky smile as he waited for Elias to tell him otherwise.

Elias raised his eyebrows at the man and took a sip of the pairing cup. *This is going to be a fun night.*

* * *

Elias spent many hours with the nameless man, neither party offering their moniker and neither bothering to inquire. It was disrespectful for nobility to address each other without exchanging names first, but it did not bother the pair as they laughed, drank, and conversed well into the night.

Elias knew he was meant to return home before the moon was at its halfway point, but he did not want to leave the man's side to check. He was enjoying himself, and any scolding he would receive from his father as a result would be worth it. The buzz that suffused him was not from alcohol, but rather a warm feeling that comforted him whenever he looked at the stranger.

A gentle brush of the fingers when they accidentally reached for the same cup. Color in the cheeks that didn't derive from alcohol. The awkward eye contact when they glanced at each other.

The warm energy whenever the stranger leaned closer as another patron squeezed by him.

As they listened to the crowds' cheering and singing that interrupted their conversation, a man-made haste between the drunkards and reached the stranger's side. He bent low and spoke words Elias could not possibly hear over the rambunctious crowd.

At once the man's face dropped, and Elias knew this night was over.

33

The messenger stood by the man's side waiting. The stranger waited until the song was over, before standing somewhat reluctantly. "I must apologize for the abrupt ending to this lovely night, but I'm afraid I have been called away, something most urgent has arisen and I must now depart."

"I thought as much. Thank you for a wonderful night. I do not get many of these and I will cherish it."

"Perhaps… perhaps I shall see you here again?" the man inquired, his face full of hope.

Elias hadn't the heart to tell him it was unlikely, and he himself wished their paths would cross again. "We can certainly hope so."

The stranger smiled and nodded them farewell as the crowd began to sing to another tune, somehow louder this time.

Geraldine had remained oddly quiet; Elias had guessed it was from the man's obvious noble status. He frowned as she watched the door, as if expecting the handsome stranger to return through it at any moment.

Elias and Geraldine sat through a couple more songs, idly sipping their remaining of their drinks before Geraldine suggested they head home for the night. Elias agreed; his desire to remain had fled with the stranger.

As they began the walk back toward the hill that served the noble quadrant, the moon had passed its peak and Elias sighed.

"Something wrong, sir?" Geraldine asked.

"I just feel… empty now. I had fun tonight, but for some reason I feel like I am not taking that excitement with me. I fear… I fear the man has stolen my emotions."

"Nonsense, sir. Lift your sleeve," Geraldine suggested.

Elias knew what she was referring to and lifted his left sleeve. His forearm was a deep blue, almost black in the darkness. Each high-ranking noble, or any person of status, was outfitted with a very light sheet of livewood, sewn into the skin of their forearm. Elias was still learning the methods used to meld it into the skin, but its color reflected its wearer's emotions. It was designed so show the reactions and sentiments towards important subjects, making it near impossible for them to hide their true intentions. It was only to be revealed in important meetings, or if requested by a member of equal status or higher.

Elias had been studying the sleeves, taking a particular interest in livewood, and knew this shade of blue represented emptiness. It was akin to sadness, but it was closer to say he had lost something precious to him.

"See? Emotions," Geraldine said, her tone a little snappy.

"What is it, Geraldine?"

"Are the memories you made tonight not good enough for you to hold onto? Did it not fill you with happiness?"

"Geraldine..."

"I sincerely hope your father is asleep before we arrive. He needs his rest, and we are already late as it is. Let us focus our energy on reaching home."

Elias was surprised at the sudden reappearance of Geraldine's professional personality. He thought she had enjoyed herself tonight, but he was clearly mistaken. They walked home in silence, Elias had already been depressed enough before Geraldine's outburst but now he felt completely sour.

He marched to his room, not bothering to check to see if his father was waiting for Elias' return, knowing Geraldine would do that anyway. As he closed the door to his room, he was holding back tears. He'd had so much fun tonight. Why did it have to end?

As he sat, frustrated thoughts stirring his mind, there was a quiet knocking on his door.

Geraldine quickly entered, face tilted to the floor in shame. "I apologize for my rudeness earlier, sir, but before I continue, I need to know something."

"Go on," Elias spoke, curiosity piqued.

"Did he make you happy?"

Elias thought on it for a moment, confounded at the unexpected question but deciding to give Geraldine the truth. "Yes."

"I think I can find out who he is."

Elias eyes widened, and he felt the spark of hope return, inflamed with a burning excitement at the prospect of actually speaking with the man again. "Geraldine, I do not know why you have been acting like this for the past few hours, but I guarantee you a pay raise if you can find him for me."

"I will try, though with a different commitment if you do not mind. I wish for you to concentrate during your training and studies, not sneaking out to see him."

Elias was surprised Geraldine cared about him that much to reject a pay increase in favor of his own benefit. He leapt from his bed and embraced her in an excited rush. "I promise, Geraldine. I will study and train harder, as long as you send him a letter from me."

"Then I shall return tomorrow to retrieve the letter and do my best to find out who he is."

"Thank you, Geraldine, you are the best."

Geraldine smiled. "Goodnight, sir."

"Goodnight," she said, and closed the door softly behind her. *Who cares what she says, she's getting a raise in rations.*

3

Maggie stood frozen in the middle of the aisle, matching the movements of the lifeless books that surrounded her, lost in her thoughts during the tedious task of going through the checklist of books. She did not resent the job—someone had to do it—but it didn't provide the stimulation that would keep her mind from venturing astray.

She had been organizing the few books they had on agriculture before her mind decided to detour elsewhere, shifting to thoughts surrounding Castor and the potential fatalities in his job. She had been advised by Audrey not to think about death, but Maggie couldn't contain the vast number of possibilities her brother faced with every wave of enemy. She had seen the metalurks on those occasions when she'd snuck out to find Castor during attacks, fearing he'd already been slain. Her memory of the creatures was a well-constructed series of paintings that played one after the other in grim scenes: Castor valiantly fighting beside his men, slaying several of the vicious creatures, all the while having been wounded. She remembered how the blood dripped from his arm and sprayed droplets whenever he swung his weapon.

She was certain he would die that day.

Distraction. Need a distraction.

She shook herself back to reality, repeating the words Audrey had told her whenever she felt an oncoming anxiety attack.

Maggie took deep breaths as she delved back into searching and organizing the shelves as the library dictated.

Her mind, however, had other ideas. It was still trying to force her into thinking about the metalurks, how Castor's men should have tried harder to protect him, convincing her that his men wanted her brother dead. She began to read the titles of the books aloud, a technique she used in desperation, hoping a title would distract her.

"*Toil and Soil*", she said then marked the book on her list and positioned it appropriately, hurrying to grab the next one. "*Crops and Weather Rotations.*" She didn't feel foolish talking to herself, the library was scarce of people. Only the head librarian, Heleen, and a solitary man resided, but they were both too far away to hear her.

"*Grow. Harvest. Survive.*" She almost laughed at that one. *Straight forward title. "Growing the Seeds of..."*

Her voice trailed away as she caught a flicker of movement in the corner of her eye. She stared into the passageway, dust particles dancing in the beams of light spearing through the windows. No one moved or made a sound. Maggie cautiously returned to her work but couldn't shake her nerves.

"*Growing the Seeds of the Future.*" She slowly placed the book in its preordained position, keeping as quiet as she could to catch any sounds of movement. As she pulled another book from the shelf, the hairs on the back of her neck rose. Someone had crept up behind her.

Maggie swung around, the book falling from her fingers to hit the floor with a lonesome thud.

No one.

She stared into the shelves, her eyes flickering between any visible gaps to catch sight of something, or someone, she was certain was there. Heart racing, her senses heightened to the point of becoming numb. Her sight and her hearing remained alert, attempting to catch the invisible predator that stalked her. Maggie's panicked, open-mouth breaths dried the moisture from her tongue.

From her periphery, she realized she had a new book in her hand, her arm raised and ready to strike.

A moment passed with no movement, and she began to ease herself down from her panic, becoming aware of her rapid breathing. Maggie lowered her arm and continued to search for whoever—or whatever—was creeping around... but she knew nothing was there.

There never was.

Convincing her mind there was no immediate threat, Maggie turned to place the book on the shelf.

"Margaret?"

She let out a small scream, startled by the voice.

Heleen, the head librarian, was staring at her, the deep lines on her face contorted into a look of concern. "I did not mean to startle you, child. Please, take deep breaths, it is only me."

She advanced, taking Maggie's hands and breathing along with her. Heleen was fully aware of Maggie's situation and provided the support needed from time to time. The elderly librarian was a considerate woman, though there were times Maggie was sure Heleen's grey hair would burst into flames when she caught anyone deliberately messing with the library or its contents.

Maggie followed Heleen's instruction and mimicked her controlled pace. She began to relax, listening to Heleen's soothing tone.

"Now, Margaret, please tell me what happened. Do not stir yourself up with the explanation, keep it short and simple."

Maggie nodded, taking a moment to think about the words before she spat them out. "I just thought someone was sneaking around."

Heleen nodded as if that's what she expected and gave Maggie a quick hug. "No one is creeping around, dear, and no one wants to hurt you."

"I know," Maggie replied softly, not entirely convinced by her own words.

"Perhaps it is time you saw Audrey?"

"I'm not to see her for a few more days."

"It is fine, child. I am sure she would understand. Tell her the truth and she will listen."

Resigned, Maggie nodded. "Okay. I'll see her once I finish going through the agricultural checklist."

"Nonsense," Heleen said kindly. "I will finish it if I have time, but there is no rush for it to be done now. Go and see Audrey, please."

"If you're certain, Heleen."

"Thank you, dear." Heleen smiled. "Do you need an escort?"

Maggie shook her head. "I'll be fine, she doesn't live far."

Heleen stared at her for a moment, and Maggie couldn't tell if Heleen was trying to detect a potential lie or weighing the consequences if she were to leave the library unattended for a short moment to escort her.

"Honestly, Heleen, I'll go, and I'll be fine."

"If you are sure?" she asked again, and Maggie nodded. "I will see you tomorrow."

Heleen escorted Maggie to the door, holding her hand the whole way. It wasn't necessary, of course, and made Maggie feel like a child, not a thirty-eight-year-old woman, but she knew that Heleen truly cared for her, and didn't want to diminish the woman's intentions.

"Thank you, Heleen. I'll see you tomorrow."

"Take care, dear."

Maggie waved as she walked away, heading towards Audrey's house. There's was no need to rush; as much as Maggie knew she had to speak to Audrey, it didn't make doing so any easier. There was a small degree of comfort during her sessions, but ultimately Maggie felt that Audrey was only giving her easy solutions to avoid particular subjects rather than addressing and fixing them directly.

Maggie decided to take the long route, playing the upcoming scenario in her mind, predicting what Audrey would say and prematurely deciding that she would not benefit from the session. She strolled through the streets, watching the people as they went about their own business, keeping an eye on anyone who headed in her direction.

She turned down the next street and hesitated. Everything appeared normal – people walking or hanging their clothes to dry, but a group of young men held her focus. Perhaps it was their demeanor, the harsh bark of their laughter, but she could not divert her attention from them. She walked forward, hoping to see or hear anything. She did not waver from the middle of the path as she neared. One gentleman looked up as she passed, his dark brown hair long enough that he had it in a plait that was wrapped around the front of his neck. It was a peculiar look, but apparently a fashion amongst the young men. Maggie saw no appeal in it, but it definitely did make one stand out. The young man's dark green eyes stayed on her for no longer than necessary before his gaze returned to the rest of the group. Obviously, he had not considered her a threat or a target and said nothing as she drifted close enough to hear their conversation.

She continued on, not daring to look in their direction, her back feeling very stiff as the panic of being caught settled in. The young men were only speaking of their boredom, providing Maggie with both relief and disappointment as she turned the corner. Relieved to have not drawn attention but disappointed she had not gained any leads. She knew they were up to something, her instincts told her as much. Maggie would swing by after her session with Audrey to see if they were still hanging around.

She journeyed on, thinking about how she would approach the boys on her way back, see if she could get a better angle on the ones who'd faced away from her.

As she came upon Audrey's house, Maggie took a deep breath, steeling herself.

Knocked.

The door swung open, revealing a middle-aged, auburn-haired woman. Her dark brown eyes widened in surprise as they came to rest on Maggie.

"Hi, Audrey. I was told to come and see you."

"I see. Please, come in." Audrey donned a smile and stood to the side, beckoning Maggie to enter.

Maggie took one more deep breath, anxiously anticipating the conversation to come, and entered the household.

* * *

As expected, Maggie didn't obtain much from her session with Audrey. Maggie said all she had wanted to say in the first five minutes, but Audrey pursued answers like a dog after a bone. While Maggie had explained why Heleen had sent her over before her scheduled session, that wasn't enough for Audrey, who was relentless in her pursuit to get Maggie to speak. It was that behavior that irritated Maggie. She would speak about her problems when she felt like it, not when someone harassed her to do so. What made it worse was that Maggie still had to attend her appointment just a few days from now.

Once the session was finally done, Maggie hurried away from the house, intent on getting home. She was uncertain how long she had been at Audrey's, but the sun was setting, and she knew nightfall was not a pleasant time for her to be out. She hated the darkness; the only place she felt safe was in her house, which was still blocks away.

In her haste, she had entirely forgotten the group of youthful men along the route she took home. She turned the corner and was surprised to see they had grown slightly in number. She knew they were up to something, and she would attempt to find out what it was.

The men didn't seem to notice her, so ducked back behind the corner, occasionally peeking to see what they were up to. Her senses heightened again, frantically searching for any others who might draw attention to her. Maggie didn't have anything on her to falsify an activity, so it was simply wait and hope.

As the sun continued its slow descent, the more anxious she became. If nothing happened in the next half-hour, she would be forced to head home. The young men sat around, talking. She was too far to hear their words, so she was hoping to see something incriminating. Maggie was still sure they were up to something. Maggie spotted a man walking down the other end of the street. It was obvious he was making his way towards the group. *This* was what she had been waiting for.

The young men greeted the man, who seemed a little stiff in his movements, standing apart rather than meshing with the group. It was clear the man was speaking to the boy with the neck braids, cautiously and periodically glancing around.

This is it.

The neck-braids boy gestured with a nod to the man and walked down the alley between the buildings, with the new arrival in tow. The rest of the group continued to laugh and talk to each other, not drawing attention to whatever was happening down the alley.

Fortunately, Maggie had chosen her spot well, and ran down the length of the building until she could peer into the alleyway the two had entered. She spied them entering the longer alleyway and check to make sure they were alone. Maggie quickly ducked behind the corner, praying she had not been caught.

Her breathing was sharp and rapid, cold sweat ran down her body as the fear of being caught lurked over her like a puppeteer. The stone building she pressed herself against seemed to tremble, warning her to flee. But Maggie stood her ground; the risk was worth it.

She slowly peeked around the corner once more. The new arrival was statue still while the neck-braids boy held a finger to the man in warning… or threat. Maggie could see the boy more clearly now, but most importantly she could see his wrist. It was what she had been searching for.

The tattoo of a skull bearing the symbol of their Gods, surrounded by a circle. She knew that symbol meant to be a sign of hope, a sign that the Gods had not abandoned their city, or their struggle. Though she had no idea what it meant when placed upon a skull. But it was the tattoo that marked them as Sandmen – a gang that specialized in the production and distribution of drugs, and most commonly, 'dreamer'.

Once the boy had finished instructing the man in hushed tones, he reached into his pocket and pulled out a small pouch and hurriedly handed it over. The man quickly stashed the pouch, his hand remaining in his pocket as if the drug might disappear.

With that, the boy went one way, and the man went the other. Transaction complete.

This is it. I have to tell him.

She abandoned her concealed position and rushed away from the alley. Maggie took turns down seemingly random streets to ensure she had not been followed, but always, she glanced over her shoulder. Adrenaline pumped through her body, allowing her to walk tirelessly, not slowing for a moment until she was certain she was safe.

After making several loops of the area to ensure once again that she was not being followed, she made her way to The Flowing Red Tavern. It was his favorite establishment at which to drink, and given the current time, he would most likely have started hours ago.

Maggie took a moment to straighten herself clothes and tamp down her unruly hair, ensuring she looked presentable. When she wiped away the sweat that clung to her face, to her surprise, her hands came away red.

She dabbed her upper lip with a clean finger, fresh blood now smeared it. *My nose.* In her mad dash to get away, she had somehow not realized the blood pouring down her face. There were even blood droplets on her once clean shirt. She cursed to herself, wiping away the blood on the inside of her shirt sleeve to conceal the incident.

Gods know how I am going to clean that out.

She double checked herself once more. Only the little bloodstains on her shirt remained, but she was adequately tidy enough as long as she didn't draw attention to the blood.

She made way inside the bustling tavern.

As expected, the tavern was quiet on this night. The limitation of alcohol did not allow for many patrons, but she knew he had connections here and they would bend the rules slightly for him.

Maggie easily spotted his dirty, light-brown overcoat. He never cleaned the thing but insisted on wearing it every night. She had to sneak away with it on occasion while he was intoxicated, feeling the need to rid the awful smell that he somehow never noticed. As Maggie made her way over to him, she found him in conversation with another man at the bar. She knew she should have waited for their conversation to be over, but there were more pressing matters to deal with.

"James."

He turned around, his expression souring as he rolled his eyes. The man James had been speaking to turned as well, eyeing

Maggie up and down with his dirty brown eyes. She stared back, noting that he was not much younger than James, and had dyed the plait of his hair a bright green. Personally, Maggie thought he looked a fool, simply trying to appear younger by coloring his hair, but she was not here for him.

"James," she repeated. He had turned away from her, clearly not wanting to speak.

"What the hell are you doing here, Mags? I told you to leave me alone."

Maggie could tell he was already a few drinks in. His short fuse a testament to that. "I have something important to tell you."

"No. No you don't. There's nothing for us to speak about. Now go away."

"James, it's really important."

"It never is, Mags! You need to leave. We have nothing to speak about." James was becoming hostile, but Maggie didn't care. Despite his apparent aggravation, she knew he wouldn't harm her.

"It's about Patrick."

James slammed his mug onto the counter. Without a word to his companion, he grabbed Maggie by her arm and dragged her outside, leading her around the side of the tavern, away from prying eyes and ears.

He dropped her arm, glared at her. "It's always about Patrick, Mags. Always. I'm sick of it. I've told you before that I don't want to talk about him. I've told you so many times to just leave me alone, we're done. That's it. No more. Stop. Please, for the love of all the Gods, just leave me alone now."

"But I found some of the people who had a hand in—"

"He's dead, Mags! Dead! Leave it alone! Get over it! Our son is gone! It's been three years now and you won't let it go!" He ran his hands down his face. "You need to find a way to deal with it. I have. Now leave me alone." Jams slammed his fist into the wall and left Maggie standing alone.

She watched him turn the corner, heart aching as he returned to the tavern. Returned to the drink he thought solved all of his problems.

I need to talk to him before he starts drinking next time.

Maggie made her way home, regret dragging at her feet even as the darkness closed in.

In the confinement and solitude of her own home, Maggie wept.

4

Arthur Va Daolin sat at his desk, back erect, eyes focused on his teacher as she continued to go into detail about Malvarkian's laws. He found the subject particularly interesting, intrigued as to when and how the laws scaled to such a high degree for seemingly low crimes. He had always been intrigued with the city's history, but so were most people. Their ancestors had found the city abandoned and simply moved in, thinking it a more favorable proposition than their home at the time. Arthur had always been curious as to why this had seemed the better option considering they had been prisoners in their own city for nearly two hundred years, living off a diet of the only vegetables and fruits that they could grow, and what limitations they had with meat.

Had the metalurks simply been in hiding, waiting until a new group of people had settled in? If they had shown such intelligence, why was that not reflected now? If they were a new threat, what had happened to the old Malvarkians?

Unfortunately, the teachings provided no answers. Their people had no historical recordings of the metalurks, nor was there any record of what had caused the Old Malvarkians to simply disappear. They weren't even sure if the previous residents had abandoned the city or had been slaughtered by the metalurks.

If they had been killed, where were the bodies? If they had left, where did they go and why did they leave everything behind?

In his other teachings with his mentor on the subject, he had discovered that the Old Malvarkians had been slowly dwindling in number before they had disappeared. It was widely believed they were cursed, and that curse had transferred to the new inhabitants once they took Malvark as their new home.

Arthur realized he had become distracted from his lesson, his mind leaping from one question to another. He quickly began taking notes once again, knowing his father would scold him should his attention wane.

All of his mentors were to report to his father at the end of every lesson, informing him of the day's teachings and Arthur's performance. Edmund Va Daolin liked to be completely involved in his son's learnings and would consistently be aware if Arthur began to slip in any way. It was true that it was bothersome, having his father and mentors constantly grading and watching him, but it was all Athur had ever known.

His father allowed leniency at times, should Arthur be up to date with his studies of course. Occasionally, Arthur was allowed to take a break where he could choose his own activities. He usually liked to walk around the city, a deep need to separate himself from his household.

As the next champion for the Daolin family, Arthur's life was defined by a very strict schedule set by his father.

Groomed since birth to believe it was normal for him to stay within the household for most all of his time, he was now in his early twenties, and it had long been apparent that his lifestyle was irregular. Still, there was nothing to do but accept it. His father would get Arthur most things he requested, and Arthur was more than aware that he lived a more privileged life than those at the bottom of the hill.

This lesson on the laws of Malvark was something his father felt crucial. Confident that Arthur would be victorious in his duel against the Noldins on the Day of Sacrifice, he planned on Arthur becoming a key member of the city, and quite possibly even join The Voice one day. The Voice dictated all laws and punishments for the city, so it was crucial Arthur knew it all by heart, even so far as devising alterations based on hypothetical situations.

The strict routine made for a strained relationship with his father; Arthur felt little more than a tool at his father's disposal. Yet he continued his notetaking, knowing he would be tested on the subject by the end of the week. His mentor on current city matters was dull, her voice so monotonous it could bore a metalurk to sleep. She truly tested Arthur's discipline, to the point he had considered on multiple occasions if his father had her put up a farce to assess his son's patience.

He glanced at the hourglass that slowly trickled, grain by agonizing grain, teasing Arthur at how close the lesson was to completion. He scribbled down ideas and thoughts for the latest law they were focusing on until finally, the last grain in the hourglass fell. Arthur immediately closed his book, prompting his mentor to glimpse at the time.

"I see, our lesson is concluded. At tomorrow's lesson, please have your alternate ruling on the stealing of livestock should everyone theoretically own chickens."

"Of course. Thank you, Madam Vardindal." Arthur bowed, showing proper respect to his mentor as he had been taught, and exited the room before she could say anything else.

He was glad to be moving again, his body needed it. He was considering skipping his next scheduled lesson in favor of tending to his garden. He was debating on informing his father of his want to do so, keen to learn more about the methods his apothecary teacher had taught him with the flowers he was growing. Edmund Va Daolin, however, would not be easily convinced, he was a man who had immaculate focus, rarely willing to detour from his day-to-day plans.

Arthur decided against skipping the lesson; he was in no mood to try and convince his father of something the man thought trivial. Arthur's flowers could wait; the teachings on his family's history took precedence.

He made way for his room, intending to swap the appropriate books over for the next lesson, and make his way down to the kitchens for something to eat beforehand. His growling hunger had not assisted in focusing on his teachings.

Despite the sheer number of items in his room, he was able to keep it all organized. He had several gifts from noble families of monetary worth on display, presented to him either because they truly wished him luck in his upcoming duel, or they wanted to look good in his father's eyes. His personal bookcase was ordered the way he preferred, and all of his clothes were neatly folded away and out of sight.

The only thing that differed was an envelope on his bed.

He placed his book on its designated spot on the shelf and retrieved the next relevant book before moving over to the mirror. The envelope was most likely another meaningless message from a noble family promising to celebrate his victory and shower him with gifts upon his return. It was becoming increasingly tedious the closer they got to the Day of Sacrifice. It was difficult to tell if any were sincere in their words; had they truly meant it, they would have spoken to him directly.

He inspected his appearance in the mirror, and as expected, he was clean and presentable. His curly black hair was kept short to avoid getting in his blue eyes. His beard was trimmed, not a hair out of place, and his fine clothes were free of any diminishing marks.

Pleased with himself, he moved over to his bed, picking up the letter as he sat.

Seal isn't broken. Father mustn't have opened it yet. Arthur pried the envelope open and removed the letter.

It has taken me many minutes to figure out how to start this letter. I was not given your name, though I am not sure if that was intentional on your part.

If it was, it worked. I am intrigued by you. Yet your name matters not to me.

And since your name doesn't matter to me, I won't share mine either. At least, for now.

Our engagement the other night was all too brief, and I long for another meeting, but I'm afraid my line of work doesn't allow me to visit the tavern very often. I hope you don't mind, but I had a friend who was able to find you and deliver this letter on my behalf.

I was hoping we could talk, even if it is only through letters. I admit that I do feel lonely and want a companion as captivating as you to speak with.

Should you agree, my friend will come for a return letter.

I hope to hear from you, I have so much I wish to talk about.

Arthur's heart raced with every word. He had not expected a letter, but he was pleased nonetheless. He had enjoyed the other night's outing, thinking of that compelling and charismatic man he had met, hoping to see him during his next sojourn, though that wasn't for another week or so. It was a long shot that he would happen upon the man again during his occasional nights out in the city but had not considered tracking down the man himself.

He was glad the mysterious man had taken the initiative to find him.

Arthur did not have to consider the proposition, immediately moving over to his desk to write his reply. He finished the letter, content with what he had written. To his side lay several pieces of paper that contained his many first attempts at starting the letter, having the same difficulty his secret sender had.

He suddenly became aware that he had lost track of time, and hurriedly grabbed his book and left, leaving the letter open on his desk to dry before…

He paused. How was he supposed to give the letter to the messenger if he didn't know who they were?

He turned to his desk, considering his options. The letter he received said that the friend would return, so Arthur would have to be patient and hope it would be soon. He hurried to his next lesson, the usual tension of being late fizzling away, finding himself not caring for his own tardiness as fond memories of locking eyes with the man commanded his emotions.

He recalled the shape of the man's captivating smile, unable to hold back his own.

* * *

The lesson felt short. Reading the letter had given Arthur a surge of adrenaline, feeling ready to tackle anything. He confidently answered all of his mentor's questions, feeling invincible with every correct response. It had been a long time since he felt this way.

With the day's lessons complete, Arthur hurried back to his room to go over his letter before he sent it off, perhaps even rewrite it to make him sound more appealing.

Don't overthink it. Just make sure it has no mistakes and send it.

He swung the door open to his chambers, startling the woman who had been waiting inside. "I'm sorry," he said. "I didn't know someone was waiting for me in here." He took a hesitant step forward. "Who are you?"

The woman composed herself, and Arthur glanced at the letter on his desk that she sat near, fearing she may have read it. Her plain clothing indicated she was not of noble birth, and her dark blonde hair woven into a basic hairstyle not common amongst any class he knew.

"I would prefer it if I remained nameless, sir. I have come for your response to the letter I left here earlier."

Sooner than I thought. Arthur closed the door, relaxing a touch. "Yes, of course. I just returned from a lesson, but I did draft a response."

The woman smiled when he pointed to the letter on his desk. He moved over, tested the ink to make sure it was dry, and placed it in an envelope. He hesitated as he grabbed his seal, bearing the symbol of his family.

"You won't tell anyone about this, will you?"

She shook her head. "I will be in trouble if anyone finds out I am here, sir. My presence and my contact with you will be kept only between us. The same goes for the recipient of the letter. I trust your discretion as well, sir?"

Arthur did not answer right away, pondering why she would be in trouble if she were caught speaking with him, but decided it was irrelevant. He grabbed a plain stamp from his desk drawer, heating the wax over a little candle, and sealed the envelope. He got a tingling sensation in his stomach as he handed the letter to the woman, who took it with a smile and made haste to the door, checking the hallway beyond before departing.

He sat on his bed, anxiety swirling in his stomach. *Is this a good thing? What am I doing?*

Everything in Arthur's body was ordering him to chase after the woman and take back the letter; it was not a good idea to talk to the man, knowing that Arthur may very well die on the Day of Sacrifice.

But he simply did not care.

5

Everyone had grown accustomed to the sound of the horn routinely bellowing throughout streets to signal the incoming attack.

It continued to instill fear, just not the same amount of panic it used to.

Castor made his way to his position atop the wall, in no particular rush. The gap between each horn blast indicated there was still time before any orders were needed. Soldiers were continuously rushing past him, bows in hand, to take their own positions at the rampart.

The elevated platform specifically crafted for General Deven was empty. The man had yet to arrive.

Castor hoped the general would not arrive at all, choosing to sit this wave out and leave Castor in charge. As captain of the East Gate, Castor wanted to show his leadership skills more often, but it seemed the general was insistent on oppressing him just enough so he wouldn't stand out.

Taking his position next to the platform, Castor watched the archers take the line. Having a battle every few days did wonders for synchronization and teamwork. He continued his watch, with naught else to do but wait as the archers stood ready for orders.

Still no sight of General Deven.

As the metalurks neared, ignoring the crops that flanked the city, the horn blasts sounded closer together. By now, the general should have at least made an appearance.

"Stand ready!" Castor gave the order for the archers.

Castor held them a little longer, watching the metalurks charge straight for them in vicious haste and ignoring the farms as expected. They may have besieged the city, but the creatures had no thought process, no tactics. Theirs was a mindless charge at the gates.

And yet, they're still winning.

"Archers! Loose!" Castor's voice resounded along the wall.

Wooden arrows arched into the night, hitting the front line of the metalurks yet stopping few in their tracks.

Like a well-oiled machine, the archers continued to release arrow after arrow.

"Resupply!" Castor called, sending the younger men who waited on the sidelines scrambling for arrows from a nearby stockpile, putting a handful into each archer's quiver as it ran low.

"You can go prepare below now, Castor," the general called out from the steps as he climbed to the rampart.

Castor stared daggers at the man. While the general had every right to wrest control from him, it was improper to do so during an attack, especially while he was giving orders.

"I can handle it, Arnald."

"I believe I gave you an order to prepare your defenses in the tunnel."

Castor knew he couldn't argue the matter. General Deven had superiority and could tarnish Castor's hard-fought reputation in an instant. Castor reluctantly complied, making way towards the stairs.

"And that's General Deven, Castor. Don't forget that next time."

Castor bit his tongue, letting his anger fester inside. He would release his frustration on the metalurks. "Steelwoods!"

His team was already in formation, and they were itching for a fight. He scanned them, noting Vance had successfully hidden to let his arm heal.

Castor wasn't sure why the general had riled him so quickly today, but he needed to vent. He waited, watching the gate shudder from the body-blows of the metalurks. Spear gripped tight, Castor was eager to begin,

The backup gate was dropped; the metalurks had already made a small hole in the gate.

Soon, they burst through in number.

Finally. "On me!"

* * *

Again, the battle was short, the creature's numbers had decreased once more. It was a regular pattern, but soon a large wave would surge. History had taught Castor that the closer the city drew to the Day of Sacrifice, the larger in number the metalurks became. They weren't sure what caused it, but Castor had been told it had to do with the Gods. Either their power drew more in number, or the monsters' goal was to reach the Gods to devour them.

It didn't matter to Castor what their intention, it only mattered that it would be his first – and likely only – time as Captain of the East Gate to defend against the largest of the metalurk waves. He considered the notion of what might follow should their defense be successful, but he knew it wouldn't be. The creatures always broke through into the city on the Day of Sacrifice, their numbers simply too great for the soldiers to handle. He knew people would die, and he knew he would have to lay down his life to prevent as many deaths as possible.

Having given his short report to the general, Castor was intent on heading to the library to find his sister for the usual check-up when Vance approached him. The soldier's arm was still bandaged, but Castor's focus was on the man's worried expression.

"Sir," Vance greeted, giving the formal salute. "Is everything all right?"

Castor frowned. "What makes you ask?"

"I watched from the sidelines, sir. You seemed... Well, let's just say determined. You left yourself open on in favor of driving more power behind your strikes." Vance hesitated then pursed his lips before speaking. "The men had to cover you because you put yourself in danger. With all due respect, sir, you taught us better than that."

Castor stared at the soldier, memories of the battle returning to him. Vance's words were true. There were times he purposely didn't defend himself so he could drive his spear a little further, knowing that one of his Steelwood soldiers would protect him.

And put themselves in danger by doing so.

Frustrated with himself, Castor let out a sigh, "You're right, Vance. Observant, too."

"You don't need to tell me what it is, sir, I just thought you'd want to know."

He did appreciate being told. If Vance were able to see it, what would happen if one of his superior's also saw him? If General Deven did? The thought made him feel ashamed of his actions. He'd been reckless during the fight to vent his frustrations, but that was no reason to put his men at risk.

Scolding himself, Castor nodded, "Thank you, Vance. I was just feeling a little frustrated today and became careless. It won't happen again."

"Go see, Maggie. Might help."

"Somehow, I doubt that."

"Not getting any better?"

Castor shook his head. "Doesn't seem like any progress, I'm afraid. I have a feeling she's skipping some of her sessions."

"I imagine it isn't easy for her."

"No one wants to talk about what they've been through, and Maggie's been through more than most. I suppose I just have to be patient and hope she turns around someday."

"The Gods eyes are on her. She'll be fine."

"Thanks, Vance. How's your arm?"

"Fine, sir. I'll be ready for the next wave."

"Excellent. We missed having you on the field. Go get a drink with the others, I think they're heading to the Grog."

"If that's your order, sir!" Vance gave a quick grin, saluted, and headed off to join the other Steelwoods.

Castor smiled as the Steelwoods began harassing Vance for missing out on the action. *They're good people. I have* got *to get our name changed, though.*

He held in a sigh and made his way to the library to see his sister.

* * *

To his surprise, Maggie was not in the library as expected. Heleen had sent his sister home early; something had been distracting Maggie, but the head librarian couldn't discern as to what that was. Castor worried all the way over to his sister's place, the thoughts of how far she may have relapsed giving him mixed emotions.

He knew today was going to be an off day.

Castor stopped at the front of his sister's house, memories flowing back to him. The once happy household had slowly decayed into a run-down home filled with misery. Nothing good came of thinking about the many sad events the family went through during their time there. Castor hated looking at it, much less going inside.

He had no idea how Maggie still chose to live there.

After a slight hesitation, Castor knocked on the door, squashing his agitation about going inside again. Maggie's footsteps could be heard on the creaky floorboards beyond the door – a problem she refused to fix, believing it would alert her of any intruders.

The door opened a crack, then wider Maggie saw him. She smiled with relief and invited him inside.

The farther he went into the house, the eerier it became. The house was dirty, cobwebs in nearly every corner, dust on most of the furniture. The mess was expected from his grieving sister, but it still disturbed Castor that she held onto her family's possessions. Her deceased son's clothes were still kept in his room, as were the toys the boy had while growing up, untouched for years. She had even kept the belongings that… that *man* had left behind.

It was apparent to anyone that Maggie could not let go of the past. The peak of her bad luck streak happened years ago, which finally caused Maggie to crack. Her son died, mistakenly executed by the city after an identity mix up. Her husband left shortly after, unable to deal with Maggie's emotional state.

Castor had tried on many accounts to convince Maggie to let go of the physical objects that acted as an anchor for her obsession and depression but to no avail. He took a seat at the table, his usual spot that was no longer covered in dust, and Maggie poured him some tea she'd brewed in anticipation of his arrival.

It was certainly odd to see Maggie act entirely normal within the house, but Castor had been instructed to leave the subject alone until she had made more progress with Doctor Grayvan's wife, Audrey.

Castor could do nothing but trust that Audrey was capable of dealing with Maggie's issues. Gods knew he didn't have the capacity to even attempt to help her by himself. He had to focus on his protection of the city, but his sister was a major concern; she was the only family he had left.
Just as he was hers.

Castor sipped at his tea. "So, how did the sessions go with Audrey?"

Maggie deflated slightly, obviously disappointed that Castor had heard about the extra session, "Fine. She did what she could."

"Meaning?"

Maggie sighed. "I still don't feel any different."

"And you won't for a while, Maggie. You have to keep going, consistently, and go in with an open mind. Right now, she's the only one who can help you."

"I still don't think she'll help," Maggie insisted. "There isn't much to fix."

"Maggie… C'mon. Isn't it a little insulting to lie to me like that?" Castor pleaded, exasperated. Today was not a day to play games.

"Fine. But I'm telling you, once I follow the Sandmen to their base, and find the man that—"

59

"Gods, Maggie! What are you doing? Following Sandmen now? Don't do anything so stupid!" Castor bit back his next words; his sister had relapsed completely.

"It's not stupid," Maggie replied sternly, frowning as she stared at Castor. "I've found one of the members, and through him, I'll find out who it was that killed my child."

"Maggie, please. The Sandmen may have gotten him caught, but they didn't kill him. You have to believe it was just a momentous screw up by the city. They thought your son was a murderer, not a simple drug transporter. Accidents happen, and I'm sorry that it happe—"

"It was *not* an accident." Maggie's voice was low, dangerous.

Castor sighed, unable to convince his sister otherwise. She has deluded herself into believing someone had it out for their family and wouldn't rest until they themselves had been killed. It has been three years, and no one had attempted to take his or Maggie's lives, but that didn't seem enough for Maggie to stray from her conviction.

"Whoever sold my son to the guards is still out there. Since the guards, nor you, believe me, I have to go after them myself."

Castor stared at his sister, his frustration building. He took a deep breath, willing calm, allowing rationality to return. "Maggie, you have to listen to me. Do *not* engage with the Sandmen, please. I fear they'll harm you if you harass them. You have got to let it go."

Maggie returned his stare, almost as if she was sizing him up. "I'll promise if you start investigating the guards, then."

"Maggie…"

"No, Castor. My son was murdered. *Your nephew*. And you don't seem to care that someone in the guards might be behind it. It could very well be a part of your Steelwoods."

"No. No one in the Steelwoods would ever stoop so low."

"But how do you *know?*"

He wasn't sure how she managed to turn the situation around and weave doubts into his beliefs. *Maybe her illness is infectious.* "The Steelwoods are not responsible for Patrick's death." Castor stared at his sister, who sat there with determination boiling in her eyes. *Gods take my soul.* He slumped in his chair. "You promise you'll leave the Sandmen alone if I investigate the guards?"

"Yes. Unless you don't find anything."

"Maggie, c'mon. There might not be anything to find."

His sister's gaze remained steely. "There is."

"Maggie, please. I'll do my best to investigate all the guards involved. When I can, at least. My priority is still the defense of the East Gate."

She finally nodded. "I'll leave the Sandmen alone for now," she said, and sat back in her chair, arms crossed.

I must have treeblood running in me. He knew she wouldn't keep her word for long. Maggie was impatient when it came to these subjects; she had always been a strong-willed woman, but now her attention was focused on the wrong areas. He just had to keep her turned towards his own investigation, dangling just enough in front of her to keep her from following her ridiculous notion about the Sandmen.

Castor sighed, the stress building in his neck. Not only did he have to defend the city, but he also now had to defend his sister from herself. He sipped at his tea, the supposed relaxing remedy now tasted bitter. He had enough stress at his job, dealing with metalurks and his oppressive general.

Maggie turned the conversation to that day's defense, worried that Castor may have suffered harm. Once her concern was appeased, he rose from his chair to take his leave.

When he reached the door he embraced Maggie, planting a kiss on the top of her head. "Don't do anything stupid, I beg you. Just leave it alone until I get time to look into the guards. Please."

"I'll wait for you, I promise."

Her words did nothing to relieve his stress; he was still unable to entirely believe her. Yet there was nothing more he could do. Castor said his goodbye and headed out. He could still feel the house staring at him, judging him. He hastened his pace, nerves churning in his gut. He sighed; it was time to begin his investigation on his nephew's accidental death, knowing there would be nothing to find.

* * *

Castor entered the Magistrate's Office, feeling ridiculous about the request he was about to make. Magistrate Linette Maldin looked up from her desk, smiling when she saw him.

"Well, this is certainly an honor. The East Gate Captain paying me a visit. I wonder what it's about this time. To court me? To thank me for the wonderful job I do? Perhaps to let me know one of my brothers died? Oh, that's grim, Castor," she mocked, causing him to feel guiltier about his intentions.

"Sorry, Lin, business again."

"Oh, that is a surprise. I had not expected you barging into my office would be about business again. Oh, let me guess, it has to be discreet? Don't tell people?"

"Lin, please. You're making this very difficult to beg a favor."

"I could bribe The Voice themselves with the number of favors you owe me. Why not go for the Gods while I'm at it?"

"Your hair is a mess, perhaps groom it, look more professional. There, one favor paid back." Castor smiled, knowing that her light brown hair was perfect as usual, intricately braided the way she liked.

She rolled her eyes at him, the green more piercing under the light. "What do you need, Castor?"

"It's an interesting one, but not a surprising one."

She cocked an eyebrow at him, leaned forward a little in anticipation.

"I need to investigate my nephew's death and the guards involved."

She tilted her head, expression puzzled. "That was three years ago. Why are you looking into it now?"

"Maggie."

"Ah, I see." She nodded, understanding his situation. "Should I take this seriously, or just give you falsified reports to appease her?"

"I think I'll need the real thing. Something tells me she'll be able to tell if the documents are fake."

"Probably because you can't lie to save your own life."

"I can lie. I just don't *like* to lie."

She scoffed, a small smile pulling at her lips. "I just told you that you weren't good at it."

"Oh really? Then show me your sleeve."

"I'll show you mine if you show me yours."

Castor sat on the chair that faced her desk and rolled up his left sleeve, revealing the pale yellow livewood on his forearm. Linette revealed her own forearm, reflecting the similar hue that indicated amusement.

"Well, that didn't really help either of us, did it?" She gestured to the color.

"What do you mean? All I see is that you're in a good mood and willing to accept such a ridiculous request."

The color of her sleeve changed to a light blue. Linette had become worried, and Castor's sleeve matched upon seeing hers.

"Why does she want you to look into it, Cas?"

Castor paused, trying to find the right words. He didn't want to seem like he was enabling his sister's skepticism and delusions, merely helping her deal with them. "She relapsed, almost completely. I'm not sure if it's part of the process of Audrey's sessions."

"She's still seeing Doctor Grayvan's wife?"

Castor nodded.

"Have you noticed it helping at all? When I first heard about them using Maggie as an experiment, I must admit, it intrigued me, but I simply don't see how she aims to help."

"Audrey thinks having someone to open up to about everything and deal with all Maggie's issues could be beneficial. I wasn't sure at first either, but I could see minor changes after each session, even though Maggie doesn't want to admit that."

"It does sound good if it works. Having your own person to talk to that has all the answers for you."

"I doubt she has all the answers, but she at least seems sincere in wanting to help Maggie. I don't understand it myself, but who am I to judge? All I know how to do is stab things with a pointy stick."

"Well, it seems to work wonders for you."

"Almost." Castor's sleeve turned a dark green, reflecting his guilt as he remembered his actions during the fight earlier that day.

63

Linette noticed, and hers returned to light blue. He leaned forward. "I need the file on my nephew's accident three years ago."

Linette thought for a moment before reacting. She moved the papers she had been working on into a neat pile. "Are you sure you want to go down this track?"

"If it'll help my sister, I have to take it seriously."

"Fine. I'll see if I can find the file. I don't know what you expect to find, though. His death was ruled an accident, and that's all the paper will say."

"I know, but I need the name of the arresting guard. I know it was Magistrate Hardale who wrongly sentenced my nephew, and he was removed from his position, so I'll find him on my own."

"But your nephew was convicted of drug trafficking, why would you go after the arresting guard?"

Castor shrugged. "Who else was involved?"

Linette seemed to accept his answer, though her sleeve had turned light blue again. Upon closer look, it was a slightly different shade of blue, a little lighter than before. Uncertainty.

"I really don't know what I expect to find," he said. "I'm just looking for now, I don't know how else to start."

"What about the gang your nephew was part of?"

"He wasn't part of the gang," Castor snapped, his sleeve turning a pale shade of red to show his irritation. He noticed Linette staring at it before he calmed himself. "They're just a bunch of kids dealing drugs. They got caught and made my nephew take the blame because they're cowards. Nothing more."

"Right, sorry. I'll trust your instincts on that one. I've seen enough paperwork about the Sandmen to know how stupid they can be." Linette gestured to the stack of papers at her desk that entailed her position going over the paperwork for criminal's sentencing.

Castor looked at the large stack, disgusted with how many there were. "They're probably the biggest cause of the increase in Dream usage, but that's all they are. Kids making coin. Not that it really matters. Most places don't use coin anymore, they're ordered by the city to distribute a certain amount to each citizen, and the city gives them the supplies for it. No coin needed."

"They probably need the coin to buy other things, like weapons."

"They're arming themselves now?"

Linette nodded, quickly sifting through a stack of papers before grabbing one and placing it in front of Castor. "They managed to get their hands on a livewood shiv. This one killed a man with it. It was confiscated by the arresting guard."

Castor inspected the document, detailing how the young boy repeatedly stabbed another man with the livewood shiv. An impractical weapon for a war, so the city stopped producing them a long time ago. So how did this boy get a hold of one? "They're becoming more resourceful," Castor noted, handing the document back to Linette, who returned it to the stack of processed papers.

"Yes. We've had to instruct the guards to take more care with them. We've had several reports of the Sandmen handling what appeared to be livewood weapons, but that has been the only confirmed case so far."

Castor's arm turned back to the light blue as he worried about what it could mean that the Sandmen were arming themselves. The streets were becoming more dangerous, and his heart dropped at the prospect of fighting a civil war along with their siege.

They would not survive.

"It's fine, Castor. We'll get it under control, that's our job. You keep devoting yourself to the defense of the walls," Linette said, but the thought of a civil war would not easily escape his mind.

"Will you get my nephew's papers?" Castor forced the conversation back to why he had come, his livewood skin remaining the light blue.

"Yes, I'll get them. I hope you're not going to bring up any trouble. The Day of Sacrifice is nearly here, so your attention has to be on the defense of the city. You have a big task coming up, we're all counting on you."

Castor smiled. "You're all counting on the general, you mean. My position is little more than a glorified assistant."

"You still get to lead the Steelwood soldiers, you have to hold the tunnel."

"But the general gets to control me, effectively controlling them. He does the job well, so I can't really complain." He maintained eye contact, smiling, hoping she wouldn't notice his livewood skin turning green from envy. He was a little relieved when she smiled back.

"One day you'll get to be a general. Surely Deven is close to retiring by now, and you'll get to be General Castor. It has a nice ring to it."

Castor scoffed at her naivety and was preparing to tell her about the general's insistence at preventing him from even being considered, when he noticed her arm was light blue again. He decided against telling her, not wanting to add to worry.

Especially since there was a chance he'd not make it through the Day of Sacrifice.

He knew better than to make any real connections to people. He had to leave as little as possible behind should he be killed. His arm turned a vibrant light blue when an image of his sister rose in his mind.

She would be entirely alone if he didn't make it. Aside from Heleen, who would thankfully watch over her after his death. It was obvious the elderly librarian already treated Maggie like family.

Castor had to do all he could to help Maggie deal with her issues before the day came. He had to help put her mind at ease to prepare her for the possibility of his death. And right now, that meant indulging her delusion so that she wouldn't put herself in harm's way. "Are you able to get the report now?"

"Of course." Lin rose from her chair. "I know precisely where it is."

Castor didn't have to wait long for her to return. He thanked her and said his goodbyes, wanting to go over the document in private. The last thing Castor wanted was for Lin to be implicated should he be discovered investigating the arrest. It had taken a long time to get over his nephew's death; Patrick was a bright, happy kid who had his mother's eyes. Castor's trust in the governance took even longer to return. Bringing up a closed matter might be seen as a slight on the judicial system and The Voice's laws. It could also harm his chances at becoming a general.

He kicked himself for adding more pressure to what currently weighed on him, but he was willing to do anything for his sister. If he miraculously got her to stop chasing illusions and nightmares, then he could be closer to peace on the Day of Sacrifice.

Though peace wasn't exactly an option to begin with.

He left the Magistrates Office, walking unhurriedly until he was confident he was alone and no one would grow suspicious of his actions He stood by a bench at what the city claimed to be a park, but instead only harbored a few starving flowers on the verge of death.

The details of his nephew's accident was laid out on the paper in his hand. It spoke of Patrick's accused crime, the proper punishment, and the punishment he received. It also addressed that Magistrate Hardale—the man who wrongly accused his nephew—was stripped of his title and position after an investigation.

Castor closed his eyes, his blood churning as memories of that fateful day rose. He had known of Magistrate Hardale, knew the man could be malicious, but Castor had to convince himself that Hardale had made an honest mistake with his nephew's identity – the man did appear remorseful.

He returned his attention to the paper, searching for a name. *There!*

City Watch Gerric Farwell.

It would be an empty lead, but it was one Castor had. The arresting guard had nothing to do with Patrick's sentencing, but perhaps he had been in the loop of what had happened internally.

Castor trekked towards the City Watch building, where he aimed to find this Gerric Farwell. There was purpose in his stride, and he hoped his rank would be enough for people to leave him be. He took twists and turns down the streets of Malvark, thankful they were mostly empty, though saddened at the realization. He could feel the weight of city's bleak atmosphere, the years of decreasing morale threatening to slow his pace.

This was a city giving up.

Castor reinforced his mental blockade against the city's dreadful attitude, in a naive belief that during his time as a high-ranking soldier, he would see the end of the constant barrage of metalurks.

He soon found himself at the steps of the City Watch. The building hosted the majority of their guards and acted as a base for the low-ranking City Watch, which was precisely what Castor was after. Someone inside would know where to find Gerric.

Castor entered the building without breaking stride, Watchmen standing aside and saluting in recognition of a superior. He made his way to one of the few offices and barged in without so much as a knock. To avoid any suspicion, Castor had to act as if he were there on urgent, official business.

City Watch Leader Brand jumped a little as the door flung open, Castor standing before the man before he could react. Brand jumped to his feet and saluted. "East Gate Captain Castor Belden, it is an honor, sir. I apologize for the mess, I was not informed you were on your way."

"No need for that, Brand, I hadn't the time to send a messenger ahead. I'm in a bit of a rush, so we can skip the pleasantries. I'm after one of your personnel, Gerric Farwell."

Brand frowned then collected himself. It wasn't polite to question a superior ranking officer, exactly what Castor had been counting on. "We do not have a Gerric Farwell, sir."

That caught Castor off guard, and his anxiety returned tenfold. "Are you certain?"

"I could ask the soldiers, sir, but that name is not familiar to me."

"I'll speak to them myself, I'm in a bit of a hurry."

"Would you like me t—"

"No need. Thank you for your time, Brand. I'll question some people on my way out."

"Of course, sir." Brand saluted.

Castor turned, leaving the man's office as fast as he'd entered it. Thoughts raced through his mind, the possibilities forming one after the other. *No, stop. That's Maggie, not me.* There must be a rational explanation for the situation. Perhaps Brand didn't know all of his men by name. How could he possibly? Castor didn't know the name of every man who stood atop his wall, but he knew the names of every Steelwood. He couldn't expect Brand to know the name of every man in the City Watch, but surely some of the lower ranks would know of Gerric.

He stopped a few men on his way out, questioning them but to no avail. It seemed none knew a Gerric Farwell. Frustration seeped through every part of Castor, and with the fear beginning to kick in, he stood in the main room, and bellowed, "Does anyone here know Gerric Farwell?"

The room immediately fell silent. All eyes turned to him as he waited for a response. No one moved or made a sound, the area was so quiet you could have heard the metalurks emerging from the forest.

Time slowed as Castor met the gaze of each and every City Watchman.

"Uh... Are you looking for Gerric?" the voice was quiet and shaky.

Castor turned to the source, watching as a man stepped from behind other soldiers frozen in their tracks.

"Um... I know a Gerric," the man continued, obviously nervous at having to address the East Gate Captain.

"Return to your work!" Castor called out, and the soldiers scrambled to follow his order. *Not exactly subtle, but it would do.*

Castor approached the man who saluted him in return. The Watchman was still young and lacked confidence, becoming increasingly nervous as Castor drew near. "It's all right, you're not in trouble." Castor did his best to calm the man, but it seemed to have no visible effect. "You know Gerric Farwell?"

"I am not certain, sir. I know a Gerric, but I don't recall his last name being Farwell."

Castor relaxed his posture, hoping it would help the nervous man. "What is his last name?"

"I don't recall, sir, I'm sorry." Fear spiked in the man's eyes after admitting he didn't have the answer Castor sought.

"That's fine, soldier, but you do know a Gerric?"

"Yes, sir. He was my mentor before he left the City Watch. He trained a bunch of new recruits alongside me but quit before our training was officially over.

Quit? "Where is he now? What does he do?"

"As far as I can tell, sir, he has no job. I see him occasionally during my shifts in the markets, but he never discloses if he has a job. Whatever it is, it pays better than this," the man said, gesturing around him. The soldiers were paid a low salary, as expected of a city without a real economy – tokens to turn in for supplies. Fortunately, the job came with a few benefits, such as larger portions of rations.

"How do you know that?"

"He dresses better, sir. New clothes, clean. Not anything a soldier could ever afford."

Castor could not believe what he was hearing, trying to convince himself it was all a coincidence. "Thank you. You've helped a lot." Castor patted the man on the shoulder, taking his leave from the City Watch building.

False name? Sudden departure? Higher quality of life? A better opportunity came along. That's all it was. No. There was more. *Gods take me, I'm turning into my sister.*

6

The curtains fluttered with the breeze, causing a chill to run up Elias' spine. The bath had cooled significantly, indicating he had been soaking in it for far too long. He wanted to stretch out his relaxation as much as possible, knowing there was more work to be done before the day's end.

He reluctantly climbed out of the tub, immediately reaching for the nearby towel to defend against the cold breeze long enough to close the window.

Elias took his time to dry and dress himself, in no particular rush to return to his activities. He had yet to finish reading his assigned book on the history of the Gods, a topic that bored him to death. Having grown up learning about their religion and history, he had no idea why his father felt the need to drive such topics into his brain even further.

However, none of it topped how tiresome his father had become in demanding Elias learn different fighting techniques. Elias did not mind the practical sessions, they were invigorating and interesting, but the theory behind them had quickly quelled his interest.

He understood his father was taking the necessary precautions to ensure Elias had the best possible chance in his duel, but it was a struggle for Elias to keep up with it all. The frequency of his combat lessons had been gradually increasing over the years, slowly superseding his other lessons.

It only stressed Elias further.

Most of the time, he did not want to *think* of his upcoming duel, but his father became obsessed with it. It seemed to be the only topic they would ever discuss, leaving Elias with no desire to spend time with his father.

The situation saddened him. Elias was all his father had left, and he could do naught but watch the man drive himself insane with the possibility of losing the only child he had left.

Elias made his way through the halls, detouring to his bedroom in hopes of avoiding his father. It was Geraldine he happened upon in the kitchen, where she was speaking with another servant. Elias had not seen her since she had delivered the letter to the man he had become infatuated with. His heart beat rapidly with anticipation, and his gut churned slowly from the fear of disappointment.

He waited patiently, pretending to be searching for a snack while Geraldine discussed work with the other servant.

Geraldine noticed him (and his poor attempt at stalling for time), and quickly wrapped up her conversation. At that moment, the kitchen hands arrived to begin dinner preparations.

Elias cursed to himself, wanting to openly speak with Geraldine.

"Sir," Geraldine said, clear enough for all to hear. "Would you like dinner brought to your room?"

Elias smiled, grabbed an apple he was too nervous to eat, just to maintain the pretense. "That would be wonderful. In the meantime, I have need of you. I think one of my clothes may need repairing, would you come look at it?"

He knew the lie was completely unnecessary; Elias could simply command Geraldine to follow him, but he did not want to give any of the staff reason to ask questions of his intent.

"Of course, sir," Geraldine responded, no outward indication that she had seen through his deception.

Geraldine followed Elias as he tried to control his pace, not wanting to outwardly display his eagerness to reach his room.

He opened the door to his chambers and ushered Geraldine in, excitedly closing the door behind them. "Geraldine, I don't have any clothes that need repairing. I just wanted to—"

Geraldine raised a hand, interrupting him. "I figured, sir."

Elias nodded, a little ashamed he let his nerves get the better of him. He thought himself at least adequate at concealing truths and emotions, but he didn't have as much of a handle on it as it seemed.

"Of course, I couldn't get past you, Geraldine. Anyway, uh… Is there a return letter?" the question barely made it past his tightened throat.

Geraldine paused for a moment, almost as if she was letting Elias stew in his own anxiety out of amusement, but she had trouble keeping her own professionalism, her face breaking into a smile as she produced the letter.

Elias excitedly grabbed it, embracing Geraldine as words didn't feel like they were enough.

Before he could tear open the letter, Geraldine stopped him. "I'll leave you in solitude to read it. I'll return soon for the um… clothes that need repairing," she said, her grin wide, seemingly happy to see Elias in such elevated spirits.

She left the room before Elias could respond. *Was she mocking me?* It did not matter. He had a letter to read.

Elias sat on his bed and tore open the envelope, cautious enough to protect its sacred contents.

His heartbeat hammered against his ribs as he unfolded the letter, his body shivering with anticipation.

Hello again.

Firstly, I want to say how grateful I am to your friend for finding me, allowing us to at least keep in contact with each other. I am saddened that I may not see you again for some time, but this method may actually have worked out better for my situation as well.

I praise the Gods for allowing me to have met you. I had prayed to them that I would get the chance to speak with you again, and now that they have answered, I do not know what to say. Words are escaping me, and I am uncertain where to begin from the multitude of conversations I wish to have.

I find it hard to confess any interests. I feel a little guilty for taking pleasure in things when our walls are constantly under threat and people live in fear. I suppose I don't share the same fear of the metalurks as most, but my fear does lie within the future of our city.

And our future, as well. If any.

Perhaps that is too soon to speak of, and we should ignore such grim subjects.

I wish to know more about you. And in turn, I will answer any questions you may have about me.

But I shall start; it seems only proper.

I am of noble status, that much would have been made clear, I am sure. I will not state my house or hint to its symbol, for both of our benefits. My father is a strict man and would not respond kindly if he discovered I am in contact with someone without his approval.

My mother is a sweet woman. She adores her children but lacks the confidence to speak against my father in matters of the family. Though I believe she would become as strong as dried livewood if one of her children were placed in danger.

I do not wish to go into further detail of my family for fear of you discovering who we are.

I would like to hear about your family, in short and in lack of details, as mine was.

I fear I may have chosen a lousy subject to begin our correspondence. I would have thrown out and written another letter, but it seems your friend is a bit anxious about departing, and I have penned many attempts already.

Do tell your friend to be careful. I don't wish any danger to befall her as a result of being our messenger.

Elias took a moment to relish the happiness that had eluded him for so long. Finally, a reason to smile other than a drink. Ignoring his prior work that was awaited on his desk, he began to write his return letter. Yet when it came time to write about his family in turn, he stalled.

Family was a subject he'd much rather avoid than acknowledge its reality. Telling the truth would most likely reveal who he was, and he couldn't afford to let that out no matter how much he wanted to divulge it all to this man who had made his heart thunder from their first meeting.

It was hours before Geraldine returned, and Elias had spent a majority of that time fixated on the letter, trying to perfect it. He was satisfied with the current contents, but his anxiety quickly returned before even handing her the letter.

Elias let the invigoration rush through him once Geraldine left his chambers with the letter, creatively covered by one of his shirts that needed 'repairing'. He went to the window, realizing there was still a little light left in the day. He needed an outlet for the amount of energy surging through him, and he had just the means to release it.

He sent a messenger for Merek, urging him to practice immediately.

Elias did not wait for a response, making his way towards the private sanctum of his training room and beginning the process of donning his armor. Merek was not far behind, joining him before he had completely suited himself.

"What is this about, Lord Elias?" Merek asked, a sense of confusion at being called upon outside the scheduled sessions.

"I need to burn some energy, Merek. I hope you'll keep up." Elias grabbed his sword, practicing a few swings to loosen his body.

"Very well, sir. I will do my best."

Merek skipped any tutoring he would have regularly done in a normal lesson, deciding to focus his efforts on the sparring. A sense of invincibility surged through Elias, constantly keeping on the offensive and not allowing Merek an opportunity to strike. He kept to the Serpentine's stance, which encouraged the most movement –to spin, step, and release a barrage of attacks before Merek had opportunities to respond.

Elias was not as invincible as he had thought.

No sooner had the thought arrived, Merek quickly swung the flat of his blade forward, smacking Elias' sword arm and knocking him off balance long enough for a follow-up. A quick blow from Merek's opposite hand, and the man used Elias' momentum to knock him down.

Elias laughed before getting up. Merek did not say a word, his eyes beckoning Elias to continue. Elias obliged, starting with Serpentine stance again. He continued his dance of moving side to side, releasing his attacks with the same frequency.

He spun, feinting with his weapon as Merek attempted the same trick of knocking him off balance. Elias shoved aside Merek's weapon with his own, following with a short push from his free hand, just light enough to stop Merek from trying it himself. He swung his weapon back up with practiced precision, resting the tip of his weapon squarely on Merek's chest.

Merek regained his balance, standing upright as Elias withdrew his weapon. They both reset their stances, continuing to spar until well into the night.

* * *

Elias sat against the wall, catching his breath. He had taken off his helmet, sweat dripping down his face, his neck, his back as he bemoaned the fact no breeze awaited him in a windowless room.

Merek panted from the lengthy session. Elias knew the man's body would be drenched in sweat beneath the armor. The metal was heavy, and the design did not allow much breathing space.

Forgot I had bathed today. I'll have to do so again in the morning.

Elias smiled to himself.

"Want to tell me what that was about?" Merek asked.

"Just felt like a sparring match."

"Oh really? So, you don't want to tell me what has gotten you so excited?"

Elias looked over at where Merek stood staring at him, expecting a response. "Just needed to burn some energy."

"You mentioned that already. I just want to know what gave you that energy. There have been times where you fought with such determination, but that was usually after a dispute with your father. This time was different."

"You can tell if I'm angry or excited?"

Merek nodded. "Of course. The way you fight changes with your mood, something you've yet to control. When you're angry, you usually take up the Stone stance. It allows more power behind your attacks, a release for frustration. This time you favored the Serpentine stance, allowing you to move constantly, attacking with swift and precise strikes."

Elias considered Merek's words, silently agreeing. His teacher was curious but had also subtly let him know Elias' emotions could be read in a duel, and therefore, his strategies.

Have to keep that in mind. "Well, you're right in part. I'm not angry. I suppose I was just in a good mood."

"You didn't drink today, did you?"

Elias chuckled. "No, Merek. No drink. You think I could have won so many times if my mind was influenced?"

"Sometimes I think it is the only way you can win," Merek teased. "But your emotions can influence the way you fight just the same."

Elias stood to remove his armor, and Merek moved over to his table to do the same.

Merek glanced over. "I know it is not what you want to hear right now, sir, but you have to gain control of your emotions before the Day of Sacrifice."

Elias grimaced slightly, his night now soured. He did not wish to think about the Day of Sacrifice, which was ignorant on his part, considering he had called Merek here in the first place. The only reason Merek taught him was for the Day of Sacrifice, so how could he avoid the subject?

Elias stayed silent as he continued removing his armor and placing each piece on the table, his mind now on his inevitable duel. The streak of losses that hung over his family reminded Elias that he was merely a scrap of meat, trained to entertain before being thrown away by The Voice.

By the Gods. By the city.

He tried to calm himself, forcing his thoughts to return to the man who ignited a fire in him; the man from whom he was awaiting a letter.

Geraldine would soon deliver it, so Elias should receive a response by the weeks' end.

Merek said no more on the subject.

Elias needed to hold onto the feeling of reading the letter for as long as he could, despite the tainting of his mood, but he should have known that any form of positive emotion would be short lived. He was not destined to live the life gifted a normal person.

He wasn't destined to live life at all.

Elias spoke no more words to Merek until they parted ways, thanking the man for obliging his whim on short notice.

As he made his way back to his chambers, tired from the long sparring session, Elias looking forward to falling asleep. He changed into his nightgown, and promptly slipped into bed but sleep did not come easy. Elias mulled over what he was going to do or say to the handsome, black-haired man when it came time for his duel on the Day of Sacrifice, deciding it best to think about it closer to the day. For now, he would enjoy the companionship through the letters, allowing himself to at least be marginally happier until the day death came calling.

$$\underline{7}$$

Maggie didn't know how long she could wait for Castor to find answers. She often saw the young Sandmen at the same spot, just loitering and occasionally dealing more drugs. Of this, she was certain. She purposefully took that street to work and home despite it being out of the way, but she was driven to keep an eye on them.

And she wasn't sure how long she could hold herself back from confronting them.

They teased her, not directly, but their existence was a promise of secrets they held. They knew who killed her boy. They knew who sold him out to the guards.

They knew. And she would discover who that was. But not yet.

First came Castor's investigation of the guards, then came the Sandmen. Maggie knew she wasn't supposed to follow them alone, understood the dangers, but this was about her *son*.

She made her way to the library, the morning chill finding its way through her shabby clothes. The extra cloth she'd wrapped around herself for additional protection did little to keep out the cold. Maggie hurried along, not wanting to be near the temptation of the Sandmen for long.

As she entered the library, dimly lit by the still-rising sun, she spied Heleen sitting at her desk enjoying her morning read with her usual hot drink.

Heleen smiled and greeted Maggie as she approached. "Tea?"

"Please."

Heleen disappeared behind the shelves to the back room, to prepare the tea, and Maggie took a seat, picking up the book Heleen was reading. *Malvark, History and Future*.

Interesting. Perhaps it was a passing interest, or perhaps Heleen planned to do something to better their situation in the city and was looking for answers.

Maggie quickly returned the book to its position and waited for Heleen to return. She stared around the library, its lack of life becoming eerie in the dimly lit passageways lined with books. Maggie felt another presence in the library that wasn't Heleen. She stared into the shelves as if she could suddenly see through them.

She felt something stare back. Something she could not see in dimly lit aisles.

Spirits? In the library? I doubt it. Why would they spend their afterlife here? They can't open the books or turn their pages. It's fine. There are no spirits. Take a breath.

The sound of the back door closing startled Maggie, momentarily forgetting Heleen was here. She watched the elderly woman carefully carry a wooden mug, steam rising from it to give away its contents. Heleen placed the mug before Maggie and took her seat.

It's poison. She's part of the Sandmen. Maggie ignored that ridiculous thought and cupped the drink with both hands to warm her. "Thank you," she said, taking a sip from the drink to prove her mind wrong. The tea's aroma was pleasant, and the taste strong, just the way Heleen liked it. Maggie didn't mind the strength of the tea, would have grown suspicious if it was anything else.

She continued to sip at her brew, watching Heleen read her book. "What are you reading?"

"Oh, just another book on our situation," Heleen said. "I enjoy reading different author's perspectives on it. How they look at our situation and respond to it, how they think we would be in a different place if we didn't do particular things, how things would have changed if The Voice or Gods commanded differently, depending on what they want to write about. I find it fascinating how people in our city can see our plague of enemies so differently despite going through the exact same circumstances. At least in relation to the enemies and Voice, not personal lives of course."

Maggie nodded along. It was interesting how there were so many books about their city, and how they viewed things so differently. Though, Maggie had not read many of them, spewing out ideas onto a page was not as interesting as the historical side of the city. It made her wonder how they could have so many books in the near two-hundred-years they'd occupied the city, and yet there was no mention of any fatal or threatening situations in the books the Old Malvarkians had left behind.

How could the city's old occupants not leave behind any warnings? Any words that described their situation? It must have been a sudden event that caused their disappearance, it was the only thing that made any sense.

"I have a tray of returned books I need you to put away," Heleen said quietly, not lifting her gaze from the page.

"I'll get to work on that." Maggie rose, leaving her mostly full mug on the table to cool down. She moved over to the small cart filled with returned books and picked up a random tome.

The Boy Who Found A Metal.

She placed the book on one side of the small cart, and systematically began organizing the books into sections for a more streamlined approach. It took her a few minutes to organize, then collected her tea, and pulled the cart along with her.

Maggie's mind wandered as she returned the books to the rightful shelves. She had trouble focusing on her job at times, and it was growing increasingly difficult of late. At least the warmth of the tea provided a comforting defense against the morning weather. The sun had only begun to peer through the windows, not properly heating the library just yet, when she felt a presence. Similar to earlier. Maggie did her best to ignore it; it was only her mind playing tricks.

However, the feeling grew stronger the longer she ignored it, sitting in the back of her mind like a bug, increasing in size if she did not feed it the attention that it craved.

81

With very controlled movements, Maggie scanned her surrounds, not wanting to let her body panic.

No one. No movement.

She peeked through the gaps of the books and shelves, seeing only Heleen still at the table.

See? Nothing.

The feeling shrank, but it didn't take long to begin growing again, insisting on convincing her there was another person in the room.

Or perhaps it wasn't a person, but some other creature. *Metalurk?* No. That was ridiculous. Metalurks weren't known for lurking, they were brain-dead creatures who charged at the walls with no finesse or subtlety.

But what if that was only a distraction for others to infiltrate quietly? Maggie tried to shrug the question off, but it stuck like glued to her. Insistent. Persistent. It would not be forgotten.

Another glance at Heleen, but the head librarian was still reading her book, seemingly unaware of the feeling that something was skulking around.

Perhaps because there wasn't.

Deep breaths. It's the same as last time. There's nothing there.

Maggie slowed her breathing into controlled, deep breaths. It may have calmed her nerves slightly, but it did not ward against the feeling that something was still watching her. She continued shelving books, hoping that keeping her hands busy would calm her mind, but to no avail. The feeling simply would not go away.

She turned, this time a little more frantically than she had hoped, and felt herself slipping as her eyes darted around, finding nothing but books surrounding her.

Someone was there. She was sure.

Sandmen?

Her mind raced through thoughts, and Maggie was aware she was spiraling but could do nothing to stop it.

The Sandmen were here. They knew she was watching them. Knew she would discover the man responsible for her son's death. They knew, and they were here to stop her.

A cold sweat broke out on her forehead. She knew no one was here, but why couldn't she convince her mind of that truth? Her eyes weren't deceiving her. No one was lurking in the aisles, no one was hiding on the ceiling beams, no one was waiting for her to let down her guard.

So why couldn't she shake the feeling?

I have to check. Check all the aisles.

It was best to face the feeling front on, to see with her own eyes the emptiness that teased her. See the truth for herself.

Maggie wheeled the small cart of books at a rapid pace, ignoring that the most logical choice of books to shelve would be in the next aisle, but today, she would start at the back and work forward. She glanced down each aisle fast enough so that if anyone were trying to creep around, she would see it.

There were many aisles, but they were evenly distributed so that she could peer down each without anything blocking her view. She hurried, aiming to set her mind straight as quickly as possible. Seeing the entirety of the library empty might finally convince her that she was alone. Aside from Heleen, of course, who remained a fixture in her seat, reading her book.

Maggie stopped once she reached the back of the library. She wasn't sure why, or if it was her mind playing more games, but back here it felt darker despite having the same amount of sunlight streaming through the windows as the rest of the library.

It felt ominous. But at least it was empty.

She tried to slow her breathing; the library was empty, but the feeling had not completely yielded. Maggie took a moment to calm herself before shelving the necessary books from the cart.

As she picked up the next book, she caught a flicker of movement in the corner of her eye. She flinched, expecting to see someone – or something – racing towards her, surely a threat to her life.

But there was nothing. No movement. No sound. Just stale air.

Her heart pounded, and she could feel blood rushing to her head, the sounds of her shoes on the wooden floor becoming muffled. Still, she continued to shelve books, recognizing her own panic attack, and knowing the best thing to do was to keep herself distracted… though she knew it was too late for that.

Her hands shook as she placed books on the shelves, no longer able to concentrate enough to ensure they were in the correct positions and lined up just so.

It's the tea. Heleen poisoned you.

The thought crept in, devouring whatever chances she had of becoming calm; she was like a metalurk with metal. Yet Maggie refused to accept it, knowing it was a lie. The creep of shadows was a lie. Her brain was lying to her, like Audrey and Castor told her it did.

So why wouldn't it stop?

Another flicker of movement sent her into a complete panic, and she backed away from the shelving, gaze whipping from side to side. She stumbled back, tripped, falling backwards into the wooden wall.

Maggie heard the snapping of wood as she fell, expecting to hit her head on the wall but instead it gave way, and she slammed flat on her back. She stared up at the ceiling, dazed and confused. It was with tremendous effort she pushed to her feet, her head spinning, trying to keep her balance while attempting to process what had just happened. As her vision came into focus, she realized she was standing in a doorway.

A doorway that had not been there a moment earlier.

The door had been made to look as if it was part of the wall. *A secret door.* The thick latch that locked the door had easily broken from years of decay.

What… is this…?

The room was very small. All that it contained was a desk, a chair, and papers. Maggie wasn't aware of any secret rooms, and by the layers of dust, she doubted Heleen knew about it either. She moved to the desk, dusting off the papers before realizing how brittle they were. Some crumbled as she tried to pick it up, so she ever so gently spread them out on the desk, trying to make sense of the words.

'I've announced my wishes against …They do not know…I will try to…'

Was this a diary of some sort? The writing was outdated, similar to the penmanship she had seen in some older books, but not quite the same.

Maggie heard the approach of Heleen's footsteps, and unsure as to why, she grabbed one of the pages that was in better condition and jammed it into her pocket. She fled the room, closing the door securely behind her.

Why was she keeping it a secret from Heleen?

Sandmen.

The thought popped up again, and she hated herself for it. Heleen was not a Sandman, she would not betray Maggie like that.

Yet she could not control her actions.

"Everything okay, Margaret? I thought I heard... Oh, dear! You're bleeding again!" Heleen ran to the nearby back room, and Maggie touched her upper lip, and immediately felt the wetness of blood.

Not again!

She held her hand just below her nose to catch any drips from falling on her clothes or the floor, though it was likely that some had already done so. Heleen returned, fresh cloth in hand, holding it up to Maggie's nose and gesturing for her to take it. Maggie wiped the blood away, finding that it had run down one side of her face from when she had been upon the ground. She quickly cleaned herself up and held the cloth against her nostrils to catch any remaining blood.

"What happened, dear?"

"Oh, um... Nothing. I thought I saw something, and came here to look," Maggie said, turning away from the disappointed expression Heleen wore. "And I tripped over. I'm fine, honestly."

Concern creased Heleen's brow, and Maggie still couldn't understand the need to lie to the woman, yet she couldn't stop herself from doing so.

"You are not fine, dear. It's okay to admit that. You know you're supposed to call me when you start feeling... excited. Nervous. Anxious. When you start becoming overwhelmed. I'm here to help, but you have to let me, Margaret."

Words Maggie had heard many times before.

Something she had to accept.

But not right now. Now she had something else to focus on. "I know, Heleen. I'm sorry, it all happened so fast, it got away from me."

Heleen's concern turned into an embrace, the head librarian trying to comfort Maggie. Usually, it would help but this time it didn't soothe her as much.

Maggie quickly ended the hug, "I'll go see Audrey, I think. I'll come back after I speak with her."

Heleen gave Maggie a small smile. "I'm proud of you for deciding that on your own. I know it's been difficult, but the fact you can say it means you've made progress."

Guilt hammered into Maggie; she was not planning on seeing Audrey, she just wanted to leave without appearing suspicious. She put on a fake smile and left the library post haste.

Once outside, she took turn after turn until finding solitude in the opening of an alleyway. Maggie retrieved the paper from her pocket, and pieces fell from the edges as she unfolded the crumpled page, and she cursed herself for not treating it well. Fortunately, it was still legible.

My fears were once again ignored by the elders.

They are growing tired of my constant insistence that what we are doing is wrong. They will not listen to me, and they have doomed us all because of their hubris.

I have to keep quiet, for I fear they will use me in the experiment.

Nothing good will come of this. The people will suffer as a result, and I do not know what I can do to prevent it.

I am but one man against many.

I might have to try more discreet methods. Haedus seemed most receptive to my claims. Perhaps I should speak with him in private. Try to convince him while he is alone, and in turn he can help me convince the others.

All I can do is pray. Pray that there is still time left to convince them. Pray that there is still humanity left within them to listen to my concerns.

Maggie read the words again and again.

Elders?

Elders was a term of respect for the older generation, but the paper seemed to refer to them as a sign of authority. No one referred to The Voice as elders, but... perhaps this person did?

The paper brought many questions that could not be answered without reading the other pages. She had no idea of the author, but by the state of the room and its contents, she guessed they were long gone. The pages had been left in the open, seemingly unfinished, and they were definitely very old.

Paper took a long time to be turned into such a fragile state, so exactly how old were these pages?

She needed to read more. In private, of course. So far there was nothing worth sharing, but perhaps there was more to this. It seemed like it was more than just a diary, and Maggie wanted to believe it was not merely some fiction being penned. It seemed genuine; someone with a reason to record their actions.

At least, that's what she wanted to believe.

She went to return to the library, intent on getting another paper, but stopped in her tracks when she realized she was meant to be at Audrey's. That guilt rose again at the lies she had told Heleen, and at how happy the woman had been for her.

Maybe Maggie should go to Audrey's. After all, she did have some kind of attack. But she hated having to go, being forced to talk made Maggie feel like she was an experiment. Audrey was a doctor's wife, and they had a belief that women who had been through traumatic events in their lives needed someone to help them through it. To help them not give up.

To help them breed more.

It was necessary for a woman in her position to see Audrey. The laws dictated that married women needed to have three kids, and Audrey gave her that exemption.

Maggie already had one kid. That was enough. She reluctantly made her way to Audrey's house, annoyed that reading more of the mysterious records would have to wait.

Somehow, she knew they held answers. Her instincts told her as much.

Instinct also dictated she not tell anyone about them.

* * *

Maggie sat at her usual spot at Audrey's dining table, watching as the woman took a seat opposite. Whether the position was intentional or not, Maggie thought Audrey was trying to create a literal rift between them, to make it clear this wasn't a personal visit but official business.

"So, another surprise visit today?"

Maggie kept her gaze on the hot tea Audrey had given her. She wasn't thirsty but looking at Audrey made her... uncomfortable. "Yes."

"Everything okay?"

"Heleen sent me," Maggie lied, not wanting to confess that she came here of her own volition, even if it was just to appease her guilt.

"Did something happen?" Audrey prodded.

The answer was obvious, but Audrey was trying to get Maggie to speak. The question irritated, and Maggie wanted to refuse to answer out of spite, but knew that it wouldn't go down well, especially if Castor found out she was being difficult again.

"Panic attack. I think."

Audrey sipped at her tea, a tactic the woman used to allow Maggie plenty of time to elaborate. Maggie didn't.

"Tell me what happened." Audrey shifted a piece of paper closer, and dipped her quill into fresh ink.

Maggie hated this. She didn't want her words, her thoughts and experiences, written down to later be read and analyzed, but she'd made a promise to her brother that she had to keep. "I thought someone was watching me. Again. I turned to see, but as usual, no one was there. The feeling wouldn't go away. The more I looked, the worse it became."

Instead of responding to Maggie as a normal person would in a conversation, Audrey scribbled notes onto her paper. She then looked up at Maggie, to confirm that she was not going to continue on her own. "You thought someone was there. Who did you think it was?"

"I don't know."

"Someone you know?"

"I don't think so."

"Why?"

Maggie thought about it. It could have been anyone, so why didn't she think it was someone she knew? "Because I thought they were going to hurt me."

Audrey wrote more notes, making Maggie wait. "I know you must grow tired of hearing this, but it is partly why you are here, but the Sandmen are not out to get you, Maggie. In the three years, how many incidents have you had with them?"

Maggie knew the answer but reflected on all the times she had seen known Sandmen. The same gut-wrenching feeling came back as she thought about them, how close she was to them, their faces, their actions.

Everything.

Nausea swirled in her gut, but it normally did when she thought about the Sandmen on someone else's terms. "No incidents."

"Don't you think that's reason enough to not be afraid of them? They wouldn't wait three years to start stalking you. I know they can be dangerous, but they're not the type to go to such great lengths without reason, if at all. They're just a bunch of kids who don't know what they're getting themselves into. You are safe, Maggie. They don't even know who you are."

Maggie knew. She would tell herself the same thing, over and over again. But it didn't make a difference. There was still an unreasonable fear burning inside of her that would not go away. She knew she should not logically be afraid of them, so why was she still so paranoid about it?

It was a recurring topic, not only with herself but with everyone who was trying their best to help her. It was the same loop of words that had now lost their meaning. Saying them again for the hundredth time wasn't going to make a difference. "You're right. But there's still something telling me they're going to hurt me. I don't know why that is, but it won't go away no matter how much I tell myself I'm being ridiculous."

"Tell me more about this lurking presence. Do you think it's the same as the others you've felt before?"

Maggie stared at Audrey, a little confused. "Are you insinuating that I'm being haunted?"

"No!" Audrey quickly responded, apparently worried she may have caused another irrational paranoia. "No, no. I was just wondering if it felt the same. If it's different every time, it might be a different issue, but if it's the same one then at least we can pinpoint it."

Maggie had considered a ghost was following her, and part of her wanted to believe it. She wanted to believe that her son was still there, watching over her, but the presence she felt was an unsettling, fearsome feeling that would not come from her Patrick. Still, Maggie considered the question, thinking back on the occasions when she believed she was being followed, remembering the familiar feeling of panic settling in and what she thought it was. "Yes. I think it's the same, but I can't be certain. I always think it's a Sandman come to get me, but it never is. It always seems like something is there, I just can't see it."

Audrey sat for a moment, frowning in thought, before clearing her throat and taking a grim tone. "Death. Death is a large theme in your life, and you are subconsciously afraid that it's constantly lurking over you. Your son died, and you've had several miscarriages. It has played such a large factor in your life for many, many years it has a hold on you. It's something we should address more often. How do you feel about that?"

Maggie stayed quiet, thoughts turning to her deceased son.
Her deceased parents.
Her multiple miscarriages.
Her husband who was drinking himself into an early grave.
Her brother who put his life on the line every few days.

Maybe Audrey was right? "I don't know," was all Maggie could mutter as she blankly stared into her cup of tea. She hated reflecting on her memories; they brought too much pain. They sapped her strength, of will. She just sat, letting time flow by as she pondered why death was such a substantial entity, forcing its gruesome tendrils into every aspect of her life.

"That's okay," Audrey replied, leaning in a little closer. "You don't need to answer right now. Give it some thought, but don't exert yourself. We can leave that topic for now, it's not an easy subject to confront."

Maggie nodded distractedly, morbid thoughts demanding her attention.

"For now, let's talk about something else," Audrey said, returning to her relaxed position, "How is work at the library?"

"Fine. Quiet, but I don't mind it. It means there are less people around," Maggie replied, trying her best to turn her attention to the conversation, but it was impossible to willingly stop thinking about the topic of death now that it had been brought up.

"Perhaps we should find you other work? Something a little more active?" Audrey suggested, seemingly unsatisfied with Maggie's answer.

Maggie had considered it before but trying anything else had fear take hold. She had no discernible skills, so the best she could do was tedious work that no one else wanted.
Besides, she needed access to the hidden papers. "I think I'm fine at the library."

"Are you sure?"

"Yes."

"All right, but if you change your mind, let me know. I'm sure we can find something else for you. We can discuss it again after the Day of Sacrifice."

Another touchy subject for her. She couldn't be certain if Audrey was bringing up the subjects intentionally to gauge her reactions, but she was hitting all the notes Maggie didn't want to hear. Maggie did not respond, not wanting to encourage the topic.

"Perhaps we should end here for today," Audrey said quietly, seeming to sense Maggie's reluctance. "Unless there is anything else you want to talk about? I know it is difficult, so I won't pressure you into saying anything you don't feel comfortable doing."

Maggie knew it was appropriate to continue talking, to speak out loud about these subjects that garnered such fear. If she wanted to get better, she knew she would have to bring out the emotions she bottled inside.

But she saw an out and she took it. "No."

Audrey waited, letting the answer hang in the air. "All right," she finally said. "Well. I'll see you again soon. Perhaps a week from today, if not sooner."

Maggie rose from her chair, eager to leave. Audrey escorted her to the door, saying her goodbyes.

As Maggie walked away, she felt... different. Normally her sessions left her either drained or irritated, but today she felt energetic. Her mind raced through thoughts that her body felt like it needed to distract her by doing something. Anything.

Her steps became rapid, trying to dispose of the excess energy that had built inside of her. She wasn't paying attention to where she was walking and realized that she had taken the detour again.

The detour that led her to the young group of Sandmen.

She paused, brain attempting to process the various decisions she could make but unable to decide which one was best. Then she remembered the hidden room in the library and its contents that awaited her. Maggie continued on her path, not wanting to turn around and look suspicious in case the Sandmen were keeping an eye on her. She hurried past them, almost running as she turned the corner to get out of view. Her heart raced, her breathing came a little faster than normal, but she did her best to maintain control as she headed towards the library.

When she reached the doors to the building, she stopped. She was still too excited, and Heleen would insist on calming her down, staying by her side until she did. Maggie didn't want to delay reaching the hidden room, so waited outside, steadying her breaths. Control was everything. Heleen would detect something was off, the woman could be annoyingly observant at times.

Satisfied she had calmed enough, Maggie entered the library.

Heleen was alone reading her book, and to Maggie's gleeful excitement, there were no visitors in the library just yet. It would be easier for her to sneak into the hidden room.

Heleen looked up, a smile growing across her face as she saw Maggie. "How did it go?"

"It was fine. I feel better now."

"That's a relief to hear. Are you okay to work? We don't have much to do, so I don't mind if you go home."

"I'd like to work. Otherwise, I'll just be cooped up in my house for the rest of the day."

"Don't push yourself, dear," Heleen said kindly.

"I won't, I promise."

Heleen smiled at Maggie again, and there was that rising tide of guilt again. Maggie smiled, and as much as her body didn't want to, she searched for the cart of books. *Still at the back. Excellent.*

Maggie slowly walked past the large table Heleen sat at, feeling rigid in her movements despite the effort to not act out of the ordinary. When she reached the cart of books, she slowly put them away as quietly as possible, occasionally spying on Heleen to ensure the librarian was still at the table. After a few minutes, Maggie decided to make her move and sneak into the back room reserved for library staff. She quickly recovered a mouth burner – an elongated stick that one could hold in their mouth, covered in a flavorful wax for comfort – from a drawer and promptly exited the room. Her heart raced, not being able to see Heleen somehow increased the fear that Heleen would catch her in the act from the opposite side of the library.

The starter candle was positioned against the middle of the wall on one side of the library – central, so they could get it without leaving it close to the books. She crept, expecting the old floorboards to creak beneath her weight at any moment. Maggie was already making up excuses in her mind if she got caught, even considered purposefully making herself known, her anxiety only being prolonged from wanting to remain undetected.

A loud creak echoed through the empty library as Maggie placed her weight on her front foot. Without hesitation, she continued her pace as normal, acting as if she wasn't skulking. She couldn't see Heleen from where the starter candle sat, but Maggie didn't hear any other sounds. She lit her mouth burner from the starter candle, and casually made her way back to the cart of books, a little voice in the back of her mind telling her she had been caught. Maggie dared not look around for fear Heleen was making her way over and would see the action as suspicious. Book after book Maggie put away, pretending the mouth burner was required so that she could read the book titles, despite the library being adequately lit.

She continued her ruse, waiting for the eternity of getting discovered to end, but Heleen didn't come. Maggie dared to look, despite her instincts telling her otherwise, and discovered Heleen had not even turned from her book. It should have eased Maggie's mind, but the worst was yet to come.

Maggie waited a little longer, keeping an eye on Heleen. She carted the books over to the next aisle, letting the wheels on the floorboards be heard. As soon as she stopped, she quickly ditched the cart, and snuck her way to the back wall. She pressed up against the boards, trying to find where the door had been.

Thankfully, one of the wooden panels gave way to her shoves, swinging inward to reveal the hidden room. Maggie ducked inside, closing the door behind her. The room immediately darkened, but her mouth burner provided enough light for her task. She frantically searched the papers on the desk, skimming the words to find one that may have held answers.

Sacrifice.

The word stood out like a metalurk amongst people. She grabbed the paper, careful not to cause any tears in the process. She sifted through the rest, a constant voice in her head telling her to leave before she got caught. Maggie finally gave in when she found nothing else of interest. She had been in there too long; Heleen surely would have noticed her absence by now. Maggie folded the paper, neatly storing it in her pocket.

She moved silently to the door, smothering the small flame from her mouth burner before opening the panel just enough for her to peek through. Thankfully it allowed her to view the central area of the library, though it was mostly obscured by shelves of books. Still, Maggie couldn't see the table where Heleen sat but hoped the woman remained there. Maggie darted out of the room, closing the door behind her. It swung open slightly, having no latch to lock it in place anymore. She adjusted the door, so it sat in place then glanced again toward the center of the library.

She froze.

Heleen was not at the table.

Her eyes darted as she searched for Heleen, peering through the gaps in shelves and books, to the empty corners of the library, with no success.

She was convinced she had gotten caught, but where was Heleen?

The door to the nearby backroom swung open, and Heleen emerged. "Oh, there you are, Maggie. I must have missed you."

Maggie did not respond or move, she stared wide-eyed at Heleen, too surprised and nervous to react.

"I was just going to ask if…" Heleen trailed off, noting Maggie's expression, "Everything okay, dear?"

Maggie could not settle her thoughts, her mind once again taking over her body. "Yes, everything's fine. You just surprised me," Maggie responded, but the words didn't feel like her own. It was almost as if she had been pushed aside in her own body, watching from afar as someone else controlled her.

Heleen did not seem entirely convinced and moved closer. Maggie dropped her arms to her sides, releasing her tense pose.

Heleen seemed cautious as she neared, keeping her distance as she inspected Maggie. "Are you sure? You seem… off."

"You just surprised me. I didn't hear you go into the back room, I thought you were still at the table," Maggie answered, her face contorting into an inauthentic smile, followed by an awkward giggle to try play the situation off as humorous.

Heleen didn't smile in return, but she did appear to relax. "I must have missed you between the shelves as I walked past. Do you want another tea?"

Maggie shook her head, declining the kind offer. "I'm fine, thanks."

"Are you sure everything is all right? I saw that you didn't organize the books like you normally do in the cart before placing them away."

Maggie, still feeling a little disconnected from herself, hesitated, trying to think of an answer. "I guess not. Maybe I am a little off. I think I'll go home and lay down."

Heleen expression was a mix of disappointment and concerned. As much as Maggie hated encouraging others' perception of her mental health, it at least made for a good excuse.

That was completely fine, for the most part.

"You do sometimes get frazzled after speaking with Audrey. Go home, dear. I'll take care of the books." Heleen escorted Maggie out without either speaking a word.

Maggie waved goodbye as she left Heleen standing in the doorway, concern still etched on the librarian's face.

Maggie hurriedly made her way home, convincing herself not to spy on the young group of Sandmen – she had promised to Castor, after all. Besides, she was eager to read the paper that was tucked away in her pocket.

8

"I am giving you this in warning so that you may prepare yourself, Arthur," his father said, black hair thinning from age, but still showing signs of its former infamous curls he had been well-known for amongst the women. His chin wobbled slightly as he spoke, a by-product from years of indulging himself on food.

It sickened Arthur to see his father in such a distasteful state. Edmund's position allowed him certain benefits, and it was clear to any that he was exploiting them. Arthur loved his father, but he despised many of his actions.

"You need to be prepared for any kind of scenario in your duel," his father continued. "So we'll be preparing you for any and all of them."

"I know, Father. It's fine. I'm sure there won't be much of a difference between what hand my opponent will use. I just have to adjust for maneuvers to be mirrored, I suspect."

"Don't underestimate your opponent, you'd be surprised on how much of a difference it can make. You'll notice as soon as you have your next lesson with Vind."

Arthur had been taught to accept any and all forms of advice, so he took his father's words to heart, ignoring how piggish his father appeared while saying it, ignoring the juice that dribbled down his father's chin.

His mother sat quietly, as usual, unless someone addressed her. Arthur was trying desperately to think of a topic to bring up, but because his life was so strictly bound to a schedule, she was already aware of what he had been doing.

"Take your older brother's duel for example," Edmund said, interrupting Arthur's thoughts. "It was a spectacular match! Gavin had the upper hand for the first leg of the fight, moving left to right, dancing on his feet and singing with his sword, the poor Noldin lad couldn't keep up with him! Then, Gavin cut the boy's sword arm, rendering it useless and expecting his opponent to surrender, but to everyone's surprise, the boy—"

"Picked up his weapon in his other hand and managed to stab Gavin because he was caught off guard, but Gavin still won the match. I've heard the story many times, Father," Arthur finished, clearly irritated. He hated how his father referred to the Noldin's champion as 'boy'. It was demeaning and showed no respect for the Noldins at all. Thankfully, his father's attitude did not rub off on his children, who were considerate of their rival family. He didn't know why his father took such an attitude, perhaps his victory over the Noldins forty years ago had not left his head, inflating it as much as food did to his waist.

Edmund showed little agitation towards being interrupted, he loved telling the story about Gavin's victory to his family, who held the secrets to the duel. His father could be boisterous at times, not caring to check for servants before blurting out that metal was used in the duel. Its existence was confidential to the participating families and The Voice, being safely kept in chambers specifically designed to block the metalurks from detecting it.

How such a delicate matter could easily escape from his father's tongue, not only on one but several occasions, was beyond Arthur's comprehension. He glanced around to ensure no servants were within earshot. Fortunately, they had all returned to the kitchens after serving the food.

Arthur looked at his mother again, noting how empty she appeared. He could only imagine what she must feel during their dinners. Her eldest son had left many years ago, and her daughter recently married off to another noble house. All who remained was Arthur and Edmund, but unfortunately Arthur did not serve as a very efficient buffer between his parents.

He ate in silence, listening to his father gobbling at his food and his mother's silent suffering. Arthur finished his meal but refused to leave until his mother had also eaten; he may not be as outspoken in supporting her as he liked, but he tried to make sure she was all right when he was around.

She was a slow eater, taking small sips from her soup, nibbling at the chunks of vegetables. Only when his father was near the end of his meal had she decided she had enough. Arthur looked at his mother, slightly gesturing to her food so his father wouldn't notice, and she just smiled slightly and shook her head.

Arthur felt useless, he knew he wouldn't be able to get her to eat more. She could be stubborn when she wanted to be. He excused himself from the table, leaving before his father could strike up another conversation regarding the duel he witnessed, and how glorious their family was.

Every time his father retold the tales, it only added to the pressure of Arthur winning his own duel. He couldn't tell if his father was doing it intentionally or was just inconsiderate. It was a reoccurring issue for Arthur, nights spent at dinner with his parents had long turned into an obligation rather than a want. He only went for his mother's sake, otherwise he would purposefully avoid either eating in the dining hall, or just wait until his father had eaten before Arthur sat down for his meal.

He wanted so badly to tell his mysterious correspondent his frustrations with his father, but he knew the information would most likely just reveal who he was. Or at least narrow it down significantly. There weren't many portly men in the city, his father probably standing out the most.

Besides, Arthur wanted to continue the mystery game they were playing, finding it both alluring and comforting. As much as he wished to reveal his identity, he was finding himself feeling disconnected from his burdens when he had read the letter.

When he wrote his reply, he was not Arthur Va Daolin, Champion of the Daolin family and next in line to take up his family's metal sword and present his life before the Gods to decide his fate.

He was just Arthur, a man with his own interests who wanted to share them, a man with a personality outside of being coddled and guided by his father's hand.

It had been days since he'd sent off his return letter, and Arthur had been thinking about the lady returning at any moment, expecting there to be a reply every time he entered his room. He had to teach himself to be patient. Arthur had no idea when he would next see a letter. He had to give it time.

* * *

Days went by without a response. Arthur focused on his studies as best he could but found himself wondering about the return letter frequently, wondering about that man who visited his dreams. He had enough discipline to not fall behind in his studies, but the process was proving difficult. He had never longed for something as badly as he did the letters, it was a difficult task to ignore their existence so he could focus on his teachings.

His sparring session was perhaps the only thing that could completely rid the letters from his mind. Not only was the physical aspect of it a suitable distraction, but ever since his teacher began using his left hand instead, it had really thrown Arthur off balance. He was surprised to see how much difference using the opposite hand could make, barely reacting in time to block or parry most of the maneuvers, few finding their mark against his metal suit. He felt himself growing frustrated, uncertain if the use of the left hand was really throwing him off, or if he was too distracted and lost his own flow of the fight.

It made him consider the letters, and if they were truly a blessing or a hinderance in his ability to fight and perform on the Day of Sacrifice. He could not afford any negative impact on his chances of winning.

If he died, the letters would have to stop anyway.

He was toiling with this decision on his way back to his chambers. Was it a mistake to agree to the letters in the first place?

But his time spent bathing did not prove long enough for him to come up with the answer.

As he opened his bedroom door, all doubt and second guesses disappeared as his eyes fell to the envelope on his desk. He didn't need to look at the wax seal to know it was from *him*. Arthur closed the door, rushed over to his desk and carefully opening the envelope, removing the letter.

The paper felt smooth and somehow warm in his fingers, and he could swear it held a slight fragrance. He unfurled it.

Well, I want to begin by agreeing with your letter that it is a lousy subject. My father is overdemanding. That's as much as I wish to say about him.

I do not blame you for raising the subject, it is quite normal, but I'm afraid there isn't much I wish to speak of.

It sounds like you care for your mother deeply. Keep an eye on her. Care for her while she is still with you.

I desire to know you more. What are your interests? Hobbies? Other than wine and clothes, of course!

I do not get much time to pursue my own areas of interest, but livewood has always intrigued me. I have wished to learn more about it, how to craft with it, how it interacts with its own sap in such a unique manner. It is truly a blessing upon our city. If only I had the strength to speak out, demand time to pursue livewood and its applications.

I am unable to traverse the town as widely and often as I wish, my commitments prevent me from doing so, but my favorite attraction is the livewood presented in the city center. I do not know what the cause is, but it always brings me peace to look at it. When you get time, take a moment to bask in the tree's shadow. I hope it brings you calm as it does me.

I hope to hear from you again soon. I'll become rather busy around the Day of Sacrifice, so I hope we have enough time to talk before then. I do not know when I'll get the time to respond afterwards. Our city will have its hands full with the Red Sea that is said to come.

I hope the city will be safe.

I hope you will be safe.

Take care and respond quickly. Our messenger requested you write a return letter as soon as you see this, she will have a small window in her schedule to pick it up shortly after she delivers it.

Arthur had little time to bathe in the warm feelings upon reading the words. He had no idea how long the letter had been sitting there and made haste to write a response. His excitement and need for a rush caused his writing to be messy. He cursed himself for looking like a citizen who had never learned to read and write, setting aside the letter and pulling out a fresh paper to begin again.

To his dismay, a hurried knock sounded from the door.

He opened it slightly, eyeing the woman who had delivered the letter. She wore a hood to cover herself, and her eyes spoke of the fear of being caught. He let her inside, making sure no one else had seen before closing the door.

"I apologize for not giving warning, but I have come for the return letter," the woman said, choosing not to sit. Arthur could still see the fear in her eyes; she knew she was not meant to be here.

"The letter mentioned you were in a rush. I have written a response, but I had hoped to rewrite it. I'll not cause any delay, I can see you wish to leave as soon as possible."

"I mean no disrespect, sir."

"Please. You are doing a great favor to us both. You could not disrespect me by making me rush. It is the least I can do to lessen your unease." Arthur handed her the now sealed letter, which she slipped into a pocket, and turned to leave.

"Do you want me to escort you out? If you keep your head down, no one will stop us on your way out."

"No, please. It's already bad enough that I am here, we cannot risk being seen together,"

The woman left without waiting for a response. *I didn't thank her.*

Arthur scolded himself for not thinking of it sooner, but his mood rapidly returned at the feel of the letter in his hands. He unfolded it again, scanning over the words again. The talk about the large wave of Metalworks that city ensured would happen did not seem as overwhelming when it came from him. Arthur lay in his bed, eyes closed, letting himself relax, enjoying the long-distance companionship. It did not take long before sleep claimed him.

* * *

Arthur attacked the next day's tasks with renewed vigor. He was attentive during the entirety of his lessons, the words sinking in despite how boorishly slow the teachers were. He felt he could take on anything.

Even the stress of his upcoming duel felt insignificant. If the letters came in regularly, perhaps they would act as a booster for his spirits leading up to the fight. It could be the support he needed, even if it were indirect.

He still considered stopping the letters early, before the two of them became too attached to each other, and before the duel but knew it was likely too late. Arthur would just have to win his fight, plant the livewood tree in the city center, and inspire the city to survive through the inevitable onslaught. If he could just survive his duel, he would take control of his life.

Arthur was happily jaunting through the hallways of his home; he had tasks to complete, but they could wait. He wanted to spend some time enjoying himself, not cramped up studying in his

103

room as he should have been. His father denied his request to leave the grounds, so all he could do was walk their gardens, so he headed there at a leisurely pace.

He turned the corner, tracing his hand around walls, feeling their tiny bumps at his fingertips. He traced over the symbols that decorated the wooden cornices, his feet drifting across the dark blue carpet. The house was created by the Old Malvarkians before his family chose it as their residence. They had replaced the carpets to match their noble house color, but had left the symbols, liking the decorations but uncertain what, if anything, they meant.

When Arthur turned the next corner, he was surprised to see his mother speaking with a few other noble wives in the main room. An activity forced upon her by his father.

It wasn't that she disliked the social activity, but he knew she wasn't always feeling well enough to properly enjoy it. Edmund did not care; he wanted to keep up to date with any gossip going on about his family, and these ladies had naught else to do but exactly that.

"Oh, he's such a taunt!" one lady exclaimed. Her back was to Arthur, but he could tell by the high shrill of her voice that it was Lady Embarrel. He resisted a shiver at the horrors his mother had to face by having a full conversation with this woman. Arthur had always found her exaggerative, constantly finding offence when things did not go her way, and always prodding for rumors of commotion amongst households. She lived off of the drama, thrived off of the eager ears that would listen to her spread personal secrets and anything that seemed suspicious. He could see his mother and couldn't tell if it was his imagination, but her smiled felt forced underneath her empty eyes. He wanted to step in, give some reason for his mother to excuse herself to get a break, but no lies came to him.

He stood near the doorway, contemplating whether his mother actually needed the help or if she would be fine, when he heard her speak.

"Excuse me, ladies, but it looks like my son needs me for a moment. I'll be back shortly." She smiled sweetly to them, rising and heading over to Arthur who politely smiled as the women turned to face him.

"Oh, Arthur is here!" Lady Embarrel spoke loudly in an attempt to steal his attention away from his mother.

"Let's go quickly before she tries to speak with you," his mother whispered but he could hear the irritation in her voice.

He retreated as Lady Embarrel placed her drink onto the table, likely preparing to stand and speak with him. His mother took his arm, and together they made haste away from convent of women and to the safety of their garden.

"Thank you," his mother said. "I hate being a part of those conversations. It's rarely anything new or worth mentioning. I don't understand why your father insists upon them so often." Evelynn's frustration was clear in her tone, but she slowly relaxed with each step away from the guest.

Arthur smiled, happy to be of help even though it wasn't his idea. *Perhaps I should come up with a reason ahead of their next chat.*

They strolled through their garden, taking in the various plants they had grown. It wasn't a large variety, cutting off trade from other cities for nearly two-hundred years limited the available seeds, amongst other things.

"So, did you have use for me, or were you simply dawdling?" Evelynn asked, much to Arthur's gratification. She was so quiet whenever someone else was around, he was pleased she at least felt like she could be herself around him.

"Honestly, I was trying to find a way to get you out, but I couldn't think of anything," he confessed, a little embarrassed.

"You always were a terrible liar, Arthur. You're straight forward and honest. I'm glad you have such a quality."

He blushed a little but was concerned that she had sounded relieved. It was as if she heard nothing but lies all day, then he remembered what he had just saved her from. It had to be tough work being around them, having to speak delicately and precisely to ensure she did not reveal or even hint to anything that was worth being taken to other noble houses.

It would be tougher than hiding metal from a room of metalurks.

"You must tire of those ladies. I know you don't go out often, so it must be quite a nuisance to have them in your home."

105

"I can't say anything negative about them. I'm sure if I did, they'd hear about it," she teased.

Arthur chuckled. He had missed his mother's sense of humor. "It's like you're having your own siege, defending your own walls against ravenous creatures who are clawing at anything they can get."

"There's just one difference."

"What's that?"

"My general is the one who lets them in."

Talk of his father sullied his mood. His mother's attitude and behavior were a result of his father's actions. Edmund controlled her life as much as he did Arthur's. He was unsure how to respond. He couldn't openly disrespect his father, his mother would surely scold him. She would avidly defend Edmund in front of company, as was her necessity as his wife, but Arthur knew she really didn't agree with him in most aspects.

"It has been a while since we've talked, Mother." Arthur placed his hand on hers where it gripped his arm. She squeezed back in turn, smiling, but not turning to face him. He wasn't sure how he knew, but he could detect her slipping away from the conversation. Away from their walk.

Away from him.

"Any word from Raelynn?" Arthur tried to change the topic, wanting to keep conversation flowing.

Evelynn shook her head. "I imagine she is still getting accustomed to her new home. It will take some time to get used to, but I'm sure we'll hear from her soon. I expect her to visit within the week."

"I know I didn't see her often before she left, but the house somehow feels emptier knowing that she's gone."

"I feel the same. But it is a necessity that we must adapt to. Raelynn will be the Lady of her own house one day, we must do all we can to support her in that endeavor."

"It's not easy, is it?"

"No."

They walked in silence for a moment. Arthur pondered topics to bring up, but conversations weren't his forte. The only thing he had worth mentioning was his meeting of the light brown-haired man, and the letters that followed. He so desperately wanted to tell her but knew it would not end well for him. She would either plead with him to stop, or command it. Playing with matters of the heart so close to his duel would only end up hurting him further.

And hurt the light-brown haired man as well.

Yet, his heart ached, begging to tell his mother.

"Father has changed my dueling routine, as you know, and I must admit that he was right. It has proved more difficult than I initially imagined. I'm having trouble adjusting, but I am making progress."

"That's good to hear."

Why must I be so pathetic at conversation? Arthur cursed himself. He could see his mother had fallen into distraction. He had naught to speak of that she did not already know, he could not demand her attention long enough for their walk. "In the spirit of speaking straight forward and being honest," Arthur said, annoyed at himself for not bringing it up sooner. "Is everything all right, Mother?"

Evelynn did not immediately respond. Instead, she remained quiet as she walked about the rest of the garden, clinging onto Arthur. Then to his surprise, she smiled. "It will be, Arthur. I will be fine. I'm going through a few things, but I don't expect you to take care of me. You have to focus on yourself. Get past the Day of Sacrifice and plant the tree. Become a symbol of our future. Become our hope. You are meant for great things, Arthur. I have a feeling you'll be a key component in releasing us from our imprisonment. I'd like to be right."

Arthur was taken aback. He knew that his mother believed in him, but she certainly had great aspirations for him. Who was he to stop the metalurks? How would he even begin with that? He had no inkling where they came from, or why. How was he supposed to achieve such a great task that none had come close to completing?

He locked eyes with his mother, face plastered with a fake smile. "Mother... I can't promise anything like that. All I can promise is that I'll do my best. And my best includes taking care of you. The greatest thing I could do right now is to make sure you

107

are happy. I don't know what ails you, but I promise that I'll take care of you, despite your wishes."

Her smile grew wider, and Arthur could tell it had become genuine. She wrapped her arms around him, and for the first time in a long time, Arthur could feel the comfort of his mother's love.

At least in that moment, she was happy.

She released him and looked at Arthur with tearful eyes. "Such a stubborn boy. I better return to the convent. If I stay away for too long, they'll turn their focus to me. Their attention wanes if I don't provide the appropriate hostess etiquettes, and then they'll surround me while my back is turned."

Arthur watched her walk away. Despite their growing distance, there was a stronger connection than ever to his mother.

Perhaps it was the short moment they had alone. Perhaps it was the bolstering courage he got from reading the letter the day before.

All he knew was that he finally reached out to his mother.

Finally said what was on his mind.

And it felt good.

9

The air smelled foul as Castor sat in the city center. He stewed impatiently as he waited. *I shouldn't be doing this.* There was no cooking at the city center that day to help alleviate Castor's nostrils. His senses were trying to warn him against doing this, but he saw no other choice.

The area wasn't bustling with activity, it rarely was nowadays. Occasionally, people would arrive to pray to the Gods through the livewood tree, and today was the appointed day for elderly to receive a small piece to eat from the nearby meat distributor. It was the most active area of the city, aside from the taverns, despite its low population.

And yet it was not immune to being stagnant.

Castor sighed, his nerves building second by second. He tried to distract himself by looking at the livewood tree, its age showing in its limp limbs and cracks at its stump. He studied the glistening, dried treeblood that had slowly bled through the cracks, but that did little to cure his anxiety.

He was waiting for a contact from the Seekers, a group of individuals who were able to track down people in the city, find answers that were meant to be hidden, supposedly capable of retrieving anything you wanted.

For a price.

They were labelled a gang, for obvious illegal activity, but it seemed to Castor they were more of an unregistered business. So far, they had been professional, courteous to a point. So, he waited at the appointed spot. The last person he spoke to had told him a man would contact him at this location, all he had to do was wait.

Maybe they're checking if it's a trap. It was obvious Castor was a soldier. Not only did he bear his rank on his sleeve, but he had the posture and stern look of an experienced defender of the wall. They would likely be scouting him and the surroundings to ensure he wasn't just acting as bait to catch them.

There was a generous reward for turning over a member of the Seekers, so they took the necessary precautions. Castor hated that they existed, being that they mostly dealt with matters of blackmail and noble house secrets. Not an active cause to help the people, but rather themselves.

He hated himself even more for needing their help.

Castor changed his position, finding the seat increasingly uncomfortable. He watched a mother approached the tree, pray then leave. He watched as a bloodbird – a bright orange bird who was attracted by the taste of treeblood – peck at the dried sap. It was a rare sight, a testament to how long he had been waiting.

"Castor, my friend! How are you?" a man called out.

Castor turned to see a middle-aged man, dark blonde hair in three separate braids, his smile surrounded by a short beard, his green eyes on Castor.

"Uh…fine?" Castor was certain this was his contact, not recognizing him, he had just not expected this approach.

"Varin," the man whispered, seating himself next to Castor. He smelled of addleberries, a common symptom of people who worked in a winery.

"Fine, Varin. How are you?" Castor replied, a little hesitant. The mock conversation was a little awkward, no one was close enough to hear them, and there weren't that many eyes to pry.

"It has been a while, friend. I understand you have an opening in your business?"

"Well…yes?" Castor answered, still confused as to why they were putting up a farce.

"You have anyone you want to put into that position?"

"Yes?"

Varin waited, as if expecting a follow up, then cleared his throat when the silence stretched. "What is this potential employee's name?"

"Gerric."

"Does Gerric have a last name?"

"Farwell."

"Sounds like a man with potential. What are his qualifications?"

"I don't know."

"Don't even know what his current job is? That stuff is very important."

"Nothing."

"Well, it sounds like he may not be right for the job. I hope it all works out." Varin stood and faced Castor, held up a hand when Castor prepared to stand as well. "I'll see you around, East Gate Captain Castor Belden."

Castor watched Varin walk away. The message wasn't very subtle, but it was very clear. He hadn't given them his full name or title. It wasn't difficult for anyone to figure out who he was, he proudly wore his rank after all, but they wanted him to know that they could get to him if he chose to turn on them.

He waited until the man disappeared from sight before departing. *I hope I did the right thing.* All he could do was wait. Wait and hope that this tactic had a payoff that was worth putting himself in the Seekers spotlight.

* * *

Castor spent the next few days waiting anxiously. The only remedy had been the wave of metalurks to attacking the wall, but the nervous feeling did not stray for long. Even his training routine had not been enough to completely distract him, and he was fairly certain the more experienced members of his regiment could detect it. It would not bode well for him if General Deven was informed.

His check-in with his sister had only made his situation worse. She claimed to have been seeing Audrey, but Maggie seemed more on edge than normal, constantly fidgeting and unable to sit still. Castor spotted her lie when she denied anything had happened, but he knew he couldn't get the truth out of his sister no matter how hard he pushed. He would just have to wait for her to be ready, but now he was anxious about that as well. Maggie insisted she was keeping her promise about leaving the Sandmen alone, but perhaps she had found something knew to pursue?

He hated not knowing. Hated waiting for answers. Hated not being able to focus on the upcoming Day of Sacrifice and the Red Wave that would inevitably follow. His nights were restless, and his food threatened to roar back up his throat, but Castor was a persistent man. He pushed past everything, all the obstacles that were placed in his way. Things would clear up soon enough, he just had to survive until then. So he made his way to the Magistrates building, to Linette's office. She usually managed to help him to calm down, even though he wouldn't be able to talk about the situation with her. The less she knew, the less it compromised her position. It was certainly difficult for a woman to gain particular roles in the Magistrate's chain, which was why they had given her one of the lower positions that dealt with paperwork all day. She had no technical authority other than the respect of being a Magistrate. Castor knew she had higher aspirations, and he wanted to do all he could to support her. She deserved it.

He paused outside her door, making sure his uniform was straight and presentable, then knocked.

"Enter," Linette called, and Castor opened the door. She smiled at him and offered him a seat across from her. He gladly took it, leaving his livewood spear against the wall. He had brought it along knowing Linette enjoyed looking at livewood weapons. "Business or pleasure today?" she asked, smiling at him coyly.

"Pleasure."

"Sounds good to me. I could use a break." Linette moved her paperwork to the side, neatly organized as usual. "So, what's the news at the wall? Have we won yet?"

"Not quite. I think next time we're just going to ask them politely. I don't think we've done that yet."

"Of course not, General Deven isn't the type of man who asks politely. He's probably demanded they leave, and never come back. Maybe they don't respond well to aggression."

"Well, I suppose our walls do look very intimidating. Maybe they just want to get rid of it?"

"Ooh, take down the wall that has protected us ever since we moved here in hope that it rids the enemy? I think I'll take my chances staying behind the wall, thanks."

Castor smiled. He appreciated Linette's attitude more than she knew. She kept her spirits up, able to joke about the situation while still taking it seriously. To him, it was a sign that people had not given into the years of oppression. At least he would like to think that, if it was more than just Linette. She was different to most other people he had met. Could ease the tension, capable of relaxing and genuinely smiling. He hated that she was cooped up in her office most of the day, her attitude should be out amongst the people, letting it infect and spread amongst them, something to make the city seem less dull.

To seem like it wasn't already defeated.

"So, you really came here just to talk? No… uh… updates?" She asked, curiosity in her raised eyebrow.

"Just to talk. I can't give you any 'updates'."

"But it's so boring here! I need something to look forward to. I feel myself draining like treeblood, pretty soon I'll turn stiff and immovable from this spot."

Castor stood, retrieving his spear and handed it to Linette. "Here, play with this for now. Just don't poke your eye out. Or mine."

"Wow, you brought me a toy!" Linette ran her hands down the shaft of the spear, inspecting it. Castor had forgotten how such things could amaze others. To him, the spear was just a stick. A tool he used to defend the city, a part of his uniform. The general population had never held a weapon, let alone livewood in any form.

"I wonder how they get it so smooth," Linette observed, standing from her chair and holding the spear by her side. It was much taller than her, though she was relatively short already.

"I assume like any other wood. I'm just not sure at what stage they would have to do it. When it contains treeblood it's softer, would that make it easier to smooth out?"

"I doubt it, though I've never held soft livewood before."

"Me either. That's left to the experts. I'm not allowed to learn the process behind it, something about leaving it to the experienced and just focus on poking our enemies with the hardened pointy end."

"You undersell the weapon."

"Tell me I'm wrong."

"You should appreciate what the Gods have given us a little more. It's the reason we're still here today."

"I probably should, but I don't even know where it comes from. They keep the plantation where its grown and harvested, a secret. As far as I can tell, we're stealing it from the neighboring city that occasionally leaves us supplies."

Linette was either distracted by the spear or was thinking about what he had said. It was true the source of the livewood was kept secret by The Voice. They would send out small groups of loggers to retrieve the wood, not wanting to lure the metalurks attention towards their precious resource, but the exact location was only disclosed to those who needed to know. That didn't sit well with Castor. He needed to trust where his resources came from. But they had survived for nearly two-hundred years without knowing, so he learned to accept it.

"I'm sure they have their reasons. If the Gods willed us all to know the location, then we would know it. Clearly, we don't have to know, or shouldn't," Linette continued, fascinated by the livewood.

Castor decided not to respond, not wanting to cause a religious debate when he had come here to relax. He let Linette inspect the weapon in quiet, listening to her small remarks on things she found fascinating… which Castor was certain was the entire spear.

She handed the weapon back and Castor returned it to its wall. She continued to stare at it, and he was unable to tell if the look was longing or concern. "Everything all right?" he asked.

"Yeah. It's just that this will end up being the highlight of my week," she said, sounding defeated as she pried her eyes off the spear and turned them to Castor.

"Oh, I see. Next time I'll be sure to leave the spear back at the equipment depository so I won't be upstaged again."

"You know what I mean!" Linette smiled, and Castor smirked in reply. All too soon Linette's expression dropped, and Castor knew her next question before she opened her mouth. "How's your sister doing?"

"If I'm honest, I don't think she's doing well. Something was... off, when we last spoke. She promised me that she wouldn't chase after the Sandmen, and her eyes say that she's telling the truth, but... I don't know. She's up to something, I just don't know what." Castor sighed, feeling the tension he had momentarily forgotten return, slowly building alongside the weight of his decision to hire the Seekers.

"Do you want me to try find out what it is?" Linette offered, and Castor could see her concern for him.

"From behind your desk, in an office?"

"You'd be surprised at how resourceful that can be."

Castor thought about it for a moment, wondering what her possible connections were, but eventually shook his head. "I don't want you getting caught up in anything she's done. You have your own things to worry about, Lin. Thank you for asking, though."

"If you're certain."

Castor nodded. The offer was tempting, but she had already risked enough. He wasn't about to let her risk her position for his sake. Linette didn't respond, but he could tell that she wanted to insist. He was about to change the topic, when the sound of the horn rang through the city.

He immediately kicked into action, standing and grabbing his spear. He opened the door but stopped himself. "Thanks, Lin."

"Any time."

Castor jogged out the door, spear pointed to the ground, dodging the people in the corridors before breaking into a run once into the city streets. It was time to defend the wall again.

* * *

General Deven was livid. "And another thing, anyone who is injured must now be sent to me for a pardon from fighting! You let a soldier sit to the side because of a scratched wrist? Ridiculous! You tarnish your position, Castor!" General Deven screamed into Castor face, knowing that he could not retort.

Castor gripped his spear tightly, metalurk blood dripping from its point. General Deven was in a foul mood today, and it seemed that Castor was his outlet. He had spent no time after the battle to take out his frustration, screaming before Castor could get a word in. And as a captain, all he could do was stand and listen to the general list the things he had done wrong, blood boiling, biting his tongue to refrain from screaming back.

"You'll never have my position, Castor. Do you understand?"

Castor stared daggers at the general, reluctantly nodding, knowing there was no other answer. His neck felt stiff, and his stomach churned.

The general stared back him, his voice a low growl. "Wipe that look from your eyes, boy. Know your place and stay there."

Castor did not salute as the general stomped away. Frustration built life wildfire within, and he could almost hear his blood rushing around in his head. He muffled a scream as he thrust the spear into the ground. It was deeply unsatisfying.

"What in our living hell was his problem?" Vance asked as he approached from behind.

Castor didn't respond. He didn't know the answer, but it was clear something had pissed off the general.

"Did you do something to him?" Vance asked, no accusation just concern.

"No." Castor kept his tone as neutral as he could; he wouldn't take his anger out on his subordinates like the general did.

They didn't deserve it.

"We have to actually report to him now for pardons from defending? Gods, he'll be the death of us."

By now, the Steelwoods had surrounded Castor, and with nowhere to direct his anger, he was gripped by a feeling of suffocation. He tried to breathe through it.

"Well, I suppose I should go see him then," Vance declared to everyone.

Castor immediately turned to the man. He had not recalled anyone receiving a serious injury, had he missed something? But Vance appeared unharmed, no obvious significant injuries. Castor looked at him quizzically.

"See, I got a scratch on my arm," he said, "'anyone who is injured' must be sent to him." A sly smirk grew on Vance's face.

"I think my leg got twisted during the fight, too," Raeden announced, following Vance's lead.

"I think there is a mark on my back, but I can't see it. I'm sure it's there, I feel something," Derrin followed, reaching at his back.

"You should see the General for that, I can't find it," Will suggested.

One by one, his Steelwood soldiers called out wounds and ailments, not even attempting to make them believable, but it was obvious their intent.

Castor's frustration melted away, replaced with a genuine smile. "The general is already red, this will turn him into something that rivals a metalurk. I am truly appreciative of what you want to do, but it will do little other than garner punishment for yourselves." Castor tried to reason with them, but he knew they were a stubborn bunch, not so easily dissuaded. If it was not a direct command from their superior officer, they would do what they wanted.

"What's he going to do, Captain?" Vance said. "Punish the entire Steelwood soldiers? No," he said, and stepped closer to Castor. "He'll listen. He'll listen to the people that defend his walls, that defend his family. We're meant to be a unit, Captain. What kind of soldiers would we be if we weren't by our captain's side?"

"The word 'stupid' comes to mind in this situation," Castor said, quashing a smile.

"Then you command an elite unit of stupid men, sir. Your parents would be proud."

I was wrong. Linette isn't the only hope this city has left. "They sure would be," he said, and watched as his men banded together, feigning injuries as they walked, groaning and complaining, while trying to hold in their laughter.

Hopefully, the general wouldn't render them entirely useless after their little game.

Castor sat on the ground next to his spear, the last of his anger dissolving. He had no idea what had annoyed the general to the point of using Castor as an outlet, but he could only hope it would be gone by the next wave. He wasn't sure how long he could hold his tongue if the man continued his tirade against him.

Won't be a General?
Yeah. We'll see about that.

* * *

The Steelwood's plan went about as well as Castor had expected. They were reprimanded and temporarily stripped of their privileges, which was mostly just an extra ration of food. Soldiers weren't allowed to be punished with physical activity, it would increase the chances of becoming either tired or injured, leaving them in a less than adequate form to defend the walls.

Castor was sure the Steelwoods were taking advantage of that aspect, already prepared to skip the extra rations.

As leader of their unit, Castor was also punished. The general didn't have the courage to face Castor, it seemed, having sent a messenger in his place.

Talks amongst the other soldiers had already begun before the days end. By the end of the week, the situation had spread like a virus throughout the city. Castor received many respectful glances, somehow being dictated as the organizer for the Steelwoods little outburst. It was true he hadn't commanded them to stop, but it was far from his idea. Vance didn't seem to mind, happy that Castor had gained the respect of the people.

Though not everyone was happy with his actions. Many saw the act as cowardice, creating drama where there was none and compromising the integrity of the wall's defenders. Castor paid the people no heed, whether they respected him or not, he didn't deserve nor did he want the attention.

However, it didn't stop him from being pleased that the general's name had been tarnished. Rumors were a dangerous thing in their city and could grow out of proportion, and soon many folks were talking about how the general had become too afraid to yell at Castor again, though it was far from the truth.

General Deven had somehow grown even more impatient with Castor during the after-battle reports. It had almost come down to a shake of the head to indicate the result, and Castor honestly preferred it that way. With the general absconding from the battlements as soon as possible, it left Castor more freedom to enact decisions regarding his Steelwood soldiers. The general had quickly put a stop to his rule of having the Steelwood soldiers request pardons from him directly, though Castor was certain there was a spy to keep an eye on them.

Castor stood in the courtyard of the battlements, watching the Steelwoods run through their training routine, while he simultaneously supervised newly recruited archers as they practiced their accuracy against the circular, wooden targets. The Steelwoods needed little guidance, the more experienced members had memorized their routine and would assist the newer recruits, but it was good for their morale if he were seen. Occasionally, he would join in sparring, but his attention was allocated between the two groups, so it left little time to participate.

As Castor was giving the archers tips on their stances, the horn resonated through the city once again.

"Reds incoming! Steelwoods to position!" Castor shouted between horn blasts. "New recruits, you're on standby! Half of you to the East gate, the other half split into two more groups, one

North and one South! Move it! The Reds won't wait for you to be ready!"

The soldiers immediately sprang into action, following Castor's command as best they could, but the newly recruited archers seemed a little frazzled about how to split. Some had already run off, but the rest were trying to organize where to go.

Was I ever this lost?

"Recruits! What are you doing? This section, go North! This section, South! It's not that hard! If the others were able to follow orders, then you should as well! You better hope the wall is still standing by the time you get there!"

The recruits responded better this time, now that Castor had to practically hold their hands.

Once everyone was on the move, Castor legged after the soldiers going to the East wall, taking the stairs two at a time as he took his position once again.

The metalurks seemed larger in number, odd for their recent pattern, but it was often difficult to predict. Castor could usually anticipate the size of each attack, but every now and then the monsters would surprise him.

It taught him to never be relaxed when it came to the defense of their walls.

The horn blasts accelerated, and the archers took the line, filling the last of the gaps along the battlements. The new recruits stood in their own line at the bottom of the steps, prepared to be called upon, though it was never needed unless one of the bows broke, which was a rare occurrence thanks to livewood.

"Recruits," Castor called down, and they immediately snapped to attention. "When the Steelwoods move forward, prepare your arrows. Slay any of the creatures that escape the tunnel!"

Based on the size of the horde, the Steelwood soldiers would likely handle the attack, but it was always better to be overprepared when it came to the defense of the city. The soldiers atop the wall would slay the majority of the creatures, the livewood slopes that dropped the boulders would crush the swarm that formed at the wall.

As the metalurks drew closer, General Deven had yet to make an appearance. Castor scanned the courtyard, but the general was nowhere to be seen, and there was no time to wait for him.

Hopefully he won't show this time.

Anticipation of finally commanding the defense on his own thrilled him to his core. He took a breath of fresh air, prepared for this moment. "Archers! Nock!"

The archers prepared their arrows, awaiting the next command. The horn blasted rapidly, and Castor eyed the scattered red creatures loping toward the wall on all fours. Even without a face, it was clear their hungry for the city.

The horn gave one final, long blast.

"Loose!"

The archers released their arrows; the defense of the wall had begun again.

Creatures fell to the first wave of arrows, and by the time the monsters reached the wall, half had been felled. The archers had aimed well today.

"Slopes! Now!"

The familiar sound of boulders scoring down the ramps sounded, followed by the wet thud as it landed, crushing several metalurks. The earth shook with every thud, and Castor took it as a sign of progress. Every tremor meant more dead enemies.

The sound of the livewood being scratched and ripped sounded from below, followed by the sound of the latticed gate being dropped from below Castor's feet.

"Officer Hendle!"

A soldier took a step out of the archers' line. "Sir!"

"Take command of the wall, I'm going below!"

"Yes, sir!"

Castor raced down the steps, content the general had yet to make an appearance. He wanted to continue shouting orders, happy with the way things were playing out, but the itch of battle was too much to ignore.

As his feet hit the courtyard, Castor yelled for the recruits to stay focused. His Steelwoods stood in formation, prepared to face the oncoming threat. It surprised Castor that no matter how many times they defended their walls, no matter how many battles had passed, they still stood firmly against the relentless attacks.

Castor was proud to be a defender of the wall.

The inevitable cracking of the gate came, and the metalurks rushed through, desperately climbing over each other. The Steelwoods met them as they slammed into the latticed gate, making short work of those that rushed ahead of the pack.

Disorganized, as usual.

With the archers capably taking down the metalurks, the remaining few monsters entered in small groups, allowing the Steelwoods to strike them down with little damage inflicted on the lattice gate. Overall, it was a very successful defense. Rarely had they managed to hold back a decent sized wave and not have them break through into the city.

Castor couldn't acclaim to much in terms of commanding the wall, the soldiers knew what they had to do without leadership, but it spoke a great deal that the general had not made an appearance during this wave. Perhaps he had gone to one of the other walls instead?

Unlikely. General Deven took great pleasure in overshadowing Castor, claiming responsibility for their successful defenses. With the threats that had been made against Castor, the general would not have stood aside willingly. Something must have prevented him from attending.

As such, Castor took the responsibility of checking all areas of their defenses to receive any issues and ensure they were replenished appropriately. He had the treeblood experts repairing the gates, and that the recruits were retrieving reusable arrows from outside the walls. Any boulders that could be reused were rolled back inside and reloaded onto the slopes. Castor handled every aspect, personally confirming that everything was on track. The only thing missing was the after-battle report.

A report that had to be given to the general. Castor decided to forgo the messenger and report to General Deven personally. He scoured the battlements, and after speaking with some of the soldiers, discovered the general hadn't made an appearance all day, rumored to be cooped up in his home from an ailment.

Castor made way for the general's home, a little spring in his step. General Deven was sick and stilled missed commanding the defense of the wall? Unlikely. The sickness would have to be life threatening for the man to miss an opportunity to suppress Castor.

The large building that homed General Deven and his family was surrounded by small gardens that added color to the dull grey of the cobblestones. Castor knocked on the large wooden door, hearing it echo slightly inside.

Footsteps sounded beyond, then the door creaked open, revealing a man in drab grey clothing, sporting the bright green of the Deven noble family in the form of a cloth draped around his shoulders. The scent of treeblood-infused candles immediately stung Castor nostrils, causing him to wrinkle his nose. He was not fond of the smell; he doubted anyone was. Treeblood candles were used as an aromatic but to signify to any visitors the wealth and status of the family.

"Captain Castor. I do not believe the general was expecting you," the servant spoke, bowing as per the proper etiquette.

"I have come to give the wave report. He should have at least expected that."

"The general has fallen ill, I'm afraid. Please wait here a moment, sir, I shall inform him." the servant bowed once more before disappearing behind another door.

Castor stayed in the doorway but took the chance to look around. There was naught of interest, just portraits of the Deven family proudly displaying each man in uniform that defended their city walls. The Deven family were generational city defenders. It was how the man achieved his rank so easily – his family's reputation spoke for him.

The servant didn't take long to return, much to Castor's relief as the doorstep had grown tiresome.

"General Deven has requested not to be bothered. He suggested you give me the details and I shall relay them to him when he feels well enough."

Castor scoffed. *He's avoiding me.* "Everything went fine."

"Is that all, sir?" the servant asked, obviously confused by the lack of details but not wanting to pry above his position.

"That's all."

Castor was deliberately being short; there wasn't much to update the general about anyway. He hoped that he had at least annoyed the man by showing up at his house personally, but... there was something was off about the general's situation, Castor could feel it in his bones. Yet there was nothing to prove the feelings right.

The general had been acting stranger than normal of late, and Castor couldn't recall the last time the man had been ill to the point of missing an attack. There was definitely more to the story, and it began to grow like a parasite in Castor's mind.

Gods curse us both, Maggie.

10

Time slowly passed, grain by grain through the hourglass. Elias was bored with the lesson on various soils the city has access to, and their benefits for crops. It was not a topic he had any particular interest in, but the same could be said for most of his lessons.

What made his situation worse was knowing Geraldine would be leaving a letter in his room during his lesson. She had informed him before she left to retrieve it, and part of him wished she hadn't. His attention should be focused on his teachings; however, being conscious of time only made it seem to pass significantly slower.

His leg bounced with impatience, his mind eager for the lesson to be over. He scribbled idly on his paper – a habit that he was constantly berated for – wishing the lesson over. He did not wish to learn about soils, but apparently this was a key piece of knowledge most noble children were taught these days.

It was as if they planned to be rid of the metalurks, break free into the open world and expand upon their crops, freeing the people of their starvation.

Elias knew all too well he wouldn't be alive to see it. Even if he survived his duel, freedom would not be achieved in his lifetime. Such a reoccurring force of enemies wouldn't simply stop; you need to kill its source. The few expeditions beyond the walls had proven there was nothing to find. The few men that survived claimed the creatures appeared out of nowhere, somehow appearing in the tracks the men left behind, cutting off any retreat to the city.

Rumor had it, one man claimed that a creature clawed its way out of the soil. They mustn't have taken him seriously if they did not include such a proclamation into their current education on metalurks, or even soils.

His teacher continued to explain the limitations of their surrounding soil, unaware that Elias did not care for a word of it. His teacher had clearly spent much of their life learning about this subject, so Elias felt a little guilt for not caring nor listening, but it was becoming increasingly difficult. His chair was uncomfortable, he continuously stifled yawns, and he was in a battle to keep his eyelids open.

Finally, the teacher declared their lesson finished, and despite Elias' impatience, he maintained the etiquette of allowing his teacher to leave first. The man seemed to take their time in gathering his notes, leaving at his own pace.

Once out of the room, Elias rushed to his chambers. Geraldine would have returned by now, and he had to control his giddiness lest he draw suspicion to himself. As depressing as it was, it was out of character for Elias to be so outwardly happy. If he began showing it now, it might arouse his father's suspicions and bring cause to investigate. He couldn't deal with that.

Despite Elias' age, his father still controlled his social life, and the man would not approve of the letters.

Elias entered his chambers, his eyes falling upon the pale yellow of the envelope laying on his bed. He waited until he closed his door to smile, relaxing himself as he picked up the envelope and sat at his desk.

I apologize for any ill feelings I may have brought upon you by bringing up the subject of family. I simply wished to learn more about your life. I did not mean to pry where I should not have. It at least seems we share some similarities in terms of our fathers, but it would be best not to explore that topic any further.

You were right about my mother. I vow to summon the courage to be more active in her life. I thought my silent support may have been enough, but I can see it was only cowardice of overstepping. I do wish to let my mother know she is loved, but I still fear that I will not be enough.

I, too, have an interest in livewood. It is rather fascinating, but I do not know much more than the basics. My studies focus elsewhere, leaving little room for my own personal fields to pursue. Perhaps in tandem with being more active in my mother's emotional state, you too should pursue your own interests further. Request the Magistrates to be taught the properties of livewood and treeblood. I will truly be fascinated to hear what you learn.

Life is too short to live with regrets.

My father has me mostly focusing on politics, he has high aspirations for me. I'm afraid that I am unable to tell if it has become an interest of mine, or if I simply wish to fulfil my father's wishes. If I give it some thought, I suppose I am intrigued with horticulture. How we've managed to grow enough food to sustain the city fascinates me. I know we get the occasional delivery from our neighboring city, but we as a people have become very resourceful. If I ever find myself with free time, I might take the opportunity to delve into it further, perhaps think of a way to enhance our situation so the people do not live with the bare minimum.

It is an ambitious idea, but what is there to life without ambitions?

In regard to the tree in town, I admit that I have only glanced at it in passing. I do not hold the same respect you appear to have for it, but I shall endeavor to see what you see. Perhaps it can bring me a momentary peace as it does you.

The Day of Sacrifice is not an easy topic for me to speak of, for personal reasons. Though it is truly a blessed day that enables our city to live, I have too many negative emotions towards the events that surround it. Namely the metalurks that you speak of. I fear what the Red Sea will do to the city once they arrive. I can only hope the defenders have preparations to prevent as many as they can from entering.

It is grim to think about, but it is an inevitability our city must face. I pray to the Gods that we will both see it through to see each other once more.

I fear I have dallied for too long, your friend must take my letter.

I must confess, your words brighten my day. It is as if they were made of metal that not even the metalurks may take away from me.

I look forward to reading your next letter.

Elias held the letter, cheerful and saddened. He'd never wanted to come out of his duel alive so badly as he did now. There was a risk of becoming too attached before the duel, and if he was honest, he had immediately became attached the night they met, the letters only cementing the feeling. Elias felt reinvigorated to win his duel, see through the Red Sea that would follow, and finally see his correspondent again.

He immediately set out to writing his reply, making sure not to mention the Day of Sacrifice or Red Sea – it was becoming too dark a topic to talk about. As the range of emotions built inside, his hand began to shake, causing some of the letters to be less than sufficient from a nobleman. He started the letter again, taking a moment to calm himself. It had been a while since he felt any kind of fire from within, it was strange to experience it now.

With the letter completed, he set it aside for when Geraldine would arrive after completion of her household duties. He sat at his desk, a warmth suffusing he thought long gone.

It reminded him of love.

That feeling disappeared the day his mother died. His father, the only member of his family left, took a dramatic turn as a result, and became obsessed with Elias' protection, hiring more guards, placing more limitations to his social life. Rarely was he allowed to attend other noble's gatherings.

It was as though his father was trying to protect Elias from a force that had haunted his father since the day of his first-born son. Trying to shield Elias from the Gods themselves.

With his father growing ever more distant as the Day of Sacrifice approached, Elias found the only connections he had were Geraldine and his mysterious correspondent.

As if summoned by his thoughts, a knock on the door heralded Geraldine's arrival, and Elias granted permission for her to enter.

"Anything you require before the night's end, sir?" She stood straight-backed and looking at Elias.

A friend, or just being kind to their employer? "Yes, Geraldine. I have the letter. I will also require a light snack before bed."

"Very well, sir. I shall have the kitchens send you the usual addleberry and grundine spiced pie."

"Uh, Geraldine…?"

"Yes, sir?"

"Would you care to join me for the light snack?"

Geraldine's expression remained unchanged, making it difficult for Elias to read her thoughts. Was she trying to think of an excuse, or was she simply caught off guard by the question?

Geraldine cleared her throat. "I appreciate the offer, sir, but if I miss tonight's opportunity to deliver the letter, I may not get another for at least a week."

Elias nodded; dejectedly accepting the response. He still could not tell if she viewed him anything other than a superior,

129

wishing to keep their relationship as professional as possible. He did not want to miss the opportunity to have the letter sent, so he did not press the matter further.

"Geraldine," Elias called as she stood in the now open doorway."

"Sir?"

"Cancel the snack."

Geraldine looked at Elias pensively. "Very well, sir." She closed the door, and Elias was once again alone.

At least until the next letter.

* * *

The next day, lethargy crept in once again. Elias was adamant to conquer his sluggish attitude, motivating himself to get out of bed and get dressed. He knew what he was going to do before he became apathetic. Elias was going to speak to his father and demand a mentor to teach him about livewood. His correspondent had been right, life was not worth living if he wasn't enjoying it.

Unsurprisingly, his father was in his study, fast asleep in his chair that faced the fire. He would often doze off and the servants had been ordered not to wake him unless it was an emergency. The vacant chair next to his father had once been Elias' mother's, but now it was his on the rare occasion he shared a conversation with his father. Elias sat on the chair and stared at his father for a moment; the man hadn't even changed into his nightwear, a small red stain from spilled wine still on his shirt.

"Father," Elias said gently, but the man's eyes remained shut. "Father," Elias tried again, louder.

Warin jolted awake, taking a deep breath and regaining his senses. Elias waited a moment while his father rubbed the sleep from his eyes before focusing on him. Warrin Va Noldin's eyes were red, though it was difficult to say why. Lack of sleep? An irritant in the air? Or had he been crying again?

"Elias, is it late in the day?"

"No, Father. It's actually early."

"Good, good." His father stretched his limbs, and few cracked from the stiffness of being seated in a chair for hours.

"Father, I want you to find someone to teach me about livewood. Particularly, how to craft with it. Extract and administer the appropriate amounts of treeblood. It's various applications. Anything and everything."

Elias waited, but Warin simply stared at his son. Was his father contemplating the request, or still trying to process the situation from just having been awoken?

"You should be focusing on your fighting techniques. With the—"

"Metalurks eat my damned fighting techniques!" Elias snapped. "You know as well as I do that I am as prepared as I'll ever be. My training regimen will remain the same, I will continue to attend them and striving for the peak of my abilities. Allow me to enjoy myself in what could be my last moments. I am owed at least that much by the city. And by you."

Warin continued to stare, and Elias let the outburst sit in the air, knowing he had just shown his father disrespect, but... it felt right.

It was time his father listened.

Elias' body tensed slightly as his father continued to stare, expression unchanged. The silence was held weight, but Elias held that watery gaze, refusing to back down. Even The Voice, who sat at their secluded home at the crest would have succumbed to his demand.

Finally, Warin shifted in his chair slightly. "Very well. I will request an expert be sent to teach you whatever you wish to know."

His father reached for the bottle of wine that sat on the table but paused as his hand made contact with it – the constant inner debate of whether it was worth the drink at such early hours of the morning. Elias knew the time of day was the only thing that would prevent his father from imbibing.

As Warin's hand rested on the bottle, Elias caught a glimpse of his father's livewood sleeve.

Dark green. Guilt.

Elias sat back in his chair, relaxing tense shoulders. He tugged at his shirt sleeve slightly, so that his livewood sleeve peeked out, allowing his father to view his own shade of dark green.

Elias watched as Warin's sleeve began to change shades, shifting between the dark green and a pink hue. His father had seen his sleeve, so he rested his arm, the unspoken apology had been received.

Warin's hand left the bottle. "I cannot fault you for having interest in livewood, it certainly is an intriguing gift from the Gods. I have wondered, from time to time, how our researchers have discovered numerous applications for it. I've also heard rumors they've discovered another use for it, yet to be announced. Though I am hesitant to believe it, Some claim it will entirely change the defense of our walls. Surely something so grand would not be kept a secret unless they enjoy the suspense."

Elias nodded; he had heard the rumors from Geraldine. The livewood experts had supposedly found a way to make livewood more than just another wooden resource, apparently, they'd developed an idea to make it live up to its name.

But right now, that's all it was: an idea. If it existed at all.

"I wish to learn all I can about it," Elias said. "What it's like in its natural state, if treeblood has any other applications. Just... anything."

Warin stared into the ashes of the fireplace. "I'm sure it has many applications. I hope the request will be accepted, though I imagine it will, given our family's status."

"They will."

The conversation died. Elias sat, uncertain what he should do. He sensed that his father wished to converse more, but the man did not utter a word, and Elias had naught to speak of that his father would not already know.

After a long, awkward silence, Elias rose from his chair. "Thank you, Father." He made for the door, his footsteps stalling when his father called out to him.

"I am sorry, Elias. I love you with all of my heart, though I know my actions might speak otherwise at times. Please, do not hesitate to speak with me should you wish for anything else. I will make sure to grant it. It is the least I can do for you."

Those words tugged at heartstrings that had long been left alone. The swell of emotion overwhelmed Elias, rendering him without words. He had always known his father cared for him deeply, but hearing those words was something else entirely.

His hands began to sweat, and his eyes began to tear-up. "I love you too, Father."

* * *

It did not take long for the Magistrates to approve Elias' request. By the following week, Elias had been appointed a teacher and it had become part of his education. And it was all thanks to his father's connections and the support of Elias' mysterious man.

Elias sat in his first lesson, eager to begin. His teacher was Victor Maewell, a man of average height, long brown hair that was woven into two separate braids; he sported a short beard, and glasses that sat over green eyes. Victor appeared to be of middle-age, but his voice was youthful and filled with excitement. From the beginning of their lesson, it was clear Victor was enthralled by livewood, and despite it being his life's dedication, it appeared that not even years of study could quell his passion for it.

"Have you ever touched the tree in the city center?" Victor asked, eyes wide with hope.

Elias trawled his memories. "I don't think I have, no. I just assumed it was like… a bad omen or something."

"Well, I suppose that might come down to the person, but I implore that you do as long as you believe it isn't disrespectful towards the gods. The one in town is now quite old for a livewood tree, they don't have a very long lifespan, but you'll find that it is almost soft to the touch." Victor frowned. "No, soft isn't the right word…or perhaps it is? It is soft in comparison to other wood, you are able to press into the tree slightly. As I said, the one in town is older than most other livewood trees, so it will be softer than most, but that doesn't make its wood any less valuable."

Victor's eyes seemed to light up further. "Another amazing quality is that its wood does not degrade with age, it's firmness – once drained of course – does not differ from the younger livewood trees. It certainly is miraculous. It shows how much the Gods smile upon us by the thought they have put behind this blessing."

Victor's enthusiasm was captivating, Elias found himself engaged with every word the man spoke, despite the man sometimes going on a tangent.

Elias nodded to his teacher. "If the Gods have not frowned upon you for touching it, then perhaps it shall be alright. As long as I do not harm the tree, of course."

"Yes! You definitely should! Though, I understand that you are not able to venture into the city as others, but I shall send a request to your father that we take a trip down there in one of our future lessons."

"You will? That will be amazing! I'm sure he would accept if it came from you. Wow, one class in and you're already my favorite mentor."

Victor blushed slightly, his livewood sleeve reflecting the positive emotions from the compliment. That was possibly Elias' favorite trait of his new mentor – the man was genuine. He had no qualms revealing his sleeve, he had walked in with it already revealed.

His mentor was here to do one thing, and one thing only. Teach Elias about livewood. No politics. No scheming. Just high-spirited teaching.

There were a few odd teachers in his past that were trying to abuse their position to further themselves, acting as if teaching Elias meant they were a higher-ranking noble. Elias did not like feeling used, and even as a child it was easy to see that some of his mentor's weren't interested in teaching, just wanted to have him as a student for bragging rights.

With their lesson over, Victor packed his belongings. He had brought notes to guide him, but they were quickly forgotten once the conversation had begun flowing. Victor seemed to be able to recall everything without the need of his notes

Elias was surprised to find that he was disappointed at the lesson ending. He had thoroughly enjoyed listening to Victor and looked forward to his next lesson in a few days' time.

After bidding Victor farewell, Elias made his way towards the dueling room for his discreet sparring practice. Merek was waiting when Elias entered but had yet to don his armor.

"Good to see you, Elias."

"Greetings, Merek. I trust you are well?"

"Indeed. Normal training today, or do you wish to get something off your chest again?"

"Are you going to ask that every time I come in?"

"It worked for you, that's all I'm saying. You just need to find the balance of letting your emotions drive you, but not letting them get you killed."

"Yes, how wonderful, I'll be sure not to be nervous on the day I am fated to die."

Merek scowled, "Such a grim outlook. You must be rid of that negativity, it's only going to prove you right."

"I know, but it's difficult, Merek. Whenever it gets brought up I… I'm not in control of how I feel about it, and you must admit that my family's reputation isn't exactly astounding when it comes to duels."

Merek's face deepened into a grim expression. "Reputation only means things that have happened, not things that *will* happen. You have the ability to change that reputation, and I have faith that you will."

Elias smiled, knowing that his livewood sleeve was exposed and Merek would unmistakably notice the greenish yellow of skepticism. "Who am I to change what our family has become?" Elias continued to don his armor but stopped when he realized Merek was not doing the same. He turned to find Merek facing him, eyes burning a hole through Elias.

"You are Elias Va Noldin, son of Warin Va Noldin, champion of his family. You hold the key to changing your family's future and reputation. You just have to decide if you're strong enough to do so. Do not sell yourself short because of the

135

past. You are not those who fell before you. It has nothing to do with the way you were born, but everything to do with your attitude. Keep your head held high, Elias, or you'll lose it."

Elias stared at Merek's livewood sleeve that he intentionally left revealed. It was burning a bright red. Passion. The passion that is tied to one's beliefs. Elias' own sleeve did not change, remaining skeptical. He wanted to believe, but he had not found yet found the strength to do so.

But things were beginning to change for Elias.

His dueling mentor had complete faith in him. Elias had finally demanded something from his father and succeeded. Had heard his father admit to something he had not said in a long time. Elias was able to contact the mysterious man that had stolen his heart the night they met.

Perhaps it was time to believe that he would make it.

Perhaps it was time to believe in life again.

11

Days trickled by slowly for Maggie. Heleen sensed that something had been off and stuck by Maggie's side while at work. The woman didn't believe Maggie when she denied having panic attacks, observing the signs and putting the pieces together. It allowed Maggie no opportunity to slip away into the hidden room to retrieve another paper.

The previous one she managed to sneak away had only provided more questions than answers, and it was killing Maggie that she was unable to pursue any leads. On one hand, she promised not to chase the Sandmen until Castor came forward with information. On the other, Heleen would not leave her alone long enough to retrieve another paper from the hidden records.

At home, Maggie sat alone in her kitchen, solitary candle burning against the darkness of night. She was too amped up to sleep. She needed a plan; the last record teased her with information but not given her enough.

Unless she had missed something.

She pulled out the paper again, reading thoroughly, slowly, inspecting each individual word as if it they were a suspect hiding the truth.

As I suspected, the demons have appeared.

I warned them again and again, but the call of power was too tempting, it drowned my words until they were little more than a leaf in the wind.

Our weapons are ineffective, but somehow, we survived, though I fear more are yet to come.

Our people are doomed. I can feel it. I can feel those eyeless faces staring at us through our walls.

They called me mad. Delusional. Hysterical.

And now we are as good as dead.

These were records from an Old Malvarkian. Maggie was sure of it. Someone did leave behind warnings for others, but they were sealed away in a hidden room no one had found.

Why? Were they incomplete? Why did they have to hide the records from their own people?

The answers lay in that room. The room that she could not slip into. She would have to just bide her time. The room could wait, there was no need to rush and risk being caught.

Unless it was time to tell someone? Perhaps the records held the solution to their metalurk problem? But then what had happened to the Old Malvarkians if they had the answer?

There wasn't just one answer. The records were little more than treasured history that would answer some questions their people had, but it would not solve their situation for them. So why wait to reveal the papers?

Because Maggie knew that if she told others, then the records would be taken away to a secure location before she could read them.

She returned her focus to her surroundings, the loneliness settling in once more. The only sound was her own breath against the still night.

James will be out late drinking again.

Maggie grabbed the candle, using it to light her way up the stairs. Each step would creak under her weight, James had yet to replace them. He was too busy with work and his social life, but he would get around to it eventually.

She made her way towards her bedroom, but as she passed her son's room, the overwhelming feelings returned, leaking from the cracks of his door, it's tendrils loosely wrapping themselves around her limbs.

Maggie paused. She wanted to open his door. Wanted to see him in his room, tinkering with some new object he found while playing with his friends. Wanted to see his smile that always reassured her she was doing a good job.

But the room was empty. She knew it was, but she could not prevent herself from dreaming for another reality. A better reality.

Her inner conflict with the closed door was broken by the creaking of wood. She immediately spun around, holding the candle out, showing that no one was behind her. The stairs were out of view and the candle provided limited vision against the encroaching darkness. She hesitated but stepped towards the stairs as quietly as possible, not wanting to give away her position.

With each step closer to the stairs, she felt them. A presence lingered downstairs. The creak was not from the wind, but from weight being pressed down onto the floorboards. She knew the sound all too well.

As she neared the corner where the stairs were located, she hesitated again, taking a short moment to gather her courage before forcing herself to spin around the corner as if to catch the trespasser off guard. She held the candle forward, shedding the light so it reached the bottom of the stairs.

No one. They were not at the stairs yet, they were below her.

No. No one is there. There never is. Remember the technique.

Maggie began to control her breathing, but her eyes remained wide as she peered down at the empty staircase as if the intruder were invisible. She stood, for what seemed like hours, but another sound did not come.

They left.

No. There was never anyone. Stop.

Her thoughts were befuddled, and her heart raced. She needed to calm herself. Maggie raced back along the hallway to her bedroom as if the intruder were right behind her. She slammed the door closed and started to barricade her door. She stuffed clothes at the bottom of the door to slow it from opening, then dragged the empty set of drawers in front of the door.

Then she sat on her bed, waiting. Waiting for another sound to tell her she had been right, there was an intruder.

Silence.

She did not blow out the candle, instead set it on the small table beside her bed amongst the collection of other burnt-out candles.

Maggie waited for sleep to claim her, though her body fought against it, insistent that someone was there, lurking just outside her door.

After hours of silence, her body surrendered, and sleep victoriously claimed her.

* * *

The morning came with a fresh perspective. She removed the undisturbed barricades from her door, and ventured downstairs, feeling safe in her own home once more.

Maggie went through her daily routine – something Audrey insisted she should keep consistent – before setting out to her day at the library. But as soon as Maggie stepped foot outside of her home, she felt uneasy. The familiar sensation of prying eyes returned. Her head tingled every time her eyes darted to a corner, as if they would land on the suspect who was stalking her. Each time they failed to catch someone in the act.

Her eyes darted from person to person as she walked the streets, wary of anyone who would try approach. None paid her any mind, going about their business just like any other day. She considered going down the street where the young group of Sandmen liked to hang out, thinking she may be able to spot a missing person in the group, but decided that it was too early for them to gather. Instead, she rushed towards the library, wanting to be behind a closed door to break the connection.

She hurried inside the library, hastily closing the door behind her. The moment it shut, she felt some of the pressure lift, but not entirely. That unease remained.

Heleen greeted her with the usual cup of freshly brewed tea. Maggie gratefully accepted the cup, letting its warmth soothe her. She did appreciate Heleen preparing her a drink each morning, it took a while to heat up the water in a stone bowl over the small fire they were permitted to have inside, away from anything flammable.

"How are you feeling today, dear?" Heleen asked as she sat her own cup down on the nearby table.

"I'm fine," Maggie lied. She didn't want to give Heleen reason to follow her around all day again. She wasn't quite certain if Heleen believed her, but she was already prepared for another full day of work. Maggie was trying to stifle her drive to enter the back room, still undecided about whether to reveal its existence or not. She wanted more time to read the papers on her own, but what if they held something useful for the city? Was it not her responsibility as a citizen to do anything she could to ease their situation?

No. Not yet, at least. If there was nothing worth sharing other than historical records, then there was no rush to reveal it.

The day went on, and Heleen kept Maggie occupied with various tasks, staying alongside her through them. Maggie should have truly appreciated Heleen's intent in wanting to help her as much as possible, but it was difficult to do so when all she wanted to do was escape to the hidden room.

The library was thankfully a little busy today, and Heleen gave Maggie the task of fetching more long-hour candles and replacing the ones that had burned out. Thankfully, the day was bright enough to provide enough lighting so that they didn't need to be replaced urgently.

As Maggie headed to the backroom, she turned and noticed Heleen was busy with a visitor. Maggie slowed her pace, watching them as she crept closer to the back wall. When there were no obvious signs of Heleen finishing up with the visitor, Maggie

141

made her way to the back wall where the hidden room beckoned. Another quick check to make sure that no one was around, but thankfully most of the visitors seemed to have found their books and were at various tables reading.

With a deep breath, Maggie darted into the back room, grabbing any paper she could with the appropriate level of caution, so it didn't crumble in her grasp. She zipped back out of the doorway, making sure to close it behind her. Her breathing became rapid, looking around to see if anyone had spotted her. No one called out to her, and there was no movement nearby.

Success!

She quickly made her way into the back room, and carefully placed the record into her pocket, cringing slightly as flakes fell from the old parchment. She grabbed two long-hour candles and made her way to the main room of the library, preparing to return to her assigned tasks, when the sound of the horn blew.

No one panicked when they heard the sound, but they all knew the procedure. Everyone left in unison as if they all followed the same routine. Maggie placed the candles down, leaning them against the wall, and made her way to the front door where Heleen was waiting, ensuring everyone left. Maggie scoured in between the aisles of books to ensure no one remained behind and ducked through the door Heleen held open.

Maggie took the horn blast as a sign that she was doing the right thing, a sign that she was meant to read the records.

With the Gods approval, Maggie returned home to delve into another record.

...should n... ve tak... soil... of ours.
...was not... nef... city... s for thei... al ga...
...eir gree... y have d...
Red...ot by e... nsport... ack t...ir rea... r doma...
An...e same t... one by one, we...
Let this...ning to... re inv...e same ri...e Eld...
Do n...ted by... power t... soi...

...is to... urn it... nce it came.
Shun... Spurn i...Let i... touched... r our de... rom th... rld.
...plan... eds of life... oil of d....
Gods turn me to metal!

Maggie cursed herself for being so careless with the document. It had broken in her pocket as she walked. The Old Malvarkians were clearly not famed for their paper treatments, the record was simply too fragile. Gaps had formed where pieces were torn off by the gentle movement, disintegrating into little more than specs of dust.

This record was useless to her now. She could not bring the pieces back together, they were simply too small and indistinguishable to even attempt.

So careless!

Maggie continued to berate herself. Her situation was only made worse by the fact that Castor was currently fighting for his life to defend the walls, to defend her while she frivolously played with history by cramming it into her pockets.

No more. No more toying around. The result of the crumpled paper was proof enough that it was not worth destroying history just to keep the records to herself. She was being selfish, and now the city had to suffer for it.

She would tell someone.

But who?

Castor would not believe her, probably. Besides, he had his own investigations to follow.

Audrey was the last person she wanted to tell, and James was too busy to help her.

That left only Heleen. Heleen, who had been caring for her for many months now, and as head librarian, she deserved to know.

Yes. She would tell Heleen. She could only hope that it was the right thing to do.

* * *

Maggie scurried back to the library, thoughts of being watched pushed to the back of her mind, no longer a priority. She needed to make sure she got to the library before any visitors so she could show Heleen discreetly. It was not a secret she wanted everyone to know just yet. In telling Heleen, she hoped she would be allowed some time to investigate them on her own.

And Heleen would believe her this time. She had proof.

She made her way inside the library and closed the door. She scanned the main room, elated that only Heleen had returned.

"Heleen!" Maggie called out excitedly, causing a worried expression to alight on the librarian face. Maggie understood, usually when she was hyped up like this, it was because someone had been following her, but she couldn't prove it. Her pursuers always left her alone once she reached the library.

"Margaret? What is it?"

"Come, I have something to show you." Maggie grabbed Heleen by the hand, walking her between the aisles to the back wall of the library. "I discovered something a little while ago, and now I want to show you. I accidentally found out a hidden panel in the wall, and inside were records. Records from the Old Malvarkians!"

Maggie almost dragged Heleen right off her feet as she dashed forwards, forgetting that Heleen was a little older and slower. The woman did her best to remain upright, and was thankful when Maggie finally let go once they rounded the last bookshelf to face the back wall.

"Look!" Maggie stood at the wall, giving it a light push. The hidden door gave way, opening to the secret room. Maggie's heart sank.

The room was empty.

Her brain ceased functioning. She could not comprehend the situation before her.

How... What? I don't... How?

"Well, I didn't realize we had an extra storage room," Heleen commented, walking inside to inspect the room, standing where the desk had been earlier that day.

"No... there were...records in here... documents... I don't... I don't understand..."

Heleen walked over to Maggie, face donning an empathetic smile. "Sweetie, do you think that perhaps you got a little excited when you found the room?"

Maggie stared at her, unable to organize her emotions to express the appropriate one. She was being called a liar. Again. "No, Heleen, there were really documents in here. A desk, remnants of papers that broke off when I touched them!" Maggie could still not believe her eyes. It was as if she had stepped into a separate room. The chair and the desk, gone. The records with them. Not even specs of the brittle paper remained.

"Dear," Heleen's voice softened, trying to sound compassionate. "Do you think it's time for a rest? Perhaps to see Audrey? I know your mind can play tricks on you. Be a smart girl, truly think about what happened when you found the room. I don't think anything was in here, do you?" Heleen spoke to her like a child.

This time, Maggie found the right expression. Her face contorted into dismay, and she glared at Heleen. "Yes. I know for a fact there was. I have a record I stole at home. I'll prove to you that something was there. Somebody has come in and taken it."

"During an attack? I doubt it, Maggie, I th—"

"That's the perfect time, Heleen. I'll return shortly with the evidence to prove I'm right. And maybe then you'll stop treating me as if everything I say is insane." Maggie spat the words, leaving behind a taste of seething fury. She was tired of playing these games, but today, she had proof.

Heleen's face dropped, taken aback by Maggie's anger, but before the librarian could respond, Maggie stormed away, leaving the library and slamming the door behind her.

Maggie carried the momentum, refusing to let anything obscure her quest of retrieving the record she'd hidden in her kitchen. She ignored glances at her, no longer caring if she was being watched. Perhaps this would be a lesson to them as well – she was not to be trifled with. Once they saw the determination in her face, they'd know she would find them. She would find them all. She would find her son's killer. Gods themselves condemn her, she would no longer wait for Castor.

She barged into her own home, skipping her usual inspection of any hidden threats, and marched right into her kitchen. She gripped the wooden handle of one of her kitchen drawers and slid it open, emptying it and removing the false bottom.

She didn't think it was possible, but her heart sank even lower.

The drawer was empty.

Maggie dropped to her knees, clutching her face. Her body was a battleground of numbness and over-stimulation. The sheer number of emotions were flowing through her, tilted her world off balance. She bent over forward, hurling the contents of her stomach. Maggie grabbed the top of the drawers, aiming to keep herself upright, but every time tried to steady her eyes, to snatch a location to focus on, it would move away as if the very fabric of reality was teasing her.

Nothing made sense anymore. She didn't know who she was. She didn't know what was happening.

She let go of the wooden drawers, keeling over into a puddle, uncertain if she wanted to fight against the tears that were slamming on the door inside of her.

With the room still spinning, Maggie closed her eyes and cried.

* * *

"Her eyes are a little red," Doctor Grayvan said, "but that's what usually happens after crying. She's showing no other symptoms of illness, but I must agree that her attitude seems a

146

little more… compliant than normal." the doctor was looking at Castor rather than Maggie. She'd remained quiet, not caring to talk or respond to the comments made about her.

Castor had found her sleeping next to a puddle of her own vomit and immediately sought medical attention. Both Doctor Grayvan and his wife, Audrey, now turned to stare at her. As did Castor and Heleen, as if they were able to see inside of her head. Right now, she had no feelings towards anything. She had poured all those emotions out of her body as she cried herself to sleep.

She knew she should feel resentful, sitting in front of them as if she were an injured child to be coddled, but she simply couldn't summon the effort required to fight it. She just sat and listened to their theories of what transpired.

Maggie knew anything she said would not be taken seriously as soon as she had saw Heleen, who had retold her version of the events that occurred at the library prior to Maggie racing home.

Everyone seemed to be unified in an unspoken conclusion: Maggie was crazy. A lunatic set to rave around the streets until a metalurk broke past their line of defense and take her life.

Maggie scoffed. At least she would act as a momentary distraction.

She stared at the four people, the only ones that remained active in her life, and listened to them dictate her feelings and actions for her. She felt distant. Alone. Even her brother wouldn't believe her if she had the energy to persuade him.

The only person that truly knew her was out drinking himself to death in a bar. She mentally damned the city for allowing the production and distribution of alcohol to be so cheap. She supposed The Voice wanted the city to be drunk, it would be easier to accept their situation then.

She detested The Voice for stealing away her husband, preying upon him in his hour of need.

James was no longer able to be by her side.

No one was anymore.

"Let me try speaking with her," Audrey said. "Perhaps she'll be a little more talkative when it's just the two of us." Audrey ushered the others outside, but Maggie knew they wouldn't stray far. She couldn't quite decipher if they cared for her or were

147

simply trying to feel better about themselves by pretending to care for someone of her 'condition' as they delicately put it.

"Do you feel a little better now, at least?" Audrey asked. "Perhaps the amount of people was a little overwhelming for you." This was Audrey's attempt to get the conversation flowing.

Maggie stared blankly at the floor; it made no difference to her who would stay and watch her like an animal in a cage.

"Are you willing to talk about what happened?" Audrey tried again. "We don't have to, if you don't want to, but I can tell your brother is deeply concerned for your health."

Maggie did not respond, but there was a sensation returning to her. Anger? Irritation? No. Impatience. She was tired of these games. It was time to re-join reality. Or at least join the reality that others wanted for her.

"I don't know if I can do this anymore, Audrey."

Audrey's expression of concern deepened, but the woman chose not to speak, sensing Maggie was finding the right words to continue.

Maggie fidgeted with her hands a little, trying to summon the courage to convince herself. She wanted to believe her own words, she needed it to have an impact. "I'm tired of being in this situation. I'm tired of people having to care for me. Having to hinder themselves just because no one believes me. Fine. I'll change. I have to."

"Why do you have to, Maggie?" Audrey whispered.

"I have to change things. I don't want to keep running. I have to confront my fears. Whether my concerns are real or not, I have to face them."

Audrey nodded, but her eyes were searching for more, something unspoken. Maggie did not want to say the words, but she could tell just by looking at Audrey that the woman already knew what those words were, she just wanted to hear it.

"Why do you have to?" Audrey repeated. "Is there something else you are worried about? Or do you just want to better your life?"

Maggie stared at Audrey, suddenly finding her throat tight. But she was tired of this. Tired of not taking the initiative to deal with her demons, deal with the unknown. If she wanted results, she would have to take charge.

"Why, Maggie?"

"Before I stand up on our walls and declare myself made of metal!" Maggie nearly yelled, trying to refrain from an outburst, but her words had meaning behind it. She had never really considered doing such a thing, but now more than ever, it almost seemed like an inevitability.

Audrey let the silence return, obviously wanting to choose her words delicately. Maggie had never admitted to such a thing before, and she was surprised to find a pressure had been lifted.

"Is that what you want to do, Maggie?"

Maggie returned her gaze to Audrey but found she could not maintain eye contact. "It just seems like it's the only option sometimes. I've grown *tired* of feeling like every day could be my last because of some threat that may not even exist."

"Are you talking about the Sandmen and how you think they are after you?"

Maggie nodded. "If they are after me."

It was the first time Maggie admitted the possibility that the Sandmen may not actually be after her, but since seeing the empty room and not finding the document at home, Maggie had begun to doubt herself even more. Had she truly made up the whole ordeal? The way Heleen described her recent behavior, even Maggie had to agree it sounded odd. Without the evidence to back her claims, they would never believe her.

But… was there any evidence to begin with?

She hated the feeling she got every time she was with Audrey. The feeling that she was broken.

Because it was true, in part. She *was* broken. Living life with an incomplete family as if they were still around.

No more. She had to move on if anyone was going to ever believe a thing she said.

Audrey made some notes on her paper, as usual. Maggie continued to play with her hands, the smell of the interrupted meal Audrey had been eating lingering in the woman's breath.

"What do you think we should do to move forward?" Audrey asked. Maggie normally found these questions irritating,

149

she could never answer them in a way that satisfied Audrey, but today Maggie had nothing.

She didn't know how to move forward. It wasn't going to be as easy as ignoring her thoughts. Maggie needed proof. She needed to know that she wasn't being chased everywhere she went, needed to know that it was safe to go outside without having to look over her shoulder, without having to fear what was around the next corner.

Then she realized what must be done, but she knew that no one would allow her to do it, but she didn't need their permission. She would do it because she decided to.

So, she stayed silent, unable to think of an answer, waiting for Audrey to inevitably answer for Maggie.

Her head throbbed slightly. She drank more of the water Castor had given her, alleviating her aching a touch, but it didn't solve her growing hunger. If Maggie mentioned her need for food, Audrey would go the extra length of providing that.

Maggie didn't want any more help at this moment. She was an adult; she could supply her own food and was feeling well enough to at least do that.

Audrey cleared her throat. "Perhaps we can start small. What would you think is the best way for you to believe that you aren't being followed? Would it be as simple as turning around and seeing that no one is there? Perhaps walking with a friend to reassure you?"

By asking them directly. "I'm not sure. I always look around, but there's a nagging feeling they're hiding from me. Just because I can't see it, doesn't mean I don't believe it isn't there."

"Well, how about having someone walk with you? Having someone next to you can provide that sense of security. I know it might be difficult to completely feel secure, we have creatures banging on our walls, but it is a start. We need to get you on track to become whole again. We need to get you back on track so that we can begin to delve into the possibility of another child. We want to keep our city strong and alive, and it needs your help to do that. I don't suppose the sense of aiding the city offers any comfort for your situation?"

Maggie shook her head. "Not really. I know what the city wants of me, but I simply can't do that just yet."

"I'm not saying right now, but as a possibility in the future. You're still a young enough woman that you're fertile, so we need to do what we can before you reach the age that having children is no longer possible."

"Okay," was all Maggie could say. She couldn't outright deny wanting more kids, it was frowned upon, and in some cases, could land her in jail. The city was strict with its governance of childbearing, refusing to do so could be seen as treason.

But how was she supposed to bring another child into this world? She's had many complications before, and when she finally gave birth to one child, he'd been taken away from her in the worst possible way. She wasn't mentally capable of having another child, regardless of what Audrey believed.

Who knew, once she was 'cured' of her paranoia, maybe she'd be willing to have more kids?

Unlikely.

"Well, let's start with the companion idea first. You haven't spoken against it, so I assume it is okay to at least give it a try. Find someone willing to walk you to and from the library every day, and we'll see how you're going as you get used to it." Audrey scribbled on her paper and placed it on the table, indicating that the session was finished.

She was thankful, her stomach growled in hunger, and she covered it with a cough. She rose from her chair, thanked Audrey for her time, and walked out, leaving the others staring after her.

Maggie knew she had to eat, but she had become preoccupied with another task. She had to find someone willing enough to walk her to work and back every day. Castor was not an option, he needed to be available to protect the walls at any given moment. Heleen was her backup option.

That left only one other person. He would say no, of course, but perhaps Maggie might find him in a better mood today. She made way to The Flowing Red Tavern again. Today was a day that drinks were limited for each person, but that didn't stop James from hanging around inside.

She entered the tavern, boisterous with laughter as people chatted all around. James still wore his dirty jacket with additions of blood and dirt.

I really should clean that jacket.

He sat next to the green-haired man again. They talked and acted as if they'd been friends for quite a while, but Maggie had never met the man when James still lived at home.

"James," Maggie called out softly. She knew he had heard when his bearing changed drastically. His shoulders dropped and he stooped over his empty cup, away from her.

"Mags, what in Gods divine prisons do you want?" His attitude was foul, but his words weren't slurred. The daily drink limitation hadn't impeded his abilities, he had gotten used to the amount.

"I need help. Can I ask you something?"

"No, Mags. I thought I'd made that very clear. We're done. No more help. No more talking."

"I promise I won't bring up ou—"

"Mags! I said go away! I can't help you anymore, you have to find someone else to throw your problems onto!" This time he had turned to face her. His face was reddening from the fury. It astounded Maggie how quickly her mere presence could infuriate him, and she felt the urge to cry again.

"Okay."

Maggie left the establishment as alone as when she'd had arrived. Lonelier, perhaps, now she'd lost hope with James. She'd known it was a long shot, but she had hoped that he would change his mind if she sounded sincere.

And sane.

But he hadn't even wanted to hear her out. He had no patience for her anymore, but she could not blame him. The years had not been kind to either of them, and she was the constant reminder of their dead son.

12

Arthur plastered the fake smile on his face as he walked around greeting guests. His father was holding a gathering to celebrate Gavin's recent promotion to High Magistrate of Defense.

Without Gavin.

Arthur's brother seldom returned home. Gavin would visit on occasion to see their mother but would scarcely talk to Arthur. There were even times when Gavin had visited and not even bothered to meet with Arthur.

Had Arthur betrayed his brother in some way? Irredeemably hurt him? But once Gavin had moved out of the family home, intent on living by his own means, the two had rarely spoken. It was not a subject that could easily be brought up, especially since Gavin found any means to escape conversation.

Drawn back from his musings, Arthur made sure to greet each of the guests personally. A tedious but customary task of the hosting family. He disliked being dragged into such obligations, but he at least found joy in the party itself. It was rare that he could be amongst a gathering of people, so he enjoyed the opportunity whenever it arose.

Their ballroom had been ornately decorated with a white and gold theme. Symbols of the various ranks their family members held were intentionally placed on the walls as a display of their achievements. Of course, so was Arthur's position as family champion.

The Daolins made certain not to wear a spec of red, and as Arthur looked out into the crowd of people, no one wore the color either. It was a bad omen to wear red, but sometimes guests would wear it to signify their distaste for the hosting family. It was not something Arthur particularly cared about – every family had their rivalries – but he didn't want the night to be complicated. He wanted to enjoy himself, not be on edge and proactive in defending his family's name by keeping an eye on any guests who wore red.

He walked with livewood cup of wine; his family splurged on buying a ludicrous amount of livewood cups for this exact purpose. Arthur did not blame his family for doing so, but rather blamed the suppliers for wasting such a valued resource on something so pedantic. The number of cups they owned could easily be repurposed to arm more men to defend the walls, but the lack of willing men was the lagging factor in that scenario. The city was comfortably well-armed, but the number of men willing to defend it was at an all-time low as morale slowly degraded over the years. The city had to resort to conscripting lower class men against their will, otherwise they simply wouldn't have enough people to fight against the metalurks. Arthur gritted his teeth, displeased at the thought of men being ripped from their homes at the behest of pointed fingers that have never held a weapon. The Voice held such power behind their curtains, and yet rarely ever showed themselves to nobility – let alone their pawns.

"Arthur!" A voice called out from behind him, and Arthur reactively winced with irritation.

He turned to see William Ka Vedyr, dressed in bright blue clothes accentuated with golden trimmings. His blonde hair was long and braided, draped around his neck as many youths were wearing nowadays. William's brown eyes stared into Arthur's as if searching for information.

"William, a pleasure." Arthur politely greeted him in the formal manor, bowing slightly.

William reciprocated. "I trust all is well?" His words lacked any honesty, and his sleeve was down, hiding his livewood skin. William's family was appointed the title 'Ka', meaning they were next in line to provide a champion, should either of the current families fail to provide another male in the next year. William was hungry for the chance to rise up and become champion of his family, and he was growing impatient as the years went on. If he missed the next duel in twenty years, he would become too old to participate in the one after that.

"Indeed. I have not befallen any illnesses and my body is still intact," Arthur teased. If William was going to feign interest in conversation, then why shouldn't he have a little fun with it?

William's cheery exterior did not slack, but Arthur could tell that the man was not pleased with the response. William scratched at his beard that grew wild and unkempt, taking his time to think of an appropriate reply to avoid disrespecting the hosting family. "I am glad to hear it," William lied, "and I hope the same goes well for your parents. Might I ask, where is the man of honor? I've yet to see Gavin and congratulate him on his recent success."

Arthur knew this game all too well. William was trying to pry into his family life, sniffing out any issues that might exist like a well-trained pup. "I believe he is running late. I expect he should arrive soon." Arthur skillfully danced around the truth. The nobility loved speaking about his brother and his strained relationship with his father, there was no need to bring up nor indicate there was a shaky relationship between his brother and himself.

William accepted the answer with false grimace, pretending to appear upset by the news. "I do hope he'll appear soon. I wonder what's keeping him, I hope he isn't in any trouble."

"I assure you he is fine, just a little late."

"Well, I shall have to wait then."

"Yes, you shall. I must excuse myself now, and see to the new arrivals, proper etiquette and all."

"Yes, of course. We shall speak again, the night is still young." William did not attempt to conceal his sly smile.

Arthur eagerly walked away, happy to be rid of the conversation and the man. At least for now. As he ventured towards the entrance to the room, he halted as a new batch of arrivals entered.

Gavin was amongst them. He had actually turned up.

Many people cheered and clapped once he was spotted, congratulating him on his promotion. Gavin accepted the greeting with sincerity, an earnest smile that Arthur had not seen in a long time.

Arthur waded through the crowd to reach his brother but found that Gavin was currently swarmed by guests. Arthur was determined to have a conversation with his brother, he would not allow Gavin to avoid him. He waited patiently, hands behind his back and a smile on his face as he stood around, greeting the new arrivals. He was close enough to Gavin to see his brother was trying desperately to excuse himself, but it was difficult to get a word in when so many people wished to speak with him.

Arthur saw his brother's eyes flickering towards the door that led to the kitchens, hear his attempts to make an excuse to depart, claiming that he was momentarily needed in the kitchens and promising to return shortly. Arthur took the opportunity to make his way to the door before his brother, disappearing behind it and waiting. He wasn't certain if Gavin had seen him, but for whatever reason, his brother was going to come this way.

He waited against the wall in the short hall, trying not to be an obstacle for the servants as they walked in and out with food and drinks.

Soon, the door swung open, and his brother appeared, the relief on his face was short lived once he spotted Arthur, who quickly slipped around a corner, out of the servants' way.

"Arthur, it is good to see you." Gavin's words were awkward, clearly taken by surprise. It seemed his brother had not planned on speaking with him at all that night.

"It has been a while, Gavin," Arthur replied, tripping over his next words a little as he struggled to find the right ones. "Avoiding the party already? You only just got here."

"Not avoiding, just stepping into the kitchens to have a word with the staff. I did not expect to find you loitering here."

Arthur met his brother's eyes. Gavin was twenty years his senior, the large gap had created a rift between them, but it seemed his brother had no interest in dissolving that rift. "I knew you would make your way here, I figured it might be the only chance I would get to speak with you."

"Then speak, please. I am in a hurry. Our guests will grow impatient if I do not return shortly."

Our guests. Funny. "Then I'll be straightforward. Why do you avoid me? I can't recall what I've done to personally offend you, but that's the sensation I get whenever we speak."

Gavin sighed, taking a step towards him. "I suppose I can see how my actions might have conveyed such thoughts. In truth, I am not avoiding you. I just thought it would be best if we did not speak, lest I say something that might be incriminating."

Arthur frowned. *Incriminating?* "What do you mean? What could you possibly say to your own brother?"

Gavin shifted slightly, revealing his impatience. Whatever his goal with visiting the kitchens, he was eager to accomplish it. His attitude had nothing to do with returning to the guests; Gavin never did care for other nobility. "I do not really have the time for this, Arthur. Perhaps another time we ca—"

"No. You avoid me, and you rarely visit. You know I am unable to venture outside on my own terms, so now is the only time we might have. You will speak to me." Arthur stood firm. He was a little shorter than Gavin, but he refused to be intimidated.

"It has nothing to do with you. It has to do with Edmund."

That caught Arthur off guard. He had not expected such blatant disrespect from a sibling. This would not bode well should any of the servants have heard. "You speak with such distaste on your tongue. Why?"

Gavin's eyes pierced Arthur's, digging for any deception. "You do not know?"

Arthur's brow furrowed in confusion. "About what?"

Gavin smiled, a mask to conceal his true emotions. "Of course, he wouldn't have told you. I know it would be kept from the nobility, and the magistrate of course, but not you. I don't know why I thought otherwise."

"Out with it."

"I denounced Edmund as my father the day I left."

Arthur was stunned. He knew Gavin did not get along with their father, he suspected it had to do with the way Gavin was treated whilst he was the family's champion, but to cut the ties as his son? What in the Gods' prisons happened?

157

"I can tell by your expression you are unable to comprehend what I've said. I cannot tell if that is a good or a bad thing. As much as I wish to, I will not disturb your relationship with our father. At least while you are champion of our family. Once your duel is complete, then perhaps I might speak about it further. For now, that is all you may know. I will not add to your worries or distractions before your duel." Gavin went to walk past, but Arthur firmly grasped his arm.

Despite the wave of confusion that threatened to overwhelm him, he refused to let his brother slip by again. "I told you, Gavin. I do not know when I will see you next, and I may not see you again. Whatever it is, I deserve to know the truth."

"No, you don't," Gavin snapped. "You might be of age to be called a man now, but you are far from becoming one. You must realize your focus lies entirely on honing your abilities before the duel. If I say anything now, it might tarnish your mind, and I do not want to have your blood on my hands." Gavin was almost seething, struggling to keep his volume down. "I know thoughts are going to be nagging at you, pecking at your mind, but you must be able to control yourself. The information could cause you to change your perception about particular subjects and people, and I cannot risk compromising your chance of success."

Arthur wasn't the best at reading people, but he got the clear impression his brother's anger was directed at Gavin himself. Whatever the information, it clearly devastated Gavin to the point his brother was unable to speak it.

Arthur knew his brother's judgement was sound – the duel should be his focus. What would anything matter if he did not live through the Day of Sacrifice?

But then he would never be given the chance to find out.

Arthur loosened his grip, and his brother returned his arm to his side.

Gavin took a moment to compose himself. His face contorted into a grim mixture of defeat and longing. "I wish we could speak more. I truly do. I detest Edmund for what his actions have forced me to do. I am sorry, but every time I see you, I want to grab you by the shoulders and scream my knowledge at you. It is for that reason that I must distance myself. I am sorry, Arthur. Truly."

Arthur watched his brother walk away, disappearing back into the party. The bug that gnawed at the back of his mind had grown twice the size, wanting answers, but he would not get them from Gavin. There had been pain in the choice his brother had made in keeping himself away. Whatever the information, Arthur did not wish to hear it from Gavin. His brother held enough guilt as it was, he could not let Gavin take any blame if Arthur were to die in his duel.

He would find another source to pry the information.

Arthur took a moment to calm himself, returning his cheery exterior that he donned whenever there were guests, and stood tall as he returned to the ballroom. His eyes darted around for his father until he spotted the portly man sitting at the table – as usual – scoffing down bits of venison as he spoke to those gathered near. It was unsightly, but no one would call him out on it, fearing reprisal from a higher-ranking noble.

With a sigh, Arthur strayed away from his father, best to have the conversation without prying eyes and ears. He decided to wander, idly chatting with guests who would greet him and speak to him about his studies. The smell of treeblood-infused candles wafted around the room, conflicting with the various aromas of the guests own fragrances. It was a wonder to Arthur why so many people insisted on having a distinct odor when it would all clash by gathering in the same room. Many had applied vast amounts of perfumes, threatening to melt Arthur's nostrils if he stood too close.

He despised these kinds of parties. No one appeared to be having fun. At least, not genuine fun. They would laugh at jokes, they would smile, but it all felt like a farce. No one drank extensively, instead sipping at their wines while critiquing it.

Arthur's hands began to feel clammy; he couldn't get his elder brother off his mind, though he admitted it would be particularly difficult considering he was at a banquet held in Gavin's honor.

He sipped at his own wine as a woman approached, her bright orange hair a beacon, and he smiled in recognition. "Irene! One of the few people I am actually glad to see."

"Hush now, Arthur, others might hear you speak ill of them," Irene responded, but couldn't hide the blush of her cheeks at the compliment. It accentuated her smooth, pale skin. Her smile was sweet and genuine, and her hazel eyes reflected her innocence.

"Ignore their jealously. I am so happy you were able to make it, I fear most of my other so called 'friends' were unable to attend, it seems."

"I am happy to have come. I always enjoy the opportunities I get to meet with you. How are your studies fairing?"

"Astounding, as usual. I have but little other choice, after all, I am confined to the house all day. How goes the livewood experiments? Found any exciting new ways to use it?"

Irene stifled her reaction a little too late, Arthur had caught the stimulated look in her eyes before she composed herself, and her livewood sleeve had changed to the bright orange-yellow of excitement. He looked at her with quiet interest, knowing how easy it was to convince Irene to tell him, she was simply too thrilled about her work to keep it too herself.

"Fine, you've caught me. This damned sleeve doesn't do much for the discretion I'm meant to have in my position."

"I don't think it's the sleeve's fault this time."

"I suggest you keep quiet if you want me to tell you."

Arthur smirked but raised a hand in mock surrender and gestured to his closed mouth in compliance. Irene leant in closer so she could lower her voice. Arthur held his amusement inside, knowing her actions would have the opposite effect. If anyone saw her leaning closer, it would reveal that she was giving information not for prying ears.

"We've hit a breakthrough. Well, almost. We're still working out the kinks, but we think we've found a way to surge ourselves forward in nearly every aspect of our city. As soon as we can figure out the appropriate methods, it can be applied in an unthinkable number of ways. What we have is the foundation of our city's next era. Our first task is to create a way to defend against the metalurks. The general is working with us to help gather ideas for the best methods before the Day of Sacrifice and the Red Sea is upon us."

Arthur's eyes lit up. If what she spoke were true, then it would mean great things for the city and its people. It would not rid them of the metalurks, but it sounded as if it would greatly enhance their defenses and they would no longer have to worry as much about the creatures running rampant through the city.

Arthur stared at her, questioning with his eyes the sincerity to her words. Irene was a terrible liar, but he wanted to ensure that she believed her own words. Her eyes were wide, and her gleeful smile told him all he needed to know without looking at her livewood sleeve.

"That sounds amazing! I cannot wait for its reveal. I imagine it will be in the coming months, the Day of Sacrifice will arrive quicker than we expect."

"We hope so, it depends on when we can work out the last few issues to get it to properly function, and then give us time to build according to the combined plans of the general and my superiors."

Arthur smiled at the prospect of attending the reveal. He felt inspired by just hearing the possibility of upgrading their defenses and the effect it might have throughout the city and for the citizens themselves. It had the potential to raise spirits once again, give their people a fighting chance.

Perhaps it even had the potential to safeguard them to another city?

It was difficult to think about without knowing the details and nature of the experiments. Even if it were able to guard large groups of their people, their previous home had been long overtaken by bandits, and it was unlikely another city would agree to absorb their citizens into their own population.

Would the metalurks even let them live peacefully? Or would they track them down to another city, cursing them in the process? Too many questions and doubts arose from the idea, but Arthur dismissed himself from the topic. It was not his place to worry about, at least not until he was victorious in his duel.

161

"Irene, I am so glad to hear of this development. You and your associates have my utmost thanks and respect."

Irene blushed slightly, smiling with embarrassment from the sentiment. Her livewood sleeve changed to a bright pink hue, and Arthur knew his words had a heavy impact on her. "Thank you, Lord Arthur. I will pass on your kind words to everyone." Irene curtsied, showing proper respect, something she had never done to Arthur before without making a display of it for the other guests.

Irene's eyes widened once more, but this time her face melted into guilt. Her sleeve changed to a pale green, and her brow scrunched apologetically. "Sorry, Arthur. I didn't mean to bring up your duel like that, I know you don't like speaking of it!" Irene rushed the words out in a hurry to express her regret.

"Please, I don't mind. I had honestly not thought of it like that, I was just excited to hear your achievements."

"But I know you don't like talking about it. I try so hard not to mention it, and here I go putting my own accomplishments before your needs. I didn't mean any disrespect!"

"Irene, we wear our emotions on our sleeves for a reason." Arthur raised his arm to bring her attention to his blue livewood sleeve. Irene visibly relaxed when she saw it, but still wore a slight amount of worry on her face.

"I really should apologize. I should have considered your circumstances before blabbering on. My parents drilled such etiquette into me for most of my life, but ever since I began to study livewood it seems I've squandered much of their efforts into making me a proper lady."

"I'm glad you have, Irene. You would be dreadfully boring if you were still the product of your parents' efforts."

"Perhaps, but I might have landed a husband by now if I were. Legally, I should have wed by now, but I've been given a small exemption so I could focus on my research. Now that the research is finally coming to fruition, I fear I'll have to marry and bear children. Don't get me wrong, I wish to support the city in any way I can, it's just that I'll miss being able to focus on my research. I'll become a housewife and mother until the children come of age before I can return to being a scholar of livewood."

Arthur sympathized with her woes. He knew all too well the troubles of having your fate chosen for you. "For the record, you would make a terrific wife and mother. Were I in the shoes of any available Lord, I would gladly seek your courtship, Lady Irene."

Irene's sleeve flared the bright pink hue again, and her cheeks blushed red. "Thank you, Lord Arthur. Might I ask, what is preventing you from doing so before your duel? It would do your parents proud to have a lady in line for when you come out triumphant on the Day of Sacrifice."

Arthur hesitated, expecting Irene to simply take the compliment. "I... I... ah..."

"You're 'not available', Lord?"

"The duel beckons me before any women," Arthur proclaimed, proud of himself for thinking of an answer.

"I just want to know if my suspicions are correct, Arthur."

"Suspicions?" Arthur looked at her quizzically, in return she stared at him with a smirk.

"Yes. Suspicions of why you haven't asked for any Lady's hand in marriage, or even inquire after them."

"Oh, I see."

"Relax, Arthur, I will not reveal it to anyone. I simply wished to know as your friend." Irene gestured towards Arthur's sleeve with her eyes. He looked down to see his own sleeve an ill green, revealing his anxiety about the topic. It quickly changed to bright pink as the embarrassment of being caught flushed inside of him.

Damned sleeves. The one time she remembers.

Arthur cleared his throat before speaking. "I suppose I cannot deny it now. How did you know?"

"Just a hunch. Certain gestures and remarks from our talks gave me some indications."

"Sounds like you haven't completely squandered all of your parents' training." Arthur's sleeve turned the deep blue of worry. If Irene was able to discover a fact about him he had tried so hard to keep personal, then who else had those same suspicions?

His lifestyle meant that he could not provide an heir to the champion title, and his family would lose all of its elevated privileges. They would still be nobles, of course, but no longer at its peak.

If any of the other noble families knew, they could possibly try to blackmail his father, or himself. His father would not take kindly to discovering that he would not be getting another daughter-in-law. He enjoyed the additional attention far too much.

"So," Irene interrupted his troubled thoughts. "Perhaps now that everything is clear between us, are you seeing anyone romantically?"

Despite Arthur's years of training, he had not mastered his own emotions as he had once thought. His sleeve flickered pink before he was able to pinch himself to force the sleeve to turn red. It was a common technique to inflict harm on oneself to change the color of sleeves to the more dominant emotion of pain. While he was no longer attempting to hide it from Irene, but if anyone were keeping an eye on him it would be too suspicious if his sleeve kept revealing the pink of embarrassment. It would invite others to join in the conversation in an attempt to sniff out information.

Irene smiled, having caught the flicker of color. "Really? Oh my, is he here now?" Irene's eyes excitedly scanned around the room, as if the man would suddenly make himself known.

"No, I kept my eye out for him whenever guests arrived. I only met him once, but it was… wonderful. We are able to communicate through letters. He states that he is a very busy man, so it is likely his job took precedence over this event."

"And miss the opportunity to see you? I doubt it."

"I suspect he may actually be a livewood expert. He has stated that he has interest in the field, but I wonder if that is to misdirect me to the fact that he already is one, so that I don't pry for information on the topic you so lovingly described to me."

Irene scoffed. "I doubt it, unless you are into men much older than you. There are very few men our age working on this project, and I believe they all have wives."

Arthur nodded, accepting her review on her associates. He had hoped she would have some insight on the man, but it appeared he was not a livewood expert after all. At least, not one working on the more discreet projects. "Shame. I was hoping you had already met him, so that you could tell me more about him."

"Well, what's his name?"

"I don't know."

Irene stared at him in disbelief. She only grew more confused when Arthur smiled to confirm what he had said. "Sounds like you two have quite the relationship."

"Honestly, I do not mind it. It was his suggestion, and it works for me, given my position and future. It was why I thought he was working with you on discreet projects. Perhaps he works as a Magistrate who works on delicate matters. It also adds that bit of extra... allure. It's rather stimulating speaking with someone whose name you do not know."

"It allows you to distance yourself, that's what you find so alluring about it. I think you aren't going to allow yourself to completely fall in love because you fear of dying in your duel."

Irene always was one to be direct, and Arthur did not dispute her logic. As much as he wanted to retort, he found truth in her words. He was definitely afraid of dying, she was right about that, but who wouldn't be in his position? Right now, his arrangement with his mysterious correspondent worked for his situation and he did not wish to disturb that.

"You're as readable as a book, Arthur. Perhaps try acting a little more proper, it might do you well to conceal such things from a properly trained Lady such as myself," Irene winked at him and the playful smile returned to her lips. "It would be best if I talk to others for a bit. You know, I have to find a man and all that."

"I wish you luck, Irene. I'm sure there are some suitable bachelors here who would succumb to your charms."

"You are aware who you are talking to, or have you fallen ill?"

"I am well aware."

Irene smile grew wider before she departed. He watched her awkwardly insert herself in a conversation amongst a group of young nobles. *She'll do just fine.*

Arthur searched for his father, the nagging feeling in the back of his mind a constant reminder of what his brother had said. He failed to locate Edmund, and as he scanned the room once more, he surmised his father had slipped away. Arthur must have been quite distracted if his father was able to escape without his notice.

Taking the opportunity at his father's disappearance, Arthur approached his mother, who was engaged in conversation with another noble woman.

"Oh, young Arthur, how pleasant it is to see you!" the woman remarked, curtseying to him.

"And you as well," Arthur replied, not recalling who this noble woman was. She was his mother's age, her face brightened as he acknowledged her, but he could simply not recall who she was.

"I know it is frowned upon to favor one family over the other on the Day of Sacrifice, but I truly hope you prevail, young Lord. It would be pleasant to see another Va Daolin in the high ranks of the Magistrates, running this city towards a better future for us all."

"Your hope has not gone unheard. I will carry it with me in the battle."

"I do not mean to be discourteous, Lady Renain, but I believe my son has something private he wishes to discuss with me," Evelynn politely interrupted.

"Oh," Lady Renain donned a mischievous smile. "Perhaps to speak of the young Lady Irene's courtship? You two were getting quite acquainted."

Arthur grimaced internally but decided to give Lady Renain nothing but a smile. He did not wish to engage the topic and the implications might do him well to gain his father's patience on the subject.

Lady Renain excused herself, walking back into the crowd of people to participate in meaningless chatter, Arthur was sure.

"Do you needed something, dear?"

"Where is Father?"

"He has gone off on a meeting, he will return shortly. Do you need something from him?"

The question he so desperately wanted to ask churned inside of him, threatening to spill out now, but he had to wait. The question was not for his mother. "I just wish to speak with him on a delicate matter. Something Gavin spoke of has left me with a question. I shall wait until the party is over."

His mother looked at him curiously. She could sense the slight hostility towards his father that he had tried so hard to hide. He smiled, reassuring her the topic was not as bad as she might assume and that he would wait.

Evelynn's eyes shifted from his, and shock took over. Arthur turned to see his brother wading through the crowd that attempted to surround him. There was something about his gait and the look in his eyes that warned Arthur something was about to go down.

"Lords and Ladies, might I have your attention for a moment please!" Gavin called loudly as he stepped onto a chair for all to see him.

Arthur searched around the room, his father had still not returned.

"I wish to thank you for your attendance, I am truly honored that you have come to celebrate my promotion to High Magistrate of Defense." Gavin paused as the crowd clapped, patiently waiting for it to finish.

Arthur's stomach sank, preparing itself for whatever was about to happen. His brother had not finished speaking, and it was about to upset the entire party.

"I appreciate you all attending, but the party must come to an abrupt end. The food and drink have been halted. You do not have to leave immediately but know that nothing more will be served. Thank you all for coming."

Gavin stepped down from his chair then strode confidently from the room, not stopping to talk to anyone.

The chatter began before Gavin had made it out the door. It began as hushed whispers but quickly rose into loud remarks and questions. Theories about what transpired loosely fired from lips without much thought, hoping it would cause further damage to the Va Daolins' reputation.

Gavin had turned the nobility into vicious metalurks and teased them with a chunk of metal without telling them where it was hidden. They spat harsh words, criticizing the reception and the family.

Evelynn could not raise her voice loud enough, trying to shout over the crowd to gain their attention. Edmund had yet to return; perhaps he had caught wind of what Gavin was doing and was hiding from the mess Gavin had left behind.

Arthur was attempting to console the guests with generic responses, ushering them towards the door. Without his father, they could not control the damage that had been done. No one would listen to them now, only interested in rumors that spread like wildfire amongst them, eager to latch their greedy tendrils over the nastiest ones as if they were factual.

He was growing increasingly infuriated, his voice drowned out, and very few chose to leave. He glanced at his mother, her tears of frustration as she helplessly tried to speak over the nobles nearest her.

Without his father here to intervene, Arthur grew impatient. He grabbed the chair his brother had used and stood upon it. "Attention!" he shouted. He knew he had not used a polite tone, but he had grown weary of putting up a farce for people who would not listen either way.

The crowd slowly quieted to a murmur as they all turned towards him. "Keep your conspiracies to yourselves. The guest of honor has called this party to a halt, so there is no reason to have it continue. You will slowly depart without any more ill speak of my family. I know many of you are just vultures waiting to feed upon a carcass, but I will not tolerate it any further." Arthur let the words hang in the air, making sure every last person who had heard him knew that he was serious.

The gathering began to disperse, slowly filtering towards the door. Some were unable to keep their words of annoyance to themselves before they departed, but Arthur chose not to speak out, choosing to scowl instead. He stood next to his mother, arm around her shoulders, attempting console her. What he had just done did not help their image, but he did not have the patience to play politics. Gavin had started a storm and simply left without facing the repercussions. He hadn't even given them warning.

Why did he stop the food and beverages? Why did he abruptly end the party?

Why did he let his family take the heat for his actions?

The last of the guests trickled out of the room. Very few stopped to express their sympathies, or to offer any form of support. Irene was one of the exceptions, of course. Seeing the anger in Arthur's face, she gave him a quick hug.

With the last of the guests gone, the room felt oddly spacious. Arthur stood alone with his mother. Still, his father had not returned from his meeting. The servants swarmed in to clean, and Arthur got the distinct feeling they were avoiding the lone Daolins in the room.

Arthur encouraged his mother to retreat to her chambers, and as he did not want her to feel alone, escorted her. Once they reached her room, he peered inside and noted that his father had not been hiding here. Arthur offered to keep her company, but she just patted his hand and told him she wished only to sleep. He reluctantly complied, returning to his own chambers.

As he walked, his emotions churned within. He covered his livewood sleeve out of annoyance as it flashed from one color to the next, unable to decide Arthur's dominant emotion. He stewed in irritation towards his brother.

Why come if Gavin was only going to shut it down? Why the display?

The unanswered questions piled up and his anger piled alongside it. Why was his family such a mess? All this talk about focusing on his duel, but how could he possibly do that when he was forced to live inside a home that had nothing but internal, unspoken conflicts?

When he opened the door to his chambers, he found that a candle had been lit.

A letter on his desk, somehow shining brighter than the candle it sat beside.

All of Arthur's worries melted away at the touch of the parchment.

13

Castor's turn at running the wall alone was short lived as General Deven made an appearance at the next wave of metalurks. The general had been uncharacteristically quiet towards Castor, not even so much as a glance in his direction. Castor paid it no mind; the current wave was his focus.

Once the wave was defeated and his men tended to, the general descended the steps. Castor stood, head high, ready to give his report and meet any aggressions the general would throw in his direction.

"Anything out of the ordinary?" General Deven asked, keeping his voice lower than normal. Castor shook his head, and before he could say more, the general turned and left. Castor stared blankly after the man, uncertain what implications their diminutive meeting might have had.

First the outburst, and now this? Something was off. Had something happened recently that kept the general's mind occupied elsewhere? At least he was well enough to lead the defense against the rampant creatures.

Castor bade farewell to his men, acknowledging their notable performance in the defense. He always made it a point to show his men that he saw their skills and appreciated their dedication; it did well for morale and Castor wasn't sure how to thank them for standing up for him. He made sure his men knew he respected them and that he had their back completely in battle.

Now that the wave had been thwarted, he made his way through the streets with a worried step. The results of the investigation he had requested from the Seekers would be given to him today, and he had become nervous with their potential findings. He was afraid that they'd actually uncovered something, which meant something nefarious had happened to his nephew, and potentially his sister.

He took a right at the next street, and his eyes immediately fell upon Varin, the Seeker.

"Castor, my friend! What a pleasure it is to see you!" Somehow the polite and warm greeting seemed ominous and a little creepy. Perhaps it was because Castor knew it was an act, but there was something eerie about the way Varin smiled.

"Varin," Castor acknowledged in return, taking the man's hand and shaking it.

"So many things I wish to talk to you about, I don't know where to start, but let's begin with the biggest piece." Varin leaned in a little closer and lowered his voice so no passer-by could overhear. "Your friend, Gerric Farwell? Well, it turns out I had a friend who knows of him."

"And?"

"And he isn't Gerric Farwell. At least, not anymore. No, I'm afraid he is much more interesting than perhaps even you suspected."

Castor heart sank. *Son of a Red.*

Varin seemed to pause, letting Castor teeter on the edge with curiosity. "He had a slight name change, and now goes by Gerric Deven."

What?! Castor barely held back the word as it tried to leap from his mouth.

Varin watched Castor's expression become perplexed, the man seemingly amused by the reaction. "Connected to anyone you know?" Varin teased, knowing full well the connection but wanting to savor the revelation.

Castor was unsure what to say. Too many questions surged forward at once, too many thoughts to sift through. A vast number of implications jumped out and Castor felt his head begin to spin.

"I see you have some questions, so let me pre-emptively answer some you might have. Gerric married into the Deven family two years ago. From what I gather, they are unhappy, which gives me the distinct impression that it was an arranged marriage. For a simple soldier to marry way above his station, he must have had some concrete information on the Deven family, or at least did a stupendous favor for them. Unfortunately, I don't know much more than that. No paper records exist of any blackmail or favors made, so you'd have to ask someone who was directly involved."

Castor remained silent, still confounded by the information. Did Gerric's marriage into the Deven family have anything to do with his nephew, or was it just a coincidence? How would he even find out? He would have to ask.

"Where does he live?"

* * *

Castor stormed up the pathway leading to the luxurious, small mansion, likely given to Gerric by the Deven family. He hammered on the door, unable to control the surge of adrenaline that coursed through his body.

Yelling could be heard the other side, and after a short moment, the door opened to reveal a man in his early thirties, his dark brown hair receding at the top, scraggly brown beard, and his green eyes wide with surprise when they fell upon Castor. The two had never formally met, but it appeared Gerric knew about him all too well.

Castor grabbed the man by the collar, yanking him out of his home and slamming the man against the pretty brickwork. "Gerric Farwell?"

The man remained silent, but his reaction was enough to answer Castor's question.

"You arrested my nephew three years ago. He died as a result. Was it a set up?"

Castor's bluntness and sudden moves had caught Gerric off guard as he blabbered about, trying to get his head around the situation. The man's aroma was a stench of addleberry and treeblood-infused candles, with a heavy fume of ale on his breath. Castor tightened his grip. "Stop stalling! I need to know now, was my nephew's arrest a set up!"

"Captain Castor... I... I... look, it was three years ago, how am I suppo—"

Gerric grunted as Castor slammed him into the wall again. "You know damn well what I'm talking about, and you're going to tell me what I need to know. What was it? Payment for a hired job, or blackmail that got you here? Did Deven set it up? Did he promise you his daughter if you turned in my nephew and got him killed?!"

"Look, I don't know what to tell you. All I was told was to arrest some kid for selling Dreams, I didn't know he was your nephew!"

Gods let the Reds take me where I stand...Maggie was right. "And the general's daughter was the reward?"

Gerric's eyes were wide with fright. "It seemed like a pretty good deal, I didn't question—"

"You didn't question it, and it killed a young boy! I should throw you over the damned wall." Castor slammed Gerric against the wall one last time before he let go of the man; he had to leave before he did something he might truly regret. The man slumped to the ground, fear and confusion staining his face.

Castor wasn't faring any better. Maggie had been right; his nephew was murdered. Or at least put in the position to be accidentally mistaken for someone else. Whatever the reason, someone had hired Gerric to arrest his nephew, and only one man in the Deven family had the power to give his daughter's hand away.

The general.

Castor's mind stirred with the vast number of possibilities. He had only made East Gate Captain the year before his nephew's arrest, why would General Deven want his nephew arrested and killed?

There were no threats from the general regarding his nephew in the lead-up to Patrick's arrest. There was nothing. So why did he do it? And how would Castor confront him? He thought about the times the general had screamed at him, berating him for a slack job.

Perhaps it was time to return the favor.

And what would he tell Maggie?

Castor froze in his tracks. He cursed himself, turning down the next street, running towards the library. He had forgotten to check in with his sister after the wave. As he ran, he mentally prepared various scenarios that might arise if he told Maggie what he had discovered. She was still waiting on his reports, keeping her promise of not chasing after the Sandmen while he was investigating.

While he had some results, it wasn't enough. If he told Maggie what he had found, it might encourage her to confront the general on her own, and he couldn't have that. She stood no chance against the man; he could simply have her thrown in jail for so much as raising her voice or standing in his way.

No, Castor had to be the one to do it. He could stand up to General Deven. He had leverage, he had the guts, and he had a pent-up storm roiling inside.

Castor grew more agitated the more he thought about it. His life was unravelling as quickly as he pulled at this thread. It wasn't the distraction he needed before the Red Sea was upon them. He had to focus on getting as many men trained up as they could, and adding to their defenses. He was supposed to be working *with* the general in the additional barricades and traps at the East Gate – it would be the most difficult to defend. Instead, General Deven was apparently after his family.

At least, he was three years ago. Now the general seemed content in keeping Castor in his place like an obedient pup. Perhaps his plan had worked? Whatever plan it was.

Castor had difficulty containing the storm, his thoughts turned to the fate of the city with the general at the lead of the defense. How as the city meant to survive if it was busy with infighting? All these politics and games people played for the sake of their own benefit, for power. How could they possibly do such things when their city was continuously ravaged by mindless creatures?

Castor rage slowly subsided, and he felt deflated.

Defeated.

Was there hope for the city? For every positive person like Linette, there seemed to be a long line of people like the general, only out for their own benefits, damning anyone who dare step in their way. What was the point of being East Gate Captain if you couldn't work together to defend the walls? What good was his position?

Castor finally made it to the library. He took a moment to compose himself; he couldn't give Maggie any indication of his discoveries just yet. He had to keep leading her along while he investigated further.

He walked into the library to the familiar smell of musty old books. Heleen smiled grimly where she sat, book in hand, at the table. Her eyes shifted to Maggie, who sat on the other end, staring blanky into the tabletop.

His sister had been like this ever since her last meltdown. Unresponsive, unemotional. Simply staring into blank space until something demanded her attention.

Castor sat next to her. She didn't acknowledge his existence, only sat and stared as if there were something spectacular that no one else could see.

"Hey, Maggie."

"Hello."

"Everything okay?"

"Yeah."

The lie sat in the air for a moment as the silence settled back in. Castor put his arm around his sister and pulled her in tight. "What's on your mind?"

"I'm not sure."

"Come on, Maggie. Speak to me."

"Stuff. Just thinking about what I've been doing recently. How much of my... life were just lies I told myself?"

Castor gave his sister a light kiss on her head. All he could do was comfort her, he could not answer the questions she had. He'd seen the room she'd discovered at the back of the library, and

175

he was told that her accidental find had excited her mind and orchestrated an entire labyrinth of lies she could not escape.

He sympathized with her. She seemed so sincere when she had told them, so sure of what she had seen. Castor could usually tell when his sister's ramblings were real or not, and this one had seemed real to her. It seemed illogical that someone had broken into the library during an attack, not only taking the discovered records of an Old Malvark, but any furniture that remained inside as well.

Yet she had been sure it existed. She had described it in such vivid detail. Could a mind truly do that to a person?

Audrey seemed to think so, but he had his doubts. His sister had previously expressed that Audrey would doubt everything she said. He knew it was Audrey's job to question her, to stabilize her enough to the point that she could continue with her life, but he had to admit the woman had never once agreed with something Maggie had said. Always seemed opposed to Maggie's claims, almost as if she disregarded them before they were even made. He was not married to a doctor, so he had no authority to call her out, he had to trust that the professionals were doing their jobs correctly.

But he had just discovered that his superior had plotted against his family, resulting in his nephew's death, so what good were the opinion of others at this point?

"Maggie, I want you to look at me for a second."

It took a moment, but Maggie looked up, curiosity in her eyes.

"Now that you've had some time to think, I want you to tell me honestly. Do you believe what you saw? Do you truly believe the records existed?"

Her eyes drifted away from his, reflecting internally before returning to him and now filled with determination. "Yes."

Despite all that she had gone through, she was still convinced the records were real. She had been right about her son's death, in that someone had been targeting him, why should he now doubt what she saw?

Castor rose from the chair, Maggie and Heleen stared at him as he made his way to the back of the library. He grabbed the starter candle and made his way into the room Maggie had discovered. He crouched, inspecting the floor by candlelight and searching for anything that indicated Maggie might be telling the truth.

The small room was completely empty. The dust that had gathered on the floor was inconsistent in places, but with the small number of people who had entered the room, it was impossible to tell who had disturbed it. There was no sign of a desk, chair, or any paperwork. If something had been here, whoever had taken it took great measures to ensure nothing remained. Maggie mentioned that many of the papers were fragile, but Castor could see no flakes on the floor to indicate such.

He searched the door frame, wondering if the thieves had knocked the furniture against the wood as they left. The frame had a few scuff marks, but it was difficult to tell how recent it was – he was no investigator.

Despite finding no proof, Castor found it difficult to believe his sister was lying. She seemed so sincere, but... her mind was addled lately. There was no way of knowing if anything had been in here unless the thieves came forward and confessed. He returned to his sister, disappointed from his lack of findings but didn't say anything to her. He simply placed the starter candle down and gestured for his sister to rise.

As part of Audrey's suggestion, Maggie was to have an escort to and from the library whenever possible. Shame washed through him for having no answers from his search the room again. He wanted to defend her claims, wanted her to be right just for the sake of her mind, but he could not logically agree. His heart believed, but his eyes couldn't attest to it.

He walked beside his sister in silence, unsure what to say. Asking about her day would result in a short, blunt answer and nothing more. She wouldn't ask the details of his fight and he did not wish to retell the events; it might only add to her anxiety about his position.

They walked slowly, in no rush to be anywhere in particular. Castor would smile to passers-by who recognized him, though none wished to disturb his walk with his sister. His eyes wandered, taking in the scenery and its people. They seemed sullen, but their faces at least grew a smile when they saw him. The few colorful plants and decorations seemed mute, influenced by the morale of the city and beginning to blend into its drab nature. They appeared as half-hearted attempts to spruce up a home, Castor admired it but could feel the slow drain of confidence in their city.

His eyes searched for more, as if trying to find a small flicker of positivity, but instead they landed on something far more interesting.

A blonde-haired man with three braids. Varin.

He was hiding around a corner of a house, keeping an eye on the pair as they walked. He made no attempt to conceal himself once Castor had spotted him, making it difficult to tell if the man had not expected to be seen, or wanted to be.

Still keeping an eye on me? Castor ignored the Seekers' existence, putting him out of his mind. They could follow him all they liked, they wouldn't find anything incriminating.

Let them waste their time.

They walked to Maggie's home and she said her goodbye. Castor wanted to accompany her for a while longer, but he got the impression Maggie wanted to be alone for a while.

Besides, he had to figure out his own next steps.

With General Deven now a lead in the case of his nephew's arrest, he had to find out why. He could simply hire the Seekers to learn why, but the less he used them, the better. They would surely watch how he intended to proceed with the information given to him, but that would hardly be discreet knowledge at this point. There would be no way to confront the general without it becoming public knowledge.

Did the General really hire Gerric to arrest his nephew? Or was it someone else who had ties to the Deven family? Perhaps there was a third person involved, blackmailing the Devens into paying Gerric's reward for arresting his nephew. But why had the prize been so significant for a task so small? Did Gerric's job truly end at just the arrest?

Too many questions, and less time to get answers. He would have to take his time to decide how to proceed, any rash decisions might have him quickly stripped of his position. Deven was looking for any excuse to do just that, and Castor wasn't about to throw it all away, not while he was still being considered as the next general, despite what Deven said.

The Magistrates would make the final decision, but they would surely take Deven's testament and recommendations seriously. With the Day of Sacrifice drawing near, the man was likely to retire should he make it through the Red Sea. As long as Castor stood out, defending the wall to the best of his ability, he would still be considered, whether the general gave him a negative review or not.

Perhaps the best time to confront the general was after the man's retirement. They could not afford any more disturbances amongst the ranks. But if he waited until after that retirement, and he was not given the position, his actions might be deemed as retaliation for not being promoted.

It was a delicate situation that had no easy answers. His mood sullied and his motivation tarnished, but he still kept his posture straight with an air of authority. He refused to let the city get the best of him. If the citizens caught wind of his attitude, it would only demoralize them further.

He held in a sigh; this situation seemed to have repercussions no matter what decision he made, but he held his head high. The general would not win by chasing away Castor's fighting spirit, not after all he'd been through.

But how long could he go without confronting Deven?

* * *

The simple task of not mentioning his discovery proved difficult at the next wave. Upon seeing General Deven climb the steps, Castor wanted nothing more than to grab the man and scream his pent-up fury. But the fight always took priority.

Deven didn't look at Castor once, and when the general ordered Castor to retreat to his position in the tunnels, the call didn't come with its usual authority, but rather an irritated bitterness for having to acknowledge Castor's existence.

179

There was no after-battle report; Deven had left the wall as soon as the call came that the last of the creatures were vanquished. Castor stood at his position in the tunnel, watching as the General walked away without turning back.

So the general was avoiding Castor, but why? Had Gerric reported the confrontation?

Whatever the reason, Castor let Deven walk away, an unpleasant taste in his mouth at the sight of the man.

"Well," Vance said, coming over to Castor and tracing his line of sight. "I've never seen the general run away like that without so much as a word. I think we might have scared him."

"You definitely irritated him. I think he has a personal dislike towards you in specific though."

The scent of burning metalurks blew over the wall, the smell not unfamiliar but still unpleasant.

"Shame, that," Vance said. "I was about to invite him to tea."

Castor smiled. "Well, now I know who your favorite superior is."

"No offence, Captain, but you heard him when he said you wouldn't make General. I figured I've got a better chance at it than you have now."

"You want to be General, Vance?"

"If a stone brain like him could do it, I figured I could as well."

"True, you could be a shining beacon for the metalurks, perhaps even serve as a momentary distraction."

"I'd still serve the city better."

Castor chuckled. Vance did well to lighten his mood, and the moods of the soldiers. Ironically, he would do well for the morale if he were General, he just needed the experience and determination to become one.

"How's your sister going, Captain?"

Castor shook his head. "I'm not sure, if I'm to be honest. Her mind is playing tricks on her, and she's having trouble figuring out what is real and what isn't, what has happened and what hasn't. She seems so sure on something, yet all evidence suggests the opposite."

Vance let out a sympathetic sigh. "I'm sorry, Captain. I was so hoping she would be getting better. It mustn't be easy for her. The city must be breathing down her neck about having more children before she's no longer able. Gods know we could always use more men, but at this cost? I'm not sure it's worth it. Our people struggle as it is, and... and I'm not sure bringing another child into it is the best solution in every instance."

Castor nodded his agreement. He figured Audrey would regularly bring up the topic of bearing more children, perhaps that might be an obstacle Audrey wasn't considering. "I think my sister is set on not having any more. She can barely take care of herself as it is, I don't know why the city would want her to have another child."

"Law's the law, I suppose. We've gotta keep this hell hole we're in going. Struggling to survive is still surviving."

"Giving birth just so that we can continue our suffrage. Remarkable."

"I'm hoping it'll at least get better soon. Rumors are going around about some extra defenses being set up to tackle the Red Sea."

Castor nodded, he had heard the rumors as well but nothing had been confirmed as yet. Only General Deven knew the details in advance, and there was no chance in Gods divine prisons that he would share that information with Castor.

What Castor did know was that the wall would be receiving several additional defenses before the Day of Sacrifice. Rows of wooden spikes for the metalurks to impale themselves upon, log swings to slam into the metalurks at the tunnel entrance, a layer of oil poured onto the top section of the walls should the monsters climb that high, and an increased number of soldiers in every aspect. There would be no retainers. All soldiers would be at the wall, defending to the death the city and its inhabitants.

If only the damned creatures didn't eat metal, they could dispose of them quickly, Castor was sure. He didn't know what properties metal held, but he assumed the weapons they used would have more weight, able to bear more of a blow without fear of blunting or splintering. They could even make their gates of metal, surely that would prove vastly more difficult to tear

181

through. Though if the creatures managed to snap off livewood, perhaps they could do the same to metal. It was difficult without knowing how metal would function, the knowledge all but forgotten in the history books.

Their people had marked several deposits of metal but feared harvesting it should the metalurks increase in number due to the amount of metal the city possessed. Even with no metal, the Red Sea was to be feared in sheer size alone. If a single metalurk broke through their defenses, it could mean the death of hundreds of citizens. All of lower class, obviously. The nobles sat high atop their hill, hoping the monsters would tire before reaching them.

It made life truly difficult, but what was the point in lamenting what could have been? Their reality was that they would continue to fight for survival until the day they died, and then someone else would take over to continue the cycle. Without the knowledge of where these creatures came from, there was no way to know how to stop them.

Castor was interested to see what this new defense would be, considering they could not upgrade the resources they currently used. As time went on, they were able to harvest more livewood, so perhaps the spike barricades would be replaced by the superior wood?

No, that couldn't be it. Why would that be a rumor and not general knowledge released to the public? There was no forward stride in their defenses, other than slowing the metalurks down a little. Sure, it would help, but it didn't match the hype of the rumors. It had to be something that drastically changed the way they defended themselves.

At least, Castor hoped so.

"Can't quite picture what they'll do," Vance said, as if reading Castor's thoughts. "The only places they could add something would probably be in the tunnels. If they put anything up on our wall then they'd block our archers," he said, staring at their wall as if the solution might jump out at them.

"At this point, any kind of defense would be better. I wonder if they considered my idea of hollowing out the walls near the tunnels to allow our men to attack the creatures through built-in slots."

"Not if the general got a hold of your suggestion," Vance scoffed. "He would shut it down out of spite."

"Do you think he'd go that far? Damning his own people just to shut down the idea of someone he doesn't play well with?"

Vance stared at him, eyebrows raised to indicate that the answer was obvious. Castor nodded; the General was probably that spiteful. Castor had been trying to get the plans to go through ever since he made Captain, but the Magistrate of Defense insisted it would harm the integrity of the wall, the metalurks could break through while they were excavating the stone.

It was a poor excuse. If they had enough livewood, they could easily reinforce the wall, probably better than as it stood with just stone. Either Deven had gotten to him, or the old Magistrate of Defense was simply too scared to take such risks.

It was understandable to a point. If the plan failed and the creatures did break through the walls, it would mean the deaths of many, but Castor was certain that livewood was stable enough to withhold the creatures. The gate and portcullis did great work in slowing the beasts down, but perhaps he didn't know enough about infrastructure to adequately grasp any repercussions from his plan.

A new Magistrate of Defense had been appointed recently, so Castor had planned to bring up the idea with the man, though the paperwork was hopefully sitting in a pile of proposed ideas.

Still, Castor would have to make time to go see the new Magistrate of Defense. He'd heard it was the eldest son of the Daolin family, but that fact mattered little to Castor. Although by all accounts, the man had moved up to his position without the help of his father. But Castor would give the new Magistrate time to settle before bringing up the idea once more. Besides, it was time to see Maggie.

14

Vernin looked apologetically at Elias as he spoke. "I'm afraid it could develop into something far worse. The signs are all there, but I'm afraid there are no preventatives. All we can do is not bother him, make sure he has plenty of water, and pray to the Gods that he will recover."

They stood outside Warin's room discussing the results of the medical examination. Elias' father had fallen ill, and it appeared to be a result of a poor diet, a lack of eating mixed with regular intakes of wine, and a build-up of stress. It was not yet fatal, but judging by Vernin's words, there was a strong possibility the illness could deteriorate into something that not even the strongest medicine—reserved for high nobility—would be able to help his father survive.

By refusing to change his habits over the years, his father had willfully chose to become sick. The only thing to do about it now was to give his father the best fighting chance by seeing him minimally and encouraging proper eating. The latter would now become difficult as his father had turned away any food that had been offered, claiming it would only make him feel worse.

"Listen, Elias. I know things seem pretty dire, but I have been your father's personal doctor for years, and I think most of his stress is revolved around your duel. I don't want to add to your own personal pressures, but you are the last living family your father has left. I think he is afraid that he'll be left alone if you perish, and his body is… rejecting that possibility in its own way. It's refusing to continue alone."

Elias nodded, having already guessed as much. The duel would obviously add stress levels, but his father had been alive long enough to see three of his family members lose their duels, his wife and daughter die at childbirth, and now his only remaining son was on the executioner's block.

The guilt rose bitter to Elias' throat; the years of disrespect and utter lack of compassion for his father had caught up.

And Warin was paying that price.

"So, all I can do is sit by and throw out encouragements to continue living?" Elias snapped, not at Vernin, but himself.

"It's not that simple. His health will gradually deteriorate, and probably hit its apex around the time of the duel. My personal judgement is that it cannot be avoided, but I have been wrong before. All you can do is ensure that he is eating right and taking the medication I've left for him. It won't cure him, but it might help him with the pain. He'll initially try to reject the amount of food, I doubt he's eaten properly in many years. He'll also wish for his usual wine, and I'm a little hesitant about that. Given his condition, I am tempted to allow him a bit of respite before he…Well, you know."

Elias buried his face in his hands, frustrated at the irony. For years, his father had wanted Elias to only focus on his duel, and now his father had fallen ill and would demand Elias attention if he wished to get better.

Uneven footsteps could be heard from his father's chambers, and the door swung open to reveal Warin, pale and leaning on the frame for support. "I'm not as frail as you might think. I am fine and I *will* be fine. There is nothing wrong with me. Don't fill the boy's head with your exaggerations. Your job is done, now leave my house!" Warin could barely raise his voice without a fit of coughing.

Vernin looked sympathetically towards Elias again before complying to Warin's demands and leaving.

"Get back to bed, Father."

"No. I am well enough to walk about my own house as I please. Shouldn't you be attending your studies?"

"My lessons have been cancelled today, in respect for your health."

Warin snorted. "I am absolutely fine, there is no need for this melodramatic display. I'll be well enough soon, just you see. Geraldine!"

The woman quickly appeared from where she had been waiting just down the hall. "Sir."

"Send word to Elias' afternoon teachers. Tell them to come at the appointed times and not to cancel without my knowledge again."

"Yes, sir." Geraldine hesitated a moment, Elias could see the pain in her face as she saw Warin's frail frame. She had been a servant for his family for many years, it was no surprise she cared for Warin's health.

As Geraldine departed, she turned back for a moment, producing an envelope from her pocket and using it to discreetly signal Elias. He gave a slight nod in acknowledgement; the letter would be waiting for him in his room.

For now, it could wait.

"You should be in bed, Father. You've sent the order for me to return to my studies, and I shall do so."

"I'm not a decrepit old man that you need to wait on hand and foot, Elias. I can take care—"

"Do you want me to focus on my studies?" Elias raised his voice, not to yell at his father, but to emphasize his point and authority.

Warin did not respond, looking away in annoyance.

"Then I need to be assured that you are doing your best to recover. You claim not to be this fragile old man that needs to be taken care of? Then prove it. Your word is only good if you can back up its claims. Eat the meals that Vernin has appointed, and take your medicine. You will stay in bed and rest as much as you can. If you want to help me, then you must help yourself, Father."

Elias spoke with authority, his tone indicating there would be no arguing. Warin looked down at Elias' livewood sleeve, seeing the red of anger. In truth, Elias wasn't angry as much as he was worried, but he refused to let worry become the dominant feeling.

He stared at his father until Warin rolled his eyes at the message being received. A moment later the door closed, and Elias heard the man shuffle back to bed.

Elias stood outside the door for a moment, both to compose himself and to ensure his father would not try to sneak out once he thought his son was gone. The illness had come suddenly, at least to Elias. He had not known if his father had begun feeling ill over the past few weeks, yet it was a secret his father would have kept. Still, it seemed as if this illness wasn't the kind to sneak up on a person.

By the Gods, Father, what have you done to yourself?

Elias headed to his room, conflicted. Warin would be locked in his room, in pain from his ailment while Elias would be in his own room, in his own joyous world of love and happiness.

The guilt rose again for allowing himself to indulge in happiness at such a moment, but he had to take these chances when they arose; they were scarce, and he couldn't afford to let them slip by.

When he entered his room, the letter was on his desk. He would let himself be happy, even for a moment. Elias would likely regret it later, but he would deal with those feelings as they came.

For the next few moments, nothing else mattered.

As much as your letter warms my heart on this frigid night, I find it spoiled by the night's events. I shall not go into any detail, keeping the mask that shields our identities, but I am sure you would ask about my woes were you beside me.

My family continues to dissolve, and I bear the brunt of my father's rage. Out of choice, mostly. I refuse to allow him to treat my mother the way he has over the years. Your words touched me deeply. I now realize how much pain I have indirectly inflicted on her by not standing in the way.

I promise that I shall cherish her. I believe you would admire her as much as I do. She is no longer her former self, but I believe her exterior shell that she has adorned still contains the sweet and caring woman she once was. Though she knows not about you, I do not doubt for a second that she would welcome you with open arms.

It is with a heavy heart that I confess she has been emotionally wounded once again, by a family member she still held hope for. I must stop writing for fear I may reveal too much, but it is all I am able to think about.

I apologize for the ill timing. I hope that when, or even if, you respond to this letter, soon I shall be in better spirits.

Though I shan't deny I have already begun to feel better by simply having heard from you.

The words felt heavy on the parchment, carrying the emotions of their writer. Even through the vague descriptions, Elias sympathized with his correspondents' position. He could only imagine what the mysterious man was going through, he had not experienced any drama within his family other than the conflicts with his father. His family held nothing but grief and loss, which led to conflicts with his father, but he presumed that it was not a similar situation. Loss was not the same as watching a family members quarrel.

Elias shouldered an enormous amount of guilt for having written such a spirited letter, but he was not in control of the rate at which the letters were sent and received. He knew his correspondent would not have held it against him – their connection was too strong for that.

At his desk, Elias contemplated his next action. He wanted to respond, of course, but he considered giving the man some time to deal with his situation. Elias would be of no help, especially when they could not describe the intricate details of their lives to each other.

He grabbed a fresh parchment, preparing to write another letter. Geraldine would not be able to deliver it for days, he assumed, so the man would have time to deal with his situation before it arrived.

With Elias' own emotions a little scrambled, he was uncertain what to write and how to write it. Every fiber of his being implored him to ask about the situation further, to pry for more information on the man's identity. His heart ached knowing that he could be told no such things as it would mean revealing his own identity in return, and that was something he could not afford to do.

With his father ill, his duel now held two lives on the line. Elias could not afford to be distracted any further. Revealing their identities would only encourage them to meet in person, becoming more attached than they already were.

Part of him wanted to allow it. He wanted to see the man one more time before his duel. There was no guarantee Elias would survive both the duel and the Red Sea, what good was withholding emotions when his time could be cut short?

The other part of him was more reserved, finding a reason to deny himself the compulsion to see the man, to know his name, to know everything him about him – his likes and dislikes, his wants and needs; the things that made him laugh. What Elias wanted more, was to know the man's sweet embrace that he had yet to feel.

It would be his reward if he won his duel. He would use it as fuel to burn the fire of determination that had dwindled over the years. This was more fuel to the fire of motivation to prevail in his fight. Perhaps that was why he had felt so hopeless about his duel. He had not taken into consideration what he might gain if he were victorious, only what he would lose when he failed.

With each letter, his negative disposition towards the duel alleviated slightly.

Throughout his life, he had been told he would aspire to be a great champion, reinstate his family's honor and continue the lineage of the Va Noldins. The deaths of his family members –

both inside and outside of the duels – had taken its toll on him. He had slowly come to accept that he was destined to die. No matter how much effort or brilliance he showed in his duel, fate had already dictated his future, there was no escaping it.

Perhaps he had been wrong. Perhaps there was more to live for.

Starting his own family was not entirely out of the question, though there would clearly be difficulties going forward. He had ignored that side of himself, thinking it unnecessary to be revealed to save the hassle and drama that would follow. Did he want to have his own family? Did he want to continue the Noldin line? It would end with his death, his father showed no signs of wanting to bear another child, and with his illness, it seemed unlikely he would even be given the opportunity to do so.

The pressures rushed back as a wave of fatigue drained him. He had been told he was the last hope for his family ever since his elder brother's death. All of his siblings had perished in one way or another, his mother along with them. Now his father edged towards death, and there was naught anyone could do to stop him.

How was Elias supposed to recover from this? How could he actively adopt a child, knowing that it would have to be a boy, so a new champion was anointed? Was he selfish if he chose not to do that? He refused to burden a child with the pressures Elias had shouldered growing up. It was a cruelty he would not inflict.

The duels were barbaric. The city praised its champions, lauded them for being sacrifices so the city could continue to survive. The reality of being a champion was much grimmer than the citizens were led to believe. Elias did not want to be champion, why should it be forced upon him?

A blessing from the Gods, the citizens called him but he was little more than a starving dog fighting for its own survival. And all the while spectators clapped as they sat in their stands, bellies full of delicacies as they cheered for the death of one of them.

How could the Gods ever have declared this outdated method of selecting a sacrifice? Wasn't one of the prerequisites for being a sacrifice, willingness? The Gods had led their people astray before. Had guided their ancestors to this city only to become entrapped by a threat that had only shown themselves when they had taken residence. How could this situation have been better than their previous home?

History taught that their people were tormented by bandits, constantly sieged and raided. How was this situation any different? Or even any better? You could at least try to reason with a bandit, but there was no room for negotiation with the metalurks; they were mindless beasts that threw themselves at the walls only to be slaughtered.

Elias would have been scolded for questioning the Gods and had quickly learned as a child not to question them. Blind obedience was the only acceptable path.

He stopped his line of thinking, knowing he would quickly find himself in an unanswerable loop of the Gods decision making. So he returned to his letter, thinking very delicately about his wording. He struggled to not to ask for further details, but he finished the letter and quickly sealed it in an envelope, hoping the action would calm his nerves but sealing the blank wax stamp did very little for his anxiety. The letter sat on his desk, nagging at him to tear it open and rewrite it.

Elias tried his best to ignore its existence but knew it would sit there for hours before Geraldine would return for it. He decided it would be best if he left his room; if he were no longer able to look at the letter, it would quell his thoughts. His next lesson would soon be upon him, so he walked the halls of his house, checking that everything was in order, expecting to distract himself with busy work. Instead, his thoughts drifted to his father's condition. So he headed to the kitchens, speaking to the staff about his father's meal preparations. They had already been informed by Vernin about the change in diet, and staff had been sent into town to retrieve the required ingredients from the stock reserved for nobility.

The cooks knew his father would be difficult with meals. They were good folk, and most of them had been working at the house for his entire life and had grown to learn the habits of his family. He thanked them, informing that he would eat a duplicate meal along with his father. The cooks were understandably shocked; Elias had not had a proper meal with his father without the presence of guests in many years.

191

His father would grow irritable, dealing with the pain of his body; Elias would at least try to alleviate some of the symptoms by joining his father for his meals, hoping to at least provide a momentary distraction. More than that, though, he wanted to form a connection with his father again. They were both practically walking towards their own deaths, they might as well bond before the possibility one of them would perishing. He had missed the opportunity to do so with his mother and brother, but it was not too late to at least try with his father.

Judging by where the sun sat in the sky, Elias guessed it was almost time for his lesson on agriculture. He would once again be discussing the city's use of the surrounding fields and what crops they grew and how they treated them.

As dull and meaningless as it sounded, he welcomed just about any form of distraction he could get. For the first time in many years, Elias looked forward to his lesson, hoping to delve into deep conversation that would demand his attention.

As deep as someone could get when talking about dirt.

15

Life was painstakingly slow for Maggie. Her paranoia remained, and she now spent a vast amount of time questioning what had been real and what might have been a trick of her imagination.

She spent some time questioning if Heleen was even real. Of the very few people in Maggie's life, Heleen was the only person not obligated to care for her, but still chose to. Heleen was at the library every day, and usually waiting for Maggie with a cup of freshly made tea. The librarian looked out for Maggie, tried to catch the signs of any panic attacks in an effort to calm Maggie. There was no way Heleen was a trick of her imagination. Maggie's mind would not be so kind.

Despite the lack of evidence to back up Maggie's claims, she still could not entirely believe the records had been falsified by her imagination. They had seemed so real, how could they have been fake?

Someone must have crept into her house and taken them. But who? If the Sandmen had been keeping an eye on her, why would they be interested in records of Old Malvark? Were they hoping to sell it for extra rations? Were they working for The Voice? The records did indicate they should not be trusted. Perhaps they had some kind of agreement with the Sandmen.

She had to begin her pursuit of them again. Castor had not gotten anywhere with his investigation yet, and now that the

Sandmen might have made a move by sneaking into her own house *and* her place of work, she had to see for herself what they were up to.

They must have been keeping an eye on her for them to discover the hidden room at the library, but how did they know about the hidden record in her home? Were they there searching for something else?

There were simply too many questions burning inside her to let the situation drop. It was time to start following the Sandmen again. She had to go further than last time. She would have to try and follow them to their base.

With the records gone, they would have no reason to suspect she had more. They would have searched her house thoroughly, possibly on more than one occasion. Perhaps they had stopped following her now that they got something of interest? It was a risk she would have to take. She wanted to recover the records to prove to everyone that she was not the lunatic they spoke about in hushed whispers.

Maggie did admit she may not be completely whole, but she knew what was real when she held it in her hands. She had read the words, had broken pieces off the fragile parchments, held them between her fingers, knew their texture and how they smelled.

They were real and no one would convince her otherwise.

She continued her work at the library, dusting off the shelves, constantly looking over her shoulder whenever the feeling of being watched returned. Her nerves churned her stomach, the anxiety of once again pursing the Sandmen had returned before she had even begun the chase. The familiar sensation of her body tingling in anticipation had also returned. She would not only find the records, but also the Sandman who had gotten her son killed.

With her work at the library complete, she walked home, alone. While Audrey had requested Maggie walk home with someone, that would only make her task more difficult. She needed to be alone; she couldn't trust anyone with her convictions. It would be easier to follow the Sandmen without someone constantly trying to prevent her from doing so.

As soon as she had left the library, the feeling of being watched amplified. Whoever was keeping an eye on her remained outside, watching what she did and where she went.

This time, she would catch them.

Maggie moved at her regular pace but made way towards the street the Sandmen regularly gathered, but the gang was not there. This late in the day meant they were probably off trying to peddle their wares.

The eyes still burned a hole in her back, so she calmly continued her pace. As soon as she turned the next corner, she broke into a sprint, trying to hide behind a building before her shadow would be able to catch sight of her again, and she ducked behind the corner of a nearby house, hoping she had been fast enough.

She poked her head out, watching the street. Time seemed to slow as she stared intently at the opening, waiting for anyone to emerge. Her breath was rapid; the anxiety began to take a toll as she had difficulty slowing her breathing.

Her eyes darted between the opening of the street and the back alleys, wondering if her shadow had taken a different path to remain hidden. She began to think that no one had come, that it was just another trick of her imagination – he had tried on several occasions to catch her shadow only to be met with no success.

This time felt different. She had more confidence that she would finally find her stalker, but as she waited, slightly hunched over and head poking around the corner, she began to wonder if anyone had actually been following her.

Maggie was about to give up waiting when a man turned the corner of the street, and she froze, her mind had ceased thinking and her body felt numb as a cold sweat broke through. The man was of average height, aged somewhere between his thirties and forties, thick, blonde hair that was woven into three separate braids. He seemed to hesitate slightly, as if confused by the empty street. It was only a small moment, but Maggie had caught it.

The man continued his stride uninterrupted, walking as if he wanted to be seen. Maggie watched, confused. Something was off about the man. He didn't appear to be a Sandman, but the tattoo could be hidden beneath his clothing. He didn't wear his braids

195

draped around his neck as was popular amongst the Sandmen group she had seen, and he walked with a confident gait.

Maggie watched in silence, the street devoid of other people or sounds.

No sound at all.

She couldn't hear the man's footsteps.

His feet landed softly upon the stone, and he was too far away to see if he wore any particular padding on his shoes. The man kept to one side of the road, close to the open alleyways as if he would escape down one of them at any moment.

He was her shadow. *He* was the one who had followed her, and likely the one who had entered her house. She didn't know how he did it, but he kept eerily silent as he moved.

As the sensation in her body returned, she was shaking, cold sweat weeping from every pore. Part of her wanted to spring out, chase after the man and confront him, but her body had given up, too anxious about what she had seen.

Maggie sat behind the corner of the house she had been hiding, unable to steady her breathing.

She had a pursuer. Despite her belief at being watched, she was surprised by her surprise to find out that it had been true. The world seemed to spin, her eyes unable to focus on anything, the only sound was her breathing.

Calm. Remember Heleen.

She closed her eyes for a moment, took a deep breath before opening her eyes once more and picking a spot on the nearby building to focus on. She remembered how Heleen tried to calm her, counting along in her head with Heleen to pace her breathing. It was not an easy task, but Maggie knew that she would get through it, she always did. *Patience.* The attack would subside, and the transition would go smoothly if she controlled her breathing.

After a moment, she felt herself returning to normal. Some of her anxiety remained about seeing the man, but she was in a stable enough condition that she could walk home.

She stepped out onto the street but immediately stopped. *What if he's waiting up ahead?*

Maggie turned down the next alleyway, weaving behind the buildings and emerging onto another street. She repeated this a few more times, taking a few extra streets than was necessary until she found herself at home.

She stopped at her front door and waited. Listened for the sounds of creaking floorboards, but the chatter of a group of women across the street was the only thing to be heard.

Maggie swung her door open; the light of the day had not yet vanished, amply lighting her house. She cautiously entered, searching each room but finding no one. Satisfied, she grabbed a candle and walked out to the street to light it from the day burner candle that was set up for this purpose. She returned to her house, hesitating once again before entering.

Sat at her kitchen table in her usual chair, Maggie waited for the anxiety to pass. They had no reason to enter her house anymore, but she couldn't figure out why she was being followed. Maggie didn't know the man, and he wasn't part of the Sandmen group she ventured by on a regular basis, perhaps they had sent someone else, to avoid suspicion. That seemed like the likely explanation. The Sandmen had become aware of her snooping and were keeping an eye on her to make sure she didn't cause them any trouble.

But they had brought this upon themselves. They'd messed with her son, likely stole the Old Malvarkian records, and they'd played with her mind.

They would get their due.

* * *

Maggie startled awake, her breaths short and rapid. She had not slept well, tossing and turning as her dreams taunted her with shadows filled with eyes. She wiped sweat from her brow; while these nights were common for her, it didn't make them any easier to deal with. Audrey had gone as far as to suggest just a small amount of alcohol each night to see if it helped with her rest, but Maggie refused, not wanting to get into the habit of a nightly drink. She chose to struggle to sleep instead, finding it easier to deal with than the demons of intoxication... even though Audrey assured her a small drink would not cause such a thing.

There was a rumor a particular type of treeblood-infused candle encouraged your body to sleep, helping with those restless nights, but such an item was way beyond Maggie's reach, reserved only for nobility. She doubted such a thing would help, anyway. How could scent relax the body or mind? She couldn't even see how particular types of food could help. Perhaps the city's restrictions and what was available to her, made this an implausible theory.

Nothing would be able to help her. Not until the Sandmen and her shadow were dealt with.

Maggie ate her breakfast of stale bread and water and dressed for work in the usual drab grey of common citizens. She had very few clothes of any other color, but she did not want to stand out today.

She set out for work, occasionally ducking around corners and peering behind her to see if her shadow had been waiting. The streets were busier in the morning, so she doubted the man would dare to follow her with so many witnesses around.

The Sandmen were not yet at their gathering spot, but she had decided to finish her work early so she could pursue them before they left to ply their trade. She hated lying to Heleen, but it would be the only way to leave without drawing suspicion.

When Heleen greeted her at the library with a caring smile, Maggie made a passing comment about not feeling well to plant the seed of her lie. As the day drew on, Maggie gave more hints to feeling ill, eventually excusing herself to go home and rest.

As Maggie made her way out of the building, the sensation of being watched returned immediately. She did her best not to give away her ulterior motive as she made her usual detour to where the young group of Sandmen liked to dawdle.

She moved at a precise pace until she turned a corner and once again dashed into the nearest alleyway. The trick had worked last time, it was sure to work again. Maggie waited patiently for her shadow to turn the corner, would wait until he searched for her on another street, then she would be free to pursue the Sandmen at her own leisure.

Her heart pounded, the familiar sharp breathing returned. She kept her eyes on the street, but her follower did not appear. Occasionally, some small children or a couple of women would turn down the street, appearing to go about their daily business, but she had paid them no mind. It was the blonde-haired man she waited on.

But… perhaps her follower had changed? Perhaps he had been replaced after yesterday's failure? The children were surely too young to be able to pursue someone intelligently, so maybe it was some of the women? Or all of them?

Maggie peered down the street, but no one fit the bill of a stalker. Did she have no shadow today? That seemed unlikely. They would probably redouble their efforts once she had lost him yesterday.

They were out there, she just had to be patient.

So, she waited. And waited. Scanning the faces of passers-by for any hints of masked intent, and disappointed when she found none. Her patience ran thin. The longer she waited, the closer the Sandmen came to dispersing. Maggie needed to make a move, but she could not be seen when she did so. *Decision time.* Leave now, hoping there was no shadow to follow her, or take the risk and try to lose him on the way to the Sandmen?

"You're quite good at this, you know."

The voice came from behind, startling her. Maggie lost her footing and fell to the ground. The cold, hard stone did little to hurt her, she was too panicked to care.

There he was. The blonde-haired man with three braids, smiling at her, conniving and amused.

Her shadow. How did he get there?

Fear lanced through her, and she waited for him to make his move. Chest heaving, Maggie crawled across the ground in search for a rock to defend herself.

"Oh, please." the man raised his hands to show they were empty. "I will not hurt you. I'm not here to harm, but rather admire your efforts."

Maggie stopped grasping at the ground for a weapon, but her eyes did not stray from his. They were captivating, demanding her focus. She wasn't sure if she believed his words. He seemed sincere, but he loomed over her, and she hurried to think of how to escape. *Scream?* What would the nearby children and women do if he attacked? It might only encourage him to complete his job faster.

"I can see your eyes, Margaret. You're scared, looking for an escape. yet you immediately sought something to defend yourself, and I caught your eyes flicker to the street for a moment to try seek help. Your decisions are there, but they're scrambled, causing you to become confused as to what you should do. Impressive, for someone with no training." His voice was calm and curious, his body still as he studied her.

Part of her screamed to get away, to just stand up and run, to take her best chance at survival, but another part insisted she listen. The man sounded sincere, sounded as if he were assessing her. She tried to speak, but the words stuck in her throat. She tried again, but they would not come.

"It is fine. Again, I am not here to harm you. Please, relax yourself. Breathe." the man took a step back to allow Maggie more room. Such a small gesture, and while he was still within dangerous proximity, surprisingly it helped immensely. She no longer felt... trapped.

Control my breathing. Her brain reached for the techniques taught to her. And all the while, the man waited, smiling, but not offering anything further in the way of calming her.

Maggie dared to stand, using the nearby wall to put her back against, as if expecting another person to sneak up from behind her. She stood near the end of the alleyway, enough so that people might be able to see her, and easier to make it into the street if she ran.

She stared at the man who waited patiently for her. He did not try to rush or encourage her, only waiting until she was ready. "What do you want?" Maggie blurted, finally unjamming the words in her throat.

"I suppose I am here to make you an offer."

"Offer? Of what? Leave the Sandmen alone or else?" She spat the words, upset at having been caught and that they had the nerve to ask to be left alone.

"Oh, I think you might have mistaken who I am," the man said, still calm. "I am no Sandman."

What? Maggie didn't lower her guard, just glared at the man as if he would confess to his lie. "You're not? But you know who I am?"

"Yes, I do. Because I've done my research. I've gathered my information. I've been observing you. Ring any bells?"

Maggie stared at him, perplexed. He was giving her pieces, but she could not put the puzzle together.

"I am a Seeker," the strange man admitted, and Maggie felt herself freeze all over again.

She had heard of the Seekers. A gang that dug for information and used it to blackmail and gain power. In some ways, they were a lot more dangerous than the Sandmen. They were more organized and better prepared – thinking before acting.

And they had been following her. Why? What business did she have with the Seekers? "The records…" Maggie realized.

The man nodded. "Yes, the records. That part was our doing. I apologize, I did not anticipate you trying to show anyone, but perhaps it might have been for the better. I understand you have some… difficulties, and I meant no ill will in taking those records. In fact, I had already planned to invite you to participate in our plans should the records be of any use."

"You." She grit the words out. "You made me look like a fool. You made me look insane to everyone!" Rage surged inside her, and she was surprised by the courage she found to yell.

The man solemnly nodded. "Again, I apologize for that. I wish I could come clean, prove that your words were true, but I'm afraid I cannot do that. The records are safely with us, and I cannot reveal myself to others."

"What's stopping me from telling them?" Maggie knew the answer before she had asked the question, but she needed to hear it from him.

"I suppose nothing. Other than more blank claims to things that don't exist," he said, the tone of his voice reinforcing what everyone had already thought of her.

As much as she tried to find a loophole in his logic, he was right. She would just seem like a raving lunatic again and Audrey would insist on more appointments, and Maggie *really* didn't not want to spend more time talking to Audrey. She couldn't stand being coaxed and manipulated into thinking she wanted another child.

"Then what do you want?" Maggie eased her posture a little but remained firmly in her spot. She would not lower her guard, it could be what the man was hoping for.

"I want to invite you to join the Seekers, Margaret."

Maggie was stunned. The Seekers were a bunch of thieves, criminals, and scavengers who only looked for ways to extort favors and possessions out of others. In a city besieged by creatures, they would extort their own people, driving a wedge between citizens, fighting against the very reason soldiers laid down their lives.

Soldiers like her brother.

She could not join a group that indirectly encouraged the breakdown of society. They were a big factor in why people could no longer entirely trust one another.

"No," was all Maggie could think to say. She wanted to lash out but feared she might agitate the seemingly calm man before her. He had shown no signs of aggression so far, but Maggie did not want to give him a reason to react violently.

"Fair enough."

The man continued to surprise Maggie. He didn't seem disturbed, upset, or even disappointed. Almost like he had been expecting her response.

"That's it?"

"That's it. But I think I've observed you enough that you want to know my plans. Your curiosity gets the best of you."

She wanted to argue, but there was truth to his words. Answers gnawed at her, wanting to know why this man was trying to recruit her. "Just tell me what you want."

"The records that you discovered – thank you for that by the way, truly a tremendous discovery – have confirmed our suspicions about something we've been questioning for a long time now. Sort of." the man paused for a moment, as if considering the weight of what he was about to say. "We think The Voice are hiding something from us. I don't mean small, common things like corruption of power, but something much grander. We also think it has something to do with livewood."

This didn't surprise Maggie. A small percentage of the population believed their governance was hiding something on a much larger scale. What did spark her interest was the man's intelligence. He would not make such a claim without having a reason, evidence. He must truly have discovered something to risk saying something treasonous. "What do you want from me?"

"Your innocence."

Why is he being deliberately vague? "You are going to have to start answering properly or I'm going to leave."

The man chuckled. "Sorry, I guess it's become a bad habit. You are free to leave whenever you want, of course, do not feel pressured into staying. You are a woman nearing her forties, no criminal past, and a history of being mentally unstable. I think you're more intelligent than people may believe. True, you suffer from severe paranoia, but I think you are aware enough to perhaps use that to your advantage."

Maggie could not find fault in what the man had said. He had clearly been observing her for a while if he was able to intricately detail her as if he were a close friend.

"And yes," the man laughed again. "I do see the irony in asking for your innocence while recruiting you to do something potentially law breaking."

"Potentially?"

"Okay, fine, definitely law breaking."

"So…You want to use me for your nefarious work because I could feign insanity and potentially get away with it?"

"That's about right."

"And I would also make a good sacrifice to cover your involvement if I got caught?"

"Well, of course it sounds harsh if you describe it like that."

"How would you describe it?"

"You have a better chance of getting away than anyone else."

Maggie examined the man but could find no indication of ill intent. It seemed like he genuinely wanted to recruit her, as if she had the makings of a Seeker. She did not see that same need; the man was clearly more insane than she was. Still, Maggie refused to relax entirely. The man definitely hid ulterior motives. "What is it *exactly* that you want me to do?"

The man took a moment to contemplate his response. "We're not sure how far we want to send you just yet, not until you become a little more adept in gathering information. We were going to start you off small, and with something that is personal to you, so you don't feel as if you are being used."

She stared at him, eyebrows scrunched in confusion and curiosity. He knew how to tempt her, teasing her with just enough information so she kept asking questions instead of just turning to leave. Despite being aware, Maggie could not draw herself away. "Explain further. Straight to the point this time, no playing games."

The man seemed amused by her answer. "See? You're more adept at this than you might think. We know all about your deceased son, and I do offer my condolences in his death. We've done our own research and we believe two things. The first, your brother knows some information that he has not shared with you. We could convince him to tell you, if you like, we are very persuasive, but that decision is up to you. Consider it a gesture of good will that we told you. The second is that we are inclined to believe that his death was not as accidental as it might seem, which, coincidentally, aligns with some of our tasks."

Castor found something and didn't tell me? That doesn't seem likely. So why do I believe this man? So many questions were popping into Maggie's head, she was having difficulty picking which one to start with. Confronting her brother would be a place to start; there had to be a reason he didn't tell her. What she couldn't figure out was how her son's death coincided with the Seekers' research. But he'd offered the one thing Maggie wanted most: an answer to her son's death.

"You'll help me discover what happened to Patrick?"

"Yes. It is only fair we assist you before you assist us."

"Before I agree to it, what is it that you'll have me do? Follow around a Magister? Pretend to be insane if I get caught chasing them?"

"We will assess you on your first task of finding information about your son. You have belief that he was involved with the Sandmen, so we'll begin there. Based on your capabilities, we will determine the best job for you. It will involve sneaking around and likely following someone, but we need time before we put you in such dangerous waters."

Maggie considered the offer. She wanted so badly to know what happened to her son, would she entrust herself to the care of the Seekers just to find out? Or had Castor discovered information relating to her son that might answer some questions? She inwardly cursed herself, knowing that either way she would find herself on the same path.

"Fine. Where do we begin?"

16

The tension in Arthur's home increased as each day passed. His elder brother's actions at the party sullied his mother's already bland attitude and caused his father to go into a fit of rage. Gavin had ordered the leftover food and wine be turned over to the market square, where any citizen was able to grab their own portion. It was deemed as the Va Daolin family's way of celebrating Gavin's promotion, gaining the respect of the general population. But it lost respect amongst the nobility, where Edmund truly cared.

Arthur could not figure out the intent behind his brother's actions, only seeing the harm that it had caused within his family. His mother spent an increasing amount of time locked away in her bedroom, and his father became irritated with everyone within his proximity, so Arthur made sure to avoid him when possible. If he saw his mother outside of her bedroom, he made sure not to stray too far should she become the target of his father's wrath.

Thankfully, she seemed to avoid him quite strategically, knowing that Edmund needed more time to cool off.

Arthur had not been able to speak with his brother further, but he had not forgotten what Gavin had told him in their brief conversation. There were questions he had to ask his father, but the situation did not provide an opportunity. Gavin would be a sore point for his father for quite some time, and there would be no telling when Arthur could ask about Gavin's elusiveness and departure.

He wanted to ask his mother; surely, she would know. But he did not have the heart to bring it up, seeing her reddened face from a night of sulking tore at his insides. Despite what Gavin thought of their father, his brother should have considered the repercussions of his actions and how it affected their mother.

His lessons with his mentor's ran as normal, but he could sense the awkwardness between them. The nobility talked, and any who associated with them became targets if the gossip and rumors. His teachers could only hope they would be an exemption since they had to teach the Champion of the Daolin family.

Thankfully, his dueling mentor Eustace was his usual authoritative self. The man didn't seem to care for the Daolin's recent debacle – he was here to do one thing, and one thing only. Train Arthur.

"Your form is becoming sloppy, boy. Keep your eyes up, do not tilt your head when you watch my feet, and for the sake of your own life, parry!" Eustace thrust forward, his armor clattered as he moved with a surprising amount of agility for a man his age, keeping Arthur on his toes.

Arthur barely raised his sword in time to block the attack, knocking Eustace's sword off center, but the sprightly man was relentless, immediately and seamlessly flowing into another attack. Again, Arthur barely parried the blow, but there was a surprising amount of power behind the attack and it instead knocked Arthur's weapon to the side, leaving him momentarily open.

He quickly rolled backwards, dodging Eustace's swipe that would have made contact with his gut.

"Good roll, bad parry. Match my strength, boy!"

Arthur had dueled with Eustace more times than he could count, and yet the man still managed to be his equal. Whenever Arthur felt himself gaining on his mentor's expertise, Eustace would simply adopt a higher level of skill. Arthur was still uncertain if his mentor was holding back. He had grown accustomed to his opponent using his left hand, something that took a surprising amount of time to adjust to.

"You're thinking too much. Move, attack, do something instead of just standing there dawdling!"

Arthur swung his weapon, putting just enough strength behind the blow to make it seem deadlier than it was. His trick worked as Eustace parried the attack but overextended his defense just enough that Arthur thrust his weapon in the gap, making contact with his opponent's armor.

"Good, but you need more power behind the final attack, or you'll never inflict a fatal wound. We've got the blade covers on for a reason, use it."

Arthur nodded, busy catching his breath from the sparring. He was about ready to finish the training session, but Eustace adopted the Eagle stance, ready for another bout, and Arthur shrugged aside his want to finish, taking on the defensive Stone stance. He knew what was about to transpire, it was how they normally finished their practice.

Eustace came at Arthur with a barrage of swift and precise attacks. Arthur parried and blocked as fast as he could, watching Eustace's feet and torso as they shifted in preparation for the next attack. A few of the blows managed to lightly touch his armor, not enough for a real blade to pierce the sturdy metal. He danced with Eustace, countering his steps so that his opponent did not get the upper hand.

Eustace's fist came flying from the side, targeting Arthur's head. Deftly rearing back, the fist scarcely missed him. Arthur grabbed the man's arm and yanked him forward, blade pointed towards his chest.

His mentor stumbled forward, striking Arthur's weapon with his own in an attempt to sway it to the side. Arthur held firm, his sword unwavering, knowing that he would have to land a fatal blow.

Eustace's armor made contact with the sword, followed by a dissatisfying lack of sound as the padded weapon landed heavily on its mark, and the man regained his footing, taking off his helmet. "That, was a killing blow, boy. Do that earlier and there wouldn't have been need for more than one strike. Remember, you must make your opponent surrender, but fatally wounding your opponent is not out of the question."

Arthur nodded. It had been drilled into him for years that he must aim to slay his opponent, not simply win a sparring match to determine the victor. Admittedly, Arthur had some reluctance in the matter. He had never killed before, not even fought against the metalurks to gain the sensation, even if they were just mindless creatures. He wasn't sure if he would have the courage to strike down another man, but he figured the sense of life or death might change his attitude in the arena.

"We're done for today. Take your armor off and clean it, fix any dents that might have been made, and then clean it again."

Arthur complied. He enjoyed the clean-up process. Not the clean-up itself, but rather finding the small imperfections in his armor and fixing them, making it appear is if it were brand new. He had quickly learned to appreciate the metal, being one of the very few people in the city who were able to safely use it, he did not want to squander that opportunity.

As he cleaned the armor, he wondered what other purposes the mysterious resource could be used for if he could only leave the room with it. Could the metalurks pierce through such a thing? It was hard to estimate when he had not personally inspected the claws of the creatures. He could not ask anyone outside of his family either, and none of them had ever seen a metalurk up close.

Arthur also wondered what made the creatures lust for such a thing. He imagined they ate it by absorbing it into their skin. Out of curiosity, he had once licked the metal when he was younger, wondering if it had a particular taste the creatures enjoyed but could not describe the disgusting feeling it had left on his tongue, as if it stained it at the mere touch. He remembered the feeling vividly and could not even imagine what made the metalurks want to put it anywhere near their mouths.

After the initial cleaning process was finished, Arthur picked up the small hammer and began inspecting his armor for any imperfections. There was very little to ever fix when they padded their blades to the point it was just a blunt object, and even then, the padding softened the blows.

With both suits of armor inspected and cleaned, Eustace called Arthur over before he had a chance to escape. "Remember, head up, eyes open, and anticipate. Don't watch where the sword will fall, learn where it will go next. There is very little I can probably teach you at this point, but that does not mean your training will ease up. I'll see you in two days."

They left the room together, locking it behind them. They took a quick look around, Eustace was always on edge about spies, but were satisfied when no one could be seen.

Arthur bid his teacher farewell and set off to the baths where a tub should be ready and waiting for him. As the adrenaline of the fight seeped away, the thoughts and problems that dominated his mind returned. An unnecessary load of burdens had been placed on him, none of his choice. He could simply just ignore his family's troubles, focusing on himself instead, but what kind of person would he be if he simply ignored his mother like that?

He undressed and entered the bath that had been prepared, rushing to wash himself before the heat disappeared from the water. As much as he wanted to dawdle and relax, he found that he simply could not. Gavin's words played on his mind, repeating over and over, refusing to be ignored until they were addressed.

He had to ask his father what happened, but would his father give him an honest answer?

There was only one way to find out.

Arthur dried and dressed himself, intent on joining his family for dinner in the hall where they should be gathering about now. As expected, his mother was nowhere to be seen, but his father sat at the table, picking at some bread while reading from a small pile of letters and waiting for the meal to be served.

Arthur signaled the servant to send another dish and took his usual seat at the table. His father did not acknowledge him, not even moving his eyes from the paper.

Unsure when the right moment would arise to bring up his brother, Arthur worked up the nerve to just blurt it out. He opened his mouth to give it voice but his father snorted.

"Oh, Gods," his father scoffed, "Can you believe that these people, guests invited into our home, dare write me about their disturbed evening? Who do they think they are, talking down to me, and through a letter no less! Why not speak to me directly? They're too scared to play real politics, hiding behind their quill and parchment in the safety of their own home. Ridiculous."

His father threw the letter down and picked up another, scanning it as he shoveling another handful of bread in his mouth.

Great. I'm sure he's in a good mood now. Arthur grimaced in anticipation of the question that teetered on his tongue.

His father threw another sheet down. "Simply ridiculous. They hear an order from Gavin in my absence, and think that he runs the family in my stead? The boy doesn't even live here anymore!"

Well, may as well get it over with before it gets any worse. "Father," Arthur interrupted between letters. "About Gavin. Why did he leave the household?"

Edmund stared at Arthur, not with a scowl but with curiosity. "He will be man of his own household, or so he claims. He will not pick another name, he wouldn't dare. Our name carries too much weight to simply throw aside. He did not agree with some of the ways I run this house, so he left. To the Reds with him, he's a stubborn boy who does not appreciate the lengths I went for him."

Not really the answer I was hoping for.

Without being prompted, his father continued, "The Gods will condemn him, just you wait. He dares to speak out against me, in my own home no less. Claims to no longer be my son but uses my name to get himself a comfortable position as Magistrate of Defense. He's no better than the creatures pounding at our walls!" Edmund's face turned red as he spat the words out.

Arthur was still dissatisfied, he was hoping for a clearer answer than just having a dispute. He was about to pry further, but his father had begun acting strangely. Edmund's face dropped from anger to panic, his face began to pale, and he patted his chest with a closed fist.

"Father?"

Arthur prepared to stand up, but his father raised a hand to stop him. Arthur complied, watching as the man began taking deep breaths.

"It's over, I'm fine now."

"What just happened?"

"A small hiccup, nothing to worry about."

A hiccup? Stubborn fool. "Are you alright? Should I send for a doctor?"

"I said it's nothing to worry about, sit yourself down."

Arthur hesitated before retaking his seat, staring at his father as if the condition might return at any moment. Edmund did not seem worried, grabbing at the bread again, his face lighting up as the servants brought out the starter soup.

Despite what his father said, Arthur took whatever just occurred very seriously. He'd seen the panic in his father's eyes but could also tell that his father had experienced it before, likely on more than one occasion. And as his father happily delved into the bowl of soup, Arthur decided to let the conversation drop. Whatever had just happened might have been the result of his body becoming too agitated. Arthur did not want it to happen again, it seemed painful, and it might lead into something potentially fatal.

"How's Mother?" Arthur asked, beginning on his own soup.

Edmund's expression to annoyance. "Unchanged. That woman needs to use her spine. She wallows in self-pity, day after day. Gods have mercy on her if she doesn't break out of this rut soon."

What?

His father just kept eating his soup, as if the comment would fly by unnoticed.

"What do you mean?"

"I'll give her a good talking to if she doesn't drop this stupid act. I don't have the time nor patience to play her silly games, we've got to pull our pants up from being spanked and move on. Learn from these experiences, not let it overwhelm us into the passive person your mother has become."

Arthur tightened the grip on his spoon. It took every inch of willpower to hold himself back, wanting to fly into a rage at his father. But why was he holding back? For the sake of his father's health?

'Care for your mother while she is still with you.' The words from his correspondent played in his mind as if the handsome man was right beside him, encouraging him to stand up.

Arthur abruptly stood, the momentum knocking his chair over as it failed to slide along the wooden floor.

His father looked at him, soup dripping down the corner of his mouth, like an innocent child who did not know the weight of the words he had just said.

"You will not speak about Mother like that. She grieves for her family, torn apart by your actions. I do not know what you have done to encourage Gavin to leave, but I know it must have been terrible to push him so far. You sold off your only daughter into a marriage she did not want in return for meaningless possessions. You have no right to talk down to Mother as if she were not a victim to your actions. It makes me sick to think of how such an obscenely, grotesque man managed to suppress the happiness and caring that Mother once had. You've kept her close only so she can bear the brunt of the consequences of your decisions. If I hear you so much as breathe in her direction and it upsets her, I swear that I will remove myself as Champion of the Va Daolin family."

Edmund placed his spoon down but did not bother to wipe the soup running down his face and dripping off his chin. "How *dare* you speak to me like that, boy! You're worse than your brother, squandering the efforts I've made so you have the best fighting chance in your duel, and you dare to deprive the family of its champion? Who do you think you are, boy?!"

Arthur no longer cared if his father had another 'small hiccup'. He leaned over, staring Edmund down. "I am the Champion of the Va Daolin family. I have the power to completely strip this family of its good name and titles. I have chosen not to bear a son before my duel, so everything lays solely on me. You have no power over me. You never did. I wish I had seen that sooner, but I was blinded by what I thought was love." Arthur's tone was low, but it did not squander the intent behind it, each word filled with as much anger as the last. He walked over to Edmund, challenging his authority as he bent over the portly man. "Just one. All it takes is one more negative word, look, or even a damned thought against Mother, and I'll disown myself from this family, and absolve the title to the Ka Vedyrs. Just one."

Arthur turned, leaving the room in a furious march, not to even glance at his father.

The anger subsided, transforming into pride. He'd finally stood up for his mother, properly. He had achieved the confidence he needed to stand against his father. Arthur still didn't know what his father had done – or still does – that caused Gavin to leave, but he now understood why. Arthur hadn't thought about disowning his title before, but the threat had come to him in the heat of the moment, and he had meant every word.

He carried the confidence with him to his parents' chambers where he sought his mother. The servants stationed out front confirmed she had not left the room that day. Arthur knocked on the door but received no response. He was in too great a mood to be ignored, so he entered the room without an invitation. His mother sat at her desk, idly brushing her hair. Arthur could see her reflection in the mirror as she stared at him, and he watched in turn as she donned a polite but fake smile.

"Arthur, dear, there is no need to check up on me. I have eaten my nightly meal."

He spotted the tray of half-eaten food and ignored the remark. "Not why I'm here, Mother. I words I wish to speak, then I will leave."

His mother turned to face him, sensing the seriousness of the situation.

Arthur took a breath, but found he was not nervous. "I have told Father to leave you alone. I do not know what he does behind closed doors, but I have demanded that he no longer treat you with contempt. He will be angry, as I threatened to leave the family and the title." He ignored the slowly dawning shock on his mother's face and powered on. "I understand the seriousness behind those words, but this can no longer go on, Mother. I am sick of the way he treats you. Do not feel guilty for my actions, they were not yours, and I am completely aware of what I am saying."

He walked over to his mother and embraced her. "You tell me if he so much as steps out of line. I will handle it. I know you feel alone, but I am not giving you a choice any longer. I will be here, beside you."

Evelynn began to weep, and Arthur could tell it was not from his actions directly, something else was bothering her.

"What is it, Mother?"

She looked into her son's eyes. "I am filled with happiness that you felt compelled to do that for me, but it will all be in vain if you fall in your duel. He will become worse." She shook her head, but like Arthur had done so earlier, she continued with her words. "He tried for years to have another son after you were born, but my body had simply become too aged. He'll replace me if you die, Arthur."

He felt like he'd been punched; didn't want to believe what his mother had just said. Evelynn had given the man three beautiful children, and he would dare toss her to the side simply to keep the rank of Va Daolin?

"What about Gavin? He has three daughters, he could always try for a son?"

Evelynn's tears did not break. "He has refused to bear more. He only risked having three children because we are not exempt from the laws entirely, but he will not have a son to act as our next champion after you."

A wave of nausea washed over Arthur. His father would go that far to keep the petty title. He would dispose of his mother, sire another child for a deathly duel all to keep it.

And no one would question or speak out against him.

The nobility would know the reason for his actions, and they would accept it as a tactical method to keep the wealth, riches, and fame.

To them, it was a completely normal maneuver.

Arthur clenched his hands to fists, resisting the urge to slam them against something, to feel something break beneath his wrath. His father was the source of all the misery and conflicts in this family. Edmund was worse than the metalurks that threatened the life of the citizens of Malvark, because his father's relentless hunger was satiated behind the safety of the walls.

Evelynn gripped her son's hand, seeing the fury held behind them. Arthur released them to allow his mother's hand to slip in, squeezing his own as she silently pleaded for him to calm. He returned the squeeze, let his anger slip only from his façade. Inside, he was a controlled storm, one of focus and commitment.

He helped his mother to her bed then stayed by her side, letting her cry herself to sleep. His father did not return to the room before he had left, and if Edmund was smart, he would be sleeping in another room from now on.

As Arthur slowly made his way to his own chambers, he cursed inwardly, refusing to let his ire be seen by others. He would keep up appearances for as long as was necessary. But he refused to let Edmund cause any more discord amongst his family.

As time draws on, I find my heart feeling heavier and heavier, burdened with the secrets of my life that I cannot share with you. Your letters continue to prove as a personal beacon, as a promise that things will soon get better.

It warms me to hear that you care so deeply for your family. Even as scarce as you describe them, I find myself compelled to learn more, but know that I must withdraw my intrigue for the sake of our mutual decision of concealed identities. Though, I find it increasingly difficult.

As much as the letters brighten my days, their magic does not last as long as I wish, dulled only by the fact that I cannot see you. Written words are one thing, but the smoothness of your voice is beginning to evaporate in my mind.

I do not know how much longer these letters will continue to suffice, but I do not want to do anything rash without considering the consequences. Yet I do not know what the future holds in store for me – or yourself – around the Day of Sacrifice and the Red Sea. Seeing you before might compromise my position as I won't be able to keep my identity a secret should we meet face to face once more.

All logic screams at me to wait until things settle down, after the Red Sea is vanquished, but my heart aches with the chance of not seeing you should one of us perish by the time that it is over. I hope you have the words to still my thoughts. It is an answer that is elusive to me, I am truly torn between two decisions, and you are the only one I can ask. I shan't put our messenger in a position to accept any guilt if things develop negatively.

My hand wavers as I write my confession. I do not know if you reciprocate the feelings, but my heart wishes to fool me into thinking that you do.

I hope you have a clearer mind to think of the answer.

I have also sent along a personal craft of mine. A livewood ring. I tried to match its color with my memory of your complexion, so it might not be seen if you wish to wear it.

Even if we do not meet, I still wish for you to have it. A token, if you will, of my feelings for you.

Arthur read the letter, having woken to find it had been slipped underneath his door as he slept. It was a pleasant surprise to an otherwise fretful night of sleep, the slight bulge in the envelope had made him excitedly curious.

The weight of emotions poured into every letter, and this one in particular, made the parchment felt heavy in his hands. His correspondent had clearly been struggling with their agreed method of communication. Though it had ailed Arthur that he was unable to see the man, he had simply accepted it as a necessity, but it appeared that the man was having a difficult time being patient.

Arthur toyed with the ring on his finger, brushing his fingers along its smooth surface. It was a delicate item performed with wonderful craftsmanship, fitting perfectly on his finger. He wondered if his correspondent had actually lied about not working with livewood before, but that was a fleeting thought.

Perhaps there was more to the situation than had been written, his correspondent clearly feared a possible death by the Red Sea. Arthur was equally afraid of death, though for different reasons. The noble district was located towards the west wall of the city, farthest away from where the metalurks usually bombarded and broke in, and situated on a rise as it was, gave the nobility that extra level of protection. Or time. Extra time to live, to wait to die. His fear of death centered around his own duel, whereas his correspondent must live in the east end of the city. The east side would be evacuated to pack as many people as they could in the western district, piling the people on the streets behind livewood barricades that were in the process of being set up.

Other than the soldiers, they were most at risk. Arthur had the safety of his own home, where his father had managed to commission livewood shutters for the windows and replace the entrance and chamber doors with livewood, to slow any metalurks who managed to get that far.

Their noble lineage also came with certain benefits, guards were ordered to protect them above the general population of the city, though in the heat of battle, Arthur hoped that each soldier would react to their situation, protecting anyone and everyone, no matter who they were.

The Voice would be safe, barricaded in the small arena where the duel would take place. This was where The Voice conferred, no one was allowed entry, not even Arthur. He would see it for the first time on the day of his duel. It would just be a small, open area for the duelists to move around in, but the arena was the most defensible place in the city, having been occasionally reinforced with livewood in every possible space.

Arthur found the lengths that The Voice went to just to protect themselves a little distasteful and a waste of livewood. They would not allow anyone else other than themselves and a personal selection of guards to protect them inside the arena. Such amounts of livewood should have been used to protect a larger portion of people, not a small handful.

That was not his concern, however. At least, not yet. If he managed to find himself in a position to speak with The Voice, he would then speak his mind on the matters, trying to convince them to reconsider, but he held no power or authority just yet, they would not hear from a champion who might become the sacrifice.

He understood why his correspondent would be so afraid of survival, crammed behind barricades like pigs waiting for the slaughter. Yet, they all were. Creatures that fought for survival, day after day, year after year. Armed with sticks and stones, grasping whatever they could to survive.

He could not quell his correspondent's fears, it was logical to be afraid of death.

He stared at the livewood ring, feeling himself renewed.

He had come to a decision.

No more running. No more hiding. No more keeping quiet. It was time for action. Time to get things done.

It was time to stop living in fear.

17

Castor's plans of one day becoming general seemed further and further out of reach the more he spent time thinking about his sister and what he had discovered about the current general's involvement in his nephew's arrest.

Not only were people plotting against him, but it seemed as if the Gods themselves held a personal disdain. A sister who was struggling with her own mentality and her grief over the loss of her child, who had a useless husband that abandoned her. General Deven seemed to have a personal vendetta against him, and they had damned sticks for defense.

He watched as piles of wooden spikes were placed along the wall in preparation to be set up for the Red Sea. It was only a few weeks away, and nerves were understandably unsettled throughout the city.

Castor had yet to speak to the new Magistrate of Defense, but it would likely be too late to prepare livewood spikes; they had probably run out a few months ago and were waiting for the new trees to grow the appropriate height before harvesting.

People gathered in groups on occasion to inspect the wall of any new defenses. They were becoming agitated and nervous, faces filled with disappointment. It seemed most people had almost accepted the prospect of dying.

Few approached him, asking for information about potential new defenses, and he gave them the truth. More wooden spikes, a second livewood portcullis, increased number of archers and soldiers, more livewood weapons spread amongst them, and the potential for a new defense that had yet to be revealed to him.

They were mixed reactions; some were hopeful, but most skeptical. A large proportion of the population had survived one or even two Red Seas, so they knew how dangerous it could be – they were a testament to Malvark's resistance, its refusal to be overwhelmed. Castor had believed there would be more of them spreading hope, but many were perhaps too afraid to see the death and destruction of the Red Sea again.

Castor had been but a child when he had lived through his first Red Sea; it had scarred him deeply. He remembered the splintering of wood as the defenses broke, the screams, the crying, the sounds of people being torn apart as the metalurks raged throughout the city. Fortunately, he and Maggie had been kept safe in one of the hidden rooms beneath their stone floor of their home. Their parents had not survived the attack.

It was the reason he'd become a soldier. The memory of him holding his sister as she shook and cried, the fear in her eyes as they prayed to the Gods for help, was still vivid.

As a soldier, he could do more than just hold someone while they cried. He couldn't ensure their safety, but he wanted to be a beacon of hope for the children. Castor wanted them to see him and feel safe, that their survival was in good hands. After years of defending the wall, his prospects of becoming a beacon had slowly diminished to a small, wavering flame. The people discarded their hope, their spirits flagged as the death toll rose each year.

Movement atop the wall caught Castor's eye. A few men were hauling a small amount of livewood, escorted by General Deven. They walked along the top of the wall, inspecting it, as though trying to determine the best location for whatever it is they were doing.

Deven finally pointed out two spots, leaving as the men got to work with their lumber. Castor was intrigued; he'd not heard anything about work being done to the wall... other than the special project he wasn't allowed to know anything about.

Over the next couple of hours, the men worked hastily, other builders had also stopped to watch and ask questions but were

221

turned away. One man declared their work finished and placed a sheet of cloth over it whatever it was they'd constructed to protect it from prying eyes.

The small constructions only appeared to be a foundation for something larger to be attached. On its own, it made no sense to Castor, so surely there was more to it. He glanced up at the sun, wincing against the brightness as he inspected its place in the sky. He figured it was time, and left the builders to continue their preparations. Castor wasn't on duty and had no obligation to stay; other soldiers had been placed to observe and report to Deven should any complications arose.

Besides, Castor had other things that needed to be attended. Audrey had asked him to meet with her and Maggie today, apparently suspicious that there is some untold activity, and wanted Castor to help her confront Maggie. He wasn't sure if he believed it himself; Maggie had returned to her usual self, with a little difference. She seemed a lot more confident in her claims, especially when it pertained to the secret room and records she had supposedly found.

Something must have happened, that much was certain, but Castor wasn't sure if it meant that Maggie was up to something. He had to believe his sister. What kind of brother would he be if he couldn't believe a word she said?

He arrived at Audrey's house, but before he could knock, he could hear that the conversation had already started. Maggie was trying to convince Audrey – again – that the records were real, but she could not prove it.

Castor opened the door, inviting himself in. Maggie was surprised to see him and, as usual, immediately became suspicious that they were plotting against her. Castor gave her a reassuring smile and a gentle kiss on the head as he greeted her. She stared at him, eyes burning with skepticism and questions.

"Margaret," Audrey said, but Maggie's eyes did not stray from Castor. "I asked your brother here in the hopes that it gives you reassurance that we only have your best interests at heart. I have come suspect that you might be doing something secretive, and I fear that it might be something dangerous. Do you have anything to say on that?"

Castor watched his sister carefully as Audrey spoke. There was a slight flicker in her eyes, but the determination behind them did not waver.

"I am not doing anything wrong."

Oh Gods, Maggie.

"I did not necessarily mean you were doing something wrong, just that you were keeping something from us. What is it that you are hiding, Margaret?"

Maggie took her time before she answered, momentarily holding Castor's gaze before turning to Audrey. "I am not doing anything wrong."

Castor knew Maggie would not give a straight answer, at least not to Audrey. The meeting repeated itself in different context in the remaining time it had left, and Maggie did not become any clearer about her actions.

Audrey thanked Castor for coming, and he escorted his sister out of the house, walking with her in silence as he tried to figure out how to confront her.

Before he could, however, Maggie stopped in her tracks, spinning to face Castor with a scowl. "What have you found?"

Castor was thrown off guard by the question. He looked at Maggie, confused, pretending to be uncertain what she was talking about. "What?"

"What have you found, Castor? I know. I know that you've discovered something, but you need to tell me what that is."

"How did you know I found something?" Castor demanded, trying to take control of the situation.

"I just know. Gods, Castor, you were meant to tell me when you found something. Why did you keep it hidden from me?" Maggie's voice fluctuated between anger and hurt.

Castor shrugged away his guilt and let his curiosity take precedence. He eyed Maggie, suspiciously. "You've been following me, haven't you, Maggie?"

"No, Castor, I haven't. I had an associate tell me that you discovered something. It doesn't matter how I know, what matters is that you *didn't tell me*. How could you not tell me? It's about my son!"

Castor's shame hitting hard this time, more so when he saw a tear rolled down Maggie's face, Castor could no longer look her in the eyes without being overwhelmed by the guilt. "First of all, it does matter how you know. If you've been following me, then I don't know how I'm supposed to trust you anymore. I suppose you might feel the same way, but I had reason for not telling you. A reason I thought was the right decision considering the circumstances."

"What could have possibly driven you to hide information from me, Castor? I thought you were the only person I could trust. I thought you were the only one who was on my side. Now, I'm starting to wonder if Audrey has managed to convince you that I'm unfit to be left alone. That I'm no more than a child you have to keep an eye on, so she doesn't get into trouble."

"Gods curse me, Maggie, you can't always assume the worst! I'm your brother, you have to give me a chance to explain myself. Instead of jumping to the worst possible conclusion, perhaps just consider that I might have logical reasoning."

"Then what is it? What have you found?"

Castor rubbed his eyes, frustrated. He had not wanted to tell her yet, he hadn't found enough information but he had no other choice. "Yes. Patrick's arrest was not coincidence. The officer who arrested him was paid, rather handsomely, to arrest him. I'm guessing he managed to pay off one of the Sandmen to set him up, planting the drugs on him. So far, I've connected General Deven to it, but I haven't found much more than that. I don't know why the general was after Patrick. It could be a coincidence, and I don't think he intended for him to be mistaken as someone else and be executed."

Maggie stared at him, another tear rolling down her face, blue eyes piercing Castor's, reflecting the pain he had unwittingly inflicted upon her.

"Why would you want to hide that from me?"

Castor rubbed the back of his head, gripping a bundle of his hair to an attempt to vent some of his own emotions. He was having difficulty even facing her, but he knew that he had to. He was already a coward for having hidden it, there was no point in continuing the façade. "I thought you might go off and investigate it on your own. I thought that you wouldn't be able to sit still and let me handle it at my own pace. You might have gotten into trouble if you began snooping around the general, I couldn't let you do that to yourself."

Maggie did not waver as Castor confessed. She stared at him, and he could feel her burning a hole through him, stacking on more and more pressure. "No, Castor. I don't believe that. There's something else."

"What?" Castor looked at her, perplexed.

"There's more. What is it? Tell me, truthfully, why you held back telling me?"

"I did tell you."

"No. You're afraid, I can sense that much, but it's not because you're worried that I'll get into trouble. It's because of something else."

"Maggie, I told you th—"

"Castor. No games."

She tugged at his emotions, prying them apart to delve deeper inside. Castor felt his heart rip, knowing where she was leading to. Something he had not confessed to himself. Something he did not want to think about. He struggled to hold back his own tears, his head feeling heavy as he had trouble lifting it to barely look at Maggie.

"I was afraid…" Castor began, the words choking in his throat as he forced them up. He hesitated, preparing himself, trying to find the courage to summon the words out from the deep hole he had buried them in. "I was afraid that you might blame me for Patrick's death. I think it's my fault, Maggie. I think I'm the reason he was killed."

Castor collapsed against the nearby wall, trying unsuccessfully to hold back his tears. He had wanted so badly to blame someone else, but no matter how he traced it back, the general had his nephew arrested because of Castor. He didn't know why. He didn't know what kind of game the general was trying to play. Castor just knew Patrick had died because of him.

Maggie crouched in front of him, and he buried his face in his hands, unable to look at the world any longer. He knew that he was making a mess of things, the few people that might stroll by

225

would see the Captain of the East Wall, the most important wall in their defense, blubbering on the ground like a child. But he could not stop himself. The wall that held back all those terrible thoughts and confessions, had broken.

But Maggie had been able to break down his defenses with only a few words and an accusatory look. He was a weak fool. How could he have ever thought to make general if he was prone to making a mockery of himself, a broken soldier weeping on the streets.

Maggie embraced him, tightly, refusing to let Castor break free, though he barely had the strength to try. "Castor." Maggie's voice was soft, wavering a little as she cried, yet still held a surprising amount of conviction. "I have been looking for my son's murderer for years. I have accused just about everyone I've ever met. I know my mind plays games with me, but *never once* have I believed for a second that you might have had a hand in Patrick's death. I still don't. There is no way you were the reason behind his death. If the general's behind it, then it's the general's fault. If he did it to get to you, then it is *still* the general's fault. Patrick's death is not on your hands, Castor. I do not blame you. Not then. Not now. Not ever."

Castor could not find the courage to speak, each word had somehow struck a nerve, not wanting to believe them.

Maggie tightened her embrace, adjusting herself so that her mouth was near Castor's ear so that she could whisper. "Patrick does not blame you for his death either."

The words lifted some of the stones that had been bearing down on Castor's soul, but his mind was not so easily persuaded. He sat for a while, listening to his sister slowly convince him, a fool of a Captain sitting on the side of the street, crying, torturing himself with the blood of his nephew.

* * *

Castor woke the next morning feeling sluggish. His body demanded he remain in bed, but he fought the desire, knowing he had to attend his training with the Steelwoods. It was going to be a long session.

He pushed through the vain attempts of his body wanting to slow down, and most of the lethargy evaporated as he walked, head held high, carrying his pride with no attempt to hide his shame. Castor knew he had been seen yesterday, crying and distraught; he was well recognized amongst the citizens, there would be no point in pretending that he hadn't. But he refused to let any rumors or his own body become an obstacle for his determination to defend the wall. The sight of him crying would likely impact his chances of becoming general, but that didn't mean he would simply abandon his post. He was, first and foremost, a soldier. No matter the rank, he dedicated his life to the defense of the city, and a few tears and whispering mouths would not deter him from continuing to do so.

The training yard came into view and Castor noted that some of the Steelwoods had already gathered. He would give a little more time for the others to arrive before commencing training.

He had been looking forward to sparring, he needed an outlet, and there would likely not be an attack today. As he entered the yard, the Steelwoods saluted him, giving no indication of having heard about his small breakdown. He saluted them in return, and they continued their conversations while waiting for the rest of the Steelwoods to arrive.

Castor spied the new recruits on the other side of the yard, a large group of inexperienced, young men practiced with their bows against the bundles of hay set up as targets. The law of the Red Sea were being enforced, recruiting any able-bodied man of age – and any willing women – to learn how to defend themselves against the metalurks. A large portion of them were trained with bow and arrow, and all were taught the basics in self-defense and the tactics for taking down a metalurk. Their priority was to protect the children by any means necessary.

The training had begun a few months ago, occurring just once a week, but as the Red Sea drew closer, training was daily to give everyone the best fighting chance to defeat a metalurk should they break into the city.

The new batch of soldier bodies to fill in gaps at the wall had quickly picked up on their training. Castor had taken the lead a few times, mostly to raise morale amongst them by having the Captain of the East Gate guide them, and they were a responsive batch. They picked up on their training well, most of them eager to help serve as defenders of the wall.

The general, as usual, was nowhere to be seen. Castor doubted that Deven had even met the men, or that the men had ever seen him at all. The chance of the man showing up that morning was slim, so Castor's best chance was to wait for the general to arrive in the afternoon.

It was time to confront Deven. There was no use sneaking around, following the man in the hope Castor would make another discovery. It wasn't Castor's style and the idea made him feel dirty. Even confronting the general seemed like a dead end; there would be no way Deven would confess to anything, and it would only increase the general's resentment, but Castor did not care.

Both he and General Deven were at a high risk of falling in the battle of the Red Sea, but the general likely had a better chance of survival than Castor. The man had already fought and survived two Red Seas, a great accomplishment for any person. Castor would be fighting in his first. As such, Castor didn't want to pass on the opportunity of finding out the reason for his nephew's death, or at least his arrest, before it was too late. Life in Malvark was short for a lot of people, and Castor preferred to be upfront and active when it came to getting anything done.

With the rest of the Steelwoods arriving, Castor called them all into formation. None asked any questions or even gave him so much as an odd glance, obeying him without hesitation.

Maybe they don't know yet. Doesn't matter either way.

He led them through their warmups, jogging around the town close to their training yard. It had the added benefit of the people seeing the Steelwoods and defenders of the wall, and he knew it brought comfort to at least some. Besides, Castor was proud of them. They were an efficient and skillful bunch, able to trust each other on the battlefield. Castor had no doubts they would be the key in breaking down most of the Red Sea.

When they returned to the yard, each picked up a staff that would act as a spear. Castor wanted them to be trained in each type of livewood weapon, should they find themselves using another on the battlefield.

Training had long become simple practice; Castor had nothing new to teach them, and they could all predict the exercises without him needing to call them out.

Castor then ordered them to set up for the mock metalurk routine. He had half the men become defenders, while the other half pretended to be the ravenous creatures trying to break the line.

They paired off, one defender and one mock-metalurk. The objective was for the defenders to lay a well-placed thrust against the attacker without being touched. A touch from a mock-metalurk meant death by sharp claws.

After a few rounds of spear practice, each side swapping occasionally, they ran through similar exercises and routines with the other weapons then broke off into their own groups of specialized weapons, sparring with each other to further hone their skills.

Castor took up a staff, gesturing for Vance to spar with him. The man happily complied; his men loved testing their skills against him. None could best him when it came to the staff, but that did little to stop them trying.

As the Steelwoods danced along to the rhythm of battle, keeping mobile and constantly on the move, Castor quickly joined them. There were no thoughts other than the fight, leaving poor Vance with no opportunity to win without Castor becoming distracted.

Vance was a formidable foe, one of the better spear users amongst the Steelwoods, but he still could not catch up to Castor's speed and precision. Castor used the full reach of his weapon, putting his trust in it completely. He spun, shifted his feet, quickly leapt left and right, anything to keep Vance on his toes.

As Castor called the sparring to a halt, the Steelwoods slumped around the pails of water, gulping from the wooden cups.

"Gods, Castor," Vance said between deep breaths. "If there was ever a day I thought I could best you, I figured it would be today. I can't believe I actually thought you might be even the slightest bit distracted."

Castor looked at Vance quizzically, raising a brow as the Steelwoods chuckled.

Albert kicked out at Vance. "That's his clever way of letting you know that we know, Captain."

Castor looked around at his Steelwoods, all the faces smiling in reassurance.

"I'm sorry, Captain," Vance said. "It's my fault they know. A friend of mine saw you yesterday and I thought it best if all the Steelwoods found out before it spread into anything else."

"And what is it you heard?" Castor kept his tone serious, but not authoritatively; he didn't want his men to think they were in trouble.

Yet.

"Not much, other than you were clearly tired and taking a rest against the side of a building. It happens with age, sir, nothing to worry about," Vance teased.

The man was barely a couple years Castor's junior, but the playful jab tactfully concealed the truth. "Being your superior ages me faster than most. It takes a lot of energy to get you to listen and understand, you stone brained twit."

The Steelwoods laughed, not giving Vance an opportunity to retort. They taunted him, repeating the insult in various new ways, but thankfully Vance knew how to take a joke.

"You're lucky that you're my Captain, sir."

"Or what? You'd try beat me with a stick? You already tried that and didn't end well for you."

Vance laughed, Castor's cheeks began to tire, making him realize just how long he had been smiling for. Training was always a good way to work out emotions, whether they were directly confronted or not. He felt reinvigorated as he joked with his men, feeling much better than he had. His muscles were now sluggish from the training rather than reluctance to move.

Castor glimpsed a familiar figure striding toward the barracks. The general. He thought that seeing the man would dampen his mood, but he was delighted to find that his spirits were still high.

He decided to carry the mood over to General Deven. What better time to confront someone than the present? Castor nodded to his men and made his way over.

The general caught a glimpse of Castor, but continued towards the barracks without pause and entered the building before Castor could reach him.

He shadowed the man until they reached the general's office, where Deven left the door open for his pursuer to enter.

"What is it, Castor?" Deven was abrupt and direct, not bothering to conceal his irritation.

Castor closed the door, and that had Deven look up, confused and annoyed. "What did you do, General? What was your plan?" Castor did his best to keep his voice level and calm. He didn't want things to spiral out of control and have the general pull rank.

"In regard to what, exactly?"

"I get the feeling you already know."

"I do, but I want to hear it," the general said. "You come here to ask me something, so stop playing games. Chin up, chest out, face me."

Castor took a step forward, lifted his chin, straightened his posture, and slightly scowled at Deven. "What was your plan for my nephew? Did you have him killed for something I did?"

The general deflated, slumping into his chair and rubbing his hands down his face. "I knew this day would come, I only hoped it was after the Red Sea and when I eventually retire. I don't suppose it can wait until then?"

"No."

The general turned away from Castor. It was hard to tell what the man was thinking, but Castor thought he had seen a slight glimmer of regret. "Fine. There is no point in hiding a truth you seem to already know. It won't matter much now, even if we both survive through the Red Sea, I'll retire in a few years, and we won't have to deal with each other any longer."

"Unless you continue to refuse me a chance at General."

"I stand by what I said, and I stand by what I've done. Mistakes happen, but I own up to what I did. Things just spiraled out of my control. When you made Captain, I could tell you were ambitious for my position. I do not take someone trying to get rid of me lightly. I gave you a few months, sometimes subtly hinting and not so subtly demanding that you remember your rank and stay there. Who knows, I might not have given you a bad review if you weren't so active in trying to replace me."

"Get to the part about my nephew."

"I am, but you have to understand why I did what I did, and how it quickly got out of my hands." the man sighed. "I thought a good way to slow you down was with a little bit of family trouble. I wanted someone close to you arrested, that way you would turn your attention towards them. My plan was to have your nephew seem like he had a drug addiction, and if you had a close relative arrested for such a serious charge, you would likely want to keep it quiet, so that way I had something over you."

"You're starting to sound as if you didn't have my nephew killed."

"That's because I didn't. My plans were in full motion. Your nephew was arrested, and I would wait a short amount of time for you to retrieve him before I came forward, wanting to crush your spirits and make you an obedient captain I could trust. Those plans went askew when the poor boy was mistaken for someone else. That part was genuinely a mistake. I do not know how they made such a horrendous error, but it was out of my control. By the time I had heard about it, it was too late."

Castor kept his mouth closed, fighting the urge to berate the man. Deven clearly didn't blame himself for putting Patrick in the position to be mistaken in the first place, and if Castor chewed him out about it, then Deven would likely find reason to strip Castor of his position. He had spent the past three years delicately stepping around the general; Castor did his job well, kept clear of any illegal activity – other than the risky situation of hiring the Seekers – and he tiptoed around the general's view whenever he could. Castor couldn't waste those years by screaming at his superior now. As much as it felt right to do so, as much as it felt necessary to make Deven understand, Castor couldn't risk it.

Even with the answer, Castor felt empty.

"Like I said," Deven continued, looking up at Castor. "It was out of my control the moment someone else wedged themselves in where they shouldn't. I did not have your nephew killed. I may have played a few games in an effort to pressure you, but I do not go as far as murder."

The man spoke as if he were a glistening star, rising above the dirt and grime of the criminal underworld of the city, acting as if he prided himself on not being a part of them. But he was no better than the thugs. The general was filth. The kind of filth that didn't get cleaned from the drab greys of everyday clothing. He was the dirt that clung to your boots after a rainy day, a toxin that led the army.

"I'd say I believe you, but then we'd both be liars." Castor spat and stormed out of the office. He had gotten his answer, what had he expected it to be? What did he expect would happen?

The general showed no remorse, not even a glimpse of sympathy. He passed off his actions as a cruel accident and that was that. How much did the man truly despise Castor? How could he just sit by while an innocent boy was wrongly executed by his indirect actions?

The man was a plague on the city. Castor had always thought the metalurks were the biggest threat they faced, but it turned out he was wrong.

18

Elias sat in his room, stomach churning with anxiety. The Day of Sacrifice was just around the corner, and despite having around twenty years to prepare for it, he was scared. His father's illness had worsened but had also somehow plateaued. Warin had lost some of his color, had become weak, unable to perform some certain tasks in his day-to-day life.

Understandably, it made Elias' father increasingly hostile and distraught.

His father was prone to fits of rage when the servants attempted to help him with ordinary tasks, which then led into excessive coughing. Elias tried to convince his father, again and again, to just relax and let the servants help. Yet his father would just yell and repeat that he was still an able-bodied young man, as if saying it often made it a truth.

Warin wanted Elias to continue his training, cancelling all other subjects – except for the new livewood class, Elias insisted on keeping that. They had just begun to explore how to craft with livewood by extracting just the right amount of treeblood from the wood before draining it entirely. It made the wood firmer, but not too firm to carve. Elias was thoroughly enjoying the process, something he wanted to keep doing for at least another few sessions, he had something he hoped to complete by the end of the week.

Merek spent more time training Elias, even going so far as staying with Elias outside of their sessions, providing some comfort about his ailing father. Merek had been upset to hear of Warin's illness, and Elias could tell Merek had come to the same conclusion: Warin would die. It seemed clear to everyone but Warin. His body was visibly weakening, he spent longer resting, and had difficulty eating his preordained meals. Elias spent each meal with his father, ensuring he ate as much as possible. The food did little good to a man who rejected his own sickness. It looked as if the man was clinging onto life, waiting to see the results of Elias' duel. His father wanted to see what would happen to the last hope of the Noldin family. It would either die with Elias or allow Warin to move peaceably into the afterlife knowing that his son would carry on their family name.

With Warin in a frail condition, and the day of the duel approaching, Elias was given a little more freedom to leave the household. He was not allowed to stray too far from home, keeping within the limitations set out by the city so he would keep clear of any of the Daolin family.

With his newfound – albeit still quite restricted – freedom, Elias frequently took walks to calm his anxiety. It did little, but at least the open space stopped him from feeling trapped in the house.

Upon one of his walks, Geraldine had agreed to accompany him. She seemed reluctant to partake in anything that wasn't directly work for her, but Elias knew she would crumple eventually. She had a soft spot for him.

"Geraldine." Elias broke their silent walk, keeping his voice low. "How can I ever repay you for being my personal messenger? The letters have truly been a blessing upon my still heart, I can feel it beating once again. I owe you a deep gratitude."

He would have thought by now that Geraldine knew how to accept his compliments, he had praised her many times before, yet she still blushed and became a little embarrassed, unsure how to respond. "It is fine, sir. It is a task that I am able to achieve for you, and as your servant, I only wish to do what I can."

"It's more than that, even if you don't want to openly admit it. I know you care for me more than your professionalism dictates. You have even increased the frequency of trading letters over the past few weeks. These favors are something I cannot possibly repay."

Geraldine blushed but turned her head away almost as if in shame. Elias shook his head; he had surely misread her reaction. "I do not expect repayment," Geraldine said. Elias was certain the waver in her voice had become more than just embarrassment, but he often had trouble figuring Geraldine out.

"Are you all right?" Elias raised an eyebrow, cocking his head slightly as if a different angle might help him with an answer.

"I am fine, sir. Just a little anxious."

"Anxious about what?"

"Your duel, sir."

"Oh, I see. It's gotten awfully close, hasn't it? Almost is if it's sprung up on me, catching me off guard. Despite knowing about it my entire life, I am still surprised that it comes."

"I have been dreading the day ever since you somehow convinced me to explore the town with you the first time. I know it is unprofessional, but I care for you as a friend, sir. I am worried of what might occur."

"Geraldine, that is incredibly unprofessional of you. You care for me as a friend? How dare you, I should fire you right now," Elias teased, trying to ease the situation a little, not only for Geraldine but himself as well.

"If you didn't fire me the night you convinced me to drink until I vomited on your pants that you cared so much for at the time, then I doubt you'll ever fire me."

Elias chuckled, expressing mock shock. Geraldine had rarely retorted to one of his taunts, it was so uncharacteristic for her to do, but it made the moments even more glorious.

"I'm sorry, sir. I'm a little on edge today."

"Something wrong?"

Geraldine stopped walking, grabbing Elias' full attention. "Have you talked to your correspondent about telling him who you are?"

Elias frowned. "Have you been reading the letters I send?"

Geraldine's eyes widened, fear and shock taking over her completely. "No, sir! I have no idea what you had written. I am so sorry, sir! Please, I have not read any of it!"

The poor girl as on the verge of tears, but Elias quickly stepped closer, trying to calm her down. "It's fine, Geraldine, honestly. It must have been pure coincidence. I know you wouldn't read my letters. My last one mentioned about the idea of meeting up. I'm struggling with it, honestly, and my stomach churns as I await his reply. I don't know if he reciprocates the same thoughts or not."

Geraldine nodded slowly. "I think that whatever he says next, you should meet with him. Only once. Maybe even just introduce yourselves if you can't find a time to meet before your duel."

Elias had considered just demanding a meet up, but everything in his body screamed at him for even thinking about it. He was scared that his correspondent might want to keep the mystery, finding it more tantalizing than the truth. And when his correspondent, this man Elias cared so deeply for, did discover the truth about his identity, what would his reaction be? Would he end things? Knowing the implications of daring to fall in love with a champion? Would he secretly hate him for making them meet right before his death? That would likely emotionally scar him deeper than if they remained somewhat anonymous.

The choices were at war within him, not one side gaining on the other. How could he declare a victor when they both had negative connotations? He wanted Geraldine to be right. He wanted reassurance from her that it was the right thing to do. He wanted his correspondent to make the same decision. He wanted other people to choose for him. Elias knew exactly what he wanted, but he still could not make the choice. Did he want others to make that choice so they would bear the brunt of the blame?

Geraldine watched him carefully. "Master, I hope I am not overstepping my boundaries, but you have declared me your friend on several occasions. Meet with each other."

Elias looked at her; her conviction strong. She wanted them to meet. She understood their situation – at least to a certain degree – and she remained so self-assured that meeting was the right thing to do. He hoped his correspondent felt the same. "When are you planning on retrieving his letter?"

"I hope to be able to cross paths with him the beginning of next week."

"That doesn't give us much time to organize before my duel. I'll be wrecked with duties. Once I receive the letter, I need you to return mine as fast as you can. We'll have to rush a little if I am to meet him."

Geraldine smiled, her lovely eyes twinkling with hope and happiness. "You're making the right decision."

Somehow, it did little to reassure him. He felt a bit light-headed at the prospect, happiness and anxiety once again at war within him

On the one hand, Elias was happy to meet his correspondent yet again.

On the other, how was he going to tell the man face-to-face that Elias would surely die?

* * *

Elias' father insisted on attending the training sessions with Merek, wanting to assess his son's capabilities with his own eyes. Warin leant on his son – complaining about not needing support most of the time – as they walked through the halls towards the training room. It had been quite a while since Elias and his father had walked together, it really put Warin's failing health into perspective.

His father hobbled and quivered, each step seemed painful, but he was adamant in not walking at a slow pace. He refused to let his body get the better of him, refusing to be seen as the frail, elderly man he had become.

Elias tried several times to encourage his father to slow down, but the man tossed the comments aside, even going so far as to try and pry his arm from Elias' shoulder. But Elias held his ground, occasionally raised his voice, and refused to let his father stubbornly ignore his illness.

Warin should have reprimanded him, should have scolded him for taking such tones, but didn't. Elias wasn't entirely certain if it was from lack of energy, or that his father knew that he was right. Warin wanted to see his son train, he had no right to complain about getting there in his condition.

Merek waited by the sealed training room, making sure the halls had been clear upon their arrival so that he could open the door. Once inside, Elias helped his father to a chair where he could watch the sparring.

"I hope he is all right to leave his bed," Merek commented quietly as they shuffled into their armor

"It was his choice," Elias whispered back. "I doubt I could have refused him. If I said no, he would likely try to walk here himself just to spite me."

"I don't mean to sound disrespectful, but despite your father's age, it seems as if he never learned to care for his own body."

"Years of drinking and eating little brought him to where he is today. I doubt even death could scare my father into treating himself right. He still probably sneaks in wine when I'm not around. He's been completely barred from the substance, yet I'm sure I'll find empty bottles stashed underneath his bed like an insolent child."

Elias had not meant for the words to sound so bitter, but he was truly annoyed that his father insisted on coming to watch the sparring when he should have been saving his strength to attend the duel. Every time Elias looked at his father, he could only see death's visage, as if the reaper had already claimed Warin.

"Your father appears to be of sound mind still, perhaps he is aware?"

"Do you honestly think a logical man would risk his health as much?" Elias shook his head. "No. A logical man wouldn't have put himself in this position in the first place."

"Well, that's where you were headed before you stopped drinking."

Elias stopped tightening the strap around his leg. Merek was right, it *had been* where he had been heading. But he had barely anything to drink in months. Ever since the letters began, he had

239

not felt the same urge for wines as he once had. It wasn't a conscious decision, the thrill and excitement he got from drinking had been replaced with the intoxicating aura of the letters, of the words that wonderful man would send him.

It was as if Elias had forgotten wine existed entirely. If he had not met the man, would he still be drinking? Did his father know about his declining health long before the doctor had told Elias?

He looked at his father, seeing for the first time what might have become of himself. Even if he survived the duel, would his drinking have stopped? The pressure of being champion would be gone, but that was far from releasing the pressures of life after that. Elias would have ended up like his father. Resenting life, family abandoning him in their deaths, raising a son only to be presented as stock for the city to sacrifice.

His life may still head there yet. But would he be able to resist the temptations of wine? To act as a companion on lonely nights? *Best not to think about it.*

When Elias finished donning his armor, Warin called him over as if to inspect the quality of the suit himself. Elias watched as his father's grizzled expression turned somber, as his fingers ran over points of the armor.

"It's remarkable what they can do with metal," his father said. "The right person can mend the holes just as if it were livewood." Warin's voice was weak, fighting back the quiver of grim memories. His fingers traced over the torso of the armor, stopping at a particular point in the plackart. Those fingers seemed to be feeling a memory, but Elias chose not to question. It was clear from his father's eyes that it was a topic best not brought up.

His father continued to inspect the armor as if he hadn't seen it in years. Once he was satisfied with the way it had been strapped on, he instructed Merek to run Elias through a proper duel, no guidance, no mentoring, just raw talent.

It was likely the session was always going to be just that; Merek had nothing left to teach other than honing Elias' skills and buffing out his flaws.

The sparring went as expected, Elias held the upper hand throughout most of the fight. Merek had slipped behind Elias in speed, only years of expertise helping his trainer keep pace. Having only one trainer meant that Elias' techniques were also Merek's; the moves predictable.

At least to them they were, Warin watched with a hollow expression, making his father difficult to read. Warin only spoke to demand another round for him to observe. Elias became uncertain if his father was here to observe his skills, or something more. He had been paying close attention to Elias' fighting sessions over the years, he was not sure what else his father had expected.

"Again," Warin called out after the Elias had won yet another round.

"No. Breath first," Elias replied as he and Merek panted heavily. He as not sure if his father even knew how toilsome wearing metal armor was during the fight; his father had never been champion, so he doubted he had ever actually worn the armor himself.

"Again. There will be no time to catch your breath in the arena."

"I said breath first," Elias said. "We will not be sparring this long in the arena. Once the covers come off the blades, the duel will be remarkably quick."

"Elias, do you recall how many duels I've personally witnessed?"

"Two."

"And how many have I been told about?"

"I don't know, three?"

"That would make five. That's how long our family has been dueling. Five duels over one-hundred years, soon to be six over one-hundred and twenty. How many have you witnessed?"

"None."

"I know I have explained this on multiple occasions, but I get the feeling it has slipped your mind. Now, tell me, who do you think has more knowledge on how these duels fair?"

Elias stared at Warin through the slots of his helmet, matching his father's stern gaze.

"Again," Warin repeated firmly. Elias reluctantly took his starting stance, Merek matching with his own, and the two began sparring once more.

They sparred two more times before Warin seemed satisfied enough to allow them a break. They drank heavily from the pitchers of water, not having been allowed a moment to drink until now.

Warin said nothing as he allowed them to rest. His eyes were fixated on an empty space on the floor, deep in thought.

Elias knew that he should likely wait for his father to speak, but he was not about to sit around all day waiting for it. "What are your thoughts on my techniques, Father?"

Warin did not immediately respond, barely moving his gaze off the floor, "Fine. It was just fine."

Just fine? That's reassuring? "What was the point in observing me if you aren't going to talk about it?"

"I don't know," Warin snapped. "Take me back to my quarters."

Merek appeared disappointed, moving to take off his armor. Elias was admittedly a little annoyed. His father was wasting their time by keeping his thoughts to himself, but Elias was not even sure if he wanted to hear those thoughts. His patience was growing thin, he had no time to play games, and decided to let the matter drop. If Warin wanted to be an irritable, stubborn man, then so be it.

Elias removed his armor in quiet infuriation, doing his best to ignore the pleading looks from Merek. His father remained quiet as the two finished the process of cleaning their armor, then Elias moved to quickly support his father, who was attempting to walk on his own. The man was hobbling, legs shaking with every step, and trying his best to keep his back as straight as possible.

Warin initially refused Elias' help, but caught himself before expressing it, taking his son's arm.

Merek covered the armors on the table and opened the door, giving Elias the signal that the halls were clear. As Elias escorted his father out of the room, Merek gave him a sympathetic look, before closing the door behind them and calling out to him.

"Elias, it is needless to repeat myself about your techniques. There is naught else I can comment on that you do not already know. We'll spar a few more times before your duel, keep your body active and used to the movement. Well done, young sir."

Elias gave him a nod in acknowledgement, but his father remained silent, keeping his eyes on the halls as if purposely avoiding the conversation. Elias gestured for his father to walk, allowing him to move at his own pace.

"I will order a cane for you," Elias commented, not so much a suggestion as a statement of fact.

"I don't need a damned cane," Warin – unsurprisingly – retorted, unable to refuse any form of help he did not specifically request. His illness had certainly made him grow more irascible. It was as though his father was angry about dying rather than melancholic.

"I don't care for your opinion on this matter, Father. If you wish to get out of bed, you will use a cane. You've ignored nearly all of the doctor's advice, and you constantly try to reassure everyone you are not in pain when even an eyeless cat can see your legs waver without proper support. You are getting a cane, and that is final."

Warin's face soured, his brow deepening into a scowl, but he kept his mouth closed.

Elias assisted his father onto his bed before dismissing himself, not another word uttered between them as he closed the door to Warin's chamber. Fighting the urge to slump against the wall from exhaustion, Elias slowly made his way to his own chambers, his thoughts finding their own way back to his correspondent and the prospect of meeting him.

He would need to gain permission to enter the town once again, it would be too risky to have his correspondent meet too close to his home. Despite the plan to reveal his identity, he did not want anyone reporting it to his father.

Elias lay on his bed, somehow too drained to even sleep. His stomach wanted to ache and toil, reminding him that the Day of Sacrifice would soon arrive, and he would have to fight for his life. Fight to continue living to see the fruits of his efforts bloom, allowing him to reap the benefits proper.

Perhaps then, in the city besieged by mindless beasts, food supplies stifled, death of old age reserved for only the noble and lucky, could he hope to find a semblance of peace.

19

Varin had proved to be quite the adequate teacher for Maggie. He showed her simple and effective ways to remain unseen and unheard. He coached her in the conduct of seeming innocent, and even worked with her on ways she could use her own instability as a cover if she were caught.

Maggie seemed like she was in some strange kind of limbo. Part of her felt that she was perfectly sane, but simply stressed to the point that other's thought she was mentally ill, and she could use that to her benefit. The other part of her was uncertain if it was just an act. Either way, she felt she was capable enough to manipulate others to get what she wanted.

She had no reason to distrust the Seekers just yet. They didn't appear to be manipulating her for their own nefarious reasons. They gave her solid information about Castor and had been upfront about her role. She would build up to a particular job for them, and if she got caught at any stage, she would feign insanity and never breathe a word of the Seekers. They weren't trying to trick her in any way; they told her she would be a sacrifice, and if she got caught, she would be on her own. If she was successful, then the Seekers got the information they were after.

But first, they had promised to help her find her son's killer.

Maggie had never known who to blame, understanding there were likely multiple people involved, but there had never been any doubt that someone in the Seekers had sold out her son. She held that firm belief for years, never wavering once, Castor's information had confirmed her suspicions, and now it was time to find that person.

After spending days shadowing random citizens as practice, she was finally permitted to pursue the Sandmen. Varin was her partner on the case, having made the promise in the first place.

She described to him the group of Sandmen she had been keeping an eye on, and Varin had smiled as she went into detail. He commented on how she would make the perfect Seeker and had already been playing her role well before he ever approached her.

Maggie was uncertain if she felt elated by the compliment in her skills, or worried that she had mischievous talents in the first place.

Varin already had information on the Sandmen in general; the Seekers naturally tried to follow them everywhere to find who they sold Dreams to – it was an easy source for blackmail.

The Seekers had information on several dens in which the Sandmen produced Dreams. Varin's plan was to spend a day observing each one, trying to note anyone of importance before picking specific targets to shadow. It would be a slow process, but Varin assured her these were the right steps to take to ensure they found every piece of information they could to discover the person responsible. Maggie had trouble holding back her excitement and enthusiasm for finally going after the person who betrayed her son to the guards.

Maggie and Varin hid in an alleyway down the street from where one of the Sandmen's dens was located. They were close enough to be able to observe people entering and exiting, but far enough away so they weren't easily spotted. They took notes of each person who came and went, marking down any differences in appearance if they existed. Varin let Maggie take charge, following her lead while occasionally providing some suggestions of his own, just to nudge her in the right direction.

Time had passed quickly when they had first arrived; Maggie was excited to finally get the mission underway, but her eagerness dimmed as time went on and she did not recognize anyone. She sat against the wall, facing the den so she could easily observe. Varin sat opposite, keeping out of sight and only peering around the corner to aid Maggie when requested.

The sun was beginning to set, soon they would no longer be able to keep watch. It seemed unlikely the Sandmen would conveniently light torches at the entrance of the den so Maggie and Varin could continue to watch throughout the night.

Maggie shifted slightly, her patience wearing a little thin.

Varin eyed her. "You know, this job doesn't have guarantees. You won't always get a result on the first day. Perhaps some idle chatter might help alleviate a bit of your boredom."

"I'm not bored," Maggie responded, not entirely sure if she believed her words. The work was a little dull, but she couldn't complain. She would sit here for a week if it meant so much as finding a hint to the right Sandman.

"Perhaps not but let us give it a try anyway. I'm sure you have some questions about the Seekers, and even though you are not technically a part of our organization, I'm happy to answer questions you might have that pertain to us."

Maggie's eyes flickered towards him for a moment then back to the den; she had just given away her own curiosity. She could see Varin smile on the edge of her vision, sighing as she kept her eyes on the den. "Fine, there are a few things I'm interested in knowing."

"Ask away."

"How did you know about the information my brother had? Did you gather some information to persuade me to join you?"

"Good question, better assumption, but unfortunately not quite how it went down. Your brother actually hired us to find that information. Well, at least point him in the right direction of a particular person, we gathered the rest ourselves. You never know when information comes in handy."

Castor actually hired the Seekers for me? I shouldn't have pushed him that far. Maggie's stomach sank a little. She had no idea her brother would go to such lengths, risking his position just to appease her. However, her guilt did not dull her intuition. "My brother hired you before you approached me. Does that mean you were gathering information on me to hold against him?"

247

Varin smiled, not bothering to conceal the truth. "Are you sure you do not want to be a Seeker? You piece things together awfully quick. That is true, your brother hired us and as protocol, we gather what we can on anyone who hires us. Think of it as a safety net; we can't have him luring us into a trap. We needed some form of collateral in case he ever tried to arrest us, he is Captain of the East Gate, after all."

"You were going to use me against my brother?"

"That was our initial idea, yes. However, there was nothing we could find to hold against him. Rather, we stopped looking once we found something else of interest."

"The records."

Varin nodded. Maggie was struggling with how to react. It was both amusing and painfully annoying that she was indirectly the reason the records she worked hard to keep hidden were discovered. She could still try blame the Seekers, though now it felt slightly misplaced.

"Luckily, we didn't end up having to go that far. Castor seems like a genuinely honest man. He sticks by his words, making him a trustworthy fellow. We decided to stop looking for leverage on him altogether."

Maggie nodded along. She doubted there was anything other than hiring the Seekers that they could use against her brother. Unless she did something stupid, such as getting arrested while snooping around. It could possibly affect his chances at making general even further. But she needed to find her son's murderers. She would have to profusely apologize to Castor, though she wasn't sure it would mean anything if her actions ended up with him being stripped of his title for having a criminal sister. Perhaps even going so far as to have a murderer for a sister. She didn't know what she was going to do when she found the people responsible for Patrick's death; she hadn't really considered it. Her focus was entirely spent on finding them, and hadn't really thought beyond that.

Her anger grew as she thought about what had happened three years ago. Anger and distress was a dangerous combination of emotions to have. Maggie felt herself hanging by a thread, not knowing where she would fall once it broke.

Night soon fell and Varin called an end to the day's work. He would not risk getting closer just yet, there were still other dens to observe before taking more risks.

Maggie reluctantly stood, following Varin as he kept out of sight. She practiced muffling her footsteps as Varin did, mimicking his steps, keeping a watchful eye on how his foot landed on the stone. It proved difficult, but thankfully no one was around to have noticed.

Varin departed, leaving Maggie to walk home alone. Her stomach grumbled, reminding her that she had forgotten to eat during her stakeout. She had not picked up her weekly rations, so she would have to starve tonight and hope she had time to gather them tomorrow.

Maggie entered her house, grabbing a candle to set flame to the streetlight. She lit a few candles in her home then searched her cupboards hoping for remnants of food, but failing to find any. She drank from her pitcher of water, barely enough left to fill half the cup, but it would satisfy her enough for the night.

She sat at the table, in her usual chair, thinking. It was strange how the moment she had begun working with the Seekers, her house somehow felt a little safer, as if it had lost a pair of eyes lurking within. The feeling had not completely gone; she still made sure the floorboards would creak underneath the weight of a person. If the Sandmen discovered her keeping a watchful eye on them, they might try to dispose of her before she discovered anything incriminating.

Her stomach growled once more. Sleep would help ignore the growing pains. She slowly climbed the stairs, testing each step to ensure it gave a satisfyingly loud creak, before moving into her bedroom and giving it a thorough study before closing the wooden latch on her door and climbing into bed.

* * *

Maggie surged awake to the sound of knocking on her door. She quickly clambered out of bed, knowing it would be Varin coming to collect her. Maggie rushed downstairs and left her house in the dim light of dawn. Varin had suggested they make the most of natural light, even if it meant watching a house full of sleeping people. Maggie had not argued with the logic, expecting some of the Sandmen to have either woken early or stayed up the entire night to make deals.

The two spent the day observing, and much like the day before, they did not recognize anyone.

Maggie began to question the plan, wondering if they were really going to sit at each den and hope for the best. Still, what other choice did they have? They needed to find at least one lead to follow. Thankfully, Varin had retrieved some of his personal rations and split them with Maggie after hearing her stomach rumble and complain about being empty. She chose not to collect her own rations, preferring to stay on site in case she missed anything important.

The next day, Maggie returned to her work at the library. She had feigned being sick so she could observe the Sandmen dens, but she worried if she played it too far that Heleen would begin to worry for her, and the last thing Maggie needed right now was to draw attention to herself.

Heleen greeted her in her usual manner, expressing her happiness to see Maggie in a healthy state. Ironically, the comment had made Maggie feel a little ill, the kind words stabbing into her like livewood spikes, knowing that Heleen was genuinely worried over a lie.

Maggie tried to stray away from Heleen for a while, keeping her distance and pretending to be enveloped in her work. The library was quiet, as usual. The general populace had little interest in the knowledge held here when they struggled to survive. Thankfully, there were still those in the city determined to improve their situation. Many of the city's researchers often delved into the old Malvarkian tomes, hoping to find information or a new angle.

The improvements to the city had long stagnated, they could grow a large number of crops, were able to feed little livestock, and learned how to stretch their supplies as thin as possible. The only thing they could currently improve was the expansion of their crop fields, but they feared straying too far from the city and getting caught out by the metalurks.

Several of the libraries frequent visitors were researchers into the mysterious creatures that pounded at their walls. The only information the city possessed on them was the research they themselves had gathered over the years. Old Malvarkians didn't mention them anywhere, but that didn't stop the researchers from being thorough and checking every book.

The only new information they could find would be in the old records Maggie had found that were no longer in her possession. She had tried asking Varin about them, but he quickly ended her line of questioning, promising to tell her once they had something more conclusive.

She wondered if the Seekers would ever reveal the information but knowing how they operated, it was unlikely they would do so for free. They were always looking for a beneficial angle and holding onto a key to the past could quickly take them as far as a personal meeting with The Voice. Though that seemed like an implausibility. The Voice did not present themselves to the public unless they had an announcement to make, which usually pertained to new or changed laws. They claimed to be the connection between the Gods and humankind, but with the growing scarcity in appearances, it seemed they'd grown accustomed to their solitude.

The Voice lived in their own little world, and the Gods had long abandoned their struggles. They claimed the livewood trees were a blessing, but what good was a blessing if it barely kept you alive? A true blessing would be ridding the creatures once and for all. Nearly two-hundred years and not a God-given sign the monsters were disappearing any time soon.

Maggie dusted the shelves, trying to make the place seem less dreary. The hidden room had had its door replaced with a proper one, now functioning as a supply room. Maggie deflated whenever she glanced over at it, reminding her of what it once held and what had become of it.

As Maggie worked, Heleen would occasionally check up on her. Maggie would poorly pretend everything was fine before finally confessing she felt slightly ill. All an act in preparation to skip work tomorrow to observe another Sandman den. Maggie knew her feigned illness would be reported to Audrey, but she would address that issue when the time came. For now, she'd try to get out of any meetings with Audrey to allow more time for personal matters.

The attack horn jolted Maggie from her thoughts, and she made her way to Heleen, waiting for the remaining visitors to leave.

"Will you be okay, dear?" Heleen's expression was soft and empathetic, clearly worried about Maggie's claims at feeling ill. She was such a sweet woman who did not deserve the games Maggie played with her.

"I'll be fine, Heleen. I'll speak with Castor after the wave. If I don't turn up to work tomorrow, it will be because I'm resting."

"Of course, dear. Take your time. Drink plenty of water and don't do anything strenuous."

Maggie nodded and smiled, guilt swelling up in her throat as the poor woman's eyes showed concern.

She turned away, walking home to wait for her brother.

* * *

Castor had once again remained unscathed, alleviating a little of Maggie's tension. Her brother was a formidable soldier, but that didn't stop her worrying about him on the battlefield. One slight mistake, taking a step in the wrong direction, reacting a split second too late, and it could all end abruptly.

Thankfully, he was fine for another few days.

He seemed skeptical about her claim of being ill. She hadn't told him she was working with the Seekers, but he could already guess she was up to something. Maggie felt like a hypocrite; she had berated her brother for withholding information, yet she was now doing the same. She couldn't tie Castor with the Seekers any more than she already had; it would surely prevent his promotion, and likely strip him of his rank.

And Varin was right about Castor – he was an honest man; she doubted he would completely accept what she was doing, even if it was hunting down her son's murderers. Perhaps she'd tell him one day, though it seemed unlikely. Castor would always be a soldier. There would be no right time to tell him about the Seekers.

Her brother left, still not believing her feigned illness, but she'd given up trying to be convincing. There would be no persuading Castor that she was doing the right thing.

She set out early the next day, meeting Varin in front of her home before he had the opportunity to knock. They planted themselves in preparation of spending the day observing another den. As usual, Maggie would do most of the watching, detailing anyone who entered or exited the premises.

Midday came, and Varin pulled out the rations he had brought along, sharing a portion with Maggie. She thanked him, slowly picking at it to stretch it out for as long as possible.

"So," Varin spoke between bites, "I've gotta ask. How did you know your son was murdered? A lucky guess? Or, did you actually notice anything around the time?"

Maggie thought back on the painful events before answering. "A mother's intuition."

Varin considered her answer, nodding as if he understood. "Something I suppose I can relate to."

Maggie raised her eyebrow. "You have children?"

"Of course. The law's the law."

"I just thought you would have found a way around that law."

"Because I'm a Seeker?"

"Well… yeah."

Varin chuckled, pointing to the den to return Maggie's focus. "I don't think the Magistrates give exemptions for being a Seeker."

"I just thought that because you're…" Maggie trailed off, no longer certain what she was trying to say.

"I'm a what? Criminal?"

Maggie shrugged.

"Well, I can't deny that, but a criminal can still have children. I still have the right to a family."

"I didn't mean it li—"

"It's all right," Varin interrupted, raising a hand to stop her. "I suppose I can understand your reasoning. To begin with, there is nothing stopping a criminal from having a family. The Sandmen you're watching now would all have relatives, many would have children themselves already. The laws do not care about what you do, only if your body is physically able to reproduce. You probably thought they were too busy enjoying being a criminal to have kids?"

Maggie shrugged, not knowing precisely why she thought what she did, but his reasoning seemed close enough.

"Not all of us enjoy being a criminal. Not all of us were criminals before falling in love and starting a family." Varin's voiced grew softer as he spoke, taking on a serious tone. Maggie felt a little guilty for having assumed the man was simply a vessel for the Seekers instead of being his own person.

Much like herself. She had a family before turning to what was legally perceived as a crime yet to her was the right thing to do. She was here to stop a murderess Sandman, perhaps it would lead to both her own personal revenge and ridding their city of a monster. Even if the Sandman did have a family, he destroyed others by selling Dreams and turning over young boys to the guards. There would be no justification for his actions.

"What made you become one? And in what order?" Maggie asked, her eyes quickly flicking over to Varin, who was staring at the ground.

"Family then criminal. Accidentally fell into it but chose to stay once I was shown the benefits."

"How do you accidentally fall into crime?"

"Well, I saw something I shouldn't have, the Seekers discovered that, convinced me to withhold the information from the guards, instead dangling the threat in front of the man I saw, and now my family gets a part of his weekly rations. My children no longer have to starve each day, and only I run the risk of getting caught. I'd say it's a good enough trade."

Maggie listened intently while keeping her gaze fixated on the people entering and exiting the den. She found herself sympathizing with Varin, though she did wonder if he gave her an embellished truth to make himself appear more sympathetic than he was. "So, you took the food out of the mouth of another to give to your family?"

"No," Varin responded sharply, as if offended by the question. "Nobles are given more rations than the rest of us. The piece he's giving me each week still leaves his family with more food than my own. I do not feel guilty for taking it, either. It's almost as if I'm taking the scraps they would soon throw away because their noble bellies are full after gorging themselves."

His words turned bitter, and Maggie knew she'd found a sore spot, though it was a sore spot most of the lower population shared. They had to squeeze their rations between all family members to make sure it lasted the week, while the nobility were allowed to eat comfortably – they didn't go through the harsh reality of those who weren't quite as lucky at birth. Maggie tried not to think about, knowing her status would never change.

But perhaps now it could?

Not for herself, of course, she had no children to feed anymore, but perhaps she could find something to help other struggling families? Something to think about once her jobs were done. Maybe she would join the Seekers after all, depending on how the properly operated and if they would force her to do any work she did not want to do.

Maggie opened her mouth but paused, the question jamming in her throat as her eyes widened in disbelief. A man had approached the den. His plait dyed bright green. A man about her age. A man she remembered vividly.

The same man that she'd seen with James the past few times she had gone to see him.

James had been talking to a Sandman. He shared drinks with a Sandman. He had been making *friends* with a Sandman.

He doesn't know. He doesn't know that the man he's been spending time with is a Sandman. She had to tell him. She had to save him from a grievous mistake.

"Maggie? What is it?" Varin asked.

Maggie looked at the sky, cursing as she saw how bright it was. *He isn't drinking just yet. Gods, where would he be?*

"Maggie?"

She turned back to the green-plaited man, watching as he entered the building. She needed to act, but she couldn't. Her body shook, screaming at her to move, but her mind could not give it a direction.

"Maggie?" Varin called louder and Maggie finally turned to him. "What did you see?"

"Someone I actually recognize. I didn't think we would have seen anything just sitting here like this but... Gods, we actually found something."

"Is he the man we're after?"

Maggie's tongue tripped over itself as she was trying to piece everything together. "I don't know. Possibly. Maybe not. I don't know."

"Calm down, take a breath. Where do you recognize him from then?"

"A bar."

Varin raised an eyebrow, waiting for Maggie to follow up but she remained panicked. "Maggie, stop. I understand getting this kind of excitement when you finally find something, anything pertaining to your investigation, but you need to calm down. Don't let your body take control, give your mind time to gather it all in."

Maggie tried to listen to him but found herself torn between trying to heed his advice and wanting to stand and run. But she wouldn't know where to run to. James wouldn't be at the bar yet and she no longer knew where he lived. She listened to Varin as he began to count slowly, realizing that he was trying to help pace her breathing.

It took a moment to properly breathe along with his counting, but thankfully he was patient. Once her breathing was mostly under control, he stopped counting and waited quietly for Maggie to do the rest, not pushing her to talk until she was ready.

"Okay, sorry, I get a bit panicky sometimes."

"I know," Varin answered softly, reaching into his pocket and grabbing a cloth, moving over to hand it to her. "Here."

She looked at him, confused, but realized what he had given it to her for. She thanked him, grabbing the cloth and wiping the blood that dripped from her nose. Maggie held it there as she felt more blood beginning to leak, catching it as it fell. "I know that man."

"Are you scared of him?"

"No, this just happens when... Well, I don't really know. Too worked up, I guess."

"So, where have you seen him?"

"My husband hangs out with him. Often, I assume. The last few times I tried to speak to James, that man was there, right beside him."

Varin kept quiet, and Maggie could tell by his frown that he was unsure of the implication. Maggie was just as uncertain. Was the Sandman part of turning Patrick over to the guards? Did he know who James was? Was the man toying with James? There was only one thing she could do. Tell James. Clearly, he didn't know who that man was, otherwise he wouldn't be anywhere near him, let alone share a drink together.

She stood, Varin following suit.

"Where to, Maggie?"

"We'll go wait at the bar my husband likes to visit."

"No tavern is selling alcohol today."

"That doesn't stop him from going."

Varin followed Maggie as she guided him to The Flowing Red Tavern, where they would wait outside until James appeared. Her stomach twisted, her head hurt, and her nose continued to leak blood. Her thoughts addled with the copious number of questions that had no answers. Varin appeared unaffected, understandably. He had no connection to James, but he still seemed just as concerned for Maggie's sake.

They sat down not far from the tavern, waiting patiently as the sky first grew brighter before beginning to dim. They scarcely talked at first, Varin letting Maggie take lead in conversations so she could control the pace. He didn't pry into her family life at first, but she soon found herself talking about it without being prompted. She told Varin of her son, her husband, and even how Castor was a part of the mess her life had become. She found it odd. She hated talking to Audrey, and Audrey would actively try to get her to speak. Maggie always found herself wanting to ignore any questions and comments out of spite, and she honestly did not know why.

But with Varin, she found that the information let itself out, as if it naturally flowed into conversation with him. She talked at length and Varin remained quiet, only asking questions when he felt a slight pause in her words. She didn't know what made him so easy to talk to, or why she even felt like talking in the first place. Perhaps it was her body getting excited from seeing the man, perhaps she was worried for James' safety, and this was the only thing distracting her. She didn't know the answer, but she didn't care.

By the time she spotted James, she felt a great tension lifted. Varin respectfully listened the entire time, nodding sympathetically. She didn't get a chance to thank him before the more pressing matter quickly approached. But a man approached James from another street, running as if to catch up. Maggie's heart sank as she watched her husband shake hands with the green-plaited man.

Maggie grew uneasy once again, her legs shaking as her stomach churned. She felt ill as she tried to summon the courage to stand. Varin laid his hand on her shoulder and she turned to him. He gave her a warming smile, making his breathing audible enough for her to hear, silently guiding her.

"Do you want me to come with you?"

Maggie shook her head. "No, I should be okay."

"I'll be here in case you need me."

Maggie took one last deep breath, stood, and forced her legs to move.

James immediately spotted her, rolling his eyes in an exaggerated fashion. "Gods be damned, not again," he cursed, and the green-plaited man gave a sly smile.

"Oh, I see. A problem with the missus?" His words grated against Maggie, as if they clawed her very center.

"Don't you dare get started," James said. "You know she isn't anymore." James directed that last comment more towards her than he did his companion.

She ignored the remark, coming up to face him instead. "James, we need to talk."

"Mags, I don't know if you understand particular words, but when I say I don't want to talk to you, it means that we do not need to talk."

The green-plaited man smiled wider, holding back a laugh. Maggie did her best to ignore him, but now that she knew who he was, his frame seemed to double in size, refusing to be pushed to the side.

"We need to talk. In private."

"Go away, Mags. I don't need your crap right now. I can't listen to you if I'm not able to have a proper drink."

This time the green-plaited man laughed, running out Maggie's patience with him.

"James, we have to talk now. I do not care if you say no, it's not something you can refuse. If you don't want to talk, then just listen."

"Oh, feisty. James, why did you ever leave her?" the man teased, provoking James to join him.

James then gave an exasperated sigh, took a step closer to Maggie to tower over her. "No. I do not have to listen if I don't want to. Go away."

He tried to walk past her, purposefully knocking her to move her out of the way. She grabbed his arm, refusing to let go. She tightened her grip in frustration, staring into James' eyes with all the fury and determination she could muster.

"We have to talk about Patr—"

"Damned, woman, don't you listen! Go inside, Ess, I'll meet you there in a moment."

The man smirked, glancing at Maggie before walking towards the tavern. Maggie waited for the man to be out of ear shot, but James was not so patient.

"Why can't you just freaking listen, Mags? I just want you to leave me alone."

Maggie realized her grip may have been too strong on his wrist, so she eased her hand and lifted his arm to inspect any damage she might have done. She caught the sight of black ink peeking out of the sleeve of his ragged jacket. He quickly tore his arm away from her, but it had been too late. Maggie had seen it.

A tattoo of a skull bearing the symbol of their Gods, surrounded by a circle.

Sandman.

"James, what have you done?" Maggie could barely get the words out, her mind unable to properly comprehend what she'd seen.

There was no way he had joined them. No way.

So why did he have their tattoo?

"I did what I had to, Mags. To survive. To stop being in this damned rut I've been in for years. I'm trying to move on, I really am, but your incessant appearances make it so damn difficult. Just when I feel like I'm making progress, you turn up and threaten to ruin the whole thing," James growled as he pulled down his sleeve.

Maggie barely registered what he'd said. Her brain nearly ceased functioning when he didn't even attempt to deny he was a part of them. How could he go so far? What did they tempt him with?

"How could you? After what they've done? Unless you had som—"

"Don't you dare say it!" James yelled, hand clenched and half-raised.

Maggie saw Varin stand from his chair, prepared to move over, but she paid him no mind. Her eyes could not stray from James. The man she had married. The man she had given a son to after several complications. The man who abandoned her when their child died. A man who turned to drinking. This man who almost raised his hand to strike her.

And everyone claimed she was the mentally unstable one.

James took a deep breath, though it appeared to do very little to actually calm him. "You!" He pointed a finger right into her face, looking down at her. "Leave me alone. I know what the hell I'm doing, Mags. Just leave me alone."

James turned and walked away before Maggie could shed any tears. He stormed down the street, not turning back once. Maggie stood unmoving. Her body numb, her arms stiff. The only thing left was the overwhelming despair.

Varin moved over, speaking quietly, making eye contact, but Maggie didn't respond to his gestures. She knew she wanted to cry. Knew it was an outlet for her. So why couldn't she cry?

Varin became hesitant, uncertain of what to do. Maggie was unresponsive, uncertain of what he could do for her either. Then Varin did the only thing that seemed logical.

He embraced Maggie. Holding her for as long as she needed.

20

Arthur spent the day walking around town with his mother. He wished to walk without restrictions once more before his duel, and insisted his mother walk alongside him to get some fresh air. In truth, he didn't know if he could trust leaving her at home alone with his father.

Edmund had grown distant, though somewhat listening to Arthur's demands. Edmund would turn into bed at later hours once Evelynn had fallen asleep. He no longer waited for her at meals and went to great lengths to avoid talking to her.

Thankfully, Evelynn had grown out of her stupor a little, leaving her room more frequently, able to avoid Edmund if she chose. Arthur was thankful his father had actually listened but was skeptical at how long it might last. His father was not the type to simply roll over and obey. Arthur feared his father was scheming something that would strike him tenfold if he won his duel.

But he was not going to give Edmund that chance.

Arthur walked the streets with his mother, allowing her to guide him wherever she chose. They first made their way to the city center's livewood tree where they prayed together. His mother reached out to touch the dried treeblood sap, as if it gave her a stronger connection to the Gods. They then walked about town, waving and greeting those who recognized them. Arthur was given many praises for being the Champion of his house, and part of the reason why they would once again be blessed with more livewood trees.

He found their words ironic, considering he had no choice to be a champion. The praise he received made him realize how deceived the city had become. Rather than apologizing, they thanked the unwilling sacrifices.

Arthur kept his thoughts to himself, not even sharing them with his mother who thankfully seemed to be enjoying herself, at least a little. She did not smile unless greeting someone, but she held her head high and kept her eyes forward. It could simply have been for appearances, but Arthur could tell it was more than that.

They headed over to the North Gate – the closest one to them – to see the new defenses being set up. They marveled at the new additions but were mostly impressed by the way everyone worked together. They did not argue, complain, or even hesitate when another asked for assistance. It was warming to see at least a portion of the city working in tangent. Even the soldiers were helping, adding more capable hands to get the job done with efficiency.

"Lady Va Daolin? And is that Arthur? My, what a lovely pleasure to see you both," a voice called out to them. They turned to see General Deven approaching, smile plastered to his face.

Arthur had only met the man on the rare occasion he attended the gatherings hosted at the Deven house. The general was a busy man, especially leading up to the Red Sea, so it was expected he was not always available. Still, the few times they had met, Arthur was uncertain of the man. Though, honestly, the same could be said for almost every high-ranking official he had met.

"What brings the lovely Evelynn and her Champion out to the North Gate? Curious about our progress?"

"Indeed, General," Evelynn responded, looking over to the wall with admiration. "I remember watching the preparations for the past two Seas. It is comforting to see we add more each time."

"Past two? That's hardly believable for such a young lady!" the general smiled, and Arthur held back the urge to roll his eyes. He hated when others pandered to them so transparently. His mother seemed appreciative of the compliment, but Arthur was pretty sure it was only an act.

"Thank you, General, but it is true. I am blessed to have reached an age where I will see my third Sea. Technically four, if you count the one when I was a mere infant."

"Well, this year will be my second time commanding our soldiers against the Red Sea."

"My compliments on your fine work, General. It is rare to have the same man in your position for so many years."

"Thank you, Lady Va Daolin. I am particularly proud of this year, we are unveiling an entirely new design of defense that could revolutionize the way we protect ourselves." Deven gestured to the top of the wall where workers were building a couple of devices that were unrecognizable to them. It looked as if they were merely attaching pieces of livewood together.

"What is it, if I might ask, General?" Arthur placed himself into their conversation, his question sounding more of a command than a request.

"Something I cannot unveil just yet, even to someone of your status," the general said. "I apologize, but I have been sworn by The Voice to not reveal it until it is ready for demonstration. I've worked with the engineers on the plans, and I must say, it gives an excited thrill to these old bones."

Arthur was displeased but understood the general's position. "When will it be ready?"

"In a few days, actually. Tomorrow we will announce the demonstration to the city. Of course, there will be a special position atop the North Gate for your family to get a good view of our new defense in action."

"We will be pleased to attend. I am eager to see what our engineers have concocted for our protection," Evelynn responded, her eyes flicking to Arthur to silently chide him his lack of manners.

"I will unfortunately not see you on the day," the general said. "My attendance is required at the East Gate, but I do pray you'll enjoy it. I'm afraid other things demand my attention at this moment, please excuse me. A pleasure to see you, Lady Va Daolin, and I wish you luck in your duel, Champion." Deven shook his hand and bowed to his mother.

They thanked him for the conversation and watched as he walked towards the wall, beginning to yell at the workers for updates.

"Why must you be so cold towards him?" Evelynn scowled at Arthur as if he were a child.

"I do not like him. I do not know why, but most of the nobility irritate me. Their smiles and words feel hollow."

"And ours aren't?"

"Well…"

"Are you all right, Arthur? You seem a little off today. Your patience for others seems a little thin, but you hold your head high with such confidence."

Of course she could tell. Maybe she noticed the ring? "Nothing to worry about, Mother. I just feel a little… alleviated, I suppose. I've finally made some decisions and it has released a vast amount of pressure. I am content and will refuse to let anyone tarnish this mood."

His mother seemed skeptical but accepted his answer. She either did not have the energy to argue with him or trusted him enough to accept the vague response.

They continued their walk, and Arthur resisted the urge to fidget with his ring, taking a small detour as they began returning home. Evelynn wished to return to the city center tree, feeling compelled to pray once more. Arthur could not say he reciprocated the feeling, but who was he to deny his mother's request?

As they returned to the city center, they noticed the tree had a surplus of gatherers surrounding it, each praying to the Gods. Mothers had their children in tow, many being scolded for not remaining still as they prayed, very few elderly citizens also prayed, though Arthur was certain they made up most of the elderly community amongst the commoners.

Without hesitation, his mother joined the large group, sitting beside them and joining in silent prayer. No one seemed to notice, most eyes were either closed or turned towards the tree, and when they were finished, they simply stood and left.

Arthur chose not to join. Instead, he looked around at those who weren't praying, and decided to walk slowly around the perimeter of the center, peering down streets and alleyways. He kept his eye on a particular man who seemed to be looking around nervously. The man seemed to be pacing up and down, eyes darting before he eventually bound down an alleyway out of sight.

Arthur dared to venture closer, trying to keep himself quiet, but didn't want to look as if he were skulking. He walked towards the entrance of the alley the man had run down, keeping himself at the corner instead of walking into full view.

There, he saw the man conversing with a younger boy. Surprisingly young for what Arthur suspected he was doing. The pair were clearly on edge, their words rushed as they wanted to get their business dealt with. That's when the young boy made a not-so-subtle move with his hands, passing something to the man.

Finally.

Arthur had come across what he set out on his walk to do, an ulterior motive to taking a stroll with his mother, something he had kept hidden from her. He clutched his ring to calm and reassure himself.

He had found a Sandman.

* * *

Arthur's senses were overloading as he dwelled on the future. He sat in his room, fidgeting with the envelope that held the unsent letter. He worried for his family and what awaited them in the coming weeks. His brother held a new title amongst the Magistrates. His sister was still adjusting to life in her new home. His mother at least fared slightly better, though still far from the woman she used to be.

Thinking about the several things that will soon befall them made him question his intentions. He could still possibly abandon the title of Champion. The duel was only days away, but perhaps there was time. His family would most likely be disgraced, but at least they would be together.

Somewhat.

His siblings would still be out of home, unlikely spending more time with their mother if they were stripped of their noble status. It could potentially cause Gavin to lose his title, and his sister to be thrown out of her new family.

Perhaps abandoning the title wasn't as well thought out a plan as he had believed. He would have to stick to his original plan, let things fall into place, don't fight fate. The best he could do was to make sure his family was better off before the likely event that he fell in his duel.

He placed the letter down on the desk, wondering when the messenger would come to retrieve it. It had important information about when to meet up with his correspondent, but the meeting could not occur if he was unaware of it even happening.

Arthur left his chambers and made for the kitchens. It was about time for their evening meal, so he wanted to make sure he got there before his mother did. He prepared to take a shortcut through the hosting room but drew to a stop once he heard voices inside.

I didn't know we had any guests. He crept closer to the door, hearing just two voices. His mother's and his sister's. *Oh Gods, not tonight.*

He opened the door, inviting himself into the room. He smiled and greeted his sister. She seemed a little disheveled, which their mother had been quietly scolding her about. It was miraculous how the two looked so much alike in that moment. He could see the unhappiness in their faces, how they truly felt about their situations and the misery they had to live.

But he would make it better.

"Raelynn, a pleasant surprise!"

"Greetings, Arthur. I've only dropped in for a moment, I haven't much time to spare."

The way the words slightly quivered made Arthur immediately distrust her. She was holding back on something, and whatever it was she was clearly distraught about it. He knew better than to push, however, he was in no mood to be patient. "Is everything alright, Rae?"

"Just fine, Arthur. I am merely tired, that is all." Her smile was false, as if forcing her face to contort in such a manner would make everything better.

"What's the matter? Are things not well in your new home?"

Evelynn shot him a foul look, quietly berating him with her eyes. Arthur did not change his expression, remaining firm in his position, reassuring his mother he knew exactly what he was doing.

"Nothing is the matter. I am still adjusting, it takes some time," Raelynn said, failing to meet Arthur's eyes. Clearly her years of being trained as a Lady had no effect on her family. The way she sheepishly avoided looking at either of them screamed louder than she could ever raise her voice.

"I know we played games when we were younger, but I thought we outgrew them a long time ago."

"Arthur!" Evelynn gasped, shocked at how disrespectful he was being towards his own sister.

He knew he was being rude, but it was a part of being blunt. He made it clear he was not playing politics, just a brother concerned for his sister.

"Arthur, I assure you, all is well. It is just different for me, you wouldn't understand. I need a little more time to properly settle in." Rae plastered the fake smile on her face again, this time meeting Arthur's eyes. It might have been his imagination at this point, wanting to see things in such a negative light, but even her eyes seemed to betray her lips.

"It's been almost a year, hasn't it? Shouldn't that be ample time to 'settle in'? If something else is going on, you must tell me. I can help."

"Arthur, go ready yourself for supper. Now," Evelynn spoke coarsely, her tone leaving no room for debate.

Arthur thought on arguing back, but his sister remained quiet, clearly uncomfortable with the situation. He let the matter drop, returning to the political façade and excusing himself from the room in a proper manner. He knew he had upset his sister further, but it was necessary to face problems so that they could be addressed. Covering a wound with a smile did not prevent you from bleeding out over time.

He quickly put the event behind him, focusing his attention on the kitchens. As he entered the dining room, his father was unsurprisingly eating bread as he waited for the meal. Edmund's eyes flickered towards him, but quickly returned to the letters that sat on the table. His father did not attempt to address him, which Arthur was fine with. He had no words left for the man.

Arthur pushed through the door on the opposite side of the room that led into a hall, turning to the door that led into the kitchens.

The head chef's eyes widened in surprise. "Master Arthur, how can we be of help?"

"Greetings, Turin. I was just wondering what the evening's meal was."

"It is the time of year we are able to receive some delicacies. We have been roasting a pig all day, preparing to serve it out over the next few days."

Ironic. "Sounds delicious. Might I see it?"

"Certainly, Master Arthur." Turin gestured over to the wall that contained the fireplace. There, a pig was slowly being turned over a small fire. It was rare they were given an entire pig, the breeding must be going well recently.

Arthur admired it, taking in the delectable scent. "It smells absolutely divine. How long until it is ready?"

"We are just about to cut it up and serve it. We were about to send a messenger to retrieve yourself and your mother. If I might confess something, Master Arthur?"

"Certainly."

"We actually received this beast ahead of time, at request from the three of us," Turin gestured to the other two chefs who were preparing supper, giving Arthur a smile. "We thought it might lift your spirits a little with your duel quickly arriving."

Well, they're not wrong. "Really? I am humbled that you thought of me and wished to do something special. You have all earned my deepest respect."

Arthur bowed to them, which they quickly tried to prevent him from doing. It was unseemly for a noble to lower their head towards a staff member. Arthur knew but did not care. To him, it was a sign of respect, and he did truly appreciate what they had done for him.

He stayed to watch them cut the beast into portioned sizes for their supper. It was intriguing watching them pry open the animal, effectively ripping it into delicately portioned sizes.

269

As the servers reached to grab the plates, Arthur stopped them. "My mother is actually meeting with Raelynn at the moment. Would you be able to serve another dish and bring the food to them in the hosting room?"

"Certainly, Master Arthur. I apologize, I did not know she was here," Turin said, dishing the left-over vegetables he had made onto another plate. Turin usually made a little extra, Edmund frequently requested a second helping, but his father would have to go without for today.

Once Turin prepared the extra plate, Arthur grabbed one for himself and one for his father, "I can take these, you send the other two to my mother and sister."

"Are you certain, Master Arthur? It is our job to serve, after all." One of the servants seemed a little hesitant, unsure if this was some kind of test.

"Of course, I'm already here, might as well take them with me."

The servants obliged – not that they had much choice – and let Arthur carry the food on his own.

Arthur placed a plate in front of his father. Edmund became perplexed seeing Arthur serve his food, but chose not to openly question it

As Arthur took his seat, Edmund had already begun eating, barely giving the food time to cool. Arthur picked at his own plate sparingly, wiping his mouth after every bite, taking his time. He remained silent, not even glancing towards Edmund, but hearing the sloppy sounds of his father devouring food. Arthur could never really tell if the sounds were exaggerated in his mind or if his father actually ate like a slob, but it did not matter.

After a few moments, his father noticeably slowed then came to a halt altogether. Arthur looked over, noting that half the food remained. His father put down the letter he was reading, looking at the table a confused. Then his father clutched at his chest. Panic set into the large man, as he simultaneously slammed his chest and the table, desperately gasping for air.

Arthur stood, knocking over his chair, adding to the ruckus his father was making. Soon, servants began to flow in, trying to respond to Edmund's wild motions.

"Call for the doctor!" Arthur yelled, trying to figure how to help his father. He tried hitting the man on the back, as if he were choking, but that didn't seem to help. The servants became terrified, standing around confused and concerned, feeling helpless. More gathered, hearing the commotion, but in what seemed like the entirety of their staff, no one knew how to react.

Edmund's face began to turn blue as his body continued to refuse to breathe, hands desperately clawing his throat.

The door to the hall swung open, and Evelynn and Raelynn hurried in, led by a servant.

Evelynn immediately rushed to the choking man, giving him a quick inspection. "Move out the way!" she commanded and attempted to get Edmund to stand, but his body seemed to refuse to rise. She tried to reach her arms around him, as if attempting a particular procedure, but quickly gave up when her arms would not reach.

"Arthur! Come here, put your arms around him!"

Arthur responded, rushing over to his father, wrapped his arms around him, fingertips just out of reach of one another.

"It's the best we can do. Position your hands around here," Evelynn shifted his hands slightly on Edmund's chest. "Now try to give quick, jarring squeezes there!"

Arthur followed, mimicking her actions as she tried to display them, but it did little to help his father. Edmund's actions became noticeable slower, his panic seeming to die down, and his body becoming limp.

Despite his mother's efforts, Arthur could not save his father from choking.

Because he knew his father was not choking.

He let his arms loosen around the man, helping his body fall to the floor softly. Edmund's blue face had deepened, his eyes now struggling to remain open.

Evelynn rushed to his side, grabbing his hand, begging for him to remain awake. Without so much as another word, Edmund closed his eyes, his last breath escaping his body. His arms fell to his side, his body stopped struggling.

Evelynn and Raelyn wept by Edmund's body, the servants standing around unsure what to do. Some gathered to console the grieving women, and a couple approached Arthur, concerned.

Arthur stood, staring down at his father's lifeless body. He did not feel sadness, nor grief, nor much of anything. He stared, wondering if what he had done was truly the right course of action. He had ridden his family of the root of their problems, but was it worth seeing his mother and sister cry?

Would they understand? Or had he doomed his family? Had he thought this through, or was it just a whim that would have passed if given more time?

The words of the Sandman echoed in his head, and Arthur now realized how true those words were.

We don't just sell Dreams, we also sell nightmares.

21

Castor listened to the howling winds that blew throughout the city. He stood in the open, feeling it rush past his body.

It was as if it were a sign of things to come.

The Red Sea would arrive in a few days. As usual, their scouts ventured into the forest, too scared to stray too deep, and finding no gathering forces of the creatures. The regular waves suddenly appearing were one thing, but an entire army materializing was another. Surely, they were amassing somewhere, assembling their forces to launch an attack that truly threatened the stability of the city.

What made them do it? What made them gather in such numbers every twenty years? The creatures had never shown organization before, so why did they swarm around the Day of Sacrifice? It was obvious Malvark's rituals were somehow connected to the Red Sea, but no one knew why.

And the wind did not hold any answers for Castor.

He let the cold of howling gales cool his body; he had finished training, and now stood in the training yard, uncertain of what he should do. He was fraught with decisions, but were they even urgent enough now? Was it worth dampening his chance at surviving the Red Sea just for some answers?

The general knew more than he let on, but Castor could not interfere with the man further. General Deven was set to reveal their latest wall defense today and Castor didn't want to impede that. The security and hopes of the people stood before his personal questions.

His hair danced on the wind, having escaped the bonds of the plait. He paid them no heed, knowing that they would simply escape again if he fixed them.

The wind couldn't cover the sound of Vance's approaching footsteps from behind, however; Castor would know that tread anywhere. "Captain."

"Vance. Something the matter?"

"No, Captain. I was wondering if there was something myself or the Steelwoods could help with. It's obvious something ails you, but we don't know what we can do. We need our Captain focused when the Sea comes."

Of course, Castor's attention would be entirely on the Red Sea when they arrived, but somehow promising that to Vance felt empty. He contemplated having their help, but he did not know what they could do. He didn't even know what *he* should do. "Your focus should be on spending time with your families before the Sea. Enjoy what could very well be the last moments of your lives. I know how depressing that might sound, but we can't avoid reality."

"Are you sure we can't do anything to help? We know you've been having some trouble with the general, but there is no way he can prevent you from a promotion. We Steelwoods won't allow it."

Castor smiled. "The Red Sea is too close to care about such matters."

"So, it must be something worse, then."

"Yeah. You could say that."

"Something you'll share with us?"

"I wish I could, Vance. I really do, but there are too many complications if I tell you. If we make it through the Red Sea, I might be able to fill you in, but with the day being this close, I won't risk anything in our infrastructure."

Vance nodded, though he seemed a little disappointed. "If you say so, Captain."

Castor sighed. "I never imagined myself being in such a position before. I thought my life was like stone. Join the army, aim for General, die in battle somewhere along the line."

"You're taking on too much treeblood, Captain."

"What?"

"You're getting soft. Take action. If you're going to be this troubled, then deal with your problems. I mean the utmost respect when I say this, Captain, but who cares if you get kicked out of the army? You can still pick up a weapon and fight. What are they going to do, stop you from defending the city? Gods, I'll even accidentally misplace my livewood spear for you. You can't mope around until the Red Sea comes. If you die, you'll die with regrets. A soldier should not have any regrets going into the battlefield, it affects the integrity of our defense, which in turn affects the lives of our citizens."

"I know where you're going, don't say it."

"Your frown is literally killing citizens."

"Remind me to send you to the Gods prisons in the afterlife."

"Bold of you to assume I'll ever die, sir."

Castor's smile was short lived, Vance's words playing on his mind. "What would you have me do, Vance? Compromise the integrity amongst our soldiers, make them lose belief in the general? I can't do that, not this close to the Day."

"Then deal with it in a way that you won't die with regrets, sir. No burdens allowed on the battlefield."

"Stop it, you're motivating me to do something stupid."

"Did you expect anything less of me?"

A horn sounded throughout the city, not the regular horn for a wave, but a smaller one that meant for the citizens to gather for an announcement. It was time for the general to display the newest defense.

"I'll think about it, Vance. But it's not like I have many options."

Castor gave him a dismissive salute before making his way to the East Gate. A portion of the citizens would be gathering there, so he wanted to take his position before it became too crowded.

He climbed the steps and took his stand on the wall, facing the crowd that began to gather below him. His eyes shifted towards the two contraptions covered by cloth to keep the mystery. They were larger than he had expected, but he wasn't entirely

275

certain what he was imagining in the first place. It was difficult to imagine an entirely new defense, but somehow the livewood engineers had done it.

General Deven arrived at the wall, servants in tow carrying colored fabrics and thin poles. Castor eyed them curiously and watched as the general pointed out a space on the wall to them, and the servants began setting up their supplies to form shades, each one with a seat.

Now that the bright fabrics unfurled, a symbol was displayed that everyone recognized, causing the quite murmurs to stir into loud contemplations and excitement.

The Voice.

They would be coming to observe the newest defense as well. Castor was certain they had already seen it, which meant their presence was much more of a performance than actual interest in the event. Their symbol already had a grand effect on the crowd before they had even arrived. Castor could see the excited looks on their faces, the smiles on their lips as they happily gossiped about how grand of a defense this must be for The Voice themselves to arrive.

The livewood gate was opened, allowing some of the population to stand outside of the walls so that more could gather to observe. They were assured the display could be seen better on the outside walls but were warned not to stray too far.

The general signaled to the guards on duty to quiet the crowd, and the chatter quickly died down in anticipation for what was to come. Deven didn't say anything as eyes turned to him, instead he faced the tower located down the length of the wall. Everyone's gaze followed, and soon the door swung open.

Normally, it would be too far to determine who had left, but their brightly colored robes and elongated hats were a clear indicator of their identity.

The Voice had arrived.

The general dropped to one knee, head bowed. Castor did the same, as was custom for higher ranked soldiers.

The gathered crowd quickly followed suit, heads lowered, and eyes closed. The area grew deathly quiet, save for the dying winds that had gone from a howl to a whimper.

The Voice's footsteps grew louder as they approached, before coming to a standstill. "Citizens of Malvark, the Gods bless each of you on this glorious day," a voice called out, giving permission for everyone to rise.

Castor lifted his head, immediately searching for The Voice. Four of them took their seat, facing out to the fields, but one stood to face the inner crowd, the top half of their face covered by a painted mask, but mouth left unobstructed.

"Before we begin, let us take a moment to pray and thank the Gods for yet another gift. They have been working through our people, guiding their hands and minds with gentle touches, allowing us to learn what it is they have created." the speaker waited for a short moment, before spreading their arms out and tilting their head towards the sky. "We praise the Gods."

In unison, the crowd responded, "And we thank the Gods."

"Let the demonstration commence!" the speaker smiled and took their seat, joining the others in facing the field.

The general stood on his raised platform, took a deep breath as his voice bellowed out onto the people. "Today you witness history. Your descendants will learn of what our people have accomplished! A blessing never to be forgotten! A great feat that will bring you comfort in sleep! Citizens of Malvark, we present to you our latest addition to our defense!" the general gave the signal, and a few soldiers threw away the cloths, revealing what lay beneath. "The ballista!"

The crowd gasped audibly, followed by quiet whispers of confusion.

Castor had a good view from his position. The device looked like a large bow attached to a wooden ramp, with a several livewood wheels located around. He could surmise that it could turn, adjust its angle, and launch much larger ammunition than a regular bow, but he was mostly confused by series of livewood wheels connected to what appeared to be a repurposed treeblood drainer.

The general gave the order to load the ballista as he continued to speak. "In the past we have attempted to create this device, but we have been unsuccessful in making it versatile and easy to use. Thankfully, through one of our researchers, the Gods guided them on a completely new method for treeblood and livewood. Observe. Soldiers, rapid release!"

Three soldiers lined up, each carrying a large wooden spike while a fourth positioned himself at the livewood wheels, placing an empty bucket on the floor, a retainer of treeblood in his hand.

The first soldier placed the spike in position then pulled a lever, launching the spike into the fields. It flew at great speed, flying at a much farther distance than their regular archers could ever reach, impacting the ground and splintering into thousands of pieces. Without pause, the crouching soldier poured a small amount of treeblood onto the thin strip of livewood that was attached to the bunch of wheels on the side. To Castor's surprise, the wheels turned on their own, resetting the bowstring in an instant, and then the treeblood drained down into the bucket.

The second soldier placed his spike and pulled the lever.

Then the third.

In less than ten seconds, they loosed three large spikes into the fields. The crowd had grown silent after the first launch, but once the third was released, the general faced the crowd, smug smile on his face as the citizens broke into an excited uproar. The crowd cheered, clapped, and celebrated, embracing each other in pure joy over the device. The reveal had brought with it the comfort and hope that had been missing for many years.

Castor stared at the device, amazed at its potential for destruction. It could impale a few metalurks before splintering, damaging entire chunks of the Red Sea, meaning they could deal with the brunt of them before they even reached the wall. Truly a remarkable device, though he wasn't sure if he'd give so much credit to the Gods rather the researchers who discovered the use of treeblood.

The general raised his hand to quiet the crowd, and the cheering slowly died down. "Of course, it wouldn't do much if we couldn't aim with it, so it has a particularly unique design, using a similar method. Soldiers, show them."

The soldier carrying the treeblood poured it onto a different section of livewood wheels that Castor hadn't noticed as his line of sight was blocked. Deven gestured to another soldier, who grabbed a couple of protruding sticks, moving the ballista with ease. He raised and lowered the aim, turning it side to side, though he could not go very far in any direction. Once satisfied, the first soldier pulled a different lever, and the ballista became stiff once more, locking into place.

Castor had no idea how it worked, but he was amazed at its functionality. In fact, it was rather similar to one of the few ideas he had before but had never mentioned it to the general or a livewood expert. Of course, his idea was simply just a larger bow that could launch larger ammunition, he had no idea how it would have worked, but he now realized that it was not such an original idea after all. They must have been working years on perfecting it.

"Each gate has two ballistae mounted atop its wall, ready to kill as many metalurks as possible before even reaching our walls. We promise to put it to as much use as possible, trust in your soldiers to defend your lives."

The crowd cheered once again. Castor looked over at The Voice, noting they all remained seated and indifferent. It was difficult from where he stood to read their expressions, or at least the half of their face that remained visible.

The general, however, basked in the glory of the reveal, standing straight, chest puffed out, smile that grew larger with each hurrah. Castor was elated as well, despite the device having been at least partly designed by the general. His pride and spite were shoved aside so that he could marvel at the device. Standing before him was a better chance at surviving against the Red Sea, perhaps even making the smallest waves even more trivial than they already were.

And there were two of them.

The general gesture for another display. The soldier's seemed oddly reluctant, but obliged.

The fetched a few more wooden spikes, placing the first onto the ballista and launched it.

The treeblood was poured and the device reset.

The second spike was placed and launched without any difficulty.

The treeblood was poured, but this time, something jammed.

The ballista got stuck halfway into resetting. The hook that held the bowstring refused to budge despite the soldier's covert efforts to knock it into position. As if by practiced routine, the soldiers stood, awaiting orders, but in a position that it blocked most people's view of the ballista. The remaining spike was held as if it were on display for its length and size so the crowd could admire it.

The procedure was clearly meant to distract people from the ballista being jammed, but they couldn't prevent Castor from noticing. The General gave no indication that anything had gone astray, continuing to encourage the crowd to cheer. As much as he hated the man, Castor had to admire his efforts in raising the citizens' morale in this moment, even if he got the distinct impression the man was taking the glory for himself.

The crowd immediately began to quiet once they noticed a member of The Voice standing to face them. It was the same member who had earlier addressed the crowd, his hands clasped behind his back as he smiled. "Despite being a Voice, I cannot put into words how much I truly appreciate the Gods for once again sending us a gift. With this device, we will hold back the Red Sea with much higher conviction and strength than ever before. We will survive another twenty years, people of Malvark, this we can guarantee."

The crowd clapped and cheered once more but were quickly hushed by The Voice raising his hand.

"We praise the Gods," he began, and the crowd finished with him, "And we thank the Gods."

The crowd erupted in a roar as The Voice departed the wall.

The general didn't put on another display but did remain for a little while so the people could draw excitement from his presence. Castor did not participate in the cheering but did smile as he looked down onto the crowd, seeing hundreds of smiling faces.

Whatever faults the imperfect device held, its intended effect was to raise the morale of the city, and it had done exactly that.

* * *

Castor carried the thrill and excitement of the earlier display with him. His impression of the device was certainly dampened by it jamming after only a few launches, but he was pleased with how elated the crowd had become.

He had not seen Maggie in the crowd, so he decided to be the one to tell her before the word spread across the city. Castor wanted his sister to understand what it had meant on a deeper level than the general population, benefits of being related to a Gate Captain.

He strode confidently into the library, meeting with Heleen who was at the front desk. His attitude soured as he saw her expression.

Maggie wasn't here. Again.

"Really?"

Heleen sadly nodded. "Her attendance has been rather sketchy as of late. I'm a little worried. She has claimed ill a few times, but lately she has stopped the excuses altogether."

"It might be safe to assume she isn't home, then."

"What is she up to, Castor? Is she getting herself into trouble?"

"Most likely. Gods, what am I going to do with her?"

"Don't berate her, dear. I don't think she'll respond well if you scold her like a child. Treat her like your older sister."

"That's becoming more and more difficult when I can't even find her."

"I know dear, but that doesn't mean you shouldn't try. She needs someone stable in her life, someone who she can rely on. As much as I tried to be that person, I don't think I can. She needs someone she is close to, like a relative."

"Or a damned husband who won't abandon her."

Heleen placed a hand on his shoulder, sensing his rising aggravation. "You're still holding onto such hate for him?"

"How can I not? He promised to be with her, they went through so many attempts at childbirth, and then he simply abandons Maggie in their darkest moments. She wouldn't be in such a bad mindset if he actually stuck to his promises like an honorable man." Castor's words poured out, almost unwillingly.

His mouth felt bitter for having talked about the despicable man again, and he found he had been frowning the entire time.

"Dear, have you ever considered what it was like for James? He lost a child, too."

"That still doesn't give him a reason to simply abandon my sister. He just up and left without a word. He crushed whatever was left of her spirits and mentality, all for a drink! How could he do that to someone he supposedly loved?"

"Not all men are built the same. As you said, he went through years and years of not being blessed with a child. He and your sister went through the same tragedies and, unfortunately, he found solace in drinking. To him, it's the only method of dealing with what he has been through. James was a very emotional man, his entire life was your sister and nephew."

"So how does a man like that, who holds family in such high regard, just leave?"

"I wish I knew, dear, if only it meant to help you better understand his position. Do not get me wrong, I don't agree with his actions, but I can sympathize with why he did them. Everyone deals with their troubles in their own way. Unfortunately, James has chosen to drink himself to death. I'm sure he would have by now if the taverns provided for him every day."

Castor spent a moment to consider it, feeling only agitated trying to understand James' reasoning, but he still couldn't get into the mindset of abandoning your family. To him, it just made no sense. "No, what James did was unforgiveable, and I won't be convinced otherwise. Anyway, I'm here to find Maggie, not talk about her useless husband. If she's not here, I'll try her house, though I get the feeling she won't be there."

"I don't think she is either. I hope she's all right, poor thing. I don't know what's gotten into her lately, but I feel like a hinderance to her all of a sudden."

Castor awkwardly shuffled his feet before taking a step closer, wrapping his arms loosely around Heleen. "You've done a lot for her, thank you. Don't stress yourself over her."

Heleen reciprocated the hug. "I have to, dear. She's the closest thing to a family I have left."

Castor let go and gave Heleen a quick smile before leaving the library in search of his sister. He knew the route she should have taken on her way to and from her job, so he made sure to carefully look around, wondering if she had seen something that caught her eye and was playing investigator again.

As much as he searched, he couldn't find her hiding around any corners, snooping around in alleyways, or even trying to blend into a small crowd of people. He made his way into her house, preparing to leave some kind of indication that he was searching for her without triggering her paranoid senses of someone else being inside the house.

Thankfully, his delicate decision was cut short when he heard Maggie walking around her own creaky floorboards. He swung the front door open, expecting to see Maggie, but instead came face-to-face with a man, who stared at him with the same perplexed and surprised expression.

Varin. Holding what seemed like a cup of water.

Castor charged forward as Varin tried to backtrack a little but could not avoid Castor's soldier grip as he yanked the man by his shirt and slammed him to the wall. "What the hell are you doing here, Varin?"

"Well, I was kind of hoping to give this water to your sister." Varin awkwardly smiled as if making light of the situation.

Castor did not find a Seeker prowling around his sister's house amusing. "I thought the job was over, why in the damned prisons are you still after my sister? I'm not trying to turn you in, you idiot, leave my family alone!"

"Look, Castor, friend, I can see why you would misinterpret the situation, I really do, but it's a little beyond that now," Varin raised his free hand as if it somehow proved he was defenseless and could do no harm.

That meant very little to Castor. "You better explain, and quickly, or I might have to change my mind about turning you in for trespassing,"

"He's not trespassing, Castor," Maggie called out from the top of the stairs. She stared down at them, neither surprised nor confused.

But ashamed.

283

Castor let go of Varin, who remained still and holding back from any sudden movements. Maggie refused to meet his gaze, and Castor rolled his eyes, rubbing them in frustration. *Just stick a treeblood drain in me and be done.* "Maggie, what in the Gods is going on?"

"I'm sorry, Castor. I really am, I just thought it would be best for the East Gate Captain to not to have any relations to them." Maggie slowly moved down the stairs, stopping halfway as Castor stared at her.

"Relations to *who,* exactly?" he asked, knowing the answer already, but needing to hear it.

"I've joined the Seekers. Kind of."

"Gods damn…" Castor trailed off, frustration building as the situation unfurled in his mind. He pointed to Varin. "You. You did this, didn't you?"

"Well, uh… perhaps, yes." Varin smiled sheepishly, as if it would somehow repel Castor's decision to attack him.

"He only offered, but I chose to accept it," Maggie said. "I'm not officially a part of them, but we're helping each other out." His sister seemed hesitant to move closer, seeing his pent-up irritation.

Castor didn't know what to think or how to respond. He had hired the Seekers' services but that was far from actually working with them. "Maggie, I don't know what to say." Castor sighed. "You're a grown woman. Though I think you're not mentally sound to constantly make the right decisions, I think you are more than capable of knowing the repercussions of allying yourself with the Seekers. And you're right, the East Gate Captain should not be related to anyone even remotely working with the Seekers."

Maggie did not smile, but her eyes at least fell onto Castor, sensing something worse to come.
"Which is why I do not know about it. In fact, I've stopped visiting my sister as of late, because she has been busy. I'm uncertain when I will see her again because she never seems to be home or at work anymore, and I know nothing of her personal life."

With that, Castor walked out the front door without another word, closing it behind him before his sister could object.

He could no longer visit Maggie, now knowing who she associated with. She was likely working with them only to find information about Patrick, but Castor had already risked enough by hiring them, he couldn't surround himself with them, it would only increase the chances of being seen together and strengthen the connection between them.

He had to distance himself as much as possible from criminal activity.

As much as it pained him inside, that also now meant staying away from his sister.

22

Much to Elias' surprise, his father still attempted to plan a celebration in Elias' honor, plotting to gather nobility to celebrate his son being Champion days before his duel. As much as Elias appreciated the idea, he could not allow his father to do so. Partly because his father was sick and Elias did not want the man to further agitate his own body, but also because Elias did not care for a celebration in his honor. He was too upset to plaster on a fake smile and pretend to be happy.

Geraldine had gone missing, not having turned up for work in days, which also meant he had not received the eagerly awaited return letter that should have answered his question about meeting with his correspondent.

In addition, his father was ill, and the duel was now only a few days away. Everything seemed to be collapsing as time drew closer to the dreaded day, as if they were signs of what inevitably awaited him in the arena.

It was as if the Gods themselves were giving him warning. His family had disappeared one by one, and now the last living member was fatally ill. His only real connections with people had ended at Geraldine's disappearance, who he worried about frightfully. It was unlike her to miss work. The other servants had not seen her, nor claimed to have heard any rumors of a sudden illness befalling her.

His life was preparing itself for the end.

Elias wasn't sure if he wanted to fight against it.

He had sent off the ring and his hopes, only to be left in the dark about how his correspondent felt. Elias alerted his family's guards about Geraldine's absence, and they promised to look into it for him, but it only made his stomach churn with fear. What could have happened to her? She mentioned that sending the messages had been risky. Had she been caught? If so, then by whom? And what had they done with her?

Surely it could not have been guards, unless his correspondent was in the prisons, and she was constantly sneaking in to deliver and receive the messages. Surely if it was anything less, she would not have been imprisoned for it, at least not without his family being informed.

Warin certainly hadn't received any messages; everything was now being redirected to Elias. His father was in no condition to handle anything, so Elias had taken on the responsibilities in his father's place.

Elias had known his days before the duel would be filled with anxiety, but he had not expected the situation to develop so negatively. The pressures began to pile on and he no longer had anyone to share his burdens.

It made him consider his unknown adversary. They had received word that the head of the Va Daolins had recently passed from an age-related illness. Despite the other champion having more living family members, it was a harsh coincidence to have a father suddenly pass only days before the fated duel.

It seemed like an ill omen was attached to the title of champion. The Gods teased them for the very position they gave, making them fret in every possible way as if trying to stir them for the duel. Though Elias was feeling more deflated and distracted than eager to fight.

The Gods must love the spectacle of the duel if they tease us this much.

Even Merek had noticed his distraction during practice. Elias' form had slipped enough for Merek to have the upper hand for the entirety of their sparring. Elias had no drive, no fighting instinct any longer.

He was giving up.

Perhaps it might just be the easiest method. Surrender instead of dueling. At least then the Va Daolins could continue their bloodline, they still had a family. Either their eldest son could provide a champion, or their current champion would have ample opportunity to sire an heir.

It seemed like the logical decision but Elias would likely be unable to forfeit his own life in front of his father. Warin clung on to the semblance of life he had left, living each day in agony, only so he could watch the duel and await the future for his family.

Elias couldn't just give up his family's bloodline like that, even though it seemed so tempting. It was selfish. He was the last brick in a building that had been crumbling for years, everyone debating whether to restore it or let it fall on its own.

He toiled over the situation in his father's study, fire crackling against the silence. Beside him sat a half-empty wine pitcher, teasing Elias with its rich fragrance, eagerly inviting him to pour himself a cup and taste its deep, sweet flavor.

Elias wanted to drink. The only thing preventing him was whether or not he could hold himself back. Would he stop at one cup, or would it be too tempting? Did it even matter anymore?

The parasite that buried itself into his life sucked away at his hope, his aspirations, his willpower. This surely could not be the will of the Gods. Why would they damn others just to test him?

Elias left his chambers, head as high as his mood would allow, and made his way to the kitchens once more. There, he asked the servants for any updates on Geraldine. They were as in the dark as he, seemingly as worried about her safety as Elias. He nodded in acceptance, and made his way to his chambers.

There, he adorned a grey cloak to hide his noble colors and headed outside. With his father ill, Elias had free rein to leave. Probably not to Warin's approval, but his father was in no condition to stop him.

Along the way, he grabbed a servant and told the man to send message to the Va Daolins that he was going into town. He decided not to wait for the confirmation word had been received, leaving right behind the messenger.

As he passed the guards stationed at the front wall, they gave Elias the appropriate greeting, placing a fist on their chest and bowing their heads. Elias smiled at them, and headed down into the streets.

The cloak was as effective as he could have hoped. Few people recognized him, and those that did he asked to remain quiet. He was not here for leisure, but rather on a mission to seek out Geraldine in the only place he knew.

The Everwall Tavern.

Not wanting to draw attention to himself, he entered the tavern as quietly as possible, and the strong scent of alcohol immediately struck him. He did a quick search for Geraldine, praying to the Gods she had suddenly become an alcoholic. The tavern was filled with guests, being a day that it was allowed to serve alcohol. Unfortunately, he could not spot Geraldine amongst its clientele who guzzled down the tempting beverages at a rapid pace.

He waded through the crowd up to the barkeep. "Excuse me, sir, have you seen a particular woman? She's about this tall, blonde hair in a servant's plait, usually looking very professional and serious."

The barkeep stared at him, either in confusion, recognition, or deep thought.

Lovely.

"Not tonight. I'm afraid this place is far too busy to keep an eye on everyone, but no lovely lady as you describe has been here," the barkeep said while serving another customer, filling several cups from the uncorked barrels.

The scent of the tavern continued to tease and tempt, slowly convincing him it was worth his time to sit down for just a drink. He nodded grimly to the barkeep, deciding to leave the tavern. Geraldine was not suddenly a drunkard, much to his dismay. Perhaps he should try the guards next. If she hadn't been arrested – mistakenly, of course – then they might have heard other news about her.

He wandered outside, peering up and down the street. No patrols were in sight, so he had to walk aimlessly until he found some.

Might was creeping in, not that it bothered him. As long as he put out the word that someone was searching for her, she should surely turn up somewhere.

It took a concerning amount of time to spot a guard, the streets seemingly abandoned as he walked them. Elias approached the pair who were stationed at a corner, conversing with one another about something irrelevant to Elias, so he interrupted without hesitation.

"Gentlemen, a moment, please."

The guards turned to him, initially scowling at their conversation being interrupted, but quickly changed their demeanors once they recognized him.

Surely the ideal guards.

One of the guard's beard had grown improperly, making it patchy and wiry, while the other sported no beard at all.

"Sir Va Noldin, how can we be of help?"

"Looking for a worker of mine by the name of Geraldine. She's gone missing in the past few days, and I've become concerned for her safety."

The guards looked puzzled, turning to each other as if in silent conversation.

"You came to look for your own servant, Sir Va Noldin? Why not send another in your place?"

"I do have others searching for her, but I would not feel right if I was not out searching for her myself. She is rather close to me, more friend than worker, and I'd like to finally get some answers on her whereabouts."

"I told you that them nobles cared about their workers. They're still a part of the city, they can't possibly ill-treat their staff," the guard with the scraggly beard said, gently hitting the other on the shoulder.

The beardless man's eyes widened as he turned towards his colleague. "I never said that, it would be disrespectful of course."

"Sure you did, you said that you'd never work for a noble because they slap around their staff as if they were brainless creatures. Don't you recall?"

"Keep your trap shut."

"Uh, gentleman?" Elias interrupted, the situation quickly losing direction. The guards turned back towards him, the scraggly bearded man smiling with mischief.

"We won't have recognized anyone today, sir. We've only recently started our shift. We can take you down to the prisons though, that's about the only place I can think of to look," the beardless man explained.

Elias was prepared for this and accepted his offer. It was a long shot, but at this point, what were his other options? He followed them as they quietly conversed with hushed tones, returning to their irrelevant conversation. The sound of rapid footsteps amongst the stone emerged behind them, growing louder and louder.

Elias turned to see a familiar looking man running towards them. As he drew close enough to speak, Elias recognized him as the messenger he had sent off earlier.

"Master Elias, I'm glad I found you," the man said between rapid breaths. "You must return, Master Elias. I sent word to the Va Noldins that you were venturing into town, and they informed me their champion was already out, the messenger must have barely missed you."

Damn!

Elias turned to the soldiers. "Gentlemen, I must take leave. Search your prisons for anyone by the name of Geraldine. Send word to me whether you found her or not. Thank you for your time."

"Of course, sir. We'll have a look right away for you."

Elias smiled as he departed, servant in tow. He hurried, taking a direct course back to his home, knowing it was imperative to avoid the champion at all costs.

They were not yet fated to meet.

It only took a short time to reach home, the empty streets providing no obstacles for a swift retreat. His bleak attitude worsened since finding no clues to Geraldine's whereabouts, or the letter she was meant to retrieve. With naught else he could do, Elias retreated to his room, mulling the situation over, slowly letting the time tick by, praying that the duel both arrive quicker and be delayed.

* * *

Elias stood with his father atop the South Gate, given a grand view of the new defenses in place. They watched with admiration at the new contraption developed with livewood and the entirely new function of treeblood.

Though Elias was still a beginner at livewood crafts, such a method of treeblood seemed nigh impossible. It was truly a miraculous feat, and the city would certainly benefit from its discovery. Ideas and images flashed in Elias' mind of the sheer possibilities the new method could do to improve the city, not only in its defense, but day-to-day life as well. But of course, his ideas were only amateurish compared to what the Magistrate surely had in mind.

Elias consistently checked on his father's well-being; he'd not wanted his father to attend but couldn't deny the man his right to witness a new age of defense.

Another spike was launched from the ballista, soaring through the sky like a bird with bloodlust, threatening to destroy whatever dared stand in its way. The tip of the spike touched the earth, splintering into hundreds – if not thousands – of shrapnel.

The crowd cheered and clapped. Elias marveled at the demonstration, but his father remained unmoved. It was likely the pains of his body interfering, but Elias had to believe that his father was at least enjoying the spectacle.

General Deven gave off more of his painfully obvious rehearsed speech, but it was enough to rile the crowd. The Voice, ironically, remained quiet during the demonstration but they did not need to speak. They had surely attended the demonstration at the other two gates; they were here merely as a formality, or to convince the citizens they had a hand in the matter.

Or they were simply here to give credit to the Gods, not that they were due much.

With the demonstration over, Elias slowly escorted his father down the steps, beginning their short yet lengthy walk home.

Warin refused to be carted around in a palanquin, insistently enforcing that he was well enough to walk, but his hobbled gait and shaky legs proved otherwise.

Still, his father refused to be carried.

Elias shuffled along beside his father, letting the frail man use him as support, thinking back on the days that his father used to smile. Slowly, Elias' spirits faded away, seeing himself slowly merge into a duplicate of his father. Life had not been kind of late, but life had not been kind to Warin for years, and it was not going to improve.

People greeted them as they walked by, but mostly left them alone so they did not draw attention to Warin's state. They could sense the frustration emanating from the man and had enough smarts to stay out of his way while paying their respects.

Many more greeted Elias, personally wanting to wish him well in his duel. It was only two days away now, and Elias felt himself once again becoming numb as the reality settled in.

He pushed back the emotions, kept his head level and his mind calm, fighting against his instincts. The people meant well, but it did not prevent him from stressing further with each remark.

Along the way, a pair of guards approached, and Elias instantly recognized them as the guards from last night. They gave the polite greeting to both Elias and his father, before addressing Elias directly.

"Sir, we have scoured the prisons and I'm afraid there is no one by the name Geraldine. Only a few matched her loose description, but none carried the name. I apologize for not being of any help," the beardless man spoke, his friend looking surprisingly professional in his demeanor today.

"Geraldine? What happened to her?" Warin asked. Elias had not yet told his father about her absence, because he already knew what the reaction would be.

"She's missing, Father."

"So, why're you looking for her? If she quit then that's her incentive, you can't go around looking for her like that. Leave her be and focus on your duel."

"She didn't quit, she's disappeared. No one has seen her and it's quite worrisome."

293

"Bah, you grew too attached to her. Look for her after your duel, you fool. You can't afford this kind of distraction."

His father was getting worked up, so Elias let the matter drop, not wanting to argue with Warin in his current state. He also noticed that the beardless man gave his colleague a quick look and a nudge, but hastily returned to being professional.

"Thank you." Elias gave them a nod, and moved on with his father.

"Sorry again, sir."

As they continued their walk, Warin's tone changed, softening as he tried to reason with his son. "You'll find someone else, Elias."

Elias looked at his father, seeing the somber expression and brow only slightly furrowed, "What are you talking about, Father?"

"The girl, Geraldine. You'll find another. As soon as you are victorious in your duel, you'll have choice of any woman you want. You don't need her anymore, just forget about her."

Elias immediately wanted to correct the man, but figured it was futile. "Yes, Father."

Warin remained quiet. Elias wondered how long his father had assumed an incorrect relationship between himself and Geraldine, as well as who else might have made that assumption. It would be unruly for rumors to spread about affairs with his staff, but it at least did well to cover his tracks with his mysterious correspondent.

It would be better to let the rumor spread its seed of misinformation for the moment, at least for his sake, he could not fathom what Geraldine would think about such an incorrect assumption.

Once they reached the courtyard of their house, they stopped being greeted by the citizens that prolonged their already slow walk. Elias escorted his father straight to his chambers, ordering some replenishments to be sent up immediately. Elias was adamant about keeping his father alive long enough to watch the duel, it was the only thing Warin strived for now.

They sat and ate together, Elias still insisting on being present to ensure his father consumed an adequate amount of food.

Once they were done, Warin lay down to rest, and Elias left his father in peace.

Quietly closing the door to Warin's room, Elias sent a messenger to call for Merek, to begin their final training session. It did not take long for his mentor to arrive, and the two were sparring within moments. Merek kept changing tactics and maneuvers to keep Elias on his toes, occasionally swapping hands to throw him off balance.

Nothing could surprise Elias now. His mind was focused, his eyes attentive to the slight shifts in Merek stance, reading his next attack before he could swing. Merek did not land a single strike. Elias parried, dodged, pivoted, applied pressure when needed to, dominating the entire duel.

Is he letting me win? The question gnawed at him, surprised by how far he stood above Merek in this moment. His mentor's movements seemed sluggish, his moves predictable. Merek had taught him, so Elias knew all of the man's moves, yet still…

Elias slammed his wrapped blade into Merek's side, the two taking a step away from each other to catch their breath.

"You're certainly focused today, Elias," Merek said between panted breaths, taking off his helmet to cool a little.

"You mean you weren't holding back?"

"Holding back?" Merek seemed offended. "This close to the duel? Why in the world would I do that? Give you false hope? No, Elias, it is you. Perhaps it is how close the duel is that your mind is finally snapping into focus, but you're always a step ahead of me. I know your moves, but I cannot keep up with your speed, your reactions to my strikes. You bested me a long time ago, but it is only today that you are letting yourself prove it."

Elias stared at Merek through the slits in his helmet, trying pierce through the façade Merek was surely putting up, but there was no falsity. Thinking back, he hadn't realized how focused he had become. Perhaps his instincts were finally kicking in. Death was right behind him, waiting for him to turn and face it.

And he just might be ready for it.

If only he still did not hold so many unanswered questions, such regret. He had to become selfish in his final moments, but he could make up for it if he survived. And if he died, then perhaps it was his form of punishment.

He had to brush Geraldine's disappearance aside.

Forget his father's illness.

Pretend his mysterious correspondent didn't exist.

"Another," Elias announced, eager to test his skills further. Merek complied, placing the helmet back on his head, and raising his wrapped blade.

Stone Wall stance.

In a blur of swings, Elias slammed his weapon at Merek, again and again, forcing the man to keep a steady blade to repel the next attack.

Then Merek shifted stances, dodging Elias next attack and filling the space with his own, fist pummeling towards his head. Elias followed his over-extended attack, quickly rolling to the side. The armor was heavy, not intended for such acrobatics, but he had practiced the move enough to know how to quickly stand again.

He met Merek's quick thrust with his own blade, slapping it to the side as if it were a mere child's strike. The man regained balance, swapping the blade into his other hand.

Long stance.

A common position. Merek was aiming to keep the distance between them, his footwork would keep him on the move, not allowing Elias to get close. It also meant Merek could not land his own attacks—a delaying tactic until an opening was made.

Elias charged, wary of the blade pointed at him. Merek thrust again, but Elias dodge to the side. Merek had clearly expected for Elias to follow with his blade, but instead Elias slammed his shoulder into Merek and knocked him slightly off balance.

Which in a duel, meant life or death.

By the time Merek regained his posture and had his weapon readied, Elias had planted his own against Merek's arm.

"Risky move," Merek said. "Not sure you'll find the courage to do it against a sharp blade."

"But it wasn't a sharp blade."

"You're not trying to beat me, you're trying to beat the other champion. The right angle and power allow these weapons to cut through the armor with ease. Just be careful, that's all I'm saying. I don't know if your duel is worth such risks."

Elias ignored the advice, confident in his ability to decide the right maneuver in the moment.

"Listen to me, Elias, do not get overconfident. This wasn't something I thought I would have to teach you, you've always been the slightest bit timid, but I get the distinct impression your nerves are getting the better of you. Certainly, you have killed me many times today, but keep in mind your adversary is not someone you have ever trained with."

"I know, I know. I'll be more wary on the battlefield, keep my wits about me and all that."

Merek removed his helmet and shook his head, visibly annoyed by Elias' tone. "You're losing yourself in this false confidence. You're scared, and that is fine, I am scared for you. I am scared for myself and my family with the Red Sea soon upon us, but at least I have my head on straight."

"You're damned right I'm scared!" Elias threw down his weapon with the outburst. It landed on the ground with an unsatisfying, padded thud. "My death is only days away, I've managed to lose a friend entirely, and my father lives in agony only to see his last child die before him. I find myself skilled in one thing, then by all means I'm going to bloody enjoy it!"

Merek slowly advanced towards Elias, gaze not wavering. "That is exactly what is going to get you killed. You need to allow yourself to be scared. You need it to fuel your instincts, work in tangent with those skills of yours. By all means, Elias," Merek raised his voice, "be bloody confident, but by all Gods keep your head on your damned shoulders!"

"Why shouldn't I be confident? It worked against you, and you claim not to be holding back! I've bested one of the few dueling teachers our city has! If I can beat you, why can't I beat him?"

"Because I'm not trying to kill you, you damned fool! You and your adversary are going to be thrown into a circle and told only one of you can leave alive! It is literally life or death for you two. In here, we have the comfort of knowing we can't be killed, but that all changes when you step foot in that ring!"

297

"I just…" Elias trailed off, trying to calm himself before words escaped his mouth without thought. "I just wanted to bloody die with a bit of happiness, even if it was a ruse. At least then I could have fooled myself into thinking it was just a lack of skill rather than the Gods growing me for twenty odd years only to harvest me."

Elias paced the room, Merek gaze following. The man gathered Elias' sword from where it lay, dusting off the handle in a show of proper care. "The Gods have not toiled with you your whole life. Perhaps it is because I am merely someone viewing it from the outside, but you and the champion of the Va Daolins are destined for something great. One of you will come out alive, move on to serve our city to the best of your abilities, while the other will be the blessing we need to survive. Both of you are held in high respect in the city's eyes, perhaps the sacrifice more so. The Gods have not left you, Elias, *you* have. I know I do not have your position, but can you at least find solace in the fact that if you perish, your life will allow all of our citizens to continue to live?"

Elias already knew all of that, but made no difference. There had been no choice of becoming champion; the respect felt hollow, and even the concept of living made him feel guilty for the other party. There was no upside to his situation. Sure, at the end of the day, the livewood trees would continue to grow under the blessings of the Gods, but why did they require a sacrifice? They seemed so giving and benevolent, how could they ask for death in exchange for a gift?

Maybe Merek was right. No one else could understand because they weren't in this position. The only other person who might relate was the other champion, but the two would not meet until they entered the arena and were told to kill one another.

They were just another crop waiting to be harvested.

Merek held out the sword to Elias, who stared at it for a while, the handle taunting him, the weight of the sword bearing more than just the metal it was composed of. Then, he turned his back and began to slowly remove his armor. He did not know how Merek reacted, but heard the man move over to the other table to begin his own removal process.

They spent the next few minutes in silence, placing the armor on the table piece by piece. Once Elias was done, he stared at the pieces laid out before him, overwhelmed. He knew he had to clean them, but somehow the task seemed larger than it ever had.

Elias left the room without another word.

23

Maggie slinked through the darkened streets, keeping to the edges, attempting to blend in with the shadows. The night sky that had once taunted her with phantom sounds had now become her ally, keeping her hidden from the eyes of the public.

She followed Varin, twisting and turning down alleyways to meet with a couple of other Seekers, finally to be given a role in their plans.

He hadn't told her much about those plans, only that it involved high ranking officials and the Day of Sacrifice. She had agreed in return for help tracking down her son's killer, but she found herself quickly absorbed into their lust for information, finding a particular thrill in discovering something hidden.

The thought of wanting to join scared her. Not because of the personal risks involved, but due to how Castor reacted when he'd found out she was working with them. Joining the Seekers labelled you as a criminal; if the guards found out of course. She knew it would raise complications for her brother, but perhaps she hadn't realized how far their actions went.

Once he stormed out of her house, she seriously considered the implications of her position with the Seekers. If the Magistrate caught wind of her involvement, they would try and trace it to Castor's position, and possibly his eagerness to make General. They might assume he had an insider this whole time, working on blackmailing his way to the top, and would be immediately removed from his position, likely jailed along with her.

But it was too late now; and it was worth the risk if it meant finding her son's killer. Hopefully, Castor would understand. Hopefully he'd forgive her one day.

Varin stopped at a door in the alleyway, barely visible in the dim moonlight. He knocked twice, paused for a moment, then knocked three times.

The door swung open, and he immediately slunk into the room, Maggie barely had time to follow before the door was closed. The room was dark, the only source of light the flickering of a lit candle in the cracks of another door. A shadow moved to the door, opening it to shed more light.

Varin entered the lit room without hesitation, Maggie followed to find three other Seekers faces silently evaluating her— two men and a woman. Maggie stood to one corner as the door was closed, the room now silent as Varin fetched a pitcher of water.

The three Seekers sat around a table full of papers and stared at Maggie, clearly skeptical.

Varin gulped down his water, moved over to Maggie's side and flourished his hands as if she were on display. "This lovely woman is Maggie, and I would very much appreciate if you didn't gawk at her like she held the last piece of bread."

"You didn't tell her who we were, did you?" the woman said, anger edging her voice. She had dark brown hair, woven into two plaits like most single women of the city. Her light green eyes were hardened by her scowl, and her drab grey clothes were no surprise to Maggie.

"No, I thought it would be best you introduce yourselves, that way she can put the names to the faces instantly."

"No names," the lady snapped. "She doesn't have the right to know. Call me Gale."

Maggie wondered if she were being tested; hesitated a moment as the woman continued to scowl. "Gale? Isn't that a name?"

"Obviously not my real one, Margaret."

"Then why do you know mine?"

"Because you aren't a Seeker, and we don't trust you. Yet."

"Okay, lovely introduction," Varin said. "She'll be more complacent once she gets used to you Maggie, she'll turn into a soft, loveable rock shortly. Moving on." Varin gestured to the man sitting next to Gale. Even seated, he seemed rather tall. His shoulder-length, brown hair had begun to grey, along with the beard he sported. His clothes were not the usual drab grey of the city, but rather the brown of a farmer.

"Remus." He nodded to her, his face expressionless making it difficult to read what he thought of her.

"And I'm Roy," the other man said. He had long, black hair, left in a mess as if no attempt was made to neaten it. His face was gaunt, as if he had been starving for days, making his brown eyes seem larger. His grey clothing was especially dirty and tattered, almost like they'd never been repaired.

"All fake names. Does that also mean yours, Varin?"

Varin gave her an apologetic smile. "Afraid so."

"That's all right, I probably should have guessed but your name never concerned me anyway."

"Well, I don't mean to be rude," Roy said, "but we're on limited time here. Varin vouches for you and that's good enough for me, so take a seat and let's fill you in." Roy gestured to a couple of vacant chairs.

Varin pulled out a chair for Maggie and she seated herself, getting a proper look at the paper's as she felt wary eyes flicker towards her occasionally. The papers varied from letters, to documents, to drawings of buildings. It seemed like clutter, but she was certain this was organized chaos. Her eyes drifted from one page to the next, eventually lighting up as she recognized some writing.

It was one of the old records she had discovered. She carefully grabbed the page, examining the words. It was not one she had read, but it was certainly distinguishable as a record.

"Careful with that," Remus suggested calmly. Maggie held the paper gently, reading what she could of the words.

"That's the page we'd been waiting for to confirm our suspicions," Roy began. "That specific page tells us the city is hiding something. The Old Malvarkians either discovered it, or created it, but whatever it was, we're certain it was the cause of their disappearance. And it'll be the cause of ours if the city keeps using it."

"Using it?" Maggie's curiosity piqued, and her nerves settled.

"Whatever The Voice or Magistrate is keeping from us, we're certain it has a use, a function. They're doing something, but we've only found scraps, and the plate they feed from is persistently out of reach," Gale answered, her stern front quickly fading away. Her rough features had softened, making her appear like an innocent young woman.

"So, you have no idea what this process is, or does, but you know it exists?"

"Yeah, that's about the gist of it."

"How do we find out?"

"Well, actually, that's where you come in," Varin began, shuffling the papers around until he found what he was searching for. "We need you to be our spy in this matter. The risk is rather high, and you'll have a better time of covering yourself if caught."

"What is it you want me to do, exactly?"

"We need someone to follow one of a few people," Varin handed her the paper. It had short list of names, all high-ranking magistrates, soldiers, or nobles.

One name stood out in particular.

General Deven.

"What am I looking for when I follow them?"

Remus cleared his throat, spreading a few pieces of paper in front of him. "We believe the key moment will be during the Day of Sacrifice. The city is preparing its defenses, moving all non-combatants to the safe zones. Fortunately, the Seekers like to take down information in case it ever becomes relevant, and we have some notes of what those particular names did during the last Day of Sacrifice. All were suspicious. Some entered a house but never left, others seemed to disappear for a few hours despite their duties, and a couple even went as far as to fake an illness on such an important day. Needless to say, they're doing *something*, and this year we'll find out what that is."

"We're certain they do it regularly, but we know for *certain* that they go somewhere on the Day of Sacrifice. That will be our chance to tail them," Roy continued.

Maggie realized that he was avoiding her gaze.

They all were.

"What is it?"

Varin chuckled. "I told you all she was perceptive." He faced Maggie, his eyes remorseful before he even spoke. "Guilt. We feel like we'll be sending you to your death, but you have the best chance to survive out of all of us."

Maggie looked at him dubiously. "You've mentioned that several times now, that can't be it."

"Well, it is. Mostly."

"Gods, we aren't here to fool the girl," Remus blurted. "Margaret, the reason we decided to bring an outsider in on this is because most of the Seekers won't aid us. They think it's either too risky, or we're shadows that aren't there. Who you see here are the only ones who wanted to be involved. The other reason we brought you in specifically makes my heart wracked with guilt, and I feel less than human for doing it. It's... We... Damned this feeble tongue!"

"It's because you have no one, Margaret," Roy said, and then the words spewed from him in a torrent. "We're sorry, we feel terrible for even considering it as a bonus, but it's true. You only have you brother left, and yes, he is a high-ranking soldier, but it's only one person. The rest of us have families we're putting at risk already, and if we get caught following a damned High Magistrate around, they'll be executed along with us."

The room fell eerily silent, and each one of them refused to meet Maggie's eyes. "So," Maggie began gently. "When you said that you didn't trust me, that wasn't entirely true, was it?"

Gale shook her head. "We trusted you as soon as Varin vouched for you. He's a capable man, he knows how to judge a person. It just didn't seem right for us to ask you to do this, but it seemed so..."

"Logical?" Maggie prompted and Gale nodded.

She couldn't lie, the concept of being chosen because she had minimal family hurt, but she also knew the pains of losing family. And how far people will go to avoid those pains.

"Maggie, if you want to leave, you can leave," Varin said gently. "We won't stop you, we won't chase you, and we will certainly leave you alone. It is not fair of us to force anyone into this. We know you're feeling guilty by even considering rejecting us, but we will not blame you in the slightest."

Maggie studied the man, then took a breath. "Let me ask, who would go if I said no?"

Varin raised his hand. "Not to brag, but I am the best of us when it comes to following someone without being seen."

"And what is it you're risking? *Who* are you risking?"

Varin looked at her, pain in his gaze just at the thought. "Mainly my children. Three of them. They would most likely be left alone, they're young enough that the city shouldn't suspect anything of them, but they'll be orphaned. I have other family who can take care of them, assuming that they won't incorrectly be dragged down with me. Stalking someone high up is bound to have large repercussions."

"Then it's that simple, I'll go."

They stared at Maggie, stunned by her sudden acceptance… all except Gale, who looked pleased.

"That easy?" Varin said, eyes still wide. "You know you can have some more time to think about it."

"It's fine, I get it," Maggie said with a nod. "You need to minimize the consequences if we get caught, and as depressing as it sounds, I'm the best fit for just that reason. I'm adequate enough to shadow someone. At least, I hope I am."

Varin's shock was replaced by an appreciative smile. "I'd say you're more than adequate."

The Seekers appeared to relax, not choosing to say anything. Maggie could see the mixed emotions were going through, each having their own internal conflict. "Well, tell me what I need to do then."

"Right." Roy cleared his throat. "First, we'll need to pick a target. I think we—"

"The general," Maggie answered.

Roy tilted his head at her, eyes narrowing slightly. "The general? That was a quick answer. Also, one of the riskier options, so I think th—"

"The general," Maggie repeated, eyes filled with determination.

"The general," Varin repeated, giving Roy a nod to just accept the answer.

"Right, Well, as long as whatever personal conflict you have with him doesn't throw you off your game." Roy moved the papers around, selecting particular ones, including a small drawing made out of smeared dirt. "We're certain General Deven goes somewhere out of the public view during the duel. A Seeker recorded his odd behavior twenty years ago, but for whatever reason, did not follow the general, only noted how he had been absent from leading the soldiers on their last day of setting up defenses. You'll need to follow him, Maggie. As far as you can. And of course, get out without being caught so you can pass on the information."

Remus leant forward. "If you enter a building, we'll do our best to stall anyone going in after you, to give you some time. We can't guarantee much, but we will do what we can without implicating ourselves as your ally."

Maggie nodded, understanding the short rope they would have to keep themselves on. The room quieted, and Maggie became uncertain if they were waiting for her to speak or had simply finished explaining. "Is that... it?"

"Well," Roy hedged, "we had hoped to have more but I suppose it literally is that simple. That's all you need to do. We have his daily routine here, though his behavior recently has deviated a little. You'll likely need to follow him the moment he leaves his house in the early hours of the morning." Roy placed the dirt-image before her. It had varying sized squares and symbols, not making much sense to her. "The general's house is in the Northern Noble district, here." Roy pointed to a square on the drawing. "It's not far from the arena, which is located just over here. We suggest trying to become familiar with it tomorrow, give you some time to get used to the area if you haven't really been there before."

Gale snorted. "The only people familiar who aren't nobles are their servants. It's not against the law for us to be there, but it's clear to any that we aren't welcome."

"It's fine, I'll manage."

"And that's just about all we can tell you, I'm afraid," Roy said with an apologetic smile. "All we have to go off is that the general acts a little suspicious, and now we have to follow him because of it."

"Seems simple enough; follow the general," Maggie said, hoping her false confidence covered her churning stomach. She wasn't very nervous, but anticipation was building, filling her with energy again. "I promise I'll start once I finish my personal business," Maggie said, reminding them she had her own matters that took precedence over reconnaissance.

Remus nodded. "As long as you have the place properly scouted before the Day, make yourself familiar with the streets and pathways." Remus sat back in his chair, a slight smile on his lips to let Maggie know they accepted her decision, not that they had much of a choice.

The room fell silent for a moment, eyes on the paperwork in front of them as if evaluating the weight of their plans.

"Maggie," Gale said, her calm face now bearing a pleasant and appreciative smile, her green eyes glistening a little as if she had been holding back tears. "Thank you for doing this."

Maggie smiled, her mouth suddenly dry and unable to respond with words. The others nodded in unison, agreeing with Gale and silently displaying their own gratefulness.

Varin then excused himself and Maggie, leading her back out into the street, back into the night. She followed him around a corner before he began speaking. "You know, you can still back out if you want to."

"You keep telling me that," Maggie said. "Do you want me to back out?"

"I just want to make sure you know you have a choice. I feel like we've pressured you and now you feel obligated to put your own life at risk for strangers."

"Not for strangers, for information." Maggie smiled as Varin laughed.

307

"Precisely, information."

"I know what I'm doing, Varin. You said so yourself – I'm stable enough to make these decisions, otherwise you wouldn't have asked me to do it."

"That is true, but I've made mistakes before."

"I'll do it. The general is connected to my son's death, so now it just feels... right."

Varin nodded. "I knew you'd choose him. I just thought you'd at least listen to Roy first, poor guy spent a lot of time gathering information so you could carefully pick a target with the right knowledge first."

Maggie winced. "I do feel kind of bad now."

"Don't worry about it," Varin said with a quick smile. "Anyway, it's dark, it's late, and you have already taken the lead from me, so I assume we're going?"

"You don't have to come."

"Nonsense, it feels right to follow you."

Maggie laughed, the sounds somehow feeling stale, but pleasant. She made her way toward The Flowing Red tavern where she aimed to speak with James. To the Gods prisons with his words; she needed to know why he joined the Sandmen, she deserved that truth.

* * *

Maggie's heart sank. The Flowing Red was filled with patrons pushing past one another to get their drinks, but James was not a part of the crowd. He was nowhere to be seen. *This can't be right, it's flow day?* She scoured the room once more to make certain she hadn't missed him. Worried, she met with Varin outside, fretting over where James could be.

"Maggie, calm down, it's fine. If he's really a part of the Sandmen now, then he might just be doing a job for them."

"Which means he is literally out there doing illegal activity? The same activity that got our son thrown in jail? No, he wouldn't do that. He's a drunk, not an idiot."

"It's fine, we'll find him. Let's just casually ask some Sandmen."

Maggie looked at him, dumbfounded.

"I'm serious. Approach some Sandmen, tell them that James offered to sell us some Dreams and that we're looking for him."

Maggie wanted to yell at Varin for even suggesting something so stupid, but she had to admit it seemed like the best method to get a quick answer. "I know where to find some to ask."

She led Varin through the streets and towards the library but he was able to keep pace with her, already knowing where she was headed. They turned down the dark street where Maggie had spied on the young group of Sandmen, and she prayed to the Gods they would be there. Thankfully, they'd kept a torch lit, as if wanting to shine a beacon on their location.

Without hesitation, Maggie marched right up to them, Varin trying subtly to slow her but to no avail.

The young group of boys stared them up and down as they stood in the torchlight, immediately suspicious. One boy stepped forward, face scowling. "Bit late for a stroll. Shouldn't the elderly be in bed by now?"

The boys laughed, but Maggie was too focused to care about insults and formalities. "I want to buy some Dreams," she blurted out, Varin desperately looking around to see if anyone had happened to be wandering by and accidentally overheard it.

The boys stopped laughing and their demeanor immediately changed.

"You guys guards or magistrates or something? You have to legally tell me if you are," the boy said as his associates tried to look around without drawing attention to themselves.

"That's not the law and we're not guards," Varin answered, his voice sounding a little confused.

"We want to buy Dreams. Are you going to help or not?"

"What makes you think that us, a group of young men, have any Dreams to sell?" the boy teased, trying to take control of the conversation.

Maggie was in no mood to play along. She grabbed the boy, yanked him close and shoved up his sleeve, revealing the Sandmen's symbol.

309

The sudden movement scared the boy, and he yelped as he lost his footing. One of his friends grabbed something from his pocket, reactively pointing it towards Maggie.

A livewood dagger.

"Easy, friend, we're not here to cause trouble." Varin tried to calm the sudden tension.

"I'm here because I want to get my hands on some Dreams, so are you going to help, or not?" Maggie demanded.

"What in the prisons is your problem, lady? Damn. Fine, follow me." the boy gestured for them to follow but Maggie stopped him once more.

"Not from you. From James. He was the one who promised he could get some for me, so where is he?"

"Who's James?"

The boy who produced the livewood dagger stepped forward, pocketing the weapon but leaving his hand close, still wary of Maggie. "I think James is the new guy, the one who's been hanging out with Harold? Oh wait, he goes by Essin, now. But you know, the guy who wears that crappy old jacket and really struggled getting his tattoo done. It was pretty funny to watch."

"Don't know him, but I did hear someone was hanging around Essin. Whatever, if that's the guy you want to see, then you should just go talk to Essin, let him deal with your crazy. He's a few streets over in a house with—"

Maggie left before the directions were given. She knew exactly where this 'Essin' would be; she had seen him there before.

Varin said something to the Sandmen that was inaudible to Maggie and quickly caught up with her as she strode away; the pressure inside of her building, building, building toward an explosion. She didn't care if her continual harassment of James got him into trouble with his new friends, he'd brought it upon himself by even associating with them in the first place.

"Maggie, do you want to stop and think about this, perhaps?" Varin pleaded.

Maggie remained firm in her steps. "No. I'm getting to the bottom of this, so then I can focus on the general and my boy. I need James to help me understand before he goes and gets himself caught, or even killed."

"It's just that, you know, walking into Sandmen territory can be dangerous in itself, so perhaps we should worry a little more about ourselves?"

"We'll be fine, James might act like he never wants to see me again, but he won't let anything happen to me."

"What about me?"

"You can stay behind if you'd like."

"That's reassuring."

"Look." Maggie stopped and spun to face him; Varin barely reacted in time to not crash into her. "You want me to do another job, which means I need to deal with my personal stuff first. The Day of Sacrifice is only a few days away, so my time is limited, I need to stop snooping in the shadows and begin demanding answers upfront if I want to get it done in time."

"Yes, that's good and all, but Sandmen don't like questions. You're going to get him into trouble by speaking with him. What happens when he doesn't give you any Dreams? What will he say when you barrage him with personal questions?"

"I'll just have to find him alone, then."

"You're being naïve."

"Perhaps, but right now, I need to do this. It's the only option I can think of."

"There are others, if we just stop and think about it, I'm sure."

"No. There's no time."

Maggie returned to her rapid pace, unsure if Varin would actually follow. She had a bad feeling about James, not something she could easily explain. Something was off; he was in trouble, and she needed to appease those feelings by seeing him for herself.

That's all she really wanted, just to see that he was alright, unharmed. They didn't need to talk, he would likely avoid her answers anyway. Besides, Varin was right, she would likely get him into trouble by getting personal.

She sped into the next street, not making any effort to conceal her presence as she marched right up to the Sandmen's base. Varin's footsteps could barely be heard behind her, she mentally thanked him for accompanying her to the den.

As she approached, a Sandman emerged from the house, spying her. He was a little older than the other boys, but just as mean of an expression. He stepped into her path, silently gauging her and Varin.

"I'm here to buy Dreams," Maggie snapped.

The man continued to evaluate them, as if he could tell they were trouble. "Who sent you here?"

"Didn't get his name. I'm looking to buy from James, and the boys sent me here." Maggie loosely gestured the direction she had come from.

The man seemed to weigh her words, debating on what action to take.

Maggie's hands began to shake. Her nerves were beginning to get the best of her as she stood in the quiet tension. She recognized the signs, knowing what was coming, praying this man would answer fast enough.

"James, huh? New guy already got himself a deal. Not bad. He and Essin just stepped out for a bit, they'll be back soon."

"How soon?" Maggie almost yelled, quickly biting her tongue to try control herself, but then an idea struck her. She twitched her fingers, shifted her stance, clenched and unclenched her hands.

The man looked at her again, his eyes drifting towards her unsteady hands, and then narrowed them onto her face. "Boy, you really did get yourself addicted, didn't you? I thought you were just some mother going through some kind of personal crisis but looks like you've been at it for a while."

She prodded her upper lip, finding blood, again. *Perfect timing.* "Just tell me where James went, please. I beg you." Maggie added a slight quiver to her voice and exaggerated the shaking of her hands.

The man smirked at her, eyes shifting over to Varin, who Maggie hoped was not about to blow her impromptu cover. "They went down the street somewhere, not far. I think they're selling Dreams to others there, so you might want to move quick before they're gone," the man teased.

Maggie saw it as a blessing, he had believed her cover. She darted past him, dashing down the street to find James. Her hands continued to shake, and her nose continued to bleed, but she didn't care. She was close to James now.

Moving quickly down the street, Maggie checked alleyways and listened out for any voices that might give away James' position. As they neared the end, Maggie's nerves continued to build with each empty alley. Granted, it was dark and she couldn't see very well, but she assumed they would at least be doing a deal by candlelight, it made no sense to do it in complete darkness.

This street had a night burner candle, so that anyone could come light their wicks from it if needed overnight. The glow of light flickered in the cracks of the wooden box that sheltered it. Her fears grew as she neared; James had yet to be seen.

Then she heard it. It was soft, muffled, but audible enough for her heightened senses.

Groaning. A man groaning in pain.

No!

She dashed down the nearest alleyway, not caring that the moonlight barely allowed her to see more than a few feet in front of her. She turned into a small opening between the back of a few houses, nearly toppling over as she slipped on something wet.

A man groaned in pain once more.

"Whoever's there, you're too late," a voice called out in the darkness.

"James?"

"Oh Gods… Mags? No, please go away!" James barely got through the words through his gasps.

Maggie darted over to where the sound emanated, slipping on something wet again. In the scant moonlight, she found James sitting awkwardly against the wall, hands clutched at his torso as a wet substance trickled through his fingers.

Blood.

His breathing was heavy. Maggie placed her hands on him, words choking in her throat.

"I'll get light," Varin said, darting out of the alley.

"Mags, please, go." His words were no longer filled with anger, but sadness. He didn't want her to see him.

313

"James...What have you done?" Maggie tried to inspect the wounds, but it was difficult without any light.

"I... I did it, Mags. I did it."

"What are you talking about? Did what?"

James gave a muffled laugh, then winced in pain.

Maggie turned her head, to see Varin walking towards them, night candle removed from its holster and in his hand. As he neared, the light illuminated a body. Slumped on the ground, lifeless. A man with a dyed green plait.

Essin. James' supposed new friend.

Maggie turned to Hames, eyes wide with horror and confusion. "James...What?"

"I did it, Mags." James began to tear up, a contorted smile on his face. "I avenged him. I avenged Patrick."

Maggie almost couldn't believe she had heard her son's name leave James' mouth. He had refused to even hear it since their son's death. She looked over at the corpse once more; a livewood dagger protruded from Essin's stomach, blood continuing to seep out. "James..."

"This bastard did it. He's the one who sent Patrick to prison. Sold him to the guards for a few measly scraps of food!" James raised his voice, though he was barely able to yell, the anger did not wane.

Maggie pushed him back gently against the wall. "I... I don't understand, James. What have you done?"

"I killed the bastard that killed our boy. That's what I did, Mags. I did it. I avenged our boy."

Tears flowed from both of them. Maggie could see the life slowly draining from James' face, could see the stab wounds that littered his torso. Essin hadn't gone down without a fight.

"Why... Why, James?" Maggie's throat tightened, choking on the words.

"I did it, Mags. I did it." the energy slowly dissolved from his voice. James was slowly becoming delirious.

Maggie pulled James to her, not caring about the blood that stained her clothing.

"I did it, Mags... I did it..."

"That's right, James. You did it. You avenged our boy."

"I did it. I think… I think I'd like to see him now…"

"Go see him, James." Maggie kissed him on the forehead as tears streamed down her face. "Tell him that I love him and miss him very much."

James reached up with a shaky hand, gently stroking her face. He brushed her hair aside, something he used to do when they were together.

When they were still happy.

James' voice trembled. "I'll tell him… I did it, Mags… Patrick…."

The last breath left James' body, his arms going limp, falling to the ground.

Maggie sat against the wall, clutching onto the lifeless body.

"You did it, James."

24

Edmund's funeral came quickly. With so many deaths in the city, funerals were reserved for nobility, and usually they took a week to plan, but the city had insisted on doing it before Arthur's duel, so that he could attend.

Arthur had hoped to skip the funeral entirely, using the duel as an excuse, but they managed to plan and execute the proper procedure with surprising speed. Someone – likely Gavin - was pushing for this funeral to happen as quickly as possible. Conversely, the service felt painstakingly slow. They buried Edmund in the allotted fields for nobility, a small stretch of land not far from the city walls. Only a small group of people were allowed to attend, not wanting to attract any metalurks.

Arthur was surprised to see Gavin in attendance. Perhaps his elder brother wanted to confirm the corpse for himself, but no one had expected him to make an appearance.

After the service, they held a gathering in their home, allowing people to pay their respects to the widow Evelynn. Arthur tried on several occasions to slip away from hosting duties, but somehow kept getting caught. He did his best to remain in a corner, hoping to stay out of sight but in all honesty, he tried to stay away from his mother. Her tears were like spikes shoved into his heart, and he could not bear to face her and her grim expression.

It was a similar story with his sister. Arthur was the source of their pain, and while he did not regret his actions, it didn't make it any easier to deal with.

Arthur leant against the wall, waiting as time slowly trickled by, counting the seconds until the gathering was over and was surprised when Gavin approached and joined him in his refuge away from their guests.

"You were awfully quiet today," Gavin said, sipping his wine.

"So were you."

"Shame about what happened to Edmund. Mother will be hurting for weeks."

"I know."

"So why aren't you?"

Arthur looked at his brother, eyebrow raised. "You aren't hurting either."

"I have my reasons. I haven't been here for a while, so I don't know what's been happening since keeping my distance. Last I knew, you were on decent terms with Edmund, I figured you'd at least be a little upset."

"We had a bit of a falling out."

"Right before his death?"

"Days before."

"So, you finally found out then?"

"Found out what?"

Gavin's stunned expression quickly dissolved into annoyance. "You mean to tell me you never found out? Did you never actually ask him?"

"It's a bit late now, so why don't you just go ahead and tell me."

"You... Gods, follow me." Gavin left, keeping his pace even so he wouldn't draw attention to himself.

Arthur followed, trying to mimic the same attitude, giving polite smiles but otherwise trying to look professional for a wake.

Gavin grabbed a lit candle and led Arthur down the hall and into a vacant room—his old room. It had been emptied when he'd left, and their Mother never felt quite right putting anything else in it. Edmund wanted to repurpose it into a function room but didn't care enough to argue with Evelynn on the matter.

His brother closed the door behind them, making the room ominously lit by the single candle. Gavin held it between them, his face was grim, clearly unhappy with the situation. "First of all, you're an idiot for not finding it out before you killed Edmund," Gavin said nonchalantly, as if it were just a matter of fact rather than something horrendous.

Arthur froze; cold sweat breaking out over his body. His brother stared at him, watching his reaction; Arthur found it difficult to control his slight movements while trying to find the right words, but he had been caught off-guard.

How did he...?

"Drop the façade, it's obvious. The man might've been a little over sixty, but he didn't choke on his food, did he? As poetic as that might have been, I just don't believe such justice would come for him."

"I did it beca—"

Gavin held up a hand. "I don't care why you did it, I just wanted to know if my hunch was correct. My statement still stands, you're an idiot."

"Just tell me what you want then, unless you're here to try blackmail your own brother."

"Bold of you to play the family card like that."

"Just get on with it." Arthur had turned from stunned silence to a bitter anger. If Gavin could tell, who else could?

"You're telling me you killed him, and it wasn't over what he's been doing behind your back? Gods, you must've hated him more than I did. But, like I said, I don't care for the actual reasoning. Tell me, has he completely controlled your training regime?"

"Naturally, he was in charge of my entire schedule."

"But you never were allowed to decide to train in areas you felt weak in? Perhaps Eustace even changed drastically one day, in the way he fights?"

The sword is in his left hand. He hasn't changed back.
"What about it?"

"You've got one sturdy wall around that brain of yours if you can't even figure it out."

"Just tell me," Arthur growled.

"He's been talking to a spy, Arthur. A spy who's infiltrated the Va Noldins and was selling secrets to Edmund. It's why you are being trained to fight a very specific style of duelist, why Eustace doesn't deviate from his stances. You're being given an illegal advantage without even knowing it."

A spy? In the Va Noldins? How is that possible? How would a spy get into their training room? "Who is the spy?" Arthur asked, still processing how this impacted his situation.

"I don't know. I left when I discovered he was doing it again. After my duel, I became suspicious of how easily I had won, then I began to piece it all together. The spy he had for my duel no longer works for the Va Noldins. I made Edmund swear that he would not do the same to you, and he gave me his word."

"But he did it anyway?"

Gavin nodded. "The sack of crap that he was, went back on his worthless word. I saw a hooded figure leaving his meeting room one day, and immediately confronted him. He could have made up a lie, any one at all and I might have believed him, but the fat old fool just smiled and said I would understand."

"Well, that explains why you abruptly left," Arthur said, trying to piece tiny clues together.

"I couldn't stay knowing what he was doing. I couldn't report it either and strip our family of all it had or endanger Mother's life. They might have suspected she were in on it, too."

"Is she?"

"In truth, I don't know. I've never spoken to her about it. She's no dull creature, but her heart and will have slowly died over the years, she might have just let it happen around her, pretending not to notice."

"Gods… an actual spy. What in these damned walls am I meant to do now? Drop out of the duel?"

"No."

"How can I go forward knowing that I already *know* how my opponent will fight? Knowing that I'll have to kill him just because our father played his dirty little tricks?"

"It is much too late to drop out of the duel. A sacrifice must still take place. You will attend your duel. You will win." Gavin moved closer, eyes locked onto Arthur's, emphasizing his point. "And you will denounce our family from high nobility. Strip us of our title, forfeit the rights to provide a champion."

Arthur seriously considered the idea. It made sense, but it did not appease his guilt at having to unfairly slay another man. His feelings would have to be put aside for now. Edmund placed him in this difficult position, he would have to try force the best outcome possible.

Which unfortunately meant still attending his duel.

"Look, I know I just let loose a metalurk in that small brain of yours, but just think over my proposition. And don't underestimate your opponent now that you're aware you know their dueling techniques. All it takes is a single moment, a slight crack in defense, a minor misplacement of your foot, and you're dead. Take it as seriously as you can."

Arthur nodded, still trying to comprehend the fact that he had been indirectly given information from a spy. But who could the spy have been? He wasn't aware of anyone snooping around the house, though that was probably the idea. Someone must've been sneaking in at odd hours, somehow either around the guards or the guards simply let them through.

Arthur's heart sank. *The messenger.*

"Arthur? What's wrong?"

"Nothing. I just… might have realized who the spy is. Maybe."

"Well, no point dwelling over that now. Revealing the person to anyone means compromising our family anyway. You'll just have to let it drop. Figure out how to deal with them later, maybe. Anyway, we should probably return to the wake. As much as I hate these gatherings, Mother needs our support."

Arthur nodded idly, eyes focused on empty space. *Could it really be her? Was she meeting with my father at the same time as sending me a message? How did my correspondent even manage to find her?*

"I'll repeat myself," Gavin said, interrupting his thoughts, his body blocking most of the candlelight as he had turned to leave, leaving Arthur in the darkness. "Mother is no dull creature. She sees and hears things you may not realize. If I figured it out… Just be careful around her."

Upsetting Mother. Perhaps I'm not too different from Edmund after all.

* * *

The sky was grey, a sea of clouds blocking the shine that should have illuminated the demonstration. Arthur sat with his family atop the North Gate, opposite to The Voice, watching the reveal of their new defense. Each time the ballista released, it made a satisfying sound as the spike left its resting place. The general was putting on a grand display of the new device but seemed to cut the demonstration short after firing only three spikes. Arthur sat beside his mother in silence. He knew she had wanted to stay home and grieve but could not miss such a defining moment in their history.

On the other side of his mother sat Gavin and his family. He had received a warm welcome by the crowd, and even acknowledged by The Voice themselves. The general promised that the Red Sea would cause less destruction this year thanks to the new devices. It would have been reassuring to hear, but Arthur had gotten the distinct impression the general was exaggerating.

The demonstration was called to an end, and The Voice silently excused themselves, all except the speaker who took the crowd through one final prayer before departing.

Arthur gave his mother a questioning look, silently asking her if she wished to leave. She slowly shook her head, her expression blank as she stared out into the fields beyond the wall.

The crowd below began to slowly disperse, chattering away excitedly about the ballista. Arthur agreed that it was an ingenious new invention but couldn't quell the feeling that something felt awry. With permission from the general, Arthur inspected the ballista closer, though he was not allowed to touch the device. He was baffled by its design, the way it functioned seemed elusive to

321

him, not something easily grasped without proper education on the subject. To him, it simply didn't seem feasible that it operated the way it did. He studied all the small pieces going on within the ballista, all the wheels, both livewood and regular wood to optimize their use of the precious resource.

He returned to his mother, impressed despite his confusion. It still made no sense to him, but that didn't squander his respect for the livewood engineers who'd designed it.

Evelynn continued her gaze out onto the fields, observing the group of soldiers tasked in returning the large spikes. They wheeled out a cart and plucked the spikes from the ground, including the one that managed to remain protruding from the earth.

Arthur watched, unsure what was so gratifying about the process, but his mother seemed transfixed by it. "Everything all right, Mother?"

"Hm?"

"You seem a little pensive."

"A lot has happened, Arthur. A lot is going to happen. I know that I should not complain in your presence about such matters, but it is not like I can simply ignore them."

"I wouldn't ask you to. A lot is going to happen."

"It's tomorrow, you know?"

"I know. My stomach is in a knot just thinking about it, but I'm doing my best to face the reality."

"I'd say you're doing a splendid job if you've managed to come out here and celebrate this new defense for the city."

"You know very well that appearances can be deceiving."

"I do, but that doesn't mean you aren't doing just fine."

Arthur noticed Gavin having conversation with General Deven atop the gate. The general had lost his smug smile from the announcement, his brow slightly furrowed. Gavin's back was turned, so Arthur could not gauge his brother's expression to determine the seriousness of the conversation. Not that it was relevant to him.

"I'm proud of you."

"Mother?"

"I just wanted you to know that."

"I do know."

"Then I am reminding you of that fact. No matter what has happened, or will happen, I am proud of you for walking into that arena tomorrow, head held high, ready for whatever may come."

Arthur could not tell if it was his own imagination or if his mother had alluded to knowing about Edmund's death. It had been toying with him since the wake, whenever his mother spoke it was as if he was going to great lengths to connect dots. He tried his best to ignore it, but it proved insistent. He did not want to wallow in self-pity until he was called for his duel. Arthur wanted what could be the last few moments of his life to be happy.

And he wanted to be with the mysterious man.

He turned to his mother, ready to respond, but the words fell away once he saw her somber face once again. Arthur rose, gesturing for her to do the same. Surprisingly, she complied, adjusting her robe against the chill breeze. Few of the crowd remained as Arthur and his mother made way to their awaiting palanquin. Gavin called out along the way, quickly catching up to them to say his proper goodbye to Evelynn. Arthur had thought his elder brother hoped to have remained hidden as they left, but it seemed with the death of Edmund, Gavin was putting in more effort to show his mother respect and care.

At least if Arthur fell in battle tomorrow, he could trust his brother to watch over her with proper care and attention.

Arthur and his mother climbed into the rickshaw and gave the driver the signal to return home. The cart rattled from the uneven stones, giving off an unusually comfortable sound, as if it helped drown the thoughts out of Arthur's mind.

As they rode through the city, waving to the people who greeted them, what Arthur noticed the most was the distinct lack of differing scents. He had never paid attention to it before, but the same stench bore through each street, never changing until they neared their house. It's as if the city had a single unique smell to it, banding them together. Though that was probably all in his mind. He had never really focused on the smells of the city before, but he had also never grasped so desperately at threads to distract himself.

323

They arrived at the entry to their courtyard, the stationed guards moving to assist Evelynn out of the rickshaw. Arthur and his mother then ventured inside, silently, looking about their garden, at how colorful and alive it seemed to be. The plants were vivacious, their stems a healthy green, and heads ranging in a wide variety of colors. It was truly pleasing to see such color against the backdrop of the dull city.

Once they entered their house, Evelynn went to part ways, but Arthur instinctively caught his mother's arm and spun her around, embracing her. He didn't say a word, simply held his mother tight, his problems melting away as she squeezed back. Arthur held her for a moment longer, scared that letting go meant returning to reality, but he knew he couldn't hide under his mother until the duel was over.

It was probably not the honorable thing to do.

He let go to find his mother smiling, a small tear falling down her cheek. Evelynn then turned and walked away, likely to reside in her chambers. Arthur stood in the front room, feeling the pressures slowly return with each step his mother took away from him. In an attempt to shake it off, he hurried towards his own room and began to change into an appropriate outfit for an evening in the town.

As he entered his room, he looked over at his desk to see his written letter still sitting there. He knew it would be there and yet he still became disappointed. *Was she really a spy? It makes sense but... was she?*

He ignored the letter that seemed to scream at him, telling him that he would never get to talk, let alone see his mysterious friend again. But he wouldn't give up hope just yet. He grabbed a coat to ward against the cold and left the house in a hurry.

Arthur ventured back through the gardens and reached the entrance of his family's estate, not hesitating in his steps to head towards the tavern where he had met the man. It was the last day for drinking until they properly recovered from the inevitable Red Sea attack.

"Sir?" a voice called out. Arthur turned to see one of the front entrance guards walking towards him.

"Pardon me if I'm interrupting sir, but I was just wondering if you had sent a messenger to the Va Noldins to let them know you'll be out in the town? We haven't seen a messenger go by."

Oh gods, how did that escape my mind? "No, I haven't, thank you. Please organize a messenger for me and send it quickly because I'm in a bit of a hurry, I can't wait around."

"Not a problem sir, we'll get right on it." the soldier bowed, dismissing himself and complying to the order.

Arthur mentally kicked himself; he could have gotten into an absurd amount of trouble if he had not sent word, thankfully someone was of sound enough mind to remember.

He made his way to the Everwall Tavern, the name and location burned into his brain from that fateful night. He was hoping to be just as lucky.

The muffled sounds of laughter, loud conversations, and music played through the walls of the building as he stood outside of it. He opened the doors to find what he had expected: the place was bustling with patrons, with barely any room to stand. He wasn't sure how he would ever find the man in such a crowd, but he wasn't about to give up that easily.

He waded through the crowd, gently pushing drunkards aside as they had difficulty moving out of his way, stumbling over others. At this rate, the tavern was probably running on empty with drinks already.

Arthur made his way to the table where he and his friend had sat, only to find it had been moved to join another table, taken up by a large group of people. It was difficult to tell if they had come in together, or had met here, as they all drunkenly slurred the words to a soldier shanty.

But the man was not amongst them.

Arthur scoured the room from where he stood, but it was nigh on impossible to pick people out in such a manner. So, he walked the room, doing his best to look at every face, at every single patron, sifting through the crowd of people one by one.

And still, he could not find the man.

Determined and desperate, Arthur rummaged through the crowd once more, hoping he simply missed him.

But fortune was not in his favor today.

325

Arthur exited the tavern, looking down the streets to find most of them barren. He slumped against the wall, deciding to wait a little longer, hoping that the man might turn up out of sheer coincidence.

But in his heart, he knew that he would not come.

He sat for what seemed like hours, the night sky darkening. It came time for him to return, lest his mother worry about his absence and send a search party. He rose, dusting himself off, giving one last, hopeful look in each direction.

When his last hope died, he trudged his way back home.

Arthur was left undisturbed on his journey back home, people either in their homes praying, out drinking in what could be their final night, or even trying to secure their valuables before they were forced to evacuate their homes and reach safety.

"Sir," the entryway guard called out to him, his tone serious and face worried. Arthur immediately became on edge.

"Yes?"

"There's been a development in the death of your father. We not long ago received word that the Magistrate suspects foul play in your father's death."

A child spread through Arthur's body. "Foul play?"

"Yes, sir. A woman had been caught lurking around the vicinity that night. Though not much has been revealed through interrogation, they think that she is connected to your father. They aren't certain how, but their suspicion is that she somehow tampered with his food or drink."

A woman? "Describe the woman."

"They said she was average height, dark blonde hair, green eyes, wore drab greys like any citizen, but also wore a dark cloak and hood."

It is her. Gods...

"Uh, thanks for telling me. Does Mother know?"

"Y-Yes, sir."

Arthur's chill melted away a little, now staring at the guard suspiciously. "Why did you just hesitate?"

"It's the uh... nature of the relationship between this woman and your father, sir. They suspect she was a mistress of his."

Would father really have gone that far? "I see. I assume Mother was told that as well?"

The guard nodded.

"All right, I'll go check on her. Thank you, again."

The guard bowed as Arthur walked past him.

As soon as he pushed through the front door, Arthur felt an eerie silence about the house. It was normally quiet, with so few people living in a large building, but somehow the silence felt different. Off.

Perhaps it was just the knowledge and rumors that would quickly spread amongst the staff and town, how quickly his family was going to become the source of conversations amongst nobility. He groaned against the idea of having to face any other nobles in this current state, and made his way to his mother's room, knocking lightly on the door.

No response.

"Mother?"

"Come in, Arthur."

Arthur felt relieved having heard her voice, and quickly opened the door. The room had several candles lit, so at least his mother wasn't brooding in the dark. She sat at her desk, looking through letters.

"I just heard the news," Arthur said, not bothering to make any idle chatter. His mother did not visibly react, still reading and sorting letters. "I really don't think he had a mistress," Arthur continued, trying to convince his mother despite her lack of response.

"I know he didn't. He wasn't having an affair with her, he was getting information from her."

"You knew?"

"I suspected. I found some rather interesting letters from her, detailing the Va Noldin's champion dueling techniques."

"So, it's all true then. I'm indirectly breaking the law."

"Don't be so melodramatic, you had nothing to do with it."

"Somehow, it doesn't make it feel any better knowing that we won't be fighting on even terms."

Evelynn picked up another letter, skimming through it and placing it down onto a pile. "Make the best out of the situation

327

given to you. Mope about it later, but do your best to claim victory anyway, make up for it later in whatever way makes you feel better."

His mother was being surprisingly cold towards him. He had expected to find her curled up in her bed, possibly weeping, but instead she was almost callous. "You truly think that she was only a spy?"

His mother placed another letter down, but this time didn't pick up another. She instead stared down at the desk, lost in deep thought. "I think for the moment she was a spy. Who knows what she might have eventually become." Evelynn's voice was low, her energy draining away with each word.

"You were worried she might have replaced you?"

"If not her, then someone else."

Arthur nodded. "Do you think she had something to do with Father's death?" the words escaped from him before he could catch himself. He needed to know if his mother suspected him and secretly despised him for it.

"No. Your father succumbed to a lack of chewing."

The worlds felt hollow. Arthur could not tell if it was what his mother believed or was simply telling people. "So, then why does the Magistrate believe there was something sinister?"

"I do not know, Arthur."

"Do you think she'll be executed?"

"Most likely, after the Red Sea is dealt with."

Arthur's stomach dropped. *She'll be paying for my crime.*

"There is something you aren't telling, isn't there?" Evelynn called out to him. He hadn't realized she had turned around to face him, now distracted by his own thoughts.

"In regard to what?"

"I don't know, but I get the sense you are trying to prod for something, or there is something sitting on your mind that is begging to be released. Did you know the woman?"

Arthur went to shake his head, but it refused to move. "Yes. But I didn't know she was also seeing Father."

"Was she a spy for you as well?"

"No, she was more than that. Almost like a friend, but we never talked. She was my personal messenger between myself and... a correspondent of mine."

"I see. You never questioned how she managed to slip in and out of the house?"

"Of course, I did, but I assumed she was only here for me. She was the one who found me on behalf of my correspondent, so I just continued to use her as a messenger between us. I didn't really suspect anything else."

"Secret letters, a secret messenger, and a secret correspondent. It's not difficult to imagine how you became blinded to her other matters," his mother said, her tone a playful slyness, but Arthur swore it hid a touch of bitterness beneath it.

"Perhaps it has, but as long as you are sure she did not assassinate Father, we should have her released."

"Nonsense. She might not have committed the crime of murder, but she did something far more sinister, depending on perspective. You are aware of what she was a spy for, aren't you?"

Arthur's head dropped, his eyes now focused on the ground, his head in turmoil. "I was recently informed, yes."

"Once that is revealed, she will be dealt with accordingly. Only The Voice can excuse such a thing, but what she has done is inexcusable."

Arthur grimly nodded. He knew that she had to answer for her subterfuge and betrayal, he just didn't want to believe that she had done it. It seemed so farfetched for her to do such a thing. He thought her timid and understanding, but apparently it was just a coat she donned when meeting him.

She had proclaimed his correspondent as her friend, but perhaps she would have also called his father her friend.

No. She was there the night I met him. She was his friend. Did...he know about her trade with my father?

The thought made his body weak, but he quickly tried to convince himself that his friend was unaware of their messenger's secret. It would likely have revealed his identity, which he was certain was still a mystery. Or he at least hoped was still a mystery, for his friend had not turned up looking for him before his duel.

"You've a lot on your mind, Arthur. Rid yourself of all matters. The Day is tomorrow and with it, your fight. It should be the only thing of importance right now, everything else can be forced aside. Until everything settles down, focus on yourself. If you are felled, don't die with a heavy heart. Smile as the Gods welcome you to their home and continue to watch over our family as you've so vigilantly done since you were a child. I consider the Gods blessed if they were to receive you tomorrow."

Arthur moved over to his mother, embracing her. Her suggestion was not so easily executed, but it did not tarnish the weight of them.

He squeezed her as she reciprocated by wrapping her arms around him.

"Whatever happens tomorrow, know that I love you. No matter what you might have done, covertly or not, nothing can possibly sully my image of you."

She doesn't know. Words scrambled around in Arthur's mind, trying to find the right way to respond. His mother needed to hear some encouraging words, but it eluded him as time seemed to fly by as he held his mother. "I… love you, too, Mother."

The words were much simpler and shorter than he had wanted, but he made sure that they carried the weight of their meaning behind them, emphasizing how much he truly cared for her.

Evelynn chuckled. "That's not what you wanted to say, was it?"

"No. No it was not." Arthur smiled. He was thankful that his mother was able to read him so well, the unspoken words he failed to find may have been lost to him, but at least they weren't lost to her.

Arthur let go of his mother, looking down to find more tears. She quickly regathered herself, wiping away the last tear that slowly formed from her eye. "You'll find it awfully difficult to sleep tonight. Have a cup or two of wine, but don't overdo it."

"Perhaps you should indulge yourself and do the same, Mother."

"As much as I find myself exhausted from recent events, I fear that not even wine will be able to aid my rest."

"Then do it for the fun of it. Wine can make an adequate companion on those restless nights."

"Are you encouraging I drink until I pass out?"

"I'm encouraging you to get sleep."

"I'll be fine, dear. Like I said, focus on yourself."

Arthur gave her one last hug before leaving the room. He quietly closed the door behind him, chiding himself for not having said more to aid his mother's emotional state, but she was a strong woman, she would manage on her own.

He made his way into the kitchens and down into the wine cellar. They hadn't many wines in stock, as per the limitations of the city, so he silently prayed that he would find it.

He scanned the last few bottles on the shelves, reading their symbols thoroughly.

No. Not this one. Ah hah! Vindlegridge's Three-Year berry solution, mixed and rested in a sweet-smoked pine barrel. His favorite.

Arthur grabbed the bottle and two cups, returning to his chambers. His stomach and mind were a mess of emotions, but as soon as he closed the door to his room and poured the two cups, he felt himself settle slightly, and poured some wine.

He sipped at his cup. "Mmm… The fragrance is certainly key. The tart of the berries mixed with the sweetness of the smoking, and the earthy freshness of the pine. Truly accentuates the thought and care behind the process of its production."

He spoke to himself, finding it lonesome, yet comforting.

Arthur stared at the other cup, thoughts threatening to race back. He downed the rest of his drink, pouring himself another. "To you. I hope we get to meet again, in this life or the next."

Arthur raised his drink to the empty space beside him.

25

Something felt off. Castor stood in his position next to the general atop the East Gate, watching a few metalurks scramble out of the forest, horn blaring through the city. The general had coincidentally been near when the horn sounded, so he was able to take his commanding position at the wall.

"Load the ballista!" General Deven shouted, and soldiers scrambled to load the two devices.

Castor watched the large spikes drop into place, the nagging feeling that something wasn't right still bugging him. It flared up whenever he looked at the ballista, his instincts screaming at him not to trust the new defense.

"Ballistae, aim!"

The soldiers used the levers to maneuver the sights to face the oncoming metalurks, then adjusted for distance.

"First ballista, release!"

The lever was pulled, and the ballista was immediately reset again before the ammo had even landed.

The wooden spike flew through the air, well past the silent storm of metalurks.

"Second ballista, adjust and release!"

The soldiers quickly lowered the sights, locking it into place again, and pulled the lever to release the spike. This time, it managed to fall just short of the creatures, who didn't seem phased by the large – and new – attack. The metalurks just rounded the spike as if it were of no significance, keeping their pace towards the city.

"Load and aim!"

The wave was much smaller than most, making it a suitable situation to test the ballista. Within seconds, the ballistae were ready again. Not quite as fast as archers, but close enough and much deadlier.

The soldiers aimed and loosed the weapons again; the eerie sensation still remained whenever Castor looked at them. The spikes flew, one too far, but the other finding its mark.

The large spike tore through one of the metalurks, completely shredding one side of its body. The creature instantly fell to the ground, missing an arm and most of its torso. The ammunition then splintered, scattering its shrapnel across all the nearby metalurks. The soldiers gave a triumphant yell, the deadliness of the ballista now shown to them.

Even Castor had to admit he was impressed. Still, it didn't alleviate his disposition towards the defenses, but it was certainly a step in the right direction. He wasn't entirely certain of his reason for his distaste of the device. He originally thought it was because the general had so proudly spoken about it, but Castor didn't think he was that callous to distrust a defense just because the general had a part in it. No, it wasn't that. It was almost like... he had been paired with a soldier he had never met before and told to defend each other.

He didn't trust the ballista. Didn't know it well enough. Didn't know its strengths, weakness, capabilities, upkeep. Anything. All he knew was that it could release deadly spikes and kill, which should have been good enough for him, but something was off when Castor has seen the demonstration. And the General had halted the display prematurely, to hide something from the people.

"Ballistae, load and release! Archers, ready!"

Well, I suppose that's one weakness. They can't aim low enough to attack the creatures who reach our wall.

The ballistae were loosed once more, and once again found a single target before exploding into thousands of pieces. The soldiers gave another victory yell in unison, except the archers who were aiming their bows, ready for the command.

"Archers, loose!"

The archers felled several of the creatures, leaving only a few remaining.

Without being prompted by the general, Castor gave the signal to his awaiting Steelwoods that they were not needed. The creatures would all be slain, possibly without even a scratch to the gate.

Normally, the general would reprimand Castor for doing so without an order, but Deven didn't even glance in Castor's direction, eyes focused on the battlefield.

Castor couldn't help but glare at the man, questions screaming inside of him, compelling him to just grab the general by the collar and demand answers. Not that there were any left to give. The general had already confessed to having Patrick arrested, which indirectly led the boy being executed, but it was clear Deven had no regrets about it.

Still, Castor couldn't find reason not to fault Deven for his nephew's death. Despite someone else making the mistake, it was still the general who'd put his nephew in that position. All because Deven wanted his little power trip, to keep Castor leashed like a malnourished pig waiting for slaughter.

It only made Castor more determined to become General. Despite what Deven said about doing all within his power to prevent Castor, the Magistrate and The Voice couldn't ignore results. Castor would prove himself in the upcoming Red Sea, capably leading his Steelwood soldiers and defending the city with a determination deserving praise.

If he survived.

He had to defend the city with honesty, which meant laying down his life in order to save others. He wouldn't be a very good General if he put up a façade, he had to have the heart to follow through as well. He fought every wave of metalurks with the same intent, placing himself between the enemy and civilians, dying was just a part of the job.

The Red Sea would be no different, just a significantly larger wave.

The soldiers called out in triumph as the archers felled the last of the metalurks. Most began talking about the ballistae as they went to recover their surviving ammunition and gather the bodies for burning. Most of the soldiers were theorizing how much easier the Red Sea will be with the power of their new defenses.

I suppose launching large pieces of wood is a good defense.

The general did not stick around, leaving Castor to ensure that all the after-wave work was completed. The metalurks didn't even reach the door, they were too few in number. One of the benefits of the Red Sea was the lack in number of metalurks leading up to it.

But that only made it more foreboding.

The Magistrate had sent out scouts once again over the past few weeks, but they found no metalurks massing on the borders or any kind of odd behavior in the forest. The trees remained the same dark brown color, the grass was still the same shade of healthy green, all growing out of the unchanged dark brown of root-infested soil. There were no signs of shelters, no tracks left of the creatures other than the entrance of the forest, no discernible proof that the creatures even existed. Nearly two-hundred years in, and still no concept of where they came from. Still, that didn't mean they would give up on trying.

Castor stared at the metalurk corpses piled up outside of the city, waiting to be taken to the burning pitch. The sky was clear, allowing the sun to shine brightly onto the bodies, illuminating the red blood that could be seen through their thin skin. It was remarkable to see. Their blood contained small particles of some undetermined substance, floating around their bodies like a puddle of water had collected dirt. Their researchers were unable to determine much about the mysterious creatures, unable to determine what allowed them to see with no eyes or hear with no ears. It was as if they were designed to be perfect killing entities.

Well, almost. They were frightfully dull.

Castor used his livewood spear to raise one of the creature's limp hands. The arm was noticeably longer and thicker than their own, the hands were also larger, but their fingers formed into sharp, bone-like claws. Castor let the hand drop, disturbed by its appearance. Another body was carelessly thrown on top, the

335

remaining half of a metalurk destroyed by the ballista splattering blood as it landed.

Seeing the destruction up close gave Castor an even better perspective at what the ballista could achieve. It seemed to have torn the creatures apart with such ease, perhaps it could take down multiple with a single shot? Perhaps finding a way to release them from the ground level for a better angle?

Taking down parts of the wall to add slits for firing was a risky move, it added a temporary flaw in the wall that the metalurks would surely exploit. Something to consider after the Red Sea, but perhaps he should make a note of it for the Magistrate of Defense. Surely, they had already thought of it, but perhaps with his request they might considerate it further?

It was times like these Castor needed the general to inform him about the plans of the wall. The Gate Captains were meant to be told all future plans, but General Deven stifled the flow of information simply to spite Castor, even though it meant the other Gate Captains suffered.

That's how petty Deven could be. The other Gate Captains didn't mind so much, they mostly just wanted to focus on surviving each wave rather than finding improvements for the wall. They figured it was the Magistrates' and researchers' jobs; the Gate Captains were simply keeping the city alive for as long as possible.

It was one reason Castor didn't get along so well with the other Gate Captains. They had no aspirations, just focusing on not dying rather than improving the city. He wondered if the general had also gotten to them, either blackmailing or crushing their spirits just enough to prevent them from wanting to become the next general.

Not that Castor minded, it meant he was the only one serious about the position, giving him a better chance at the promotion despite Deven's efforts.

Castor headed back to the city, the fire now raging as it burned away the corpses. With the last of the duties finished, he felt empty and... odd. He knew he couldn't see his sister, not anymore, but it had always been routine to visit her after a wave. Actively fighting against that urge felt wrong, but he knew it was a necessity. He felt heavy with guilt, but he had to stay strong. His sister was an adult; she could make her own decisions, and those decisions had repercussions like these.

Though Castor felt he was the one being punished.

He walked through the gate and into the tunnel, directionless, dragging his feet. As he exited the other side and into the open city, he was greeted by his Steelwood soldiers.

"Captain, off to see Maggie?" Vance called out.

Castor glumly shook his head. "Not today."

"Something wrong?"

"She's busy."

"That's a shame, Captain. What'll you do in your spare time now?"

"Honestly, I'm not sure. The defenses are already set for the Red Sea, the soldiers are being trained routinely. I haven't a lot to do, it seems."

Vance looked around at the Steelwoods, gauging their faces. "Perhaps we should move our plans ahead of schedule now that the captain is free?"

The Steelwoods agreed, nodding and smiling, and Castor stared at them, curious yet cautious.

"Let's go, Cap, we'll give you something to do," Vance said with a grin.

"Where? What?"

The Steelwoods responded, one by one.

"No questions, Captain."

"You'll see."

"Just relax, let's go put our weapons back."

"Take my weapon, I'll meet you guys there."

"Me too, I should tell my missus where I'm going."

Castor watched as a few departed and the rest made their way back to the barracks to drop off their weapons.

"I'm concerned," Castor said in a stern voice.

"Trust me, Cap," Vance said, a mischievous smile spreading across his face. "You'll enjoy it."

"If you say so," Castor responded skeptically. He didn't like surprises, but he trusted his ability to adapt.

He also trusted the Steelwoods.

Castor followed his me to the barracks, watched them store their weapons in the allocated cart, and then make their way back out where they led him to the south side of the city, stopping off at a building unfamiliar to Castor. A few entered while the rest remained outside, refusing to fill Castor in on what was happening, only telling him it was Vance's plan.

They returned shortly, carrying several barrels.

"What have you guys done?" Castor was bewildered. The sound of liquid sloshing around in the barrels told Castor that they weren't as empty as he initially thought.

"Between the lot of us," Vance started, "we've been stockpiling our limited drinks. It took us quite a while, but eventually we were able to get enough to fill the barrels. No more excuses now, Cap. Come have a drink with us." Vance genuinely smiled, no mischievousness hiding behind it. The other Steelwoods urged Castor, encouraging him, each with a hopeful look.

"I suppose I can't use my sister as an excuse to escape you sorry lot today. I should have thought of something else," Castor teased.

The Steelwoods laughed with joy as they escorted Castor outside of the South Gate. Vance talked to some of the soldiers stationed there, and it appeared he had an existing deal with them. Normally, people weren't allowed to leave the city walls without express permission, such as tending to the crops, but Vance was able to find a way to convince them to let them out for a few hours.

Castor looked at Vance questioningly as they strolled through the front gate, and the man simply gave him a shrug.

They chose a position not far from the wall and placed the barrels down. They waited for the few missing members to turn up before each taking a cup and scooping some ale from the barrel.

Vance raised his cup. "To the captain, for not thinking fast enough to weasel out of this situation!"

The Steelwoods raised their cups in unison. "The captain!"

The each downed their cup until it was empty. It had been a while since Castor had a proper drink, but he was still able to down the ale in a single breath. He cheered with the Steelwoods, doing his best to relax. It wasn't easy, but his comrades aided him. Eventually he was able to laugh and chat, all his worries forgotten.

They sat around drinking for hours, talking, joking, and complaining about the general. The sky began to grow dim, but no one seemed to mind. They were too busy enjoying themselves to care about such trivial things as darkness.

"I'm telling you," Vance said. "The South Gate hates the General as much as we do!" the man was almost in hysterics. "He barely visits them since it's the Gate that gets the least action, so they feel ignored. That can be just as damaging as his foul attitude has on us at the East Gate!"

"Not a chance!" Raeden rebutted, taking another gulp of ale. "I'd rather be ignored and left to do my own thing than be constantly yelled at for doing my job!"

Vance snorted. "Maybe it's because you're sick of the general breathing down our necks, but you gotta see it from their perspective. They think General Deven favors us just because we're at the East Wall, like we're all his little apprentices. It's why so many of them treat us so poorly, they're jealous!"

Castor didn't participate, not wanting to openly speak against the general so close to the South Gate as they were. He stared at Vance, whose face was now serious, ready to debate anything thrown at him. Castor chided himself for not realizing that Vance was surprisingly perceptive and open minded. He also seemed to have good relations with the other soldiers, probably others as well. *He'd make a good captain. Or even a general.*

Raeden leaned toward Vance. "Do they think the general treats us harshly because he wants us to get better? No way! This isn't a tough love situation, it's just tough! The general comes in, gets his little power trip over the captain then ditches us just the same."

Vance's face lit up. "See?! There! That's the thing! The South Gate has heard about Castor and the way he stood up to the general, and they've started to come around! Castor is a legend to these people, as soon as I told them we wanted some privacy with our captain, they were more than happy to let us out!"

Derrin scoffed, holding tight to his cup of ale. "What? Even the South Gate Captain?"

339

"Even Captain Gratch," Vance responded, wide-eyed, "He's not a fan of the general either, so anyone bold enough to talk back to Deven immediately gets into his good books."

"Wow, Captain," Raeden said. "You should yell at him some more, maybe we'll get ourselves an audience with The Voice." Raeden grinned as the Steelwoods laughed along.

Castor gave out a semi-drunken but genuine laugh. "Maybe, though I'd prefer to yell at someone the Magistrate of Defense hates, perhaps I'll be given general then."

The Steelwoods laughed again, Melvin finding difficulty to speak as he was losing breath. "Could you yell at my kids next? My wife thinks I don't punish them harshly enough when they mess up, maybe you could earn her respect for me."

"Oh yes," said Vance. "That would make quite the title for Castor when he gets promoted. 'General Castor Belden, the Child Screamer'."

This caused an uproar amongst the men, ale spilling from cups as they failed to maintain proper control of their limbs, bellowing over with laughter. Even Castor spilled some of his drink as Vance leant on him, unable to react fast enough to support the man.

Castor wiped the tears away from his eyes then looked around at his Steelwood soldiers. His friends. Smiling, laughing, enjoying themselves. Happy. Something he had wanted to bring to the city for a while but had been oblivious to the fact that he had lost it himself along the way, melding into the bleak attitude of the city, believing that he would one day change it.

Change didn't take hope. It took action.

It could be as small as sharing a drink with friends once in a while, or as large as slaying an unlimited supply of enemies who had besieged your city. It needed the vision and want for change, with a proactive attitude.

Castor was naïve to think things would change just because he would be general. He needed ways to actually make the city a better place rather than just defending it as a higher rank. He finished off his cup, and without hesitation, Vance grabbed it and gestured for Raeden to fill it. They were relentless, making sure Castor had no excuse to leave.

Raedon cleared his throat. "I know it's a bit of a glum change, but the Red Sea is almost here. Just a couple more days and we'll face the largest horde of metalurks we've ever seen. First time for us all, too." Raeden's eyes seemed a little distant and his smile faded. "Think we'll pull through, Cap?"

Castor considered the question. His answer would bear a heavy weight upon his men, but he couldn't give them false hope either. "Not without great losses, but as a city we'll survive."

"Shut your trap, Raeden, we were having a good time," Vance scolded the man, giving him a light tap on the head.

"I'm just saying, this could be our last time doing this," Raeden said. "It might be the drink talking, but it has been a real honor fighting by your side. Even you new guys."

"We thought the same after our first fight," Mark called out on behalf of the newest recruits. They had only been with them a few months, but they were still a part of the team, no more or less than any other member. Bonds formed quickly on the battlefield, and those bonds ran deep.

Vance nodded to Raeden. "You might have had a bit too much to drink, Raeden, but now that you've brought it up, then yes, I am thankful I was put into East Gate Steelwood's. I think about after the first week, I stopped fearing death as long as I had you guys, which brings me to the next depressing topic." Vance clumsily stood, filled his cup with ale and raised it to the group. "To those on our team we've lost."

Everyone scrambled to get a cup in their hand, empty or not, and raised it. Castor respectfully raised his, reflecting back on those he had failed over the years he was leader of the Steelwoods. He had lost fourteen in his first year, which many claimed to be a record low number for losses, but that didn't change his disposition. He had met, trained, and talked to every one of them. Formed the same bond as he had with anyone else he fought alongside. He also remembered each of their corpses vividly. Flashes of memories forced their way to the surface, but Castor was surprised he was not despaired. Vance was one of his men who had taught him not to dwell on the fallen members, but to highlight their sacrifice in servitude. They died defending the city and its citizens, and they didn't go down without taking many of the creatures with them.

"Let us meet in the Gods divine realm," Castor toasted, downing the last of his drink. Everyone else followed. "If you fall, take as many of those bastards with you," Castor continued after the drink.

"You've probably slain the most, haven't you, Captain?" Mark asked.

"Only because I'm one of the oldest members of the team, and only because I'm able to fell them through the portcullis. I think without that particular defense, Owen would have me beat."

Owen gave a smug smile. "What can I say? I'm good at what I do."

"If I had defined muscles like that, I'd be good at swinging a branch around too," Raeden taunted, gesturing to Owen's well-defined arms.

"Aww, I didn't know I was your role model, little Rae! I can teach you my training regime if you want." Owen spoke in a child-like voice, mocking Raeden who almost choked on his drink.

"No thanks, I'm hungry enough as it is, I don't know how you manage to train with such small portions of food."

"Because I'm not a glutton and I know how to stretch out the rations I'm given."

"What are you trying to say?"

"I'm trying to say I know how to make the best of a bad situation, instead of eating my feelings away and then complaining about hunger."

Raeden's eyes widened. "You mean to tell me you ain't always hungry?"

"I've taught myself to get used to it, I thought we all would have by now. I think someone's becoming spoiled."

"Right, that's it, next fight I'm gonna let a Red shred you to bits."

"You think they can get through as thick muscles as these?" Owen flexed his arms in Raeden's face.

"Absolutely, if they can get you by surprise!" Raeden quickly tried to grab for Owen's leg, but stumbled, the effects of the alcohol dominating his coordination. He fell forward, scrambling and clutching onto Owen's leg from the ground. The Steelwoods laughed at the display as Owen dragged Raeden across the ground with ease.

"As a soldier, I have the right to arrest you. I have anchored you down, give up!" Raeden called, flat on his back but still gripping tightly to Owen's leg.

"Arresting me? For what?"

"I'll think of something later, but for now, you must obey!"

"I think I technically outrank you."

"Yeah, well, I arrested you first, so it doesn't matter."

"Well, I think I'm bigger and stronger, so I say it does matter."

"You know what, you asked for it. Steelwoods! I call upon your aid to chain this beast!" Raeden drunkenly rallied.

Mark and Kasen surged forward, Kasen latching himself onto Owen's other leg while Mark surprisingly leapt onto his back. Owen remained standing; though he was significantly slowed, he still took steps despite being weighed down.

"No fair, only Castor can order us around," Owen complained, taking another step, dragging Kasen through the dirt.

Castor stood and took a deep breath. "Steelwoods!"

Everyone froze, stunned by the sudden command, each turning to face him, even those currently attached to Owen.

"As your Captain, I order you to aid Raeden in arresting that man!"

Vance was the first to leap to his feet. "Yes, sir!" he saluted and ran towards Owen.

The rest followed in a mad dash to pile onto Owen. Surprisingly he managed to withstand quite a few of them before they eventually toppled him, falling into a pile of drunken bodies.

Somehow, Raeden managed to weasel his way to the top of the pile, raising his arms in victory, "See? I am the greatest Steelwood soldier! I even tricked the captain into obeying me!"

"Steelwoods!" Castor called out once more. "Arrest that man too!"

Castor laughed as Raeden's triumphant smile quickly molded into shock as several arms grabbed and wrestled him to the ground.

343

He watched Owen and Raeden struggle to break free for a while, but there were simply too many ale-fueled bodies weighing them down. Castor looked at the sky, seeing how dark it was becoming. Soon they would lose the last of the sunlight and no longer able to see without a torch or candle. He moved over to inspect the last ale barrel. It barely had enough for a few cups, but it was against common sense to empty it out.

"Vance, come give me a hand," Castor called out to the pile of wrestling people. Vance's head popped out of the pack like an obedient pet and he made his way over.

Castor gestured to fill the cups, then he lifted the barrel to empty its contents into the cup Vance held, doing his best not to spill any drops.

It was technically punishable by law to waste food and drink by spilling it on the ground, so Castor poured with extra caution out of habit.

"I know this might not be the right moment for it, but I doubt I'll get an opportunity over the next few days as we prepare for the Red Sea," Vance said, soft enough so the others didn't overhear. "Is everything okay with Maggie? I got the impression that she's not as busy as you claim."

Castor didn't look up, concentrating on pouring. "Perceptive as ever, Vance."

"Not perceptive, I just know how to read your expressions in particular, sir."

"I suppose I should consider that dangerous from a subordinate, but as a friend I find it rather warming."

"Either way, I come out on top."

Castor stifled his chuckle. "I can't go into details, but Maggie is technically busy. I'm not seeing her because of that though, there are other reasons th—"

"Say no more, Cap. Just wanted to make sure my hunch was right, that's all."

"Yours usually is Vance. Trust it."

With the last of the ale emptied, Castor placed the barrel down and turned to the wriggling pile of drunken wrestling. "Three cups left, whoever wants them come get them!"

Somehow their wrestling efforts were doubled, now that they were all attempting to desperately reach the last of the drinks.

Owen got his revenge, the men now too focused on trying to escape they weren't pinning him down anymore. He easily pushed some of the men aside, grabbing the front runners and reaching the cups first. He grabbed and drank an ale with one victorious motion.

Mark was surprisingly second, managing to slip free of the hands that grabbed him and reaching the cups.

Just behind him was Evan, a more experienced member, managing to slip out of the side of the pile and run around them, grabbing the last cup.

Raeden lay on the ground, panting and defeated. "I can't believe it. Thwarted by my own captain!" he exclaimed, barely able to raise his arms.

Castor and Vance smiled, drinking from their own cups. "Red Sea is in a few days, men," Castor raised his voice to grab their attention. They quickly became quiet, giving their captain the attention he deserved. Even Raeden got off the ground. "I just want to say how proud you've all made me over the years. We won't come out the other side unscathed, but I know that every one of you will gladly lay down your lives to defend the city. Even if I never become general, I'd be proud to continue leading the Steelwoods. Though I would change just one thing."

The men's expressions became puzzled and concerned, growing impatient as Castor paused to add suspense.

"I really hate our name," Castor admitted, groaning in annoyance.

The Steelwoods gave a mixture of laughter and shock to the news.

"You hate our name, Captain?" Mark called out, perplexed.

"But we sound so terrifying! *The Steelwoods!*" Owen exaggerated their name, giving it a dramatic effect.

"It's stupid!" Castor said, ale fueling his tongue. "We don't even know what steel is other than metal! We should be called something more appropriate," Castor tried to argue, but the men were unconvinced.

"How can you say you hate our name, Cap? What better name do you have?"

"I don't know, honestly. Just something more accurate, like... Livewood Warriors, or the Big Stick Soldiers." Castor threw out whatever words came to his head. In truth, he had given it thought, but hadn't come across anything he liked.

"Oh, I am quite fond of Big Stick Soldiers," Vance said, nodding approvingly.

"Big Stick Soldiers..." Owen said, frowning as though deep in thought. "Hmm... Yeah, that could work!"

"Look," Castor started. "All I'm saying is Steelwood is misleading. We use livewood, not steelwood, that's not even a thing!"

"No, no, sir," Vance said, raising his hands. "You're right. Big Stick Soldiers it is. I'll bring it forward to the general, or even the Magistrate of Defense?"

"All right, that's it, everybody go home," Castor picked up a barrel and the soldiers began throwing their empty cups inside, repeating 'Big Stick Soldiers' as if seriously debating it. "All of you better be sober for preparations tomorrow," Castor announced as he placed the lid on the barrel. "Steelwoods, it was an absolute pleasant night. Thank you for tricking your captain into drinking,"

"Anytime, sir, but there is just one thing..." Vance said, gesturing for the men to stand in line.

"Don't."

"We're Big Stick Soldiers!"

The saluted, nearly in unison. Castor rolled his eyes and returned the salute, dismissing them.

Gods, they're idiots.

But they're my idiots.

26

The Day of Sacrifice.

It had finally arrived.

Elias sat in his room, alone, unmoving. Unfeeling.

Was he overwhelmed? Or calm?

It was difficult to tell. He knew he was nervous, but was he confident in his own abilities enough to ignore it? He knew he should be getting ready by now, dressing into his finest clothes. He was scheduled to leave for the arena that morning, arriving before his competitor.

But his body was not his to command. It needed time to process.

A knock sounded at his door. Loud, impatient, demanding. "Elias? Are you in there?" the voice of his trainer called out.

"Yes."

The door swung open and Merek entered, dressed in a skillfully crafted bright blue and white outfit, complete with a livewood replica of a sword on his belt.

"What is wrong? You haven't even begun to dress, and we must leave shortly."

Elias looked through the bright cracks of the morning sun through his window, "Sorry, I guess I misjudged the time."

Merek sighed, closing the door and moving over to where Elias' clothes were laid out. "This is no time to let your mind get the best of you. You must come to terms with what today means, not what might be awaiting you by the end of it. Now quickly, get dressed. Your father is waiting."

Merek threw Elias' pants at him, causing him to instinctively catch them.

Alright. Let's do this.

Merek left the room, waiting outside in the hall. Elias quickly got changed, still taking the time to make sure his outfit looked neat and proper. *Take enjoyment in the small things. Focus on those.*

The distraction helped slightly. Elias would take anything he could get to get his mind off of what fate would befall him. It was a surreal feeling. Waking up one day, knowing that by the end of it you would either kill or be killed.

And it was entirely up to his performance.

There was little solace in trying to convince himself there was meaning in being a sacrifice to allow a new wave of livewood trees to grow. He never wanted his life to be dedicated to trees. Then again, he never knew what he wanted his life to be. The fear of death dominated any sense of another future, as if it were inevitable.

Small things. Check the stitching, make sure it's all intact. Elias ran his fingers along the seams of his shirt, feeling the smooth bumps of a master tailor. He donned his boots and left his room, attempting to get ahead of his thoughts.

Merek greeted him outside, gesturing to a box on the ground. Elias nodded, picking it up awkwardly. It was slightly too large to be carried alone, but it was custom for a duelist to carry his own gear to the arena.

"You had it padded, right?" Elias asked, shaking the box. It barely made a sound, but he could feel items slightly shifting inside.

"Of course. The inside of the box is layered with the material so that it cannot be detected by the creatures. I have also grouped the equipment and wrapped them for extra protection." Merek spoked in a hushed tone, wary of any who might be within earshot.

Satisfied, Elias carried the box and walked with Merek to the front entrance where his father was waiting for them amongst a group of servants. Somehow, Elias was still disappointed that

Geraldine was not amongst them. She had still not been found, but his naive hopes of her suddenly reappearing did not wane.

"Father," Elias greeted him.

Warin was heavily leaning on his cane, but his expression did not carry its usual grouchy demeanor, but rather one of pride and worry. Especially when he smiled at Elias. "Elias. This spiteful day has finally come."

"It has." Elias sighed in agreement. They both held bitter memories of the Day, his father more so.

"Well, let us see what this day has in store for us once again." Warin smiled weakly and gave the signal for everyone to depart. The servants opened the door and led them out to the front gate where a surprise was waiting for Elias.

A horse tied to a cart, with seats built in.

"By the Gods…is that a horse-drawn rickshaw?"

Warin beamed brightly at Elias' shock, taking joy in his son's excitement. "Yes. I figured you were too young to remember this part. We have been leant a horse that the soldiers use to chase down the creatures, for the purpose of taking us to the arena in style. A gift from The Voice to their champions."

Elias placed his box in the back of the cart and immediately moved over to the horse. A man stood next to them, dressed in black and white clothes. Not of nobility, but still someone of importance.

"Greetings, Lord Elias Va Noldin. I am Henrik. I'll be taking you to the arena." the man bowed respectfully. Elias gave him a quick greeting, but his eyes were fixated on the horse, marveling at the creature.

"May I touch it?"

"Certainly, my Lord. Just be wary, he's not particularly fond of hands near its eyes."

Elias placed his hand on the large beast's side. It felt furry and muscular, a strange combination for Elias, but he loved the sensation regardless.

Geraldine isn't here…

"Merek, come!" Elias excitedly called his mentor over. Merek approached but kept his distance from the horse. "Touch it, Merek!"

349

"I shouldn't, Master Elias. He was a gift to your family, not me."

"Oh, stop being so pedantic. If it's a gift to me then I allow you to touch it. In fact, I demand you touch it."

Merek sighed but complied. Elias could see the flickers of wonder in Merek's face, unable to keep his curiosity hidden. Merek placed a hand on the horse and was immediately amazed by the texture.

"It feels... strange."

"It's amazing!"

"Okay, Elias, that's enough. We should be off, now," Warin called, moving over to the steps of the cart.

Elias was reluctant to stop inspecting the horse but moved to help his father into his seat. He climbed in after, making himself comfortable in the seat.

"Master Elias, Master Warin, I shall meet you both at the arena. Enjoy your trip!" Merek bowed to them. Elias was a little disappointed that Merek did not get to join them, but there was little room on the cart to begin with.

"Full disclosure, my Lords," Henrik spoke up as he climbed into his own seat at the front. "I've been instructed to take a detour to parade you through town."

"That's all right, it's part of the ceremony," Warin responded, not sounding like he was entirely pleased but accepted it anyway.

Henrik grabbed some kind of rope attached to the horse and gave it a quick flick. The horse began to slowly walk, dragging the large rickshaw along.

As foretold, Henrik wove in and out of streets, zig zagging his way to the arena. The city was lively today, the excitement of the Day fresh and plentiful amongst the citizens. They cheered, waved, and thanked Elias as he was put on display. He politely responded to the crowds as they gathered in the streets. He had never seen so many citizens out before. Never seen so many smiling faces, or such a positive atmosphere.

He had never seen the city so alive.

His expectations of the city center were surpassed as he was driven through. The crowd cheered in a loud uproar, clapping and praising Elias. The sound was almost deafening, as if the hundreds of gatherers were trying to cheer over each other. Despite his personal attitude towards his own position as champion, he felt honored by so many people coming to celebrate him as he made his way to what could turn out to be death. The only thing that sullied his mood was seeing the empty space in the city center.

The livewood tree had been removed in preparation for another being planted. Elias felt as if his brother had been forgotten. His memory replaced by whoever would be the next sacrifice.

The same thing will happen to me.

As they drove out of the city center, the thoughts trickled behind him, but he was doing his best to rid himself of them. They wove through more streets, eventually making their way into the vicinity of the arena, where soldiers formed a blockade to prevent any citizens from getting close.

Somehow, the arena now seemed foreboding as Elias drew close. The building loomed over him, intimidating, as if entering meant he could never leave.

And then the fear of death slowly settled back in.

Henrik drove the cart up to the entrance, positioning it so Elias would have to exit to the side facing the crowd. Henrik also left his seat, running around to help Elias escort Warin down.

The crowd cheered, and Elias gave them one final wave and a half-hearted smile before picking up his box and entering the large doors of the arena.

The slamming of the doors behind him seemed to echo throughout his mind, mocking him for ever stepping foot in here. He stood in a short tunnel that led into the open arena. As if drawn by unseen forces, Elias moved over to see the arena in full view.

It was big, but somehow seemed smaller than Elias had anticipated. It was a large circle, surrounded by layers of seats to allow a huge crowd to all observe at once without obstruction. The floor here was covered in a thick layer of dirt, but it was firm enough that Elias could tell there was stone beneath it.

Before he could wander in further, Warin called out from behind. "Back here, Elias. We must enter through here where you will prepare and wait for the other champion to arrive. Come, I'll wait with you."

Warin walked towards a door that Elias had walked past, oblivious to it once he was transfixed by the arena itself. Through the door was a lengthy hallway that had a slight curve that led to a large room.

"That door will lead to the arena as well. You'll enter through there once you are called upon. For now, put on your armor and warm up."

Elias placed the box down, trying to suppress the nerves from building further.

"Elias." Warin spoke softly, but the large, empty room made it easy to hear. "I... I am proud of you, my son. You are all I have left, but do not let our situation guide your attitude in the battle. Do not feel guilty if you lose, instead know that either way, I am proud of what you will become. What you have become. Who you are. You became the best person you could have without a mother, and with a pathetic excuse of a father."

Elias turned to his father, who was trying to hold back the tears. Not of pride, but of pain. His last living relative was about to be put up for possible execution. "Don't be so harsh on yourself, Father, we've bo—"

"No." Warin cut him off harshly. "Do not make excuses for me. I know we've both suffered a lot, but I am fully aware that that is no reason for me to have behave the way I have. I all but abandoned you in favor for an intoxicant so I wouldn't have to spend another day with my own thoughts. I've been a selfish fool, but I couldn't let us depart today without telling you that I am aware of it. That I am sorry for it. You've been such a great son. Even when I fell ill you still put in so much effort to support me. I didn't deserve that. I don't deserve you. But you are not a creation of mine, you are a creation of yourself."

Elias wasn't sure what to say. He wanted to argue against his father speaking so negatively about himself, but it was clear that Warin was adamant in his views. His father would argue, he was stating as if they were facts. And perhaps they were, but Elias could not blame his father. Not everyone was capable of shrugging aside the deaths of many loved ones.

"Just…I am proud of you."

Elias held back his own tears, his father's words both frustrating and comforting. He wanted desperately to retort, to convince his father that he was not the awful parent he claimed to be.

But it would be no use.

"Thank you, Father."

They fell silent.

Elias removed the lid to his box and began to don his family's green armor, preparing for the fight of his life.

* * *

Arthur slowly put on his dark blue armor, each piece feeling heavier than usual as he grabbed it out of the box. It was late morning, yet the day had felt as if it had been going on forever. The ride to the arena was pleasant, the citizens out to celebrate his fight provided little comfort, but he appreciated their efforts.

His mother had been quiet during the ride. When the horse-drawn cart had arrived, his mother gave them a fond look, but she bore a grave sadness upon seeing the cart once again. Fear flooded back to her, and Arthur knew she recalled the last duel. Seeing her expression only made Arthur stress further about what awaited him.

And now that he was here, at the arena, preparing for his first ever fight, part of him thought it only a dream. As if he had left his own body, watching his shell unwillingly prepare itself for the fight. He was alone in the large room, his mother had left him to wait in the stands to greet his siblings when they arrived.

He fidgeted with his livewood ring that he had never taken off since he had received it. No one had noticed him wearing it, or at least not mentioned it to him. It was the perfect tone to blend in with his skin, and even if he had gotten caught, he no longer cared.

Arthur reluctantly put on the gloves, covering his ring, but he still felt its presence.

He picked up his sword, unravelling the layer of cloth and the engineered material to prevent metalurks from detecting it.

The sword seemed dull in the dim lighting of the room. There were no windows, so he had to prepare by the light of several candles. He gave the weapon a few practice swings, quickly moving into warmups of his stances and maneuvers. Time still seemed stagnant as he tried to pry his mind away from it, hoping to become distracted enough until the time that he was called.

The sword felt deadly now, and Arthur began to feel the seriousness of how easily one could be killed by metal. He should have felt privileged, but the nagging thought that a metalurk could burst in here at any moment suffocated any notion of it.

Without so much as a knock, the door swung open, and Gavin entered. He was dressed in his appropriate red and white garments of Magistrate of Defense and not his family colors. "Hello, Arthur. Are you ready? I suspect they'll call upon you soon."

"Greetings, Gavin. I'm as ready as I'll ever be." Arthur panted slightly from his short practice. He looked at his brother who seemed just as serious as ever. "Do you need something?"

"Our relationship has dissolved so far that I cannot wish my younger brother good luck?"

"It wasn't something I suspected you to do other than from the audience stands, amongst witnesses."

"I suppose I deserve such a harsh judgement. I haven't been the best son, brother, or even husband lately." Gavin's face surprisingly relaxed as he sighed and moved over to sit by where Arthur stood.

Arthur wasn't sure what Gavin was up to. His brother always seemed to have some hidden agenda for his actions, he wouldn't suddenly just become a regular person, would he?

"I've been so centered on hating Edmund that I've lost sight of other things. For what seemed like an eternity, I strove towards Magistrate of Defense, trying to achieve something important without any aid from that man. And yet, I somehow can't shake the feeling that he had something to do with it that I have not seen."

"Probably from him having run your life for the first twenty years."

"It is the likely answer, but I became obsessed with it, constantly looking for a phantom answer to persuade myself that he had meddled in my life once again. It has created a few… rifts between people."

"Could have fooled me."

Gavin gave a weak smile. "I only realized all of this thanks to you."

"Me?"

"When Edmund died, I felt… empty. Like I was missing something. It took me a little while to realize that so much of my life had been consumed to keeping that man out of it, I didn't have a focus or a target anymore. That's when I realized that I had the wrong target all of these years. Combine that with my younger brother fighting in the Day of Sacrifice, and well… Here I am."

"To say good luck?"

"No. To say I'm sorry. I don't know exactly what will happen to you today, but I've already got enough regrets in my life now. I don't want to have anymore. I wanted to tell you before your duel that, despite our age difference and me leaving the household the way that I did that… I still love you, even if I never showed it. I was so angry on the day of my fight, I just wanted to make sure you wouldn't make that mistake, too."

Arthur looked down at his brother, confused, but feeling a little eased. It was not exactly something he had been fretting about, but it was released some unknown tension. "Take care of Mother, will you?" Arthur asked, keeping his voice straight and serious as he spoke around the topic of his death.

Gavin looked up at him, smile growing. "Of course, brother. And Raelynn too, I promise."

Arthur nodded, offering his hand to Gavin. His brother stood, straightened his back and accepted Arthur's handshake.

"I better get back to the audience stands, but before I do…" Gavin put his hand on Arthur's head and ruffled his hair like on does a child. "Good luck, little brother."

Arthur smiled and flicked Gavin's hand away. "No fair, I can't fix it with these gauntlets."

355

"That's fine, it'll be hidden by the helmet." Gavin chuckled quietly as he left the room, leaving Arthur alone once more.

This was the part that Arthur hated the most. The waiting.

He looked down into the box, all that remained was the helmet. Arthur picked it up and stared at it, taking deep breaths. The helmet was threatening to suffocate him if he wore it, but he wouldn't let his mind be the death of him. Not today. Not after all that's happened.

To the Gods prisons with his nerves! He was now a man of action, a man who would get things done, a man who accepted fate. If fate deemed his death necessary, then so be it. Without hesitating further, he jammed the helmet onto his head and dove back into practicing until a horn sounded.

It wasn't the defense horn; this was different. It had a sharper pitch and seemed to be playing a small tune as it sounded loudly.

The duel was about to start.

They were letting all the citizens waiting outside the arena and who were not permitted to observe the duel, know that the match would be starting in a moment.

And soon they would have their sacrifice.

The door that gained entrance to the arena swung open and, in the doorway, stood a masked man in ceremonial robes and an intricately designed pointy hat.

A member of The Voice.

"Arthur Va Daolin, are you ready for your duel?" the man's voice was deep and smooth, both commanding and guiding.

Arthur stepped closer, bowing as much as his armor allowed. "Yes, I am."

"Then accept the blessing I bestow upon you from the Gods themselves and carry it with you in your fight. Do not forget, this is for their display, they will choose which of you becomes the noble sacrifice for our city, so it may continue to survive. Please, kneel."

Arthur complied, placing his sword on the ground. The masked man took a step forward and began to recite the familiar chants of the churches.

"Rise, Champion, and follow me."

Arthur gathered his sword and followed The Voice out into the arena, ignoring the constant threats of his nauseated stomach. His body was not his opponent today, it deserved no attention.

As he followed the man into the center of the arena, he spotted his opponent in a similar routine.

As they grew near, The Voice gave them orders to remain standing where they were and wait for them to call for the duel to start. They made their way back to their stands, joining the rest of The Voice.

Arthur reactively fidgeted with the ring through the gauntlet, despite not being able to touch it directly, just knowing it was there provided some comfort.

For a moment, the opponents stared at each other. Arthur noted the details on the dark green armor of his opponent, trying to spot differences from his own. The only things he managed to find appeared to be insignificant details that only changed the design, not the function. His mysterious opponent stood oddly still, feeling the eyes penetrate through the slits of their helmet and pierce his own armor, gauging him in turn.

Something is... off.

Their attention was grabbed by one of The Voice standing, arms raised to grab the attention of everyone present.

"Va Daolin, and Va Noldin, The Voice welcomes both families today in the arena under the watchful eye of the Gods. Both families have provided a champion, and so you have both received thanks from the Gods. They know that today is a difficult day for all, and so they appreciate you all following through with your promises." He spoke loudly for all to hear, enunciating each word precisely. A practiced speaker. "In the arena we have two fighters who will duel under the gaze of the Gods to deem who will be the sacrifice for our dire city. Champion Arthur Va Daolin, and Champion Elias Va Noldin, are you both willing, and prepared?"

Arthur nodded.

His opponent nodded.

"With the blessings of the Gods placed on both of you, I now call this duel to begin!" The Voice raised his arms once more and the same horn blew louder and sharper, signifying the beginning of the duel.

Arthur raised his sword and adopted his stance, watching his opponent do the same.

His eyes widened in surprise, his mind racing, trying to piece things together as it couldn't immediately make sense of the situation, the horror of possibilities flashing one after the other.

He's not left-handed.

27

Maggie felt lonelier than ever.

Her husband had died, and she was unable to share that pain with her brother due to the position she chose to put herself in. She could not go to Heleen either. When Castor discovered she was a Seeker, she decided to take a short hiatus from the library to focus on her work with them.

There was no one left.

The only thing keeping her going was the kindness of a stranger. Varin.

He did his best to try and console her, but it was difficult when she had only recently met him. He provided comfort, but she still carried the weight on her shoulders as if waiting for Castor to appear.

She needed to tell him. He needed to know.

He needed to know that James was not the bad man Castor thought he was. But that seemed far into the future now. She wouldn't be able to see her brother until her business with the Seekers was over. Which meant after the Red Sea. An extremely hazardous event where her brother had a high risk of dying.

And their last exchange ended with his disappointed expression. She had learned by now that she should not dwell in the past, but somehow the lesson felt wrong. The past was all she had left. There might not be a future.

She shifted in the wooden chair at her kitchen table, feeling continuously uncomfortable. Varin sat next to her, his drabs merging with hers as he leant over to embrace her once again. It was all he could seem to think to do, words had little effect in this situation.

He let go, looking at her with regret. She knew what he was thinking. He had brought it up multiple times, and each time it seemed to guilt him further. She knew he would say it again, but she did not stop him.

"We do need to think about tomorrow's plan, Maggie. The duel will commence around midday, but you'll need to be shadowing the general as soon as he leaves his house in the morning. I know that it may fall on deaf ears right now, but we must try to push aside the grief until we have time for it later. It's a heartless thing to ask, I know, but this opportunity may not rise again. The general is not a young man anymore, he will likely retire after this Red Sea, so this is likely our last chance."

I know but... I just can't make myself move! Maggie inwardly cursed herself, her stone-like appearance difficult to overthrow. Sorrow had taken over, but she knew she must throw it aside for more urgent matters. Yet it seemed impossible to move. James' actions had completely taken her by surprise, let alone his actual death. It was not an easy thing to just walk away from momentarily.

Varin sighed, pushed his chair back and stood. "I had not wanted to do it, but it seems like I have little choice. I'll return shortly. I think it is best if I get your brother. Perhaps giving you a moment to properly grieve with him will help you out of this rut."

"No, please don't." Maggie turned, grabbing his arm to prevent him from leaving, "I can't drag him back into this. I'll get to work, I promise." Maggie tried to keep the momentum of breaking her rigid posture going, keeping herself active. She grabbed the pitcher of water and poured it into her half-empty cup and began sipping at it.

Varin's face dropped even further, the guilt swelling itself into his eyes. "Sorry, Maggie. Now," Varin said, and retook his seat. "Once you are following the general from his house, I'll do my best to follow you. I'll be sticking to the public crowds, so it is likely that I'll lose you at some point. The others will be near me at all times, but… you need to understand that we won't risk ourselves by going too far. If you go somewhere we cannot follow, or you find yourself in immediate danger, then… I don't think we are able to help. It will implicate more than just ourselves, and we—"

"I already know, Varin, you don't have to keep explaining it to me. I'm following the general alone, plead insanity if I get caught. I'm not daft, I know the risks and I know the consequences."

Varin glumly nodded, unable to keep his eyes on Maggie. "Very well. Go as far as necessary to uncover whatever it is the general is hiding. We're sure he knows something, so as long as you find anything at all that can give us a good lead to follow up on later, it will all be worth it. Get in, get the information, get out."

"And I'll meet you all at the house that night, or the day after if my business runs that long."

Varin nodded again. "As usual, I think we have underestimated you. Despite your occasional, uh… bump in emotions, you are still fully aware of what needs to be done. I think you'll do just fine, but there is one other thing."

Maggie looked at him, concerned. His voice had a poorly concealed quiver, and his hands shook slightly as he reached into his pocket. He produced a livewood dagger and placed it on the table. "I took it from the uh…your husband. I thought, in the rare event that fighting is the best option, at least this will help. It is surprisingly sharp."

Maggie was stunned. She had no idea that Varin had even taken the dagger, and now he offered it to her as a means of protection. And she was glad that he did. She slid her fingers over the handle, feeling the wood beneath her palm. She was familiar with the sensation, Castor occasionally let her handle his weapons under his care. "I hope I don't have to use it, but at least I have it," Maggie said, lifting the dagger, feeling its light weight.

"I just thought that, if you were caught, the general may not care about the level of sanity you have. Others might, if you are caught by them, but if the general wants whatever he is hiding to remain a secret, well then, he wouldn't want any witnesses."

361

Varin's eyes occasionally flickered towards the knife, but his face was a mixture of emotions, making it hard to tell his reasoning behind disliking the weapon.

Maggie pocketed the livewood dagger. "Thanks, Varin."

Varin did not respond, instead he rose from his chair once more. "Well, you have the rest of today to relax and do whatever you wish to prepare. Come morning, I'll meet you here and escort you as close as we can to the general's house."

"Varin?"

"Yes?"

"Would you come back for some tea and split some rations later?"

Varin seemed to contemplate the response, clearly not having expected it. A genuine smile appeared on his face as he looked at her. "Of course. I have to go see my children now, but I'll come back."

Maggie found a small amount of energy to give a faint smile in return.

Varin nodded to her and left, the floorboards creaking under his weight before he disappeared through the door.

And once again, Maggie found herself alone.

* * *

Maggie awoke the next morning feeling surprisingly motivated. Her nerves about following the general bothered her little, seeing the job as a means to get equal with the man who had her son arrested.

She moved downstairs in the dim light of the morning. It made it difficult to see within her house, but she would not be here for long. As she rounded into the kitchen, Maggie momentarily froze. Varin was sitting in a chair at her table, asleep.

Did he not go home?

He had kept his promise and returned at night, sharing pleasant conversation and a meal with her. She had welcomed the company and was deeply thankful he had returned at her request.

She didn't care if he was doing it all for the sake of job, she was just content having someone around.

Maggie moved over to him, gently shaking him awake. He startled, quickly regaining his composure as he took in his surroundings.

"Morning, Maggie."

"Morning, Varin. I didn't realize you had planned to stay the night."

"I hope I wasn't intruding. I just thought, given how late I was here, that it would be easier if I were to just stay. I would have asked, but I only thought about it once you had dozed off."

Maggie blushed, realizing that in her exhausted state, Varin had actually assisted her up the stairs and into her room. She must have fallen asleep while he was still there. "Sorry, I suppose I was more drained than I thought."

"Nonsense, you were as drained as anyone should be in your position. Anyway, shall we get to work?"

Maggie pocketed some dried fruits and meats, preparing for a full day of shadowing the general. "Yes. I think we shall."

Together, they headed towards the Northern Noble District, idly chatting away. Maggie was full of energy, ready to catch the general in something incriminating, something worthy of stripping the man of his status and honor. *Maybe I could even use it to make Castor the general?*

No. Stop.

The thought process scared her. She did not want to become a proper Seeker, she was only here to do the job. Castor wanted to obtain the rank by his own means, in proper fashion. He would not want it simply handed to him. She would do this to take down the man who arrested her son and fulfill her promise to the Seekers. She would not use whatever information she uncovered for anything else.

Assuming she discovered something and made it out alive to tell anyone.

Upon reaching the Northern Noble District boundaries, they made their way to an entry point Varin had scouted for her. She had become preoccupied with grieving that she had wasted time better spent investigating and getting used to the area.

363

The streets were surprisingly busy this early in the morning, the nobility wanting to get to the arena as early as possible for a good view of the champions passing by on their way to their duel. Thankfully, it also meant quite a few servants were mixed with the gathering crowds, though even their clothing stood out from Varin and Maggie's, but it allowed them to weave through without being asked any questions.

Varin guided her to the general's house undetected. He offered to stay and wait with her until Deven made an appearance, but Maggie insisted she would be fine to do so alone. He wished her good luck before quietly sneaking away to find his own place to observe her.

The chatter of nobles was constant as Maggie waited in her crevice between buildings. The houses here were slowly emptying as each family made their way towards the arena's surroundings. Of course, they wouldn't be allowed into the arena itself, but getting close to it was just as good for them to make themselves feel superior to the common citizens.

Maggie watched the general's house with a careful eye, trying to spot any movement going on at any side she could see, in case the man tried to sneak out the back. With the Seekers existence, the General might take extra precautions to avoid his secret being discovered, at least, it would be the logical thing to do.

She kept her eye on the house, occasionally checking her surroundings for anything unusual. Nobles were mingling with one another as they awaited their rickshaws, though many chose to walk instead. The morning was cold, the sun not yet fully risen past the walls to heat her up as she sat huddled against the wall. She was trying to distract herself by focusing on the job, but it was difficult when the job was so boring, just sitting around until something happened.

Nobles paid her no mind, the few that passed her in rickshaws were too busy putting on their own displays of showmanship to pay any mind to a peasant woman huddling in the cold against the wall in an alleyway.

Many of the nobles had their livewood sleeve revealed despite the morning chill, most of the colors were a bright orange-yellow, though the color meant very little to Maggie. She looked around, trying to see if she could spot Varin, but there were very little places to hide in the alleyway. It was likely he found a different place to observe the general and would follow.

She sat in the shadow of the wall, eyes focused on the house waiting for movement, hand wrapped around the livewood dagger in her pocket, letting it provide her comfort in this tense situation. Then, finally, the front door of the general's house swung open, revealing the man in the doorway. He was dressed in his usual leather armor, the only missing component was his livewood weapon at his belt. It would likely be at the barracks, though she thought that the general would have one on him at all times, for the sake of appearances.

He barely glanced around, looking at the nobles filing out of their houses. Many greeted him, stopping to chat with him for a moment.

Maggie watched Deven's body language. She could see the small fidget of his hands, slight shifting of his feet. He was impatient, wanting to be elsewhere. She also observed that the nobles surrounding him had their sleeves revealed, but he chose to keep his hidden. It seemed casual conversation, so it wasn't a necessity to reveal it. Or at least, that's what Maggie thought. She didn't entirely know the rules surrounding the sleeves and their proper etiquette, she could only guess by combining the few facts she knew about them and the rumors she had heard.

The general politely excused himself, wanting to escape before another noble tried to stop him for a friendly chat, and Maggie made her move, observing the General's direction and quickly rushing down the alleyways to follow.

Without proper reconnaissance, she wasn't certain how far she could travel in the alleyways before being forced to find an alternate path. Fortunately, they provided long enough for her to follow the general most of the way down the street, before he made a turn away from the path of nobles traveling to the arena.

She hastily made her way into the sparse crowd, standing near the servants, waiting for the right time to merge with another, keeping her head down and trying not to draw attention to herself.

She then slowly made her way to the side, disappearing into an alleyway before any could call her out.

Maggie wasn't certain if she had been seen but this was no time to sit around and wait to see if the guards were called. She quickly moved down another alley, praying that it led her somewhere to observe Deven. Quickly finding an exit leading to a street, Maggie made her way there while trying to prevent the sounds of her own footsteps. She looked down the street, relieved when she saw Deven rushing on.

She followed the man, doing her best to keep out of everyone's sight. First, she followed him to a house where he met with a man she did not recognize. They talked briefly, no smiles or friendly gestures, only business. She could not risk getting closer to hear, and they talked in whispers.

The general then moved across the city with purposeful stride, barely acknowledging the city folk as he passed them by. Judging by the direction, it seemed as if he was heading towards the barracks.

No surprise there.

Still, she stuck to her job, following the man carefully and discreetly. He disappeared into the barracks, and that was where Maggie froze, uncertain what to do. Most of the city guards would be at the arena, but there were still a surmountable number of soldiers in and around the building, how could she get in?

If I look confident, perhaps no one will stop me?

It was worth a shot.

Cursing herself for not having a stealthier plan, she strode in, head straight and face full of determination. Some of the soldiers glanced in her direction, a few confused, but all let her pass without question. It was a different story once she was inside.

The general was nowhere to be seen, but the likely answer was the man was in his office. Maggie stood in the front room, confused. She wasn't sure where that office was, and her presence began drawing the attention of the soldiers. A few were giving her scrupulous looks and her nerves began to get the better of her.

Breathe.

She picked a random hallway and veered towards it.

If I can just make it there, I can d—

"Lost?"

The question was obviously directed at her. She stopped, trying to turn as if it were a natural reaction, trying her best to seem surprised. She faced a soldier whose brow was furrowed with confusion and suspicion. He was relatively young, but the status of a soldier was not lost on him, clearly used to the kind of power he could demand.

"A little," Maggie hesitated in answering, hoping the act was convincing. "I'm actually just looking for my brother, Castor Belden."

"Castor Belden? Castor… Castor…" the man repeated, Maggie was uncertain if he was toying with her or genuinely thinking about it until he turned to another soldier. "Hey, Ronny, heard of a Castor Belden? Sounds familiar."

The soldier who was just a few steps away from them turned, frowning. "That's the East Gate Captain. You should know this by now. Why?"

"This lady here says she's looking for him."

Maggie had to do her best to maintain control of her reactions as she spied General Deven entering the room from another hall, making his way towards the exit. She shifted her position to hide behind one of the soldiers, watching as Deven quickly made his way towards the doors.

"Oh yeah? What business do you have with the East Gate Captain?" the older soldier questioned, forcing her eyes to peel off of the general and onto him.

"Oh, uh, I'm his sister. I haven't seen him in a while and was wondering if he was all right."

The older man grew a smile. "Oh, so you're Margaret! I've heard your name a few times around some of the Steelwoods, seems like your brother cares for you deeply."

Maggie watched as Deven disappeared outside, giving her only a few moments to escape this conversation so she could follow him. "Yes, yes, he does. Do you know where he is?"

"Sorry, I'm not too certain. I know he isn't here, but he might have gone out to train with the Steelwoods? Or even help prepare defenses at the wall? He's a busy man."

"I thought as much, but I at least thought I'd try. I'll go search for him at the East Gate, thank you for your time!" Maggie brushed passed them, eager to leave. The older man tried calling out after her, but she was afraid she might lose sight of the general if she stopped for more chatter, so she pretended not to hear him. Thankfully, he wasn't insistent on stopping her, and she managed to leave without any more obstacles.

She spied the general hastily moving down a street.

Does he know I'm following him? With no time to consider, she began pursuing him once again, sticking to alleyways whenever possible. She followed him until he stopped at a particular house, knocking on the door. Maggie dared to move closer to get a better angle but was unable to see whoever opened the door and allowed the general inside.

Damn! Maggie checked her surroundings. The streets were sparce of people, most of them would have gathered at the arena by now. *Breathe. Calm. Now!*

Maggie rushed across the street, flattening herself against the wall of the building the general had entered. She crept to the side, out of view of the main street, hoping to find a window where she could overhear any conversations.

She withheld a cheer as she spotted one, moving over to it. The shutters were closed and attempting to pry them open slightly revealed that they were locked by a wooden latch on the inside. She could hear footsteps and hushed voices inside, indicating that she might be missing out on valuable information.

Maggie inspected the shutters, finding that one of the wooden boards was lose. She stood, wary of anyone else who might be walking by, and moved the board slightly, allowing her to peek into the room. The inside was dim, all the windows closed allowing for little light to enter. She observed Deven with a man dressed in dark robes, standing and chatting in angry whispers. Maggie couldn't make out their words, and as she pried the wooden board further, realized she was shedding more light into the room. She slowly let the wooden board slip back into place, cursing no one in particular for being unable to overhear or even see what the general was up to.

Pressing her ear against the window, she prayed she could hear something, anything at all to help her.

"… do… certain… today!" the general was finding it difficult to keep his voice low. He was angry, but it was impossible to tell why.

The other man had more control over his emotions, not raising his voice enough for Maggie to define what he was saying, but his tone was adamant in whatever position he was taking.

"I do not care, just do as you are told. This is your last chance. Do as ordered or I will throw you into the deep prisons myself!"

Deep prisons? There were rumors about the deep prisons. Reserved for those who would never again see the light of day for their heinous crimes. Murderers, traitors, blackmailer of a magistrate or high noble. Anyone who deemed to harm the city, any who dared threaten their chances of surviving, were thrown into the deep prisons. The city and their strict laws had little to no tolerance for such matters, so the deep prisons were created for criminals to waste away if execution was too generous for them.

But why would the general threaten to throw this man inside? Was the general blackmailing him? It was feasible, seeing as Deven had already confessed to the act before. But who was this man, and what did Deven want him to do?

More questions than answers. A Seekers job was apparently never done.

With the general's careless control over the volume of his voice, the conversation was finished. Heavy footsteps could be heard as the man stomped his way out of the building, marching down the street. Maggie could only see the back of his head, but even then, it was obvious he wore a deep scowl.

Fortunately, it might mean he was now slack in judgement, allowing Maggie an easier time to shadow him. She had found nothing incriminating thus far, but she made a mental note of the house. She wanted to signal Varin, but he was nowhere to be seen.

Good. He shouldn't be following me anyway.

The general appeared to be moving faster than before, determined to get to his next destination as quickly as possible. They were approaching the arena, and with the sound of the crowd

369

cheering and clapping, Deven turned and began to skirt the large building, still a few blocks away. He ventured into the back streets, eventually picking one that lead to the arena.

Unfortunately, guards were still stationed here. It seemed as if they thought it necessary to completely surround the arena rather than just protect its main entrances, and this certainly wasn't a main entrance. In fact, Maggie could not see an entrance at all. The guards split apart, allowing Deven entry as he silently strode past them in a seething anger. He would quickly disappear from view if Maggie did not move.

But she couldn't. A wall of soldiers barred her entry, and it seemed as if there were no way past them. She could try find another side, one perhaps weak enough that the soldiers were slacking so she could sneak through, but if such a path existed, it would likely be too late to see where Deven had gone.

She was stuck. The general walked to the arena wall and turned to follow one side of it, disappearing behind a building.

No... I can't. This is it. This is why I've been following him, but how do I get through? Maggie was out of ideas. She couldn't fake an excuse to get on the other side of the soldiers, they wouldn't allow anyone through no matter the reason.

The sounds of a fight broke out in the quiet street. Maggie turned to see two men, their grey clothes dirty as they rolled on the floor, throwing punches and desperately trying to grab at the other.

Two men fighting over... is that food?

The contents of a bag spilled around them as they tussled. She couldn't make out their faces, they were facing away from her, but she could tell they were angry, one man raising his arm and slamming onto the other with all his force.

"Hey! You!" one of the soldiers called out, but the fighting men did not respond. The soldier moved closer, calling out to them again. When he drew close, he pointed his wooden spear at them to force them apart. The pair reluctantly stood, barely resisting the urge to lash out again.

Maggie smiled upon seeing Roy and Varin, panting and angry as they stood in front of the soldier. A trickle of blood poured from a small scratch on Varin's forehead, likely from rolling around on the ground. *Wow, that's dedicated.*

Angry words were exchanged before Roy tackled Varin again, and they quickly locked onto each other, throwing punches and insults. The soldier lost control of the situation, attempting to latch onto one of the men to force them apart, but was clearly having some difficulty.

The other soldiers advanced, one going to assist while the other two walked closer for a better look at the action, amused by the show.

As soon as they passed her hideout, Maggie took cautious steps forward. They were still dangerously close, and the soldiers would soon force Roy and Varin apart again. She took a few more steps before quickening her pace, wanting to disappear from view as quickly as possible, hoping to catch up to Deven before she lost track of him.

Instead of moving closer to the arena wall, she turned behind the last building. Her heart was racing, and she began to panic when she couldn't immediately spot Deven. Her eyes traced the arena wall, spotting something unusual. Part of the wall was slightly askew, before something unseen moved it back into place, becoming indistinguishable with the wall once again.

Another secret door? Maybe I really should become a Seeker.

Maggie kept low, unsure what kind of eyes would be prying in her direction, but with no cover to shield her, she moved purposefully to the wall, tracing her hands over the section that appeared to have been open only a moment ago. Desperately searching for an answer to open the hidden door, the anxiety of losing Deven once again sent her into a panic.

She found a small hole, enough to get a couple of fingers in, so she attempted to pry the door, pulling as hard as she could. Either she wasn't strong enough, or there was another way to open the door. But why the small hole? Was it always there? No. It seemed unnatural. She couldn't see into it without a light source, her head blocked the natural light of the sun if she tried to peer in.

Maybe it needs some kind of key... Something small... The dagger? Maggie produced the dagger from her pocket and quickly pushed it into the hole, glancing around to see if any of the soldiers had seen her.

371

With no one else in sight, she pushed the dagger as hard as she could, until the door unlatched, allowing her to pull it free. The door was still heavy, and Maggie had difficulty swinging it open just enough for her to slip through.

Inside was a hallway that sloped downwards. She quickly pulled the door closed, losing all traces of sunlight and enclosing herself in darkness, the door echoing down the tunnel.

That made the faint light easier to see.

Flickering down the hall from a source just out of sight.

Gods this is dangerous. I hope he didn't hear the door.

Maggie moved forward as quietly as she could, walking at the edge of the light so it illuminated her path. She crept down the sloping hallway, deeper beneath the earth. It seemed to twist and turn, but keeping her rough location somewhere beneath the arena.

She dared to venture further into the light, moving forward cautiously around corners, scared to bump into Deven. He hadn't stopped moving, indicating he may not have heard Maggie enter, and he likely wouldn't lead her so far.

Perhaps he was hard of hearing in his age? Or perhaps he was luring her into a trap.

Either way, she followed the light. This was what she had been waiting for. This was what Deven was hiding. Whether or not The Voice were also involved, it didn't matter, she only cared that the general was a part of whatever they hid from the city.

And he would get what was owed to him for having her son falsely arrested.

Maggie crept deeper, the light growing brighter as she drew near its source. She could hear the footsteps of the torch bearer now, not far from where she followed. Her heart pounded in her chest, her senses trying to ward her away, telling her to turn around and go home before she was discovered.

It's too late now. Even if I get caught, I can't play the insanity card to get away. Did they know that? The Seekers? Am I just a patsy?

The thought stuck in her mind, refusing to be torn away. She didn't want to believe it, how could they have known she would be here? Why did she enter when she could have left?

No, she chose to do this.

The slope finally levelled out, and the hallway began to widen. She snuck a peek around the next corner, finally laying eyes on Deven, who was no walking into a very large room.

Maggie immediately became uneasy. Something was wrong with that room. She could feel it in her bones. It felt…bad. She wasn't sure how she knew, only that she did.

The room was high-ceilinged with strange stonework spiraling down as if it were some kind of slide that began at the center of the roof. Torches were placed all around the natural walls, lighting up the strangest thing of all.

Dirt.

Dark dirt. Almost pitch black. Something more than that scared Maggie. The dirt almost seemed to rhythmically shift. It was only a slight movement, Maggie questioning if it was merely her mind tricking her, but for a moment she stared, mesmerized. It kept beating. Almost like a pulse.

A small platform was elevated in the middle, made of the same black dirt but for some reason it seemed purposefully raised, not natural. Not at all. The stone slide seemed to lead there, but there was no explanation for it.

The dirt seemed to whisper to her, not words as such, but warning her it was not to be trifled with.

The lower section of the black dirt was what frightened Maggie the most. It was lined with people, either prisoners or slaves, it was hard to tell. They were each bound to a stick protruding from the ground, worried looks on most of their faces.

Is this…the deep prisons?

The prisoners seemed scared. Many glancing around, frantically looking for an escape.

What is going on?

There were several others in the room, moving around and ensuring that each person was adequately tied and had no chance of escaping. There seemed to be other pathways leading here, indicating multiple other entrances.

"Everything in order?" Deven called out, his voice echoing a little in the large cavern.

A soldier approached him and saluted. "Yes, sir. All prisoners are tied and ready, the next batch are waiting. The duel has commenced, we are just waiting for the blessing."

"Excellent. There is something else, however."

"Sir?"

"Throw her with the others waiting to join the dirt." Deven turned and stared at Maggie.

She froze, losing all of her senses as she stared, wide-eyed and frightened back at him.

Maggie could no longer tell if she were even alive, no longer able to feel her body. Her thoughts were no more, simply vanished, and her heart could no longer be felt beating in her chest. Her instincts abandoned her, so she made no attempts to run. She could only remain where she crouched, watching as the surprised soldier slowly moved over to her, unhooking the rope that coiled around his body.

This was it. She was caught. Insanity would do nothing for her, especially in her stunned state.

I thought I had more control than this, was the last thought before the man's shadow covered her.

Then, everyone's attention was drawn to the roof as part of it opened, a strong beam of sunlight spearing down into the ominous cavern.

28

Elias gripped his sword tightly, letting it go meant he lost his life. His adversary in dark blue armor seemed confident, immediately falling into the Wind stance. Elias adopted the Stone stance, fighting the trembles of his body as he compelled it to move closer.

He and his adversary then began to swap stances, adjusting to each other's as they circled, beginning their dance. Elias hated the tension, but there was only one way to stop it.

He lunged, swinging his sword at his opponent's torso, but it was easily deflected.

The sound of metal clashing with metal sent a ringing in the air as the two opponents stared at one another.

Merek was right. I am starting to feel the sense of kill or be killed.

When the swords had met, it sent a signal into Elias, slamming the realization of the situation into his core.

This was not a practice. This was no time to consider taking another's life.

It was either him or his opponent.

He didn't expect to be convinced so quickly, but he was happy he had been. It might have ended poorly for him if it took any longer.

Elias stepped forward, using the reach of the sword to keep his opponent at a distance, not swinging to hurt but to test. He needed to gauge his adversary, find a weakness to exploit. And he would have to do it fast, because his opponent would be doing the same.

As Elias swung his sword, he felt something was off. His opponent was strictly focusing on defense, wasn't trying to counterattack, simply trying to guard himself against Elias' swings.

Is he scared? Or patient? Why isn't he attacking?

Elias stopped his attacks, purposely creating an opening for his opponent to swing, prepared to defend against it.

But no attack came. His opponent stood, sword pointed at him, as if waiting for another attack.

What is he doing? Elias didn't want to wait for his opponent to attack; if the man was only going to defend himself, then Elias would break that defense.

Adopting the Stone stance again, Elias struck down, slamming his opponent's weapon with enough force to create a small opening. He thrust forward, controlling his strength so he would not overextend.

The man in blue armor tried to step to the side, but his free arm did not move in time, and Elias' weapon managed to find its way through the armor, piercing the flesh.

A trace amount of blood was left on the weapon, the sword had not struck very deep. The man in blue armor seemed unphased, sword at the ready again, but still not attacking.

Elias continued strong-arming his attacks, forcing his opponent to try and meet his strength. He struck several times, allowing himself to be blocked, then he quickly feigned another attack, causing his opponent to overextend his defense.

Elias swung horizontally, the sword scratching along the surface of the blue armor.

Not far enough!

Elias quickly stepped back, expecting an attack to follow, but none came.

He looked his opponent up and down, confused at the strategy of prolonging his defense.

Is he still trying to learn my moves?

Arthur breathed heavily inside his helmet. His opponent in the green armor changed his stance again, so Arthur responded with his own.

Come on, Arthur! Attack! You've watched his moves enough!

His opponent thrust towards Arthur's neck. He quickly side stepped the attack, prepared to swing back, but he hesitated once again, fearing that his opponent was faster than he was and would strike again.

Damned limbs! I'll die if I don't hit back.

His opponent then let of a series of strikes, forcing Arthur to parry each one.

The attacks kept coming.

And coming.

The green-armored man seemed relentless.

No more! Come on!

Arthur, finally summoning the courage, shoved his opponent's sword to the side, clearly catching him off guard, not expecting the sudden retaliation, and Arthur swung his sword, cutting through his opponent's armor, finding flesh beneath. He withdrew his weapon, and his opponent clutched at his side where the sword had struck.

I can do this. If I've hit him once, I can do it again!

Not allowing his opponent time to adjust, he attacked again. His opponent moved with surprising nimbleness, rolling to the side in his heavy armor, quickly regaining his stance, hand still placed on his side.

Arthur swung again, his opponent parrying the attack, left arm stinging a little as he felt the blood trickling down his arm.

Nothing fatal.

He swung again, dropping into Stone stance and slamming against his opponent's weapon, trying to disarm him with the sudden force. His opponent held firm, refusing to let go of his weapon, so Arthur struck again, this time aiming for his opponent's sword arm.

The green armored man sidestepped, counterattacking. Arthur quickly ducked as the blade skimmed the top of his helmet.

He reactively took a couple steps back to create some distance, panicking at how close that attack had been. *He's got the upper hand. They really drilled into me the moves he would be using, but these aren't it!*

Sword raised, they circled each other, as if dancing with death itself. His opponent lunged forward, unleashing a series of thrusts that forced Arthur to parry. Trying to create an opening, Arthur tried to sidestep the last thrust, but his opponent managed to catch his free hand again, this time piercing deeper. But Arthur did not want to miss this opportunity, the shock allowed him to momentarily ignore the pain, thrusting his own weapon into the green armored man's shoulder, breaking through the armor and drawing blood.

They each took a step back, clutching their fresh wounds. The green-armored adversary tried to raise his sword, but it shook slightly against the pain of his shoulder. Realizing his sword arm was now useless, the man swapped hands, preparing to fight with his left.

That's a little better.

Arthur raised his sword, blood dripping down his arm, pain flaring beneath the armor, hand beginning to sweat, mixing with the blood.

It's so damn hot!

Arthur thrust his sword into the earth, enough to stand but not as deep as he thought as it seemed to strike something solid. He ignored it and took off his gauntlet, the blood that had been collecting inside spilling to the ground. Somehow it brought relief, whether it was real or not, Arthur felt more comfortable like this.

He picked up his sword again, as his freehand mindlessly fidgeted with the livewood ring.

Come on, Arthur. Do you want to see him again?

* * *

Elias could not ignore the pain that burned with a blazing fury in his shoulder. His opponent had struck deep, though hopefully not deep enough to be fatal. He watched as the man took off a gauntlet, as if freeing himself from its confinement made a difference to his wounds. Elias watched as blood dripped from the arm, gauging the effectiveness of his own attacks.

Not fatal, but quickly losing blood. Just like me.

The man charged forward, as a new surge of confidence flowed through him, attempting to take control of the fight.

Elias blocked his first attack, parrying the second as it came with surprising speed. The man's demeanor had changed significantly, taking the offensive and forcing Elias to take steps back as the blue-armored man continued his forward momentum.

Their swords met with each blow, the arena quickly filled with the clang of metal clashing with metal. They danced, each striking as the other blocked or dodged. Elias had felt he had the upper hand before, but now he felt even with his adversary.

His opponent had forced him to use his opposite hand, which was not his favored side, but he was still formidable enough to put up a fight.

Between the attacks and defenses, Elias was trying to spy an opening. *If he wants me to use my opposite hand, perhaps I'll force him to use his. His freehand is already damaged, so maybe…*

Wait… what is that?

Elias saw a glimpse of something odd, but his eyes were quickly taken away as the blue-armored man roared with a reinvigorated fury, swinging with all his might down at Elias, who had been a little too distracted, unable to dodge the attack, so he tried to match it with his own strength but was unable to summon it in time.

He felt his arm jolt downwards as his opponent's blade met his own with a greater force. He immediately tried to recuperate, knowing that an opening had been created. Elias tried to fall backwards, hoping to move his body out of the way as watched the sword thrust towards him, as if in slow motion.

The blade seemed to grow in size as it drew closer. Elias had not reacted fast enough, and the blade glided through his armor and his flesh.

This time Elias fell backwards as the blade was removed from his body, dripping with his blood. He tried to stand, but the pain of the fresh wound caught him by surprise. He stumbled as he stood, knowing that his opponent may not relent while he was on the ground.

He stood, breathing heavily. *Father was right. This did not end as quickly as I thought.* Elias felt himself slow, the wounds he had received quickly catching up to him. *I need to see it again.*

Elias raised his weapon again, new focus in mind. He attacked, knowing his opponent had the upper hand, but that would be his downfall. He could sense the blue-armored man growing overconfident, thinking he had control of the fight, but Elias was not to be underestimated.

To the Gods prisons with his wounds and pains, he had to ignore them if he were to stand a chance. He adopted the Long stance, keeping his opponent at a distance. He toyed with him, keeping the gap between them constant, taking a step back when necessary.

As expected, his opponent fell for the bait, charging forward in an attempt to close the gap.

Elias quickly rolled to the side, ignoring the pain that flashed through his entire body. He quickly stood, charging into the blue-armored man with his wounded shoulder, knocking his opponent down.

He stood over the Va Daolin champion, sword pointed. Elias should have attacked to guarantee his victory, but his instincts told him otherwise. This should be satisfactory for The Voice to declare him the winner, but he was no longer concerned with that.

"Let me see your left hand," Elias demanded, gesturing towards the bloodied hand.

His opponent complied with the request, though it was obvious even with the helmet that he was confused. He man raised the bloodied hand, fresh blood still dripping. Elias thought he had seen the blood obstructed by something on one of the fingers.

And he needed to confirm what he saw.

A livewood ring.

"The duel has completed! Elias Va Noldin is the victor!" a voice echoed through the empty stadium. Elias ignored them, his attention now demanded by something else.

"Remove your helmet," he demanded once again, sweat dripping down his body as he waited anxiously.

His opponent sat up, slowly taking his helmet off to reveal a young man with black curls and gorgeous blue eyes.

"No..." Elias was stunned. The man looked confused, wondering what was happening.

It's him. How is this possible? "No! I surrender!" Elias shouted, throwing his sword to the ground. "I refuse to fight!"

"What? But you have already been declared the victor!" The Voice shouted back, angered and confused. "Wait there, we'll be over to sort this out!"

"What are you doing?" the handsome man asked, becoming perplexed with the events unfolding before him.

"I... It's... Uh..." Elias stuttered, struggling to comprehend the situation himself. Then he removed his own helmet.

"No... *What?*" the man stared, wide eyed in disbelief.

"I refuse to fight," Elias said, beginning to remove the various pieces of his armor.

"What are you doing, Champion Elias?! Keep that on!" The Voice shouted, enraged, but Elias did not listen, continuing to take off his armor.

"I also surrender and refuse to fight!" Arthur stood, beginning to remove his own armor in defiance. They silently stared at each other as if they were each an illusion.

"It's you... But..." Arthur began but found himself unable to continue speaking.

Before they could completely remove their armor, The Voice had reached them, escorted by guards they had apparently been keeping out of sight.

I thought no one else was allowed in here?

"Grab Champion Arthur and place him in the center, like usual," The Voice commanded, and the guards immediately obeyed, grabbing Arthur and beginning to drag him. Arthur did not struggle against their grip, but that did not stop them from forcefully escorting him.

"No! I said I surrender!" Elias yelled in anger, chasing after Arthur.

"Champion Va Noldin, there must be a sacrifice for the Gods to bless us with more trees so that we must survive, and you have already been declared the victor! What is your issue? Why do you protest?" the member of The Voice had trouble calming himself, clearly agitated.

"I said, I surrender. Take me instead!"

They threw Arthur to his knees in the center of the arena, letting go of him but standing nearby as if he might try to run.

"Son, please! You're the victor, just take it! I beg of you!" the frail voice of Warin called out as he slowly approached.

Elias was unable to face his father, knowing that his actions would only harm him. "No! I can't let you take him!" he demanded, taking a step towards Arthur.

"Elias! No!"

"Champion Elias Va Noldin, it is a simple matter. Arthur has been declared the sacrifice, and on top of that, he surrendered in addition to you. We must take someone, and he has been chosen. Please, see reason," another member of The Voice said, but Elias was determined in his stance.

"Elias… It's a nice name," Arthur said, trying to make light of the situation in an attempt to calm Elias.

"I'm glad to have finally learned your name, Arthur, but don't let them take you away from me. Not now. Not like this."

"I'm sorry we couldn't meet before this, but I am not sorry that it is me going instead. Please, I want to. I don't want anything happening to you either, and they've already decided I am the sacrifice, so let me go, Elias."

"But we just met again. I can't. We have so much to talk about and… and I just can't let you go now!"

"Champion Elias, there is no negotiations here. We must give a sacrifice to the Gods, and you cannot change that course. Let the sacrifice be sent to the Gods, we will pray for him as he is sent!" A third member of The Voice gave a signal to someone out of view.

Then the floor beneath Arthur opened up, and he quickly sunk beneath the earth and out of view.

"No!" Elias dove in after Arthur, not caring what waited beneath them.

The last thing he heard was everyone's shocked reactions and attempts to dissuade him from diving in, mixed together in a meaningless mess.

All except his father's. His father's last plea stood out from them.

Arthur and Elias found themselves sliding down a stone surface, before it abruptly ended, and they landed on soft soil. They tumbled as they landed, grunting and hissing as their wounds flared once again. Elias forced himself to his knees, trying to gather his surroundings. Arthur had already stood, his body in a panic as he sensed something distressing.

They looked around the room, realizing they were on some kind of raised platform made out of black soil. Below them the soil continued, but was lined with people tied to sticks, those who were able to crane their neck stared at them in horror.

Soldiers surrounded the soil, as if afraid to be near it, but still on duty to prevent…something.

But what?

Elias began to feel heavy. "I don't… feel…"

"Me too," Arthur said. "I feel…"

"Drained," Elias finished. Like they were being drained by the soil itself.

They looked at each other, panic taking over.

"This is the sacrifice," Arthur whispered.

Elias nodded. Whatever this soil was, it would take their lives.

It was too late.

Elias immediately began to throw the rest of his armor off, not wanting to be restricted in death, but rather gain the false sense of freedom as his last living choice. Arthur followed, struggling to take off his armor, clambering towards Elias in the process. Elias caught him as he stumbled forward, aiding him in removing the final pieces of metal from his body.

Elias felt his life being sapped away, pulled into the ground by an unseen force, and he knew Arthur was experiencing the same. He looked at Arthur, worried. Each sleeve nearly entirely black, the color of fear. They had finally met again, and it would soon be accompanied by death.

But Elias was surprised to see a smile on Elias' face. A sweet, loving, genuine smile that calmed him. He knew they would die. But they would die together.

And in their final moments, that's all that mattered.

Arthur wrapped his arms around the man he had been missing since the day they had met, their letters were not an ample replacement for the joy of being in his presence. Elias reciprocated the embrace, finally able to be in the arms of the dark-haired man with the captivating blue eyes. Their sleeves slowly shifting from black to a pinkish red.

The world around them melted away, as if no longer relevant. In their final moments there was no worry, no fear.

Just each other.

They smiled at each other, and in their last moments, kissed.

One final surge of warmth and happiness before reality transformed into nothing.

29

Maggie stared, dumbfounded. Her mind unable to believe what her eyes were seeing.

A hole in the roof appeared and two people fell through, sliding down the strange stone chute. They landed on the dirt platform, clearly injured, but still managed to rush to each other to embrace.

Then their bodies began to change. From Maggie's angle, it looked as if their legs sunk into the ground slightly before their bodies slowly melded into wood, and soon they each began to take the shape of a tree.

She watched, eyes wide and mouth agape as the two men turned into trees, twisting and dancing with each other until they each stood tall and strong, intertwined with one another. Maggie's brain slowly began to function, constantly screaming and sending off alarms in her head.

Secret. Run. Sacrifice.

Once the tree seemed fully grown, almost in unison the people tied to the sticks cried out.

Not in pain, but fear.

Fear of death.

Trees. Secret.

The prisoners then seemed to repeat the process, but slower, melding into the earth and slowly taking the shape of trees as their screams muffled and died out.

It was horrifying to watch as their lives were slowly drained from them, turned into the resource their city raved about.

This was the Gods blessing.

RUN!

Before the General and the soldier turned around from watching the spectacle, Maggie scrambled to her feet and darted back the way she had come. Unfortunately, her body was still not entirely in her control, and she made much more noise than she had intended.

"Get her!" Deven screamed and Maggie shortly heard footsteps chasing after her.

Maggie ran, sweat dripping down her body, heart pounding against her chest as if reminding her she was still alive, at least for the moment. She ran in the darkness, but the light from the torch her pursuer carried slowly began to gain on her, lighting up her path ahead but reminding her she was slower than he. Her adrenaline and panic allowed her body to ignore how tired it was becoming by running up a slope, promising her life if she could only make it out.

She slammed into the door, but it did not open.

No, no, no! Where does it open... how...

"Stop!" the soldier called behind her. She turned to see him standing only a few steps away, rope in one hand and torch in the other. The young man did not immediately approach, as if waiting for Maggie to respond.

She turned and fumbled at the door again, searching for a way to open it from this side. The soldier then rushed forward, throwing the torch on the ground and grabbing Maggie by her shoulder. She fought against the grip, trying to pry it free, but it had a tight hold on her drabs. She turned, trying to shove the man away as he struggled to try get the rope around her.

He managed to place it around one arm, but Maggie scratched at his face to prevent him from getting the second. This only made him redouble his efforts, tackling her to the ground. They continued their struggle, Maggie fighting desperately to break free.

Before she knew it, she had the livewood dagger in her hand, placing it against the soldier's neck.

He immediately stopped moving, fear sinking in as he realized what she held.

She stared at him, holding her arm firmly in place. The boy was young. Afraid. If this happened at every duel, then this would be his first time he'd seen the events that unfurled before the both of them.

The soldier slowly let go of the rope, raising his hands. He was defenseless, given no weapon of his own, clearly not having expected to have dealt with this kind of conflict.

She watched as he breathed heavily, staring at Maggie as she held his life in her hands.

And she hated it.

She leant in, keeping the dagger in place, keeping her voice low. "You saw what happened, didn't you?"

The boy nodded, as much as his head would allow with a dagger at his neck.

"First time, right?"

He nodded again.

"How can you let that happen? How could you send those prisoners to their deaths like that? How long did you know?"

The boy choked on his words, stuttering as he tried to piece his mind together for an answer, a tear rolling down his cheek. He mustn't have fought at the wall, or at least never stared at death before.

The guilt inside Maggie grew but knew that holding the dagger there was the only thing keeping her from being captured. "Okay, stop. Did you know that was going to happen?"

The boy tried to breathe before speaking, but it appeared difficult to control. "I-I knew that something like that would happen, y-yes. I just didn't know e-exactly. But they didn't tell me about their screams."

The boy broke down crying. Maggie got the feeling it wasn't from death, but the event scarring the poor boy. She had to admit, she didn't come out unphased, but she had more pressing matters that took precedence over her mental stability.

"Their screams... Oh Gods... I didn't think they'd be so terrified. I was told they were waiting to join the Champion in sacrifice but... they seemed so scared. So afraid. Why would they

387

scream like that if they were joining the Gods? I mean... I knew most of them would have been against their will, but still, i-it was horrifying!" the boy crumpled to the ground in a mess. It was obvious he had never dealt with such a harsh situation before. Perhaps he might have been strong enough to resist it, if Maggie had not held a dagger to his neck.

Fearing that she might be being played for a fool, she kept the dagger pointed at him, but reared it away from him slightly. "Listen. I said listen, you need to stop crying for a moment. I need to tell the city out there what has happened here. I need to tell them what The Voice is doing, this can't go on. this—" Maggie was cut off by the sounds of footsteps echoing up the slope.

He's coming.

"Will you let me go so I can tell the city?"

The boy stared at her, contemplating. She turned to the door, thankful that the soldier had brought the torch as her eyes landed on what she searched for, the hole that would open the door.

She turned back to the boy, who seemed lost in thought, the footsteps growing louder. "I need an answer, now!"

"Okay, yes, tell them! I can't get their screams out of my head! There are more prisoners lined up down there, I'm going to have to hear it again and again, oh Gods!" the boy began to cry again.

"Then you have one more choice. Stay here or run with me. I need a decision, now!"

The steps grew louder.

Maggie began to panic, the boy was taking too long to answer. "I'll make the decision for you, and I am really sorry to do this, but I hope it stops you from getting into any trouble." Maggie gripped the dagger tightly, psyching herself up before driving it in the boy's side. Not deep enough to be fatal, but enough to wound him.

He cried out in pain, clearly taken by surprise.

The steps grew faster. Maggie rushed to the door, prying her now bloodied dagger into the hole and unlatching the door from whatever mechanism held it. She opened it, breaking out into bright day of the city.

She instinctively began running, as she heard the door behind her swing open again.

"Guards! Guards!" Deven shouted, his voice bellowing through her head as if he had been right behind her.

"Guards! Stop her!"

Maggie ran, refusing to stop.

Castor. I need Castor. She didn't know why she thought of her brother, but for some reason she believed he could protect her. She needed her brother, he would shield her against the general.

Somehow.

He would believe her. He had to.

They were family.

The wall.

She raced towards the East Gate, not knowing if the general was chasing her, or if there were only guards.

She turned into a street, bumping into a soldier who was part of a human barricade, knocking him down. Maggie didn't slow her momentum, she didn't care. She had to run for as long as her body would last.

And it wouldn't last long. She was no young woman anymore, and her chest already began to ache as her legs threatened to buckle at any moment.

But she had to run. It was the only choice. One of the soldiers abandoned the barricade to chase her, she could hear his footsteps.

She paid him no mind, compelling her feet to move faster.

As long as she reached Castor, she would be safe.

Then the sound of the attack horn blasted rapidly throughout the city.

30

Castor's body began to shake with fear and anticipation as he reached the steps of the wall at the East Gate. The attack horn blared throughout the city, but its frightening aspect was the rapid pace at which it was being played.

There was no way the creatures could have snuck so close to the city, so it must have meant something else. As leapt to top of the wall, his body shook as his fears were confirmed.

The Red Sea.

They poured out of the forest, barely a gap between them as they filled the fields surrounding the city.

How? They weren't meant to come until tomorrow!

The soldiers were already stationed atop the wall, awaiting their orders, and the general was nowhere to be seen. There was no time to wait for the man. They had to act, and they had to act now.

"Archers, unleash as soon as they're within range! Ballistae, release! Now!" he bellowed, shaking off the fears in order to face the Sea with a clear mind.

The soldiers sprang into action, unleashing the large wooden spikes into the sea as it rapidly encroached their surroundings. With the sheer number of enemies, it was almost impossible to miss with the ballista. The large ammunition decimated several creatures. Impaling three, four at a time, but scattering its shrapnel all around, slowing some down or even outright killing them.

"Slopes! Rotate and prepare for the drops!"

The wooden platforms the rock slopes stood on were rotated, facing outward rather than towards their gate. A large rock was loaded on either side, waiting for Castor's call.

The ballistae unleashed again, killing a large portion of metalurks. Well, a large portion in comparison to their usual amount. It only made small dints in the army that charged towards them.

Castor looked back towards the city; people were frantically fleeing uphill, towards the back of the city, where the safety blockades and shelters were, clearly not having expected the attack to come so soon.

We have to hold them for as long as possible. Why? Why have they come now?!

The monsters reached within archer distance and the soldiers unleashed their first volley, hitting several metalurks but only felling a few.

The ballistae continued their attack, rapidly firing and taking down chunks of the creatures at a time. Castor was thankful for the added measure of defense, it would be the reason they might make it through the Red Sea, though they would still suffer heavy losses.

Castor peered down at the entrance to his gate, spying his Steelwoods in formation. The horsemen waited farther back, prepared to chase down the metalurks that broke through, but Castor knew they would not be enough. They had to try make a wall of their own within the city, a human barricade to prevent the metalurks from coming through.

Thankfully, his thoughts were answered as he also spied the extra regiment of shieldmen marching towards their positions. Regularly, the shields weren't as effective against the creatures, but it seemed like they had reinforced them with small bits of livewood to make them sturdier. They were also quite large in size, requiring both hands to wield effectively. It was really more like using a large door rather than a shield. They would form walls at the street entrances, backed by any and all soldiers.

He returned his attention back to the fields. The Red Sea was nearly at their wall, but thankfully the ballistae were taking down more than their fair share.

Until one of the ballistae jammed.

391

The soldiers cursing turned Castor's attention towards them. They were standing at the ballista, smacking and jolting it as if trying to lodge it free from whatever was preventing its function.

"Don't do that, you idiots! Let me try and fix it before you break the damn thing!" the soldier in charge of the treeblood berated them, inspecting the cogs at the side of the device.

"What's happened?" Castor called to them, demanding an answer.

"I think one of the wheels stopped turning, but I'm not entirely certain. It could be a number of things, but I can fix it if these idiots can stop hitting it for a moment!"

"Hurry! We need that ballista running! They're taking down a large portion of them!" Castor said and watched the frustrated soldier attempt to fix it a moment longer, but the metalurks were only seconds away from their walls.

"Slopes! Drop!"

Several rocks were rolled onto the unsuspecting creatures, crushing piles of them at a time.

Where is the general? I need to get to the tunnel!

"Keep at it, men! We're chipping them down!"

The archers were relentless in their attacks, firing as fast as possible at the cost of accuracy, but they didn't really need to aim. It normally took several arrows to fell a metalurk, it was nearly impossible to pierce their skulls with their wooden ammunition.

Castor watched as the runners restocked the archer's quivers with bundles of arrows, slowly draining their stocks.

The General still had not made an appearance. Today, of all days, the man seemed to be held up somewhere else. He would not be at another wall, the East Gate was the most vital.

Thankfully some of the creatures spread themselves out, realizing there were other doors at the North and South, alleviating some of the force that would slam itself at the East Gate. If the enemy thinned themselves out along the walls, then it would make the job easier for everyone.

Some of the metalurks tried clawing at the stone walls, finding no other place to attack. Few tried scaling it, using their sharp claws to find spots to cling onto, but the wall not that easy to climb. Soldiers focused their efforts on any who tried, slaying them before they got very far, only to be replaced by other metalurks attempting to do the same.

Below, Castor could hear the roars of the first lot of metalurks reaching the large livewood gate.

"Got it!" the soldier fixing the ballista exclaimed, and it was quickly loaded and loosed again.

Castor stood, listening to the sounds of battle.

The ballistae being released.

The rocks rolling down the slopes and impacting heavily on the creatures and earth below.

Archers calling for a resupply.

Soldiers down below preparing to face the inevitable Sea.

The creatures, eerily silent and determined.

The sounds of the fight going on below.

Wait... why don't I hear the gate being torn apart?

"Officer Hendel!" Castor called, and the man came running towards him.

"Captain?"

"The general isn't here, and we can't rely on him. I need to get below to face the creatures about to break in. We need those ballistae and rocks to kill as many as they can, but if you fear for the men's lives then retreat behind the barricades we've formed. It's a lot of responsibility, but right now, you need to accept it without question. Good luck, Hendel, and I pray I see you on the other side."

"Leave it to me, sir!" Hendel saluted and Castor returning the gesture. He raced down the steps, the sounds of screaming and surprised exclamations sounding below.

As he descended, he saw the metalurks had already broken through the livewood gate with unnerving speed. He could not make it down far enough to inspect the tunnel, he was too busy running towards his Steelwoods.

Who were all retreating for some reason.

Castor was about to shout an order to keep them in line, but he noticed several had abandoned their weapons, adding to his confusion.

A metalurk broke free from the pack, so Castor jumped down to meet it. It ignored him, running for someone else, so he took the chance to thrust his weapon into the creature.

The weapon sunk into the creature with no resistance. Castor felt no impact as he drove the weapon in, and the creature seemed unfazed, continuing to run. His livewood spear moved with it. The creature remained unharmed, untouched. Only half of Castor's spear remained.

He stared, his brain unable to process what had just happened. The weapon definitely sank into the creature, but instead of piercing it as it normally would, it was… absorbed? Consumed?

Like metal would?

He turned, watching as his Steelwoods scrambled to grab a regular weapon, having already discovered the new fearsome defense of the metalurks.

"Castor!" a feminine voice called out, and he looked around but found no one trying to get his attention.

"Castor!" the voice grew slightly louder, trying to yell over the sounds of the soldiers screaming, desperate to find an effective weapon.

Gods please, no… Is that Maggie?

He knew the voice all too well. He turned to see his sister in the distance, running towards him. He was about to respond, to yell at her to get away, run to the shelters, demand she leave, but the sound of his men rallying as they finally grabbed ordinary wooden spears and clubs drew his attention once more.

His men yelled, thrusting and swinging rapidly in an attempt to slay the creatures as fast as possible. Soon, the area surrounding the tunnel filled with red, metalurks trying to crawl over metalurks, stepping on the bodies of their fallen as if it were a minor inconvenience.

The gate and portcullis that were their main means of impeding the enemy had been useless with this newfound power of the metalurks. The crux of their defense, the sole reason they had been able to survive, the very blessings from the Gods themselves.

Now completely useless.

The Steelwoods tried to push back but were unable with their less-effective weapons. Castor ran back up the wall, grabbing a regular spear off a soldier and informing Officer Hendel of the situation before retreating to his men.

Soon, pairs of his men found a rhythm. The spearmen would strike the metalurks, piercing their torsos and holding them in place long enough for the maces to crush their skulls. Effective, but it was not enough to keep up with the enemies surging into the city.

Castor momentarily joined the fight, slightly distracted by the presence of his sister. He knew her general location, but he could not spend the time to try and spot her. He felt their position slipping, little by little. He had to stand and watch as some of his men were slain by the creatures, unable to protect them with his stick. A stupid, gods be damned *stick*.

His attention was redirected quickly as a small group of metalurks broke free in the direction he had last seen his sister.

"Vance!" called hopefully, having not spotted the man.

Breaking free from the line, Vance appeared, slightly scratched but still standing, "Cap?"

"Take over!"

"Cap?"

"Just do it! You're capable enough, I'll try make it back!"

Castor pierced the skull of a charging metalurk, its body adding to the pile that quickly filled the area. Without waiting for a response, Castor charged off into the direction of the creatures, his spear breaking. He grabbed another off the corpse of Mark, one of his Steelwoods, unable to spend the appropriate time to mourn.

As soon as he broke free of the line, he saw his sister fleeing towards the city. *What in the Gods prisons is she doing here?!* He ran as fast as he could, chasing down the creatures that were either pouncing after her, or aiming to get deeper into the city. Fortunately, one of the horsemen caught up and struck the farthest one down. Thankfully, the rider had a regular wooden spear, adjusting to the situation. He then expertly danced with the other two, keeping them at a distance as they tried to lunge after his horse, who kicked at them.

Castor caught up, striking the closest metalurk down with ease as its back was turned. He and the horseman struck down a few more, but the last metalurk managed to claw the horse's hind leg, rendering it useless and toppling the horse.

The rider became pinned underneath the horse's weight, and the metalurk sensed his opportunity, moving in for the kill. Castor thought it would target he rider, but instead it slashed at the horse again, instantly killing it. It gave Castor enough time to pierce the creature's back, turning its attention towards him.

It appeared to mouthlessly roar at him, sounding like a suffocated scream, its eyeless head somehow tracking his movements as he lured it off of the horse. With another yell, it lunged at Castor, who quickly rolled to the side to avoid its claws. The creature was fast, talons reaching towards Castor as he thrust his spear into the creature's chest. It was not enough to wound it, and the metalurk's claw found its way into his arm.

At first, he only felt a slight sting, his mind too focused on the battle to care for a non-fatal wound. He pushed the spear that was already impaling the beast, shoving it backwards. He pulled it free from its torso, and struck the beast several times over, each time shoving it back, keeping it off balance so that it couldn't attack.

The beast finally succumbed to the wounds, falling limp to the ground. Castor immediately rushed over to the horseman, finding the man conscious but struggling to pull his leg free.

Castor flipped his spear around, shoving the blunt end as far as he could underneath the horse, using it to life the heavy animal as far as he could. He managed to create enough gap for the man to pull his pinned leg free.

The rider tried to stand, but his pinned leg was unable to bear any weight. Castor helped the man up, escorting him over to the human barricade. It split open, allowing him entry, and he handed the man off to someone else with the order of taking him to a shelter to sit out the rest of the fight.

Castor frantically scanned the streets until he spotted his sister being dragged, kicking and screaming, likely towards a shelter.

He ran closer, his impatience building as the fight continued at the wall. "Men, hold it! Release her for a moment, I wish to speak with her."

The soldiers, confused, obeyed the order. They let go of Maggie and returned to the front lines in search of any other civilians. Maggie stood, panting. Castor scowled and prepared himself for some insane excuse. "Maggie, what are you doing here?" he almost growled at her, the irritation growing.

"I… I needed help…The general is after me," she said between breaths.

Gods please, not today. "Maggie, what have you done? What did the Seekers put you up to?"

"I chose to do this for them in return for a favor, which I'll tell you about later, but for now you need to protect me! I can't go to the shelters, it'll be too easy for him to catch me there!"

"And so you think running through the streets as the metalurks break into the city is a safer option? Gods, Maggie, what is going through your head? This seriously couldn't wait until after the city is safe again?"

"No."

He stared at her. She had answered firmly, her eyes screaming for him to listen, scowling as if silently threatening to never speak with him again if he abandoned her here. Castor sighed. "Fine, but be quick, I should return to the fight."

Maggie stepped closer to lower her voice, eyes scanning their surroundings for any soldiers who might be within earshot. "There's something underneath the arena, a large cavern thing that they take prisoners to. Don't ask why, just trust me, but I followed the general there, and what I saw… Castor, the livewood trees are *people!*"

"What? Maggie, that's ridiculous!"

"I said trust me, Castor! You have to believe me! I'm not some deranged psycho who would make this up while our city was being threatened! I wouldn't be this close to danger if I wasn't serious! You have to believe me! The champions, the ones that fight every twenty years, they're sacrificed to become the main tree!"

"None of this is making sense."

397

"And none of it will, but it's what is happening. It has something to do with the soil they plant the prisoners on. It's dark, too dark for soil. It beats like a heart. It doesn't look right, and it feels…creepy. Something is wrong with it, and whatever it is, it turns anyone who touches it into a tree. I know it sounds stupid, but damn Castor, I saw it with my own eyes!"

"And the general?"

"He found me. I managed to escape, but he was chasing me and sent men after me. I lost them about the same time the horn sounded."

"The Red Sea came quicker than we expected. The cursed creatures appeared from nowhere! And now our damned livewood is useless against them."

"I… have a theory about that too, Castor."

"I do as well. Look, we don't have time. I'm sorry for not believing you in the past, so I'll assume you're right. It's the soil."

"I think so, too, but I don't know how. The forest soil is normal, isn't it?"

"Who knows. Maybe at the surface?" He shook his head. "Soil that turns people into livewood?"

Wait…

His mind returned to watching the soldiers use the ballista and fixing the livewood gates.

Treeblood.

So much he didn't know about the substance, but the times he had seen it in action, the way it interacted with livewood, it all somehow made more sense to him now. How it had a unique interaction with the very tree it came from, how it oozed out of things like… well, like blood. He still couldn't believe it entirely but—

"I don't think it's just the soil, Castor," Maggie said. "The general seemed… afraid when the duel ended."

"Afraid?"

She nodded. "Only one champion was meant to be sacrificed. I saw two bodies fall into the room, they were wearing some kind of… shell or something, but they were definitely two men. They turned into two large trees, different from the others. I don't know why, but the general seemed frightened. And now—"

"And now the Red Sea is here. Two sacrifices amplified… whatever in the Gods Prisons is going on. I haven't the slightest clue how this all works. Maggie, and I'll likely be branded a deserter for doing this but… would taking down the tree stop them?"

"I don't have the faintest idea. At worst, it might stop them from returning? It might not send them back from… well, wherever, but it might stop more from attacking our city."

"So…our curse can be lifted?"

Maggie nodded, her face revealing her uncertainty.

"The Red Sea can be defeated. We can deal with the trees afterwards, but right now I have to focus my efforts on defending our city."

"Without livewood? And what about me?" Maggie asked, concerned. In truth, Castor wasn't sure. He just knew he needed to fight the metalurks, it was his job. If ridding themselves of the tree wouldn't stop the army, then he couldn't risk it. He had to place his life between the metalurks and the civilians, but now he had the added task of protecting his sister.

"Go to the Magistrate's shelter."

"What?"

"It's near the arena. I can escort you there, but we have to be quick, my place is on the front lines. I have a friend in there who can protect you from the general. At least, I hope she can."

"Hope?"

"I don't know what else to do, Maggie!"

"We should burn the tree down!"

"I can't risk that! If burning the tree won't rid the metalurks rampaging at our doorstep, then I can't! I'll have to fight them using the most basic of resources, but by the Gods I'll slay every one of them with it!"

"Fine! Just protect me from the general!"

"I can't if I'm fighting the damned Reds, Maggie! I need to—"

The sounds of men screaming turned their attention towards the shield wall. The soldiers were desperately trying to hold the metalurks back, and apparently the Steelwoods had retreated behind the wall.

399

Or at least what was left of them.

The shields were quickly rendered useless, only hindering the enemy's movement slightly.

Before he could move, the wall split apart and the metalurks poured in, once gain clashing with the Steelwoods. "My men…"

"Castor! If you're going back in there, then I need to survive so I can tell others what I've seen! Take me to the Magistrate's shelter, I'll try keep myself alive from there!"

It took all of Castor's strength to turn his back on his men, guilt flaring through his body in a threat to shut him down, but the information his sister held was vital to the city. Possibly the answer to ending the curse that ravaged them for nearly two-hundred years.

He grabbed Maggie's arm, tugging her behind him so that he could keep his eyes ahead without worrying about losing her.

Castor dragged her through the streets, feeling her stray away from any soldier they neared as if any of them might suddenly lunge at her. A group of metalurks had managed to wriggle their way past the guards, running in their direction before splitting apart, leaving one charging at them.

Castor shifted himself to be between Maggie and the metalurk, spear in hand preparing to meet it head on. He gripped his spear tightly. He had not used regular wooden weapons since he had joined the Steelwoods many years ago, and he felt himself once again feeling like a small child with a toy.

Maggie's words replayed themselves in his mind as he prepared himself for the advancing enemy, her words simply not making any sense to him. But he had to believe her. She seemed so sure. Maybe the prospect of ending their curse clouded his vision, but he would accept whatever fate held for him if he was mistaken.

Maggie moved to the side of the street, hiding behind a building as the metalurk drew closer. Castor pointed his spear and waited.

Years of fighting these creatures allowed him to learn how they fought, and what their instincts were, so occasionally he was able to predict what they would do. And as expected, this metalurk pounced in an effort to overpower him, leaping into the air to pin him down with its weight. Castor crouched, thrusting his spear forward into the creature and using its momentum to propel it over him, slamming it hard onto the ground. He quickly withdrew his weapon and pierced the metalurk's skull to confirm its death.

Maggie looked at him, frightened and stunned. She had never been so close to the metalurks before. At least, while they were alive. Castor ran over and took her hand again, either to try and give her the courage to move, or forcefully drag her if necessary.

The street they had come from was now overrun by the metalurks as they slowly swarmed into the city. The next wave of soldiers met them, slowing down their movements. Castor continued to lead Maggie away from them as fast as he could, but he could hear the fight behind them. It wasn't going in their favor.

He tried to ignore his guilt as he ran from the fight, questioning himself again. His sister had put him in a difficult position, now feeling like either decision led to abandoning them in this dire time.

He ran harder, nearly pulling his sister off her feet, but she was doing well to keep up with him considering the difference in their physical stature. As they ran, it seemed not all the civilians had yet retreated to the shelters, possibly coming back in search of missing family members.

A few soldiers were attempting to escort them, but some resisted, attempting to reach their houses to make sure it was clear, but the soldiers were under strict orders not to allow that.

Castor cursed the metalurks for being ahead of schedule, it had completely thrown off their defense and preparation. They used to be predictable, but if Maggie's claims were accurate, then no one could have seen this coming.

Well, no one except those involved with this secret.

The Voice.

The noble families who produced the champions.

The general.

If only they had prepared for a scenario like this, but they were apparently confident enough in their plans to have prevented this.

And now, here they were.

Livewood was useless.

Maybe we should try to destroy the tree? I don't know if we can survive without a proper weapon.

They drew closer to the arena wall and Castor was left with a decision. Have Maggie lead him to the trees to be destroyed or take her to the shelter where she could tell others if they survive the Red Sea.

He slowed his pace, looking behind him and seeing the creatures beginning to spread into the city, like a plague. *What do I do?*

"What is it, Castor?" Maggie asked, worried tingeing her voice and her eyes.

"I just...I don't know what to do anymore, Maggie! I can't stop them. Not on my own and with this damned tree branch!"

"Then let's do it, Castor. Let's go burn the trees down. All of them."

"What if it doesn't work?" he asked, his conviction fading.

Maggie stared him straight in the eyes. "What else can we do? If it doesn't work, then we still have to face them."

Behind them, a group of metalurks sprinted towards them, quickly gaining on them. With no more time left to think, Castor dragged his sister towards the arena, still undecided but knowing he needed to at least keep moving. As they ran, the sound of a galloping horse grew louder, and quickly appeared by Castor's side.

"Captain Belden! Sir!"

Castor stopped. The metalurks quickly closing the gap, but the horseman seemed like he had something urgent to deliver, his horse kicking a metalurk who had reached them.

"Captain! A message from Vance of the Steelwoods! A group of citizens still remain at the city center for some reason, and with no other authority left at the wall, Vance has called a retreat there to protect them where he plans to try hold the enemy back! He requests you go there when you are able!"

Castor nodded in acknowledgement of the message, and the rider directed the horse towards the arena before veering off towards the city center. He grabbed Maggie once more, and they took off again, fearing the creatures were gaining on them. Castor wouldn't be able to stop them all, not without a livewood weapon.

The wall grew larger as they drew nearer. Castor's heart raced, feeling for the first time in his career as a soldier that they may not make it through. He'd been somewhat confident about facing the Red Sea at the appointed time and with the appropriate defenses, but now that control of the situation had been taken from them, hope slowly slipped away.

Castor wasn't sure where he was running to anymore. He'd still not decided if it was worth trying to find this tree and destroy it, if something did exist that tied the creatures to the tree, destroying it might not stop them from rampaging throughout the city. His eyes alighted on a figure up ahead, standing out in their green outfit atop the grey stones of the street, waving something undiscernible in the air.

A civilian? What are they doing? Castor glanced over his shoulder; two metalurks had managed to run ahead of the small pack, edging closer.

"Run!" Castor yelled at the figure, but he wasn't sure if the man heard. He waved frantically, trying to signal the person to escape, but they continued to walk towards them, waving the same object around.

Details slowly emerged as they neared the mysterious person. It appeared to be an elderly man, very sick as he hobbled with a cane, likely a noble based on the colors they wore.

"Come at me, you bastards! I'll fight the lot of you for taking him from me! You damned creatures!"

What is this old man doing? And what is he waving?

The old man wasn't talking to them, in fact he ignored Castor and Maggie entirely, focused only on the metalurks behind them.

"Run!" Castor repeated, but the old man did not listen. Castor stopped as he reached the noble, turning to see the two metalurks within a short distance.

"You have to leave! Now!" he yelled, almost hysterically as he was perplexed by the old man's actions.

The object the man held was peculiar, it had the shape of a sword, but was a reflective grey color. The old man continued to wave it in challenge to the beasts.

"What is that? What are you doing old man?"

"Getting my revenge on these damned creatures! They took my son! Now they can take me, but I'll strike one of them down before I go! With my son's own sword! Those bastards will pay!" Tears streamed down the old man's face. Castor could see the man knew clearly what he was doing.

"Sir, I can't let you—"

"Do not touch me! I am the last of the Va Noldins! I will not be left alone in this city! I have chosen my fate, now leave me be!"

Va Noldin? As in the champion?

It was too late. The metalurks had drawn too close, and the man was clearly too frail to run.

"Maggie, hide!" he shoved her behind him once more, pointing his spear. The metalurks split, one charging at Castor and the other at the old man.

Castor met the creature front on, using its own momentum to easily pierce its skin with his spear. The creature did not fall, continuing its attack, forcing Castor to dodge to the side. The spear broke in half, leaving the detached portion sticking out of the metalurk.

Damn! Castor faced the creature, now only holding a thin club. He felt the presence of the rest of the pack growing nearer, beginning to fear for the life of himself and his sister.

The metalurk lunged, Castor quickly dodge aside, striking the creature in the head, momentarily dazing it. He swung again.

And again.

And again.

Slowly bludgeoning the creature to death. He stood over it, panting, the remaining half the spear splintered and cracked.

He threw the remains of the weapon down, turning to confirm his suspicions of the other fight.

The old man had been killed. He lay lifeless on the ground, blood pouring from multiple wounds.

The creature he fought was still moving, though it was clearly in pain. The peculiar weapon the old man had used was loosely stuck in the creature's side.

Then metalurk shifted, trying to stand, and the weapon fell.

It hit the ground, giving off a peculiar sound, one Castor had never heard before. It rang through is ears, as if whispering its name to him.

He bent and picked up the weapon. It felt sturdy, surprisingly light, and sharp.

Metal.

Castor could only guess, but he wanted to believe that it was the forbidden substance. He looked at the beast, slowly standing in an attempt to face him. Castor thrust the weapon, easily breaking the skin as it glided deeper inside.

I thought metal didn't work on them?

The creature fell, dead. He turned to face the oncoming pack, sword in his hand. Somehow, this felt right. He was drawn to the weapon, and it filled Castor with a new surge of strength he'd never before experienced.

He pointed his sword, standing against the small pack alone.

But he was not afraid.

He was confident.

He was prepared.

He was Captain Castor Belden, leader of the Steelwoods, defender of the city.

Death would not take him today.

The sharpness of the blade easily drove itself into the metalurk, slaying the first with a single strike.

He killed each one as it drew close enough to strike. The weapon pierced and sliced smoother than anything he had ever used. As a test, Castor struck the weapon into the last metalurk's neck. The blade sank deep enough to kill, but it did not decapitate the mindless creature.

He stood amongst the slain pack of metalurks, metal sword in his hand. It was hard to tell if the sword had suffered any damage, there were no visible signs to him, but this was the first time seeing such a weapon.

"Maggie," he called to her softly, his eyes stuck on the new weapon.

"What in the Gods is that thing?" Maggie crept out of her hiding place, staring at the weapon and slain metalurks in awe.

"I think it's the answer to our situation. Listen, Maggie, can you destroy the tree alone?"

"Alone? The general might still be in there, I won't be able to fight him alone."

"I'm sorry, but you'll have to. Either that, or retreat to a shelter."

"Where are you going?"

Castor raised the weapon in the sunlight, watching the light gleam against the peculiar material, feeling his hope renewed. Feeling like they now had a fighting chance. "I need to save my men. And the people of the city."

Maggie looked disappointed but could see that Castor had made up his mind. She turned away from him, preparing to leave but hesitated. Without a word, she wrapped her arms around him, giving him one final embrace. Castor hugged her back, knowing that it might be their last. Right now, it didn't matter if she was a Seeker. Nothing mattered except surviving this Red Sea.

And hopefully ending their curse.

They ran off in different directions along the arena wall, each with their own objective of saving the city.

Castor ran as fast as his legs allowed, rounding the arena until he reached the front where several guards were lined up in defense of the front entrance, livewood weapons in hand.

There must still be nobles inside.

"Livewood weapons are useless," Castor yelled as he passed. "Grab yourself something else to club them to death with." It was the only advice he could give as he made his way towards the city center.

It was overrun with Reds. He could not see any soldiers or civilians left, at least from where he stood, but the metalurks still seemed as if they were after something on one side of the market.

Metal sword in hand, Castor ran forward, confident in his ability to slay any creatures that might turn to him fight him. But they were quite distracted by something, none of them turning to face him as he approached. He slashed his way into the pile of scrambling enemies, cutting through their backline and hacking away their numbers.

Through the cracks and the growls, he could hear what they were after. There were still men fighting, forming whatever barricade to fight against the metalurks, their backs to the building they defended.

Castor let loose a rallying cry that caught the attention of many of the enemies, but his new blade cut down all of those around him swiftly, carving a small path through the middle of the enemy, allowing him to join the remnants of the soldiers left to defend the city center.

"Captain!" Vance exclaimed, blood dripping down his arm and from his head, but still happy to see Castor.

Castor looked past him, realizing what they were here for. He could hear the cries and muffled screams of people inside the building. They must have gathered them inside in one last valiant attempt to protect them.

"Vance, you've done well. This is all that's left of our Steelwoods?" Castor looked down the line, saddened to see how few there were. Vance gave a nod and a glum smile. His weapon was cracked and near its breaking point, and his back was against the wall with nowhere else to run.

"It'll do."

Castor turned, facing the enemy that the Steelwoods desperately held back, raising his sword in display.

"Protect them with your lives men! We will get through this!"

With another rallying cry, Castor dived back into the fray.

31

Maggie's hope had been with Castor protecting her from General Deven. Without her brother, she knew she wouldn't be able to survive if she was caught again.

She traced the wall with her eyes, trying to spot the hidden door again. She wasn't sure if the general had returned, or had gone off looking for her, or possibly joined in the defense of the city. Either way, she needed to get into the cavern and destroy that tree. She wasn't sure how yet, but she would.

There was no other choice.

She could hear the growls and yells of the city under attack, hastening herself to find the door. Finally, her eyes fell upon the hole she was looking for. She quickly inserted her livewood dagger, popping the door open. She swung it just far enough for her to slip in, but she stopped.

The crack of light that poured into the tunnel seemed to act as a warning, letting her know that something dangerous waited below. Even without the general, the number of guards would stop her. She didn't know if they still remained to harvest the newly-made livewood trees, but she couldn't assume the cavern was empty.

The growls behind her grew louder, and she realized that some of the metalurks might have found their way to this side. She stood in the entryway, uncertain. Looking into the tunnel only gave her an overwhelming feeling of dread but looking back into the city told her there was only death.

It's a stupid idea that might get us all killed, but it might work. She opened the door fully, standing at the entrance, cupping her hands near her mouth as she prepared to shout into the city.

"Hey!" She yelled, waiting for a reaction. "HEY!"

She waited for a moment, but there was no movement. *Damn, I'll have to get closer.*

Maggie took a few steps towards the buildings surrounding the arena but stopped as a metalurk came rushing around. It stumbled a little as it realized she was there, changing its course to follow her.

Maggie did not freeze, she'd already turned and entered the tunnel, running past the spot where she'd stabbed the soldier. The tunnel was dark, but she didn't care. She traced the wall with one hand, the other held out in front of her to warn her of anything she might run into.

Growls echoed down the hall, the sounds of claws against the earthy rock growing loud inside of her mind as she feared the creature was gaining on her.

Finally, she could see the tunnel becoming lighter as she drew near its bottom. She rounded the final turn and broke into the open cave beneath the arena.

Right into the general.

He grabbed her by the arms, tightening his grip. She tried to pry herself free, but his strength was simply too much for her.

"Stop struggling. Stop!" he demanded, and something about his tone caused Maggie to listen. He wasn't commanding, but rather trying to persuade her. "Now isn't the time for your damned snooping again. You've seen what you've seen you needn't have come back. We're trying to destroy the damned thing!"

Maggie didn't believe him. She couldn't believe him. She looked behind him, watching as several of the soldiers were trying to place planks of wood atop the black soil in an attempt to create a path to the main tree. "Destroy it?"

"Yes. I'm not a fool. When I chased you outside, I heard the sound of the horn, and I knew it immediately. The Red Sea is here."

Maggie glared at him. "If you knew, then why are you here and not out there fighting?"

409

He sighed, loosening his grip but still keeping hold of her. "Like I said, I am not a fool. I've been alive for sixty odd years, and I have been here for three duels. This is the first time I've seen two sacrifices fall into the pit. This is the first time two trees have grown at once. This is the first time the Red Sea has attacked us, not only on the same day, but almost immediately. The Voice probably realizes how it works, and they've manipulated us into thinking it had no connection to the damned beasts. Maybe they don't know, I'm just speculating, but right now, we've got to destroy it."

She stared at the General, her perception of him fracturing a little. She still thought him a harsh old man who was ruthless and self-absorbed, arrogant and entitled, but at least he was rational. He knew what had to be done in order to protect the city and he immediately tried to rectify the situation, but it still didn't squander his role in her son's death.

The growls from the tunnel grew louder. The general stared past her, horrified, then looked back at her, wide-eyed. "What have you done?"

He pushed her to the side, yelling for soldiers to retreat out the other entrances. They had no weapons to defend themselves and no way to fight any creatures that discovered them. The general was making his way to the back tunnels with his men as the creature rushed into the cave.

Maggie scrambled, trying to catch up to the general and his soldiers, but she was too slow. The beast was already on the move, roaring and hungry. She ducked, hands over her head as if it would do anything to protect her. She heard the creature's claws scrape across the hard floor, listened to it leap into the air.

Then all sound seemed to fade away. Dying out as if the air had become still. For a moment, nothing existed, not even her.

Just the darkness of her closed eyes, waiting.

She was not greeted with death.

Maggie wasn't sure how long she had been crouching, but as she opened her eyes, she realized she was still alive. She dared to raise her head to look around for the creature.

It was walking across the black soil with a small amount of difficulty. Its movements were slow but its goal was clear: the two trees that stood tall, embracing one another in their twisted forms.

What... is it doing?

She watched as the creature clawed its way up the soil platform, growling in anticipation as it neared the trees.

Maggie put her back to the wall, flattening herself against it as if it would hide her from the metalurk's attention. She slowly edged across, making her way to the back tunnel where the soldiers and general had fled, watching the creature with both marvel and fear.

It finally made it to the top of that soil, stood tall, muscles trembling as it faced the entwined trees.

And then it pounced, landing against one of the trees.

She couldn't tell what it was doing. It wasn't attacking, it was barely even moving, but the tree was fading away at a slow rate.

Like it was being... absorbed. Consumed.

It pressed itself against the tree, trying to get as much body contact as possible. As pieces of the tall tree disappeared, it moved itself into a better position.

Maggie stared in wonder, uncertain about what was happening. *Is this good...or bad?*

She traced where the creature must have run across the soil. Several trees must have been in its path, as small pieces of it were missing as if it brushed past. Maggie could only watch as the tree disappeared, chunk by chunk. It was a slow process. Whatever the creature was doing, none of it made sense. The way it appeared to absorb the tree matched the stories of many years ago when the creatures were said to consume metal.

But why was it consuming the livewood trees? Wasn't it the key to their entrance into their world? Unless Maggie had been mistaken entirely about the situation. It was definitely feasible, she was only going off of what she could piece together, it left a lot of room for mistakes.

Her ears perked up as she heard more growling and scratching across the walls and ground. More of them were coming down the tunnel. Seeing the open door must have attracted their attention, unless…

Unless they could sense the tree? Was that something they could do? They had to have a way to see, they fought against the city and the soldiers without eyes or ears, there had to be a way for them to perceive things.

Maggie shuffled into the back tunnel, standing deep enough to give her a head start should she need to run but still giving her a view of the torchlit cave where the group of metalurks poured in. They spread themselves out across the soil, latching onto the outer prisoner-trees, while more attached themselves to the main two trees.

The ones at the ground level were consumed faster, disappearing at an alarming rate in comparison. They methodically went to each tree, consuming every last piece of the livewood before assisting the others with the main two trees.

Maggie watched as what was once two men, comforting each other, loving each other in their last moments, slowly faded away. She wasn't sure what made those trees different from the rest, it certainly looked taller and thicker, but it still held the same color as the others.

But clearly it was different but she had no inkling as to why that was.

The last of the twisting trees melted into the metalurks, disappearing entirely.

With nothing left for them to focus on, she expected them to notice her, so she began to quietly back away, unable to turn her gaze away from them. She had no idea what she had just seen, but it had fascinated her.

The metalurks that she could see at ground level stood in place for a moment. It was hard to tell with their faceless heads, but it seemed as if they were uncertain what to do. As if they were lost.

Maggie quietly continued to creep away, doing her best not to bring attention to herself while still keeping an eye on them. She was terrified running might alert them to her presence, so each step was methodical and slow.

The creatures in the cave perked their heads up and Maggie froze. *Did they see me?*

Her back was still to the wall, pressed against it as if flattening herself meant anything to these creatures. Their heads began to make jarring movements, rapidly facing different directions, only adding to their ominous behavior.

And in a flash, they simultaneously ran. For some reason the soil still slowed them, but they disappeared from her view as they made a mad dash for the other tunnel.

Maggie watched as those from the pit climbed their way back down, following the others, their ravenous attitudes back as they found a new target. Her heart raced as she watched them leave, one by one, now feeling the full effects of her cold sweat. She waited until she could hear neither clawing nor growling before summoning the strength to move her legs back into the cave.

She dropped to the ground, sitting against the wall, relieved. The creatures had gone. She huddled herself up as tears began to freely fall from her. Her intention was to only have a single metalurk follow her, to keep the general and the soldiers occupied. She thought them capable of taking a single creature down, but she did not anticipate further metalurks entering the tunnels.

She was thankful they soldiers had fled, they surely would have perished by her actions.

Maggie to the time to reflect on what the general had said about wanting to destroy the tree, wondering if her actions were too hasty. But it no longer mattered. The general and the soldiers had escaped safely, and the metalurks that had swarmed the trees had now returned to the surface.

And she was safe. At least, for the moment.

She gazed up at the black soil platform, now seeing it as a hungry beast waiting for its next meal. She noticed the pieces of that strange green and blue material had been knocked off the platform and to the soil below. Maggie was far too frightened to attempt walking on the soil, remaining still where she sat as she tried to process how close she had been to death. The colored materials reminded her of Castor's sword, but she couldn't be certain why. Perhaps it was the way the torchlight flickered across

413

its surface that reminded her of the sword in the sunlight, or perhaps it was just her instincts.

Metal. The creatures didn't absorb this one either, but… weren't the men wearing it?

Wearing metal? That seemed ridiculous. Such a sturdy substance surely couldn't be worn, at least not with ease.

Seeing the two men fall to their doom earlier only brought further questions about everything that was transpiring. But right now, she couldn't focus on that. She thanked the Gods for her safety and asked them to watch over her brother who was fighting for his life and the lives of others on the surface.

Staring at the empty platform, she silently thanked the two men for their sacrifices.

Maggie had never personally known them, nor did she even know if they had planned this or if it was unintentional, but it didn't matter.

Their actions had caused Maggie to learn a great deal about the metalurks, livewood, and the actions of The Voice. Maggie needed to find her brother, urgently.

Their sacrifice would lead the city into a new age.

32

Castor, bloodied and exhausted, continued to fight against the creatures, doing his best to keep them at bay and prevent them from reaching the civilians. But the metalurks just kept coming. Crowding in, adding themselves to the pack just as fast as they were slain. There was no end to them.

But that didn't stop Castor and his Steelwoods.

More of them had fallen, but that did not diminish their fighting spirit. Castor's blade did exactly what he had expected it to, bring hope and inspiration to his fellow soldiers, seeing how easy the creatures could be struck down.

Metal could once again be used. These creatures no longer stood a chance against the city. Well, after today, hopefully. They still had to rid the creatures that had broken in, and surely their numbers had to be dwindling.

Surely.

Castor struck down another metalurk who tried to flank him, the sword quickly and efficiently cutting its neck and dropping it to the ground. He had never felt such power. It was a significant improvement over livewood.

Children in the house behind him cried as their parents tried to calm them, barely holding back their own resolve. It drove the Steelwoods that protected them to fight even harder, summoning strength they should no longer humanly have. They barely kept the Reds in control, their own numbers falling as the fight went on.

The sturdy force of the East Gate Steelwoods had been chipped away to nearly nothing. There were now only eleven of them left, most of whom were already close to death. But they did not dwell on the situation, it would do them no good. They accepted their fate, knowing this would be their last stand but making it last as long as possible.

Another Steelwood fell and their line shortened.

Vance fought by Castor's side, protecting him with a broken weapon, trying to batter the enemies away long enough for Castor to slay. They were woefully unprepared for this event, and had relied too heavily on livewood, and now there were reduced to literally hitting the enemy with a broken stick to keep themselves alive.

They continued their delaying tactics with the enemy, knowing they could not kill them all if the monsters kept receiving reinforcements. Then the enemy's attack faltered. For a slight moment, none of the metalurks moved or attacked.

Castor and his men became confused but knew that they could take no chances in their position, and did not relent in their own attack. Unfortunately, Castor had the only real weapon left, and he cut down a few metalurks while his men tried to stab the creatures with splintered weapons.

Then the creatures began to move again, slower, but seemingly reacting to the Steelwoods attack. The front line of metalurks returned to normal, but the ones that remained behind seemed confused. Castor did not care why, they needed any form of relief from the fight. The enemy's sudden change in demeanor would have originally concerned him, but he was in no position to stop and think, he could only attack. Slicing and cutting any metalurk who happened to be within distance of his sword.

The moment quickly faded, and all of the metalurks suddenly returned to their onslaught. Whatever had happened, it appeared to have changed nothing in the end.

Another Steelwood fell and once again, their line tightened.

As if they had been rallied, another wave of metalurks appeared, adding to the sense of imminent doom. Castor knew that returning here would likely mean his death, but he did not regret his decision. Without him and his metal weapon, the Steelwoods would not have lasted this long. They would have died without their captain fighting by their side.

He was East Gate Captain Castor Belden, leader of the East Gate Steelwoods, and a man driven to become general.

In the face of death, he admitted to a few regrets, but ultimately was content with the way he had lived his life.

Another Steelwood fell.

He prayed that his sister was alive and safe, that she would be the key to driving this city into a better life in his absence.

Another Steelwood fell.

Their backs now literally to the wall, the remaining Steelwoods kept their burning limbs moving, refusing to buckle underneath the strength of the enemy.

Castor moved to stand in front of his men, his weapon the only thing that could truly prevent the metalurks from reaching them. His soldiers were tired, so he tried to delay the enemy for only a moment so they could catch their breath.

He swung his sword, trying to scare the metalurks away, but their brainless bodies willfully entered the weapons reach only to be cut down.

But the numbers did not relent, and the formation that surrounded the Steelwoods grew larger.

Stay safe, Maggie. I'm sorry.

Castor dispatched another metalurk then another but something drew their attention. Several of their heads turned to Castor's left, focused on something he could not see. After a short moment, one side of the enemy's formation broke away, and in the newly formed gap came three men, each hacking at the enemy with their own swords.

What?

He wasn't sure who the two elderly men were, but Castor recognized the man who led them. The newly appointed Magistrate of Defense, Gavin Va Daolin.

They ran to join Castor's defense, easily hacking the enemies down.

"Captain Castor Belden?" Magistrate Va Daolin asked, unable to turn his attention from the metalurks that surrounded them.

417

"Yes, sir," Castor replied sluggishly, his body exhausted.

"I apologize for the tardiness, but I just received word we could now use metal. One of the soldiers from the arena saw you wielding it and reported to me. I know a man like you is going to ask questions, so I'll make you this promise. Fight and survive along my side, and I'll answer any questions you have to the best of my ability, once we eliminate the Red Sea."

"Fight by the Magistrate of Defense's side? An honor, sir."

Finally, Castor had received reinforcements. Not in number, but certainly in quality. They easily felled the creatures, one by one the bodies dropped to the ground. It felt as if it had been hours, but with the added help, they finally slew the last of the creatures that had filled the city center. Thankfully the enemy had no inclination towards tactics, making their movements easy to read. They simply kept throwing themselves at the men but were easily hacked down with no sense of defending themselves.

Within moments, the four men who wielded the forbidden material stood amongst a small field of metalurk corpses, panting and lightly wounded, but victorious.

The remaining Steelwoods had stayed close, keeping some of the creatures in line whenever necessary, lacking the weapons to properly slay the creatures. Castor had only a moment to explain how proud he was of them before finally escorting the citizens towards the shelters. There were few metalurks who had ventured deep into the city, making their retreat simple and quick.

Castor gave the options for the Steelwoods to remain in the shelters as well, seeing how hard they had fought and how wounded they were. There were now only six, after another had died from his wounds. Castor wanted to keep as many alive as possible, but he knew he couldn't order them to stay behind, they likely wouldn't listen to him anyway.

Two of his men chose to stay, feeling faint from their wounds and hoping to seek treatment from someone in the shelters that were stocked with medical supplies.

The slab was momentarily lifted from the ground, and the citizens rushed inside, followed by the two Steelwoods. The slab was then placed back to block the entrance, leaving the citizens safe, but terrified.

The fight was not yet over.

But it soon would be.

Magistrate Va Daolin ordered the two unknown men to the south-east section of their city, while he and Castor ran to the northeast side. They would then rally the soldiers into pushing the enemy back and eliminating them entirely.

The metalurks would not retreat, it was simply not in their nature, but the Malvarkians would fight until the very last was slain.

The western side of the north and south walls would be able to defend themselves, few creatures would have ventured there, and they would be capable of holding the enemy back even if they could not use livewood.

After listening to Magistrate Va Daolin's plan for defending the city, Castor called his Steelwoods to join him, finding regular wooden weapons for them, and followed the Magistrate of Defense back into the fray.

With a metal sword tight in his grip, Castor's confidence grew tenfold. The creatures had no defense against the sharp edge of a metal blade.

Or the conviction of a Steelwood.

* * *

Castor stood at the city center at the Magistrate of Defense's side, listening to the general's reports from his scouts. Deven had made a sudden appearance near the North Gate, and if the Steelwoods connections were to be believed, he had been outside the walls with a group of soldiers, but they gave no explanations to anyone as to why they were there in the first place.

The general explained that his scouts scoured the city, finding no creatures left in sight. He detailed what they had seen, giving Castor the occasionally scowl, quietly resenting that the East Gate Captain stood by the Magistrate of Defense's side.

Castor and Gavin had formed a quick bond, protecting each other on the battlefield as they rallied the remaining soldiers and reformed their line. They had personally seen the massacre at the East Gate, the stone floor of their city almost completely obscured by bodies on both sides.

They had also seen what had happened to their soldiers atop the wall. Officer Hendel had made a decision to go against Castor's orders to retreat. Instead, he and the soldiers had pried the ballista bases from the ground and moved the devices over so they could turn it around completely and had begun firing at the creatures who poured into the city.

It was a move that meant they would inevitably be killed, but their heroic sacrifice had slain many of the creatures, making it an easier time for the four swordsman and their soldiers to slay the remaining forces.

The general's report continued, including that The Voice remained safe, no creature had been able to break inside the arena where they had remained, not having anticipated the sudden attack.

With the report completed, Magistrate Va Daolin visibly relaxed, dropping his shoulders and wiping away the sweat from his forehead.

"Thank the Gods this ordeal is over. Almost." Gavin looked around, making certain that only he, the three other metal swordsman and the general were alone. "What are the theories for why metal works and now livewood does not?"

The general's eyes flickered towards Castor for a brief moment, before turning away. "I wish I knew the proper details, it might be something The Voice could answer for us, but I'm honestly not certain. There are two differences between the results of this year's duel and previous years, so I think that our method of producing the livewood might be relevant, and if I may ask," he said, glowering at Castor. "Does he have to be here?"

"Yes," Gavin responded without hesitation, and with a sternness that didn't allow for any arguments.

"Don't worry, General, I already know the crux of what's going on." Castor smiled, knowing that his approved presence hit a sore spot for Deven.

The general rolled his eyes, knowing where Castor had got his information. He cleared his throat and continued his explanation. "The first difference is that, obviously, there were two sacrifices instead of one. Without knowing how any of this truly works, I can only hazard a guess that it brought on the Red Sea sooner rather than later, assuming that the Reds are tied to the tree, of course. And if they are, then the second difference is that both men stripped themselves of their armor before they... well, were sacrificed."

"It seems like I have to have a little word with The Voice. In fact, I think we all might. You said that The Voice was safe, are they still in the arena?" Gavin asked, his voice growing with controlled anger.

"Yes."

"Gather all the remaining soldiers who are able to stand within a few blocks and meet me at the arena entrance."

"What's the plan?" the general asked.

"To get answers."

The General obeyed the order, yelling off commands, sending the soldiers who had been relaxing into a scrambled mess to comply with the demands.

Castor waited by the Magistrate of Defense's side, perplexed.

Neither of them know the details? Damn, what have The Voice been doing?

Within moments, the soldiers had gathered, confused but disciplined. They stood in a loose formation as the remaining few fell into position. Castor was growing eager. He had never cared for seeing the arena but knowing what it held on the other side brought a driven purpose to enter.

His eyes caught the flicker of movement to the side, between the buildings. His head reactively turned, eyes scanning the terrain, fearing that a metalurk crept about.

But he found nothing.

I need a rest. He shook off the growing fatigue, pushing it back to be dealt with later.

Beside him, Magistrate Va Daolin took a step forward, and raised his voice. "Men. Once we enter the arena, you must obey two things. The first is to heed my every word. We are going in to demand an audience with The Voice where they will answer

421

questions about today's events. The second, is to go nowhere near the center of the arena. Now, follow me."

Gavin turned, walking up to the heavy-set doors and swung them open. He marched forward with determined step. Castor had only met the man once before but could see the conviction and seriousness this man had towards his position.

A superior truly worthy of respect.

Castor walked by his side, not too impressed by the arena. It was simply a large, enclosed field, nothing grand about it. On one side, amongst the stands where an audience might sit and watch, The Voice raised themselves from their seats, immediately repositioning their guards in front of them.

"Castor," Gavin said. "Take small group of men and march around the opposite side. Leave the rest in the arena itself."

Castor nodded, smugly smiling knowing that the general would be infuriated by the Magistrate of Defense calling on him instead.

Gavin called for ten men to follow him, walking into the stands and marching towards The Voice.

Castor led the rest to the front, making sure to stay close to the wall to avoid the center of the arena. There was nothing there to be frightened of, at least that he could see, but Gavin had made it very clear to stay away from it.

He ordered ten men to follow him, telling the rest to remain where they stood, and walked into the stands from the opposite side, effectively surrounding The Voice. He quickly scanned the arena, noting a few extra people had tagged along Gavin's group, but an enraged voice drew his focus.

"Magistrate Va Daolin, what is the meaning of this?!" one of The Voice yelled at him, outraged. "Only a select few may enter these holy grounds, what are you doing?!"

Gavin climbed the steps behind them, taking on a higher ground so he stood above The Voice. He ripped off the rest of his tattered sleeve to reveal his arm to all, the deep red of anger nearly matching the red of his blood. "I want you to tell them," Gavin said and pointed to the soldiers, who were all just as confused.

"Tell them what?"

"Tell the men who fought to defend this city. Tell the dead who died to protect this city. Tell these people why they had to fight today. Tell them why their weapons were suddenly ineffective."

"You forget your place!" one of The Voice snapped, but another held up his hand.

"Gavin, have you lost your mind? How are we to know the will of the Gods and the—"

"Stop hiding behind that farce! The Gods would not have allowed us to live this hell! They abandoned us long ago, and your ancestors put on their dead masks! Tell them! Tell the people of this city that they are nothing more than an experiment! That they exist purely for your own people's benefits!"

Gavin drew his metal sword, pointing it at the man. He stood out of reach, but the threat was still there.

The crowd was confused by the remark. Gavin spoke as if the Voice were an entirely different race. Yet they were still human, weren't they? Malvarkians like them?

Even through the mask, the man was visibly scared. He looked for help from his guards, but they seemed to not react, apparently waiting to hear what The Voice had to say.

"Gavin! If you want the truth, then fine! But you can't have it spread across the city, it'll ruin everything! The people won't be able to hear it, they won't understand! Take my offer to teach you everything!"

"You've taken us for a fool for the past two-hundred years. This is your last chance, speak with us or be thrown in the prisons where we'll force the answers out of you. I've done my research, I've climbed my way up to this position, and now I have the information I was searching for this entire time!" Gavin beckoned a man over, someone Castor did not recognize. He handed Gavin what appeared to by old pieces of paper.

"My records!" Maggie exclaimed loudly, but quickly hushed herself. Castor quickly shot her a curious look but returned to Gavin who held the papers aloft as if making a proclamation.

The voice looked to his fellow members, who all remained frightened, but adamant in their position.

He looked back at Gavin, meeting his gaze, "The prisons, then."

"Lift your sleeves and tell them! Tell them now what you have done to us! Tell them that we are all a test for your own people! I want to hear you all admit what you are, and what you have done to this city, for Gods knows how many hundreds of years before us!"

Beneath their masks The Voice were seething with fury. Gavin was taking control away from them, piece by piece. Even their own guards would not protect them. None lifted their sleeves, it was custom for The Voice to not reveal their arms as none could demand it from them.

"We are trying to better this world, you fool!" a member of The Voice shouted. It was a man who had remained the entire time, one who scarcely made any public appearances or speeches. It seemed as if The Voice didn't wish for him to speak, each turning to try and calm him, but he was immune to their pleading. "You have no idea the power of the soil! We are trying to discover its full potential, use it for ourselves so that our people may benefit from them!"

Gavin took a couple of steps down, glowering at the man. "And what people are they? Malvarkians? Or Evelkharians?" Gavin's arm had not wavered from the red of anger, but now it seemed to begin slowly transitioning itself to a blue as he tried to control his emotions.

"And pray tell, what are Evelkharians?" Castor asked, gripping his sword tightly by his side. He feared the answer, knowing what it was before Gavin even began.

"The people of Evelkhar. The only city that supposedly cares enough to give us those packages occasionally. They were making sure we stayed alive long enough so that they could carry out their research!" Gavin responded, not daring to move his eyes from The Voice. His arm now the shade of the bright blue of truth.

Murmurings broke from the crowd of soldiers. They were becoming angry. Gavin's demeanor was infectious, and the way The Voice stood, not bothering to counterclaim the argument, screamed a horrifying silence.

"You heard the man earlier," Gavin spat. "Arrest them. As of today, The Voice is abolished."

"The people won't stand for this! They need someone to lead them, they need a council that will guide them, a faith that keeps them alive! Evelkhar will act if they hear of this rebellion!"

"I'm sure we can figure it out."

"No, you cannot take us! This place will be damned! We'll all be slaughtered, and they'll just start again!" a female Voice yelled, struggling against the soldiers.

"Your head shall be first, Gavin Va Daolin! You, personally, have doomed this city! Count the last of your days, for they will be short!" another yelled as the soldiers continued to advance.

The soldiers moved in, placing ropes around The Voice, who continued to fight back, trying to persuade any and all to take their side, promising safety in return for protection.

None took them up on their offer. They forcefully guided The Voice away, the soldiers a mixture of anger and triumph.

All throughout their shouts and threats, Gavin's arm remained blue, revealing to them that their words had no effect.

"Will you get any answers out of them?" Castor asked as Gavin climbed down the steps.

"Unlikely, but we don't have to. I'm sure we can piece it all together."

"Uh, if I may?" a feminine voice called out from below. The soldiers seemed surprised to find that a woman had snuck in, standing behind them without their notice.

Castor was just as surprised as any when he first saw his sister, but the relief of seeing his sister alive was replaced with a groan and a quite curse, dragging his hand over his face in exasperation.

"Who is that?" the Magistrate of Defense asked.

"My sister,"

"And what is she doing here?"

"I assure you, I have no idea, but I would advise listening to her. She seems to have a knack for being in places she shouldn't be and holding a surprising amount of information."

"You mean like a Seeker?"

"No, of course not, sir."

425

Castor watched as his sister climbed the steps and walked up to him, preparing himself to listen to her explanation. To his surprise, she instead embraced him.

"Thank the Gods you're alive, Castor. I was really worried."

Castor hugged her back, elated to see her unharmed.

"Shame on you, Cap. You know the rule about seeing your sister after a wave," Vance called out from behind them. Castor smiled at the remark, letting go of his sister and gesturing towards Gavin who had been waiting patiently.

"I found some old records a while ago, those records you have, left over from the Old Malvarkians. I didn't get to read them all before they were stolen, but it has to do with the black soil. The Old Malvarkians... or, now the Evelkhar? In any case, they discovered the soil and its use, but it brought the metalurks. It brought their untimely death, not having prepared to fight them, though I think in their case it was much more dire. Whatever they did caused them all to completely disappear, not just slain. Otherwise, there would have been bodies left for us to find."

"I know," said Gavin. "I read the records. I'm still trying to piece everything together myself. So... the very thing that kept our people alive against the siege is the very thing that caused the siege itself?" Gavin asked, trying to understand.

Maggie nodded. "Yes. I think it also has to do with what is sacrificed. I have a feeling that it's not just the people who are sacrificed, but also whatever they carry or wear. The two men stripped themselves of metal before turning into the trees, so I think that might be the reason."

Gavin stared at her, brow burrowed in confusion. "Why do you speak as if you saw it yourself?"

"Oh, uh... No reason."

"Of course. What of the livewood? Neither man had any livewood on them at the time of the sacrifice, so why did our salvation suddenly become useless?"

"That... I'm not sure about. Maybe my theory is wrong," Maggie said, seeming a little deflated.

"Well, I suppose there is one way to test if the soil is connected. Burn the trees down and prohibit use of the soil. We'll have it removed before Evelkhar ever hears word of this."

"They're already gone. The beasts, uh… I'm not sure how to explain. They didn't eat it, they kind of just… absorbed it, into themselves. It disappeared at their touch."

"I can confirm that the trees have gone," the general cut in, as if trying to remain relevant.

"You mean to tell me you watched them do this?" Gavin ignored his remark, not turning from Maggie.

"Yes."

"Brave. It seems we have much to discuss, perhaps meet with me at a later point, along with your brother. For now," he turned towards the soldiers who remained intently listening, "I am swearing you all to a vow of secrecy. Keep this to yourselves until we figure out how to fix this mess The Voice has placed us in."

"Sir?" Castor asked, grabbing Gavin's attention. "What of Evelkhar?"

Gavin sighed, visibly uncertain of the future. "We'll figure it out. If they plan to attack, we'll defend ourselves. We need to have a serious discussion with the Evelkhar we just imprisoned. Get some information before we take any actions. In all honesty, I'm angry, but I'm tired of war."

"I think we all are, sir," Castor agreed, Maggie nodding alongside him.

Gavin called everyone who had gathered to attention, vowing them to secrecy until he addressed the city personally.

The soldiers saluted. They were likely bitter that they couldn't tell others what they had witnessed, nor what they truly were, but they understood the necessity for secrecy. They were also ordered to remain quite about The Voice until the shock of the Red Sea cooled down. The soldiers were dismissed and ordered to begin the clean-up of the city. Word was sent to the shelters to let them know it was safe to leave, and the lengthy process of cleaning the city began.

* * *

Castor was allowed to keep the metal sword in recognition of his efforts. It was explained that it had belonged to the Va Noldins, but the family ceased to exist with the death of the old man Castor had obtained the sword from.

Over the following days, they prepared themselves for another attack that never came. They waited a full two weeks before celebrating the end of the metalurks.

Maggie gave her late husband a proper funeral. As the ceremony ended, she felt a weight lift from her. She no longer clung onto the death of her son, James had taken that burden from her when he moved into the afterlife. With the help of Varin, she was able to return to a regular lifestyle, though Castor remained skeptical about her connection with the Seekers.

East Gate Captain Castor Belden felt a sudden emptiness with the metalurks gone. There were now so many options for the city that it was hard for him to pick a direction. He felt himself renewed, happy with the fact that he even had options to pick from in helping the city grow.

Atop the wall, Castor stared out into the forest where the metalurks had once emerged. It now seemed like an ordinary forest, no longer emanating an ominous darkness from within. He looked to his side where his sister stood, a smile on her face as she finally seemed to be at peace.

He took pleasure in this moment. The fear of being besieged gone. The sky feeling open. The air fresh as it entered his lungs. The walls no longer feeling like a prison.

The city of Malvark was finally free of its curse.

EPILOGUE

Castor Belden stood atop the East Gate, watching as citizens tend to the crop fields. With the metalurks gone, they could properly expand their fields to reach further, eventually allowing the city to no longer starve.

It was comforting to watch them. Watch them work without worries of metalurks emerging from the now placid forest. They no longer had to peer over their shoulders, to prepare themselves to flee at any moment.

They could just work. Grow and supply food for the city.

In silence.

The bell had not rung since the devastation of the Red Sea many months ago. It was odd to not hear its song dominating the city, warning them all to hide and prepare.

It was peaceful.

Castor was skeptical about how long that peace might last. Magistrate of Defense Gavin Daolin had made contact with the neighboring city of Evelkhar, the very city that had been allowing them to barely survive with their limited food supplies. They had treated them like animals, using them as testing grounds for something Castor was certain was a weapon. They tried to control the black soil that drew the metalurks to their city, attempting to find a way to control them, to expand their dominance.

The revelation had not been announced to the city. They could not afford their people to become enraged, sparking another war. Evelkhar would be key to their prosperity and survival, so Gavin Daolin had to peacefully negotiate an alliance. But those who did know the truth began to question their history. Were they truly pushed out of their home by bandits? Or was that also falsified? Were they ever in any danger? Were the bandits just Evelkharian's in disguise?

Questions that had to be pushed aside. Their confusion and anger had to be controlled so they would not spark any conflict with Evelkhar.

It was difficult for Castor to hide his feelings, but as he looked across at the unknowing citizens, watching them smile for the first time in years, it satiated him. Malvark was finally out of its eternal battle, he could not draw it back in, even if it were right to exact revenge on Evelkhar.

The wind blew, its chill blaring against his exposed skin. He turned to his side to check on Maggie, who stood in silence, a smile on her face.

Normally, citizens weren't allowed atop the wall without permission, but no one questioned her while she stood with him. He pulled her in under his arm, squeezing her tightly as the wind began to pick up. He looked down at his sister, feeling warmer by seeing her smile. She was not entirely over her personal issues, but she had improved significantly.

Especially since she had been seeing a new man.

"You know," Castor began, drawing his sister's attention. "If Varin is blackmailing you into seeing him, I can have him arrested."

Maggie pulled away from him, chuckling as she rolled her eyes. "When are you going to trust him?"

"I know what he is. That makes it a little difficult to trust."

"What he *was*," Maggie corrected. "He left the Seekers. I don't know why you don't believe us when we tell you that."

"Sounds exactly like what a Seeker wants you to believe." Castor gave her a smile to let her know he was only teasing. He did have his reservations about Varin, but he could not question the improvements he was making with Maggie.

He could only keep an eye on the two of them.

Maggie crossed her arms. "And what about you? I heard that you've been paying many visits to a certain secretary. Something you want to tell me?"

"Linette's not a secretary," Castor corrected, but realized he had fallen into Maggie's trap as she smirked at him.

"So, there is a woman then?"

"Like you didn't know with your Seeker of a boyfriend."

Maggie laughed alongside her brother. It had been years since they had joked like this, it was a relief to be able to once again.

"General!" a voice sounded as footsteps approached them.

Castor turned to face Vance who stood, saluting him. "Captain." Castor returned the salute, both dropping back into an informal stance.

"Maggie," Vance greeted her.

"Hello, Vance."

Their interaction stuck with Castor. He wasn't sure what it was, but something about how casual they were in their few words spoke loudly to him. "So, it wasn't a Seeker after all." He eyed them both, reading their reactions.

"General, important news," Vance said, looking guilty and cutting the conversation short. "Magistrate Daolin requests your attendance. Sounds like you'll be escorting him on his next venture to Evelkhar."

The news did not come as a surprise, but rather as pleasant relief. Castor knew he would eventually attend alongside Gavin but had simply been waiting until the Magistrate of Defense felt it necessary.

"Thank you, Captain. Any reports from our lookouts?"

"Nothing yet, sir. No one has been seen spying on our city or skulking about the forest. No movements whatsoever."

Castor mulled over the report for a moment. "Seems unlikely. Surely, they want to gather their own information on us. Make sure they're following proper routine, we can't let anything slip by us. Not now."

"Yes, General." Vance saluted. He bid farewell to them both and set off.

"Wow, you'll be visiting Evelkhar? That's so exciting!" Maggie smiled, eyes wide.

"It's serious." Castor tried to calm her. "But...yes, it is exciting."

431

"Do you think you can smuggle me in? I'd like to see it as well," Maggie jokingly asked, knowing that it would be forbidden.

"I don't know if I could even stop you if you wanted to go. I just ask that you wait until I give you permission."

"I'll try," Maggie chuckled. "You better go. Come see me once more before you leave."

"Of course." Castor smiled in return. The pair descended the stairs together before parting ways.

Castor wandered through the city, in no rush to reach Gavin's office. He took his time to relish the mood of the people. Their faces that had lifted from the ground shone brightly even with the faintest of smiles, life returning to their eyes by the day.

Somehow, Malvark didn't seem so bleak anymore. The grey of their stone didn't feel so dull, people moved about rather than feeling at a standstill.

Malvark was in motion. Its foundation may have be built on betrayal, blood, and years of fighting, but the city had not given up.

It would thrive and prosper.

And General Castor Belden would do anything he must during his visit to Evelkhar to ensure these people would never hear the sound of the bell ever again.